W9-DDR-079

Meri 11/5/15

The
Memory
Weaver

Center Point
Large Print

Also by Jane Kirkpatrick and available from
Center Point Large Print:

An Absence So Late

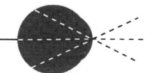

The Memory Weaver

JANE KIRKPATRICK

CENTER POINT LARGE PRINT
THORNDIKE, MAINE

This Center Point Large Print edition is published
in the year 2015 by arrangement with Revell,
a division of Baker Publishing Group.

Scripture used in this book, whether quoted or
paraphrased by the characters, is taken from
the King James Version of the Bible.

This book is a work of historical fiction based closely on
real people and events. Details that cannot be historically
verified are purely products of the author's imagination.

The text of this Large Print edition is unabridged.
In other aspects, this book may vary
from the original edition.
Printed in the United States of America
on permanent paper.
Set in 16-point Times New Roman type.

ISBN: 978-1-62899-757-6

Library of Congress Cataloging-in-Publication Data

Kirkpatrick, Jane, 1946–
The memory weaver / Jane Kirkpatrick. — Center Point Large Print
edition.
pages cm
Summary: "As a child, Eliza Spalding Warren was taken hostage by
Indians during a massacre in 1847. Now the young mother of two
children, Eliza faces a different kind of dislocation; her husband wants
to move, which will mean returning to the land of her captivity. Eliza
must face her childhood trauma and find peace with what's left"
   —Provided by publisher.
ISBN 978-1-62899-757-6 (library binding : alk. paper)
1. Large type books. I. Title.
PS3561.I712M45 2015b
813'.54—dc23
                                                        2015028533

Dedicated to Jerry,
with whom I've shared
a lifetime of memories

The difference between false memories
and true ones is the same as for jewels:
it is always the false ones that look
the most real, the most brilliant.
Salvador Dali

The past beats inside me like a second heart.
John Danville in *The Sea*

Cast of Characters

Eliza Hart Spalding	the mother, early missionary to the Nimíipuu/Nez Perce People
Henry Spalding	husband of Eliza, father of Eliza Spalding Warren
Eliza Spalding Warren	the daughter, keeper of her mother's story
Henry Hart Spalding	Eliza the daughter's brother
Martha Jane Spalding	younger sister
Amelia "Millie" Spalding	sister and youngest of Spalding siblings
Andrew Warren	husband of Eliza
America Jane Warren Martha Elizabeth "Lizzie" Warren Amelia "Minnie" Warren James Henry Warren	children of Eliza and Andrew Warren
Rachel Jane Smith	Boston teacher and second wife of Henry Spalding
Nancy Osborne	Brownsville resident, friend of Eliza

Matilda Sager	young friend of Eliza, survivor of Whitman tragedy
Lorinda Bewley	young friend, survivor of Whitman tragedy
Timothy	early Nimíipuu/Nez Perce convert of Spaldings
O'Donnell brothers	drovers with Andrew Warren
John Brown	son of owner of Brown and Blakely's store
Bill Wigle	Brownsville businessman
Matilda	Nimíipuu/Nez Perce friend of Eliza Spalding, the mother
Tashe	Eliza the child's Nimíipuu horse
Nellie	Eliza Spalding's Brownsville horse
Maka	Eliza Spalding Warren's horse
*Yaka	the Warren family dog
*Abby	the Warren cattle dog

*fully imagined characters

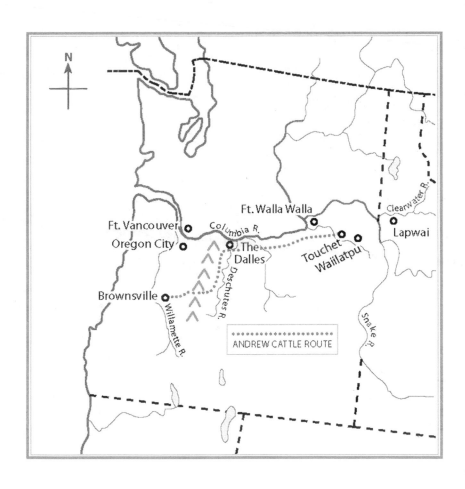

The
Memory
Weaver

❯❯ Prologue ❮❮

1847
Along the Clearwater River
Oregon Territory

The woman rode sidesaddle, holding the leather reins like long ribbons in her sturdy hand.

"Mama, Mama, wait!"

The woman turned, looked out beneath her bonnet as her daughter ran forward, carrying a late-blooming iris in her nine-year-old hand. The girl's Nimíipuu horse with freckles across its rump followed behind the child.

"Why, I rode right past it, didn't I, Eliza?" The woman inhaled the flower's scent as the child handed the blue iris up to her.

"I notice things."

"Yes, you do." It was good to see the child's smile light up her usually serious face. "But I notice that you are not on Tashe's back. I dare not dismount from this sidesaddle to help you get back up."

"I can mount all by myself."

"Can you?"

"I'll show you. Come, Tashe."

The horse followed like an obedient dog as the child made her way down the bank of the Clearwater River. At what she decided was the perfect

13

spot, the girl stopped the horse, ordered the mare to "Stay," then scrambled back up the bank, the horse below her. The mare switched her tail but waited.

"Watch, Mama." Certain she had her mother's full attention, the child leaned over to grab tufts of the horse's mane, inhaled a deep breath, then leapt like a frog, landing astride, her dress covering the blanket on the horse's back. She reached for the reins, then sat up straight as an arrow.

"Oh, that's wonderful." Her mother clapped her gloved hands. "You're so smart, Eliza."

"I am." The satisfied smile revealed two front teeth almost grown in.

"We must ride more often in the morning like this, so I can witness how wise you are, how much you've grown into a young lady."

"Just you and me, Mama, and none of the rest."

"Yes, just the two of us."

It was a promise the woman wished she'd kept, but events intervened as they always do. Still, the girl would remember that last solo ride with her mother: the sweep of the landscape, the scent of the flower and the horses, the sound of the Clearwater River chattering on its way to the faraway sea, and her mother's approving smile. She would weave those memories into what happened later, trying to make sense of those threads, praying they would support rather than threaten her own life as a woman, mother, and wife.

Part One

1

IN THE BEGINNING

My earliest memory is of laughter inside a waterfall of words. I'm in a half-barrel that once held flour. Tree rounds act as wheels. My bare feet tease the knots of rope bored through the barrel's end; my dress covers my legs stuck straight out. My hands grip the smooth sides of the half-barrel. A Nez Perce boy, with shiny hair as black as a moonless night, tows the rope over his shoulder, pulling me in my makeshift wagon across the rubbled ground in front of our cabin-school-church. I lay my head back, close my eyes, feel the sun on my face, let my child belly jiggle over the rutted earth, laughter joined to theirs. Ecstasy.

A sudden jolt. The wagon stops. Eyes pop open. Before us stands my father, hands on hips, elbows out, eyes black as turned earth. Absent our laughter I can hear my mother's distant voice speaking to her Nez Perce students inside the school, then Nez Perce voices repeating as a song: English. Nez Perce. English. Nez Perce. I let the words wash over me, as comforting as a quilt.

I found no such comfort many years later at the grave-digging of my mother. I was thirteen. I didn't know then that the healing of old wounds

17

comes not from pushing tragic memories away but from remembering them, filtering them through love, to transform their distinctive brand of pain. That frigid January day in 1851 I wanted to forget my mother's dying and so much more. Then laughter interrupted my sorrow as the chink, chink of the shovel hit dirt. Laughter—that made me wonder about my first memory. Perhaps it wasn't true that I was comforted by Nez Perce words mixed in with my mother's those years before. Maybe I didn't even hear what I thought I did. Emotions wrap around memory. We don't recall the detail in our stories; we remember the experience.

Deep in the pit, pieces of ice floated in shadowed puddles. I had slipped out of a grieving house in Brownsville, Oregon Territory, leaving my brother and two sisters behind, with my father holding his head in his hands. I ought to have stayed at our cabin for my sisters and brother, comforted as an older sister should, been a shoulder to let them cry on. We all ached from the loss. But I'd had enough of tears.

The laughter came from one of the grave diggers. He stopped when I approached. A light rain pattered against his felt hat, dotting the brim. I took his sudden silence when he saw me as respect while Mr. Osborne, the father of my one and only friend Nancy, continued to dig. I hadn't minded the sound of laughter.

Mr. Osborne looked up in the silence. He introduced us. "Andrew Warren, meet Eliza Spalding."

Mr. Warren's eyebrows lifted. "But I thought—"

"Same name as her mama, Eliza Spalding, who we're working for here." Mr. Osborne nodded at the grave hole they dug for my mother.

Mr. Warren's smile when he gazed at me from the pit was a clear drink of refreshing water that, when I swallowed, soothed a throat parched from tears. I noticed his shirt had a scorch mark against the white of his collar and wondered if his mama ironed it for him or if he did it himself.

"Wishing it wasn't so, Miss Spalding. A mother's love can't be replaced, only remembered."

"Thank you, sir."

"No need to call him sir. Not much older than you, he is." Mr. Osborne winked.

Andrew Warren seemed much older and wiser, his observation of my loss and memory wrapped together a profundity to me at such a vulnerable time. His brown eyes looked through me, and when he removed his hat to wipe his brow of sweat, a shock of dark hair covered his left eye. He had a clear complexion, his face free of whiskers, revealing a young man who chewed on his lip. I'd learn later he was nineteen.

He did not attend the burial or at least I didn't see him. My eyes and heart were focused elsewhere, and my hands were occupied with my siblings—Martha, four, but a year older than Baby Amelia, and Henry, named for my father, eleven—as we listened to one of my father's preacher colleagues read the Scriptures. It was his intent to give us comfort and to try to capture my mother's story at the grave site. Her amazing story. He failed, in my opinion. But who could capture the fleeting life of a woman who gave her all to the Nez Perce people, Indians who later sent us away.

I saw Mr. Warren next that same spring. Muck still marked the Territorial Road, but rhododendron with their red and yellow hues edged the dark fir forests. My mother never lived to see spring in this new town my father had moved us to.

That May morning I walked to Kirk's Ferry with Nancy Osborne to pick up needles and thread at Brown and Blakely's store. I could have asked my father to bring needles home since that's where he worked as a postmaster, but in truth, I loved the walk with my friend. Nancy understood my quirky ways, my wanting to stop and inhale blossom fragrance or seeking tiny trillium that peeked through the dense forest shade. I had to point out deer hooves that had crossed our path and sent her eyes upward at an owl gazing down at us from a fir. It took forever to walk to the store, I stopped us so often.

Out of nowhere, Mr. Warren appeared, sitting astride a horse, wearing brogans, heavy duck pants with shiny pocket brads, a white collarless shirt, a sweat-stained hat. His hands rested on the pommel, reins loose, as though he waited for me and had not a care in the world.

"Like a ride into town, little lady?" Andrew's soft drawl warmed like honey on a johnnycake. I couldn't let him know of such thoughts, though. But neither was I one to be coy nor play those games I'd seen other girls tease at with boys.

"I prefer my own two feet." I looked up at his sable eyes shaded by his hat. "And I already have a companion. Miss Osborne, meet Mr. Andrew Warren."

"So you remember me?" He sat a little straighter on his horse. "Well, I am memorable."

"For such things as you may not wish to be remembered for. Free-speaking to young girls could be a caddish act." I stifled back a grin of my own.

"Hmmm. Well, my horse could use a rest. Any objection to my walkin' beside you precious ladies?"

"The road belongs to everyone."

Nancy giggled as the May warmth gathered around us, puffy white clouds like cottonwood fluffs drifted across the sky. The pleasant weather gave me strength enough to deal with my father should he learn of my walking down the road with any young man. My mother could have tempered him. But she wasn't there.

His horse clomped along the dirt path and stopped us once or twice to tear at grass. Mr. Warren—I thought of him then and later, too, in that formal way—talked to us about a model of a revolver he hoped to buy one day, "a cap and ball firearm Samuel Colt called a Ranger, but they changed the name, call it Navy."

"You like guns, then, Mr. Warren?" Nancy asked the question. She'd turned eleven but was wise beyond her years. Tragedy does that to us.

"I like the feel of them, their smooth barrels and the weight in my hands. I'm partial to the smell of gunpowder too. I plan to defend as needed against any old Indian uprisin's that might come my way."

"There's a certain alacrity in your voice, Mr. Warren."

"Don't know the meaning of that word, Miss Spalding." He frowned. I admired his ability to express his lack of knowledge.

"Eagerness," I said. "Or maybe enthusiasm might be a better word."

"Ah, that alacrity—that's how you spoke it?"

I nodded.

"That alacrity would arrive on the horse named coincidence, my coming upon you girls walking and letting me join your path."

"I don't believe in coincidences." Then I sermonized as though I knew all there was to know. "I believe the Lord sets our path and whatever befalls us has some meaning and purpose." My mother believed that, and at that moment I was certain of it as well, even if I couldn't explain what happened, what sort of purpose the Lord could have for all those grievous deaths at the Whitmans'; all the pain and suffering that hollowed us still.

"Then I thank the Lord." Andrew didn't seem the least fazed to have been "taught" twice in the same number of minutes nor did he seem to mind the certainty with which I spoke about God and life.

I told him we were digging bulbs and he offered to help, holding the gritty tubers in his wide hands. He had stubby fingers, not long like my father's. Nancy and I pressed a deer antler into the ground beside the blooms to loosen and pull them up, just as we'd seen the Nez Perce and Cayuse women do in spring. We were a little late for gathering the camas or other eating roots, but the iris was what I wanted to plant at the grave. My hands in the warm earth brought my mother to mind. But then, everything reminded me of her.

Mr. Warren's horse trailed behind, didn't seem to need to have a rein held. I commented.

"A well-schooled horse is one of man's finest accomplishments. Do you like horses, Miss Spalding?"

"I do. I miss Tashe, the mare I had at Lapwai."

"An Indian pony, was it?"

"Nez Perce. Spotted hindquarters like freckles on a pale white face. She, too, followed behind without reins held when I walked."

We had that in common then, the value of a well-trained horse. Relationships have been built on smaller foundations.

We chatted about the early feel of summer. I wiped sweat where my bonnet met my forehead, finished our digging.

"I can lend a hand planting these."

"They're for my mother's grave."

"I've been watching you since that sad time." His volunteering this made my skin tingle.

"I'm not sure I like the idea of a man watching a mere girl." I kept my eyes forward, caught Nancy's look, her eyebrows raised in question.

"You aren't no girl. You're an old soul. I saw that from the beginning. You weren't no whimpering mess like some girls hit with harsh living."

"You seem certain of your insights, Mr. Warren."

"Ain't sure of much, but I see courage when it walks beside me."

That day his claiming he saw courage in me proved a comfort and comfort was what I needed more than truth.

It became a habit, his meeting me weekly, closer to the schoolhouse than might have been wise. I knew my father would object. My father objected to everything after my mother's death. Yet there was a thrill to wondering what my father would do if he caught us. How strange to think I wanted the tingling of danger but I remember that I did —until a day when my father met me at the door, my brother standing behind him. I could tell by his set jaw and narrowed eyes that he was angry.

"You will not cavort with that man!"

"Who—"

"Don't play naïve with me. That Warren."

"I merely walk to town and he walks beside me, Father. We're rarely alone. Nancy joins us. And Henry watches too, as you know by his . . . tattling."

"Don't blame others for your transgressions." He raised his hand but did not strike me. He never did strike his own children, though he had been severe in punishment of the Nez Perce children. He used harsh measures with my brother too, more so since my mother's death. He once put a wooden laundry pin on Henry's nose, forcing him to wear it all day at school in humiliation for some perceived lack in my brother's character that day. Had my mother been alive she would have stopped him. She did not believe in shame. And speaking of shame, I did not act to protect my brother either.

My father continued his diatribe, ending with,

"The man is too old, too loose in his direction, Eliza. Your mother had high hopes for you, as do I. You'll continue your education. And we have work to do together, you and me. Work interrupted by, well . . . you know." His voice had softened. "You must stay away from Mr. Warren. Or any young man. You are too young and I can't afford to lose you too."

He stomped outside, leaving me and my brother staring at each other. I'd gotten off with a switch of my father's tongue instead of a willow stick. Yet his words haunted. *Or any young man?* What future had my father planned for me?

We'd left the mission at Lapwai in a hurry. Forest Grove, where most of the missionaries landed in the Willamette Valley, was a settled place. My father helped start a school there and my mother taught in it. It was a good place for recovering from all that had happened. Then the trial happened and Mother became ill and not long after we moved to Brownsville. I had traveled with my father, making sure he ate before his hours of preaching as he started new churches in Albany and beyond. I saddled the horses we rode, listening to the stories of hardships told by new immigrants and older settlers alike. If my mother was up to a journey, then we all went and I tended my siblings and took on the task of making certain my mother ate as well. After her death, I became my father's sole preaching companion. I wondered if that's how he saw my future.

I glared at Henry Hart for tattling about Mr. Warren, surprised at the intensity of my upset. I slammed my purchased lye on the table with a bit more force than necessary. Soap had to be made. My father earned little money being the post-master, teaching, and preaching, so I made soap, did the laundry, stitched patches on my father's and Henry's pants, let out the hems on Martha's and Amelia's little dresses.

"Thanks, brother."

"I only want to protect you. Father says Mr. Warren is not a nice man."

"I can take care of myself. I've done it often enough."

His mouth turned downward in a frown. "I only said you had man company going to town. I didn't think Father would mind, not really."

"Anything that isn't his idea he objects to." Henry nodded, stared at the floor. "It doesn't matter, Henry. Mr. Warren merely likes to give his horse a rest and so he walks. Father will get used to it, if it continues."

"I could walk with you." He rubbed at a cut on his finger.

"You could." I lifted his chin. "But if Papa thinks Mr. Warren is a poor influence, then he'd punish you as well for associating with him. I need to look out for you too. You and Martha and Amelia."

"We look out for each other."

"We do."

I smiled then, and later when Henry Hart came to me with apology wildflowers in his eleven-year-old hand, I accepted them and hugged him. It's what my mother would have done.

He lingered for a time, but as he saw I held no grudge against him, he left to chop the wood we'd fire and turn to ash for making soap.

As I worked preparing supper for the five of us, my mind did wander onto Mr. Warren. His hair was the color of good earth, eyes the same as otter fur. Charming is the word that came to mind, beguiling, with just the slightest hint that what he presented might not be all there was to see. Was I drawn to the mystery of him? Or was testing destiny with Andrew Warren the distraction I longed for, pushing out the losses that had moved into my thirteen-year-old heart and threatened to stay?

❯ 2 ❮

FINDING THE CENTER

"You let the taters burn." This from Millie, in her five-year-old-missing-front-teeth voice.

"Potatoes," I corrected. Mama would want me to continue to keep our grammar and pronunciation pure. It was my job to correct when I saw it was wrong.

"Well, you lets them burn."

"I did let them burn." I scraped the spider pan of the mess, tossed the remnants in the chicken bowl, and started slicing potatoes again.

"I'm telling Father. Waste not, want not."

"Do what you must. And while you're at it, maybe you can tell him about the broken crockery pieces I cleaned up. He might wonder how they ended up so wasted."

She pooched her lower lip out. "I'm sorry, 'Liza. I won't say nothing."

"Anything. Off with you, then. Let me concentrate on our supper. Eggs and potatoes."

"I loooove potatoes."

She wiggled her nose and began to set the table with our tin plates. We only used my mother's ironstone on special occasions. It would bring her with us as she always tried to have a little beauty and "back East" civilization on the table. A flower might grace the center. A candle scented with lavender. But since her death, Father didn't want any of her things used and he didn't want us having joys. It was as though we were to suffer more because we lived and she didn't. We mourned and we'd do it properly, according to my father.

Had he always been so hard or did it happen with Mother's death? Or the massacre? Or his growing hatred toward the Catholics, whom he blamed for the troubles at the missions. "All went well until the bishops arrived," he pronounced on Sundays from the pulpit at the Congregational Church. Blaming was a second language with him, one I hoped I wasn't learning. Finding fault with everything is tiring and breathes no hope of change.

The time between the massacre and my mother's death was often a fog misting up from the river. All I'd known before November of 1847 was the happiness, joy, and laughter among the Nez Perce and my family. The massacre changed my father, made him angrier. I wondered if I'd ever get my intense but loving father back. Had my mother wondered too and died of a broken heart?

Despite my father's warning, Mr. Warren became a regular part of my week, appearing on the

Thursdays when I went to town. That fall, when school began, for a few months after harvest but before the heavy rains made travel treacherous, Mr. Warren enrolled in my father's school. He wasn't so old he couldn't. Many young men spent summer months working, and then in winter when Father held school, boys as old as twenty would settle their lanky legs out in the aisles leaning against the bench backrest, slates in hand.

Mr. Warren didn't take his schoolwork seriously, but he paid attention enough that Father found it hard to send him on his way. He was a paying student, after all. His parents had a farm on the north side of Brownsville. They'd named a creek there after themselves. But Mr. Warren dreamed of running cattle on a spread—it's what he called larger acreage on unclaimed land in the eastern part of the territory. Mr. Warren painted pictures with his words of lowing cows and riding the "range," of shooting coyotes and wolves that threatened, of branding his own mark in spring-time—or fall—to show that he owned all. He had big dreams of how he'd tame a wild country, beat back Indians who warred. "They best get used to us being here and them having memories of once livin' here but making no more memories in this place."

I cringed at those words, though truth was in them. I could see that. Despite the massacre and uprising that followed, I held no animosity toward Indians as a whole. But I did resent the betrayal of the Nez Perce—to my parents, but also, to me. They'd invited us, and then after the tragedy they sent us packing. I never understood it. The Nez Perce had had no part in what happened except to invite my parents and the Whitmans to come west and bring the Book of Heaven with them. One even saved my father's life when all was chaos.

Mr. Warren reminded me of my father in odd ways. Grandiose ideas, full of visionary hopes. My father wanted to save the Indians from a hell they did not know of, to give them the light and love of Jesus. It was what the Nez Perce had asked my parents to do, bring them that light, and they had done so with a purpose, building lives in that remote place, on their own, and printing books. Books! Aside from our Lord, what greater gift than to give a way to hold one's story inside a book.

Mr. Warren's hopes weren't wrapped up in faith. He believed, I think, but such views were secondary to his wishes to make his mark on a new land. *His* mark. He'd come west from Missouri, a lush, green place not unlike this Brownsville country. But he sought the wide vistas of the prairies and plateaus he'd traveled through while heading west. I hadn't had the privilege of overland travel, having been born in the territory. My father would say, "The first white child born here who survived." It was how he introduced me at his preaching events. I had a unique status, associated with the Whitmans' child who had been older than me but drowned while very young. What I lacked were the happy stories of the overland journeys so many spoke of— stories like Mr. Warren's.

"I want to settle one day in those fields of thigh-high grasses, near . . . where the Indians did their dastardly acts." Andrew looked away. We had sat beside the Calapooia River that summer day, the year after my mother's death. It was the first time he'd brought up the terrible events of November of 1847.

"I'm familiar with the place." He tossed pebbles into the stream while I crocheted tiny stitches around a linen square, my fingers suddenly cold. Later I'd embroider a flower onto it and give it to my sister Amelia—Millie, we called her—as a birthday gift. I had no problem with his mention of where the "dastardly acts" had taken place. It wasn't the directness of a mention that took me away but more a certain smell or sound. Of blood, for example, when I had to kill a chicken for our supper. Or the scream of a mountain lion in an early morning, so like the cry of anguish of Mrs. Whitman, seeing her husband's mangled body just before the hatchet struck her down. The sound of horses running on frozen ground, raising puffs of snow. Once when I ironed my white apron, then held it up to hang and caught the whiff of it, I nearly fainted with the memory of a day I covered my face with a bloody apron so as not to see more killings. Those are the things that take me to another place where my heart beats hard, my breath gasps as though I'll choke, and images flit across my eyes as real as my sisters bending to their dolls, and I disappear. Perhaps it is the surprise that takes me away.

When Mr. Warren mentioned that place, I knew of what he spoke, and odd as it is to me, I could see what he saw, the wind-driven grasses rising to a horse's chest, meadowlarks chirping their song that sounded like they were saying *Why-e-la-pu is a pretty little place*. I could see what he imagined and I longed again for those wide vistas, the hills hot and brown in summer, cool and verdant in spring and fall, snowfall blanketing us in winter, my family happy and intact in a landscape as nurturing as a mother's arms. Every season seeking singular recognition, bringing change and wonder and a memory of when I loved the Nez Perce people like my family.

"Yup." Andrew picked up a stone. "That's where I'd like to settle one day. Near the Touchet River. You remember that one?" He tossed the pebble, the plop like a baby's cough. "Not so much a big stream but the grasses are lush. And there's flat ground enough to build on, and timber in

34

surrounding hills for corrals. We can drive beef to the fort at Walla Walla—well, a man can. It's a good market. And travelers on the trails heading west, they could stop at our place to resupply dried beef. Then there's the hide market. All sorts of opportunities."

"And where will you start your herd and what will you do until you have enough cattle to run and slaughter and sell?" My bone crochet needle felt smooth in my fingers, cold as they'd become. I blew warm breath on them.

"There are cows coming on the trails across. And I hear that a group of fellows gathered up longhorns from the Mexican missions in California, brought 'em into Oregon. A bunch not far from here. They were wild as a troubled hornet's nest but likely tamed, some. Fort Vancouver has stock to sell. You'll see." He sounded petulant, as though my asking questioned his dream.

"You've done some thinking on this then."

" 'Course I have. I'm working for my pa, hoping he might stake me. Maybe find others to invest. They'd have a good return. I'd make it worth their while."

I thought of "investors." My parents' investors were those who supported the foreign missions, the Mission Board, and all the faithful people in the East who offered sustenance of various kinds to us as we labored among the Nez Perce. And how that support could shift with changing circumstances both back East and with the news received from the West. My father wrote diligently to the Mission Board asking they reinstate the Lapwai Mission. That he and my mother had done good work there and "our" Nez Perce Indians had not been involved in the trouble. I was embarrassed for his pleadings. It was over. Lapwai was over. My parents and all the missionaries were at the mercy of the Board, who ultimately owned everything we had at Lapwai— house, barn, mill, printing shed, printing press, hoes. Maybe even my mother's dishes, I wasn't sure. Maybe that was why my father didn't use the good dishes. He'd have to replace them if one broke. His begging letters shamed me. The Nez Perce didn't want us back anyway.

So Mr. Warren sought investors. I wondered if he knew that doing so would limit his control, shade his dreams a bit with different colors than what he had in mind. I didn't say that as we sat beside the river. Instead, I tried to erase what he had taken as a slight on my part, questioning how he'd accomplish what he set out to do. Facts do little but annoy big dreamers, or make them more determined to show the naysayers wrong. And I found I didn't want to distress him. I wanted to please him, to make him happy. "How many cows do you think you'd need to have?"

"Not milk cows, now. I'm talking beeves."

I nodded, picked up a stitch I'd dropped.

"'Course I'd let you have some milkers, for the little ones and all."

I blinked. "Was that a marriage proposal, Mr. Warren?"

"Kind of." He had a charming grin, the ease of it bringing a shiver to my belly. He plopped another stone into a quiet eddy of the stream. I watched it ripple outward. He reached for my hands. "They're cold."

"I'm fourteen, won't be fifteen until November," I reminded him. "My father would never approve. I've schooling to attend to. My father intends for me to return to the Tualatin Academy in Forest Grove."

"You're smart. You should do that, I suppose, but you can learn from places other than books." He kissed my knuckles. "I wonder if he'll let you. You do a lot for him."

"As long as I have books to read, I'm always learning." I pulled my hands from his. I dropped another stitch I had to go back for. Would my father let me marry, ever? "I can take care of my siblings. No, marriage to you is quite out of the question. I'm responsible for my brother and sisters. I'm the oldest. It's what my mother would want."

"Bring the little ones with you. I like that toothless Martha."

"Her front teeth are in."

"And Amelia is a minx. She's game for anything. Got me to give her a ride on my horse last week and hand over the reins to her. What is she, five?"

"She's six. She'll say 'six and a half.' And yes, she does sometimes take a risk or two and is pretty certain of herself."

"Runs in the family, does it?"

I'm not a risk taker. "With horses. She's very good with horses."

"Not unlike her big sister." He leaned toward me then and I thought he might kiss me.

He did.

The crochet hook dropped into my lap. "I'm fourteen." I swallowed what I was going to say next.

"I know," he whispered. "And tall. And beautiful." His voice was gravely low. "And kind." He kissed me again, hands warm against the back of my head. I hoped my twisted braid would stay atop it. "And the smartest girl I've ever known."

I might not have allowed the final kiss of that afternoon if he hadn't added that last. I don't know why, but it mattered to me that he saw competence. Perhaps because I struggled so with seeing it in myself. I'd made mistakes. Like at Waiilatpu. I hadn't listened to my mother's pleas to keep me home that year. I knew my father wanted me to go to the Whitmans' school at Waiilatpu and I wanted to be with other children, away from my brother and sisters for a time. I wanted the new adventure too, of being in a new place, to hear new stories. So I'd sassed my mother, who only longed to keep me home with her to continue teaching me herself. She could have schooled a toad to give up its hopping if she'd set her mind to it. Brilliant, people said of her teaching. I told her we should do what Father wanted. He was head of the house, after all.

" 'And the servant of the Lord must not strive; but be gentle unto all men, apt to teach, patient . . .' Second Timothy 2:24," my mother had quoted. "This means one must not be quarrelsome, Eliza. But always kind, to everyone, be open to learning new things, and allow God to whisk away resentment as I hear in your voice." I shamed myself with her calm reminder that my tongue could get me into trouble.

Because of my selfishness that day, my desire to resist the higher order that my mother wanted for me, I'd ended up in tragedy, unable to stop it, fearing for my life, my parents' lives, wondering if I'd ever see them or my brother and sisters again. I'd erred. Made many, many mistakes that I carried in my basket of shame. But only briefly did I wonder if sitting there kissing Mr. Warren was one of them.

I clung to him, felt the safety of his arms around me, having missed the touch or warmth of caring. The smell of his sweaty collarless shirt comforted, and his words held the hope that I could choose wisely. My heart pounded and I felt tingles in my bodice pressed against him. "One of the smartest people" he'd ever known, he'd said. And what fourteen-year-old ever considers that a boy twenty probably hasn't met many people at all, let alone so many that one young girl stood out in his field of intelligent people who had crossed his path. For all I know, I was likely the only fourteen-year-old girl he'd ever spent a moment with, let alone kissed.

The crochet hooks poked against me. "We'd better go." I pushed him back with gentle force.

"You didn't answer." He traced my cheekbones with his thumb.

"When you make a proper proposal, Mr. Warren, I will consider it. For now, I will cherish your dream with you. And pray that God will guide you to that place where all good things come from him, not only from your sound efforts."

He pulled back. "You preachin' like your pa?"

"I'm telling you what I believe, what moves me. Not just your warm kisses, Mr. Warren, but your heart must woo me. And I must know your heart seeks Jesus." I didn't know why I threw that condition in. Maybe to placate my father when that time came, or in memory of my mother who was so faithful. "My mother knew her path was set by the Lord Almighty and that was how she endured the trials she did, and she and my father were faithful to each other and their work. She changed a hundred lives with her commitment, her kindnesses, her—"

"I get it. Your mama was a saint. Oh, I ain't mocking, I'm not." He held his hands up to ward off my scowl. "She was. Everyone says so. Even my pa, and his kind words are stingy as mosquitoes in December." He rose, pulled me up to him, our bodies pressed together as close as iron to apron. "I have to think on how I feel about what you're talkin' on." He thumbed my cheek, sending shivers. "Jesus and what-not. That's needed before you'd consider hitching up to my yoke?"

"It will never be a yoke, Mr. Warren, if the Lord chooses it. We'll team up together, yes, but I'll not wear a heavy collar saying I must always go just your way whenever you choose."

"I'll be ponderin' then, Miss Spalding."

I'd given Mr. Warren words to consider. My mother would be proud. I knew what was important in a marriage. I knew what was the center. But I harbored a terrible fear that perhaps Mr. Warren might not come to choose the faith, and what then for us? He rode off. I touched my fingers to my lips so recently caressed and wondered if I would be strong enough to resist the warmth his kisses promised, whether he met my conditions or not.

The Diary of Eliza Spalding

1850

I have often wondered what is important in a marriage, besides a shared faith, how two separate people somehow come together for a purpose beyond themselves; and then see it fractured and believe they've contributed to the problems but not how, nor how to stop it. I've no answers. So I've taken to poring over old notes, translations, lessons, and letters while Mr. S and Eliza are gone to the trial. I write then in this journal hoping I can find some understanding as to what happened, why it happened.

This morning, I watched my twelve-year-old daughter's slender body walk away from me, again. She wore my old cape instead of her own. We hadn't been allowed to take much with us when we escaped, and funds to replace things have come as slow as high country spring. Her bonnet hid her face, but I knew, as a mother does, that she stared with eyes focused on the past. She turned. A painful, pleading look; me, powerless to stop it.

Earlier, my husband and I quivered inside the space of silence as when a walker comes upon a mountain lion, wondering if in that moment destruction would slice the gap or if each would honor peace and allow the other to go along its path. I asked him not to take her, that she was so young and still shaking from that dreadful November day. What I did not realize then was that we all still shook from it, from the powerlessness and wondering why our work had failed in such a way that God had turned his back on so many. These would not be words I could say to my husband, but then I often struggled to find the words to express myself to him. Even before the great tragedy at Waiilatpu.

"I have need of her here." That's what I'd told him, of my need. But truly, I believed it was God's need to protect her yet again. God as the center. That's what I so wanted Eliza to understand, to experience. Instead, it was her father's passion for justice or perhaps revenge that drove him to take her with him to Oregon City.

We'd adjusted to yet another landscape, our little family. This one in the Willamette Valley of the Oregon Territory far from the land I'd come to love, which we called Lapwai and the natives described as "the place of the butterflies." From the mighty rivers of the Snake and Clearwater and the stark, round hills rising like the humped backs of sleeping bulls we moved—escaped— to the Tualatin Plain where tall timber closed in the sky and where I hadn't heard a word of Sahaptin, the Nez Perce language, now for nearly three years. I miss the Nimíipuu people, the language, the work, my life 350 miles away.

I'd pleaded with my husband this morning, using the same words as when he sent Eliza to the school when she was nine. That my husband would insist my child leave (and be a part of that Narcissa Whitman's life! Forgive my sin of jealousy, Lord, especially when I live and Narcissa does not) and then not even take her to school himself because he was too busy doing the Lord's work? Is not tending our children also the Lord's work? I must not dwell there. I will think of better things.

Matilda, our Nimíipuu helper, took my child, the two riding on separate horses the 120 miles to Waiilatpu where Eliza was to remain until the spring. My daughter left a happy child. She celebrated her 10th birthday at Waiilatpu, away from us, among the Cayuse and with the Whitmans. I'd failed in my efforts to keep her home with me then, though some would say I was obedient to my husband, which is of greater import. I'm not certain of that. Standing for a child is of the highest order to my thinking. Now, after all our chaos and moving and moving again, he wishes to attend the trial, insisting that Eliza is the greatest witness, that his Eliza spoke the language, interpreted for the hostages, so of course she would testify, as she must to secure justice. I wonder if having her repeat the trauma expresses the mercy our Lord commanded. The Cayuse responsible are captured; there were other hostages freed, older, to testify. A twelve-year-old child has seen enough and I believe repeats the events in her nightmares. She does not need to see the accused nor hear again the agonies of those terrible days.

I wanted Mr. S to let her stay with me, help with her younger brother and sisters, be a child again, to walk beside me in the forests that we might discover together this new landscape. When I would be well enough to walk again. But in the silence, that pause of walker meeting mountain lion, I knew that I had lost. I watched his face turn red, his fists tighten. He would take her, and my resistance to him would falter as it always did. Well, not always. I did once insist she learn the Nez Perce language as I did, and in the end, that may have saved her. Saved us all. No, the Lord saved us. Even in this diary I must acknowledge that. But I did teach her the language, didn't I? I played some small part in my child's survival, didn't I? I am shamed for not standing up and insisting she remain at home, with me. I didn't stand that day; I let her go to Waiilatpu. One often never knows if what one stands for will in the end be for naught or be the bridge that gives a child a way to go forward.

She mounts her horse, takes the reins. She looks back once and I see a small hand raised, waving.

Forgive me, Lord, my own rambling. It will never be the same for any of us. Especially not for Eliza. Pray help me accept. Help me accept what I do not understand.

≫· 3 ·≪

THE RIVER'S EDGE

Many things about my behavior I do not understand. My meetings with Mr. Warren, for example. By the spring of 1853 I'd been breathless with him, often, seated beside the Calapooia, at some risk. We'd catch each other on the way to Brown and Blakely's or while riding to the Osborne farm. He'd come upon me as planned in the moist heat of blackberries ripening in July. He'd put his arm around me at the graveyard, comforting, my mother having been joined by another settler that year. The iris bloomed. I missed her so! Nothing would be the same with her gone, I knew that, but I kept imagining her with me, wondering what she'd say about Mr. Warren.

I had been too young for my mother to talk to me of love between men and women. Only on that journey to school the fall before the killings did I gain some small insight into marital love. That wouldn't have happened if my father hadn't insisted I go to school, overruling my mother. Then at the last minute he gave Matilda, a Nez Perce woman, a list of supplies to bring back and directed her to take me to the Whitmans at

Waiilatpu. I adored the five-day journey with Matilda. I was nine years old, almost ten. At first I felt abandoned by my father for not riding with me. I also felt incomplete without my brother along; but after what happened, I was grateful he had not been sent to school with me and wasn't there to spoil my time alone with Matilda either.

Matilda had friends among the Cayuse, who often intermarried with the Nez Perce. She looked forward to a few days with them before returning, possibly bringing relatives back with her, a friend or two. We had five days together and they were precious. I've often thought since then that God gives us great joys that fill us so we can draw upon them like a well when times turn tough. I think that's why after the massacre my mother often spoke of the arrival of the printing press, a remembered joy for when she suffered sorrow beyond words.

Matilda didn't treat me as a child who shouldn't be going off to school, who needed me at home. That was how I saw my mother's wish to keep me close then. Matilda treated me as her friend. She told stories of others who lived close to our Lapwai mission, of the trapper Mr. Craig and his sometimes sneaky ways, or of the arguments over men her aunties had. My mother would have called this gossip and forbidden it, but Matilda spoke of life, of how people got along—or didn't;

how they fell in love—or out; something my parents never spoke of.

"Do you have a husband?" I asked Matilda. Birds hopped their way along the deer trail we followed beside the river. I watched the world between Tashe's alert ears.

"I did. He died. I might find another."

"Where do you look for husbands? Are they hiding?"

She laughed. "Some do. Celebrations are good places. Singing and dancing and eating and game playing. One can find a good husband if one looks with clear eyes and is willing to haul them out of their activity." She used the word *hol*, meaning to drag or pull. I imagined a husband stuck in a mud pile and laughed with her. Then she turned serious. "*Aiat hayaksa.*"

"Women hunger?" I clarified. "I'm not hungry."

She smiled. "It will find you one day."

And so it did four years later. With Andrew Warren.

Mr. Warren had begun attending my father's church services in the fall of 1852 shortly after I had turned fifteen. Perhaps to convince me of his faith or to convince Father that he was a worthy mate. Still too young and with the added responsibilities of the younger children, I hadn't considered Mr. Warren's earlier proposal much, instead enjoying the pleasantries of his company, not the least of which was a feeling of exuberance for doing so—taking his company—knowing that my father would object if he knew. I wanted a distraction from my father. He stayed up hours at night by candlelight writing long letters. He drank copious amounts of grain coffee and expended rare funds we didn't have on elixirs he claimed built his concentration. He worked himself into a sweat chopping wood beside my brother, then forgot to bathe before the Sunday service. Several evenings former mission men came for meetings, and I heard them talking late into the night, sometimes my father shouting about Catholics causing all his troubles and shouting of justice "not being served until the Catholic part in this is understood far and wide."

"The hangings are enough, Spalding," I heard one of the men say.

"Never!"

"Vengeance is not ours, Reverend."

"Don't talk to me of vengeance. You still have a wife! You still have daughters not warped!"

I'm warped? How was I twisted or deformed? Didn't I do everything he asked me to do? Didn't I fill my mother's shoes as best I could? Didn't I care for my baby sister, whom he teased while I prepared his meals? How was I misshapen?

"Not all Indians are troublesome," my father said. "The Board must come to understand that. Marcus is the one who created the issues and he paid the ultimate price at the Cayuse hands. But we were asked to come, begged to come by the Nez Perce. Why can't we return? Why can't the Mission Board see that?"

His voice held a wail to it that made my heart ache for him. He and my mother had done so much with the people they served for ten years. I knew he longed to return to that Lapwai valley, to the work that had sustained him. But a part of me knew he could not go home again. My mother wouldn't be with him. I wished he'd stop talking about it.

He mourned, he did. He took Henry with him on road trips, leaving me to tend the girls. Then other times without warning he would change his mind, tell Henry he had to stay and take care of the little ones and that I should pack for two days. We'd be starting a new church, he'd tell me, in some far-off valley. "I can still save souls," he'd say. "Regardless of what the Board says." Yes, he grieved. And some of how he mourned—his unpredictability and frenzy—frightened me. Andrew Warren was a steadier stream.

It was about this time that I began to hear rumors about Mr. Warren. Nancy Osborne told me one or two, that he met up with fellow farmers—ranchers, he would call them—and they played cards. He sometimes lost "sums." And he had a taste for liquor, I learned. I remembered Matilda's stories, and thought these were just ways men played and kept their spirits up until they settled down to hearth and home. I did once venture a conversation with Mr. Warren about what I'd heard. He and I had made our way up the hill behind his parents' farm; our horses were hobbled as we looked out over the valley below. There'd been some moments of holding, kissing, deep breathing, our bodies lying face-to-face along a quilt my mother set aside for picnics. I could stop the forward motion with my words and I did that now.

"I hear you have a taste for liquor, Mr. Warren." I sat up, brushed my bodice, and breathed in the scent of his cologne still lingering at my throat.

He pushed his chin down and jerked away from me. "Whose lips are you listening to? Every man likes a little taste. Medicinal, that's all I take it for. Helps me with the pining you're putting me through."

"You are singled out for such behavior. At the back of Brown and Blakely's, I'm told. On a Saturday night or two. While others drink only to relieve their thirst, I hear that you drink beyond quenching. You've even been loaded on your horse and led home, or so I'm told."

"You hear wrong. Haven't any other good occupation to commit my efforts to. A certain young lady won't commit herself."

"I've told you the conditions." In fact, if he had

expressed his faith in God, I wasn't at all sure that would be enough for my father's blessing on our marriage. I knew I'd have to work on that, but his reluctance to commit suggested I had time. And during that time I looked forward to the kind things Mr. Warren whispered to me, the gentle stroking of my arm, the way my heart beat faster when he came near, how time stood still when I was with him and did not start again until I heard the pounding of his horse's hooves leaving me, my breathing and heart rate once again becoming as steady as a metronome.

"Then let it be known that I do accept your conditions. That I intend to speak to your father about your hand in marriage. I've secured a position in Oregon City, working at the docks."

"You have?" Oregon City was some miles away, across a ferry, though on this side of the Willamette. It's where the trial was held. I didn't like to go there.

"The docks? But I thought you were a cattle-man."

"I need to earn funds to buy those cattle, and working for my pa isn't making that happen fast enough. They need strong arms to load and unload cargo. I'll come back on Sabbath days. That's when I'd like to see you, proper."

"I don't think my father will—"

"Does he intend to keep you cloistered in that house until your sisters are married off?"

"I . . . I don't know. I just know that he needs me now."

"I need you too." He crooned the words with that husky voice he used at times that thrilled me. Yes, that is the word, I was *thrilled* that someone loved me—someone who held me, told me I was precious, adored, who cared for me. And who now was leaving in order to earn money so he could marry me. I wasn't sure I wanted that . . . but I didn't look forward to the drudgery of caring for my siblings and my increasingly erratic father despite what I knew my mother would want. "I need you to say yes to me, to make my longings honest."

"You understand."

"Yes." He pulled me back down onto the quilt. "I understand that I love you, that I cannot live without knowing you love me too. Just say the words, Eliza."

I wanted to. And yet a part of me believed that once I did, all would change. My strength would dissolve and then what? What if the rumors were true?

"I'll keep you safe, Eliza. No one else on this earth will ever love you as I do."

"And what if I can't ever say it?"

"I would still marry you. I love enough for both of us."

Could that be? Could one person love enough for two? I didn't know. I wished I could ask my mother if one's love was enough. I only knew my heart pounded, and that if he threatened to leave, I'd race after him shouting that I loved him. Then I'd be sunk, buried in the well of needing to be loved by someone other than my Lord and living in the depths of consequences such a separation would entail.

The Diary of Eliza Spalding

1850

Today, while they are gone to trial, my mind races backwards like a tongue on a broken tooth, always hunting for familiar, something worthy to think upon following my daily Scripture reading. I used to daydream as a young girl, of having an education and then marrying a man who adored me, promised to keep me safe. I wanted a dozen babies to play at my feet. I love S so. Yet how greatly my life has changed from those youthful thoughts. But today, while my child is grilled by lawyers, forced to recall that wretched time, I pray for her, that she will find happier things to think upon when the questions cease. I must do the same, pray I find happier memories to dwell on.

The day the printing press arrived at Lapwai! Oh how grand a day it was! We had hoped for so long for a way to bring the Word to the Nez Perce people who had welcomed us with such delight. They gave us a skin home to live in while they cut logs and built our house. Fish and elk and deer meat appeared at our door that saw us through that first winter. I saw then God's grace in my not having a child to keep. Compared to

Fort Vancouver, the "New York of the West" as I called it, our log hut in Lapwai was primitive at best. But it was home and our Indian neighbors warm and inviting, unlike what we heard from the Whitmans, settled among the Cayuse. Unlike what we'd been told to expect before we traveled west. I held no fear of the Indians then. None. I could observe the different ways The People did things, like the baby boards that kept a child secure as well as entertained while a mother cooked over an open fire. Older children ran free of the constraints of clothing, small loincloths for the boys; short skirts of leather for the girls. The People willingly gave me the names of items I touched, and I was ever grateful that the Lord blessed me with the gift of taking in languages with ease. With the printing press, I could give the language back.

Mr. S insisted that we plant a garden quickly that next spring, and the Indians worked beside us digging earth as well, though we had no plow, just hoes. He begged the Mission Board for money to buy plows, but such expenditures were not approved, just one of the many frustrations with us being so far—in a foreign field—on our own. While we worked, I learned words in Sahaptin more quickly, I found, than they could grasp our English. *Shikam* is what they called their handsome horses, many a light color with black spots sprinkled like bits of nutmeg across their rumps. Ravens or *Koko* flew above us as we worked. Each thing I saw was new, and when I pointed, Matilda or Timothy or Joseph would give me the Nimíipuu or Nez Perce name. I once asked what The People's name meant and Joseph was thoughtful. "English give it the name for pierced nose. Those who did this are not of The People. We say Nez Perce means 'We walked out of the woods through the forest.' Before we had fine horses. But the English . . . maybe Clark used that nose name." He put his palms up in surrender. "We are the Nimíipuu, The People."

"We English spread from one thing to many," I said.

Timothy answered: "It is as you say."

I would remember that conversation later, after Waiilatpu and the Board's decision forcing us to leave. But the language-learning! It was as though I was back in Hebrew and Greek classes sitting on hard wooden benches beside my husband at Western Seminary in Cincinnati—but here I sit on a Hudson's Bay blanket with blue sky and fluffy *Ipalikt* (clouds) over us rather than the rafters of the college. I knew I would need to know their Nez Perce word, their Sahaptin language, if I was to share with them the stories of our Savior's love. And that was why I had come all that way, to bring that good news to lighten the dark days of The People. The Nez

Perce had come east to plead for teachers to bring them the Book of Heaven. I was prepared to meet that call in the everyday routines as God allowed.

Mr. S would soon ride off to place orders with the Mission Board and also spend what little cash we had at Fort Vancouver. Or he'd have meetings with the missionaries who came after us, taking their calls among the Spokane and other tribes. He left me alone during those travels, but I found the time a respite from his constant activity and direction. He so wanted our Mission to succeed, as did I. The women learned weaving and carding quickly, and the summer the printing press came, we plain wove 23 yards of flannel.

The Hall family came with the press. Dear Sarah Hall endured a difficult pregnancy and could not walk. She'd made the trip all the way from the Sandwich Islands where their mission work had been so successful. Having our own printing press was a luxury and we saw it as God's divine gift for furthering our work. We did not hold it over the other sites that we had this gift, but I sensed envy, even then.

Little Eliza was but a year old when the Halls and Mr. Rogers and their giant boxy press arrived, the size of two pie cabinets with rollers and gears. Mr. Rogers would help S put all the parts together. Flats of typeface and reams of paper, precious paper. The party also arrived with Indian paddlers who had brought Sarah Hall lying on her back in a canoe while the men rode overland on horseback with the press, meeting Sarah at evening time, the men preparing the meals at the water's edge. Once arrived, the Indians faded into the Nez Perce community as though family, but I heard one woman paddler, tall and stately, speak soft French and English. Sarah called her Marie and said she was of the Iowa Tribe. "She's a long way from home. She arrived with the Astor Expedition of 1811." She had been an over-lander too, one who, like me, remained.

"We are all come from faraway places," I said, to her agreement.

We settled the Halls in, placing Sarah on a pallet laid upon two timber rounds inside the house so she could be with me as I chopped potatoes and washed greens from our abundant garden. She spoke to Eliza as though she was an adult and I liked that. Baby talk never appealed to me, and after Eliza's close call with death the first month she lived, I treated her like a companion.

"What's she saying?" Sarah asked. I listened.

"She says you have pretty hair."

Sarah laughed. "I'm not sure how it can be as I haven't had a chance to wash it since we left Vancouver. I just hope the lice have not found their way as they did on board ship."

"We'll settle your clothes in cedar bark just to be sure. Something in the bark kills the fleas and ticks and might kill lice too. And later, if you wish, Matilda and I will wash your hair."

"Lovely." Eliza stroked Sarah's golden hair and I saw the woman close her eyes in blessed rest.

"Come," I whispered to my daughter. "Let Mrs. Hall sleep."

The Nimíipuu, Matilda especially, sensing the festive nature of the arrival of the Halls, brought fresh fish and planned a gathering in their honor. I found The People looked for any excuse to sing and dance and play their stick games. (It was only much later I learned that the stick games amounted to gambling, and I had some consternation over my having learned how to play the games and finding such delight in the sleight of hand, not knowing that such actions might mean the exchange of horses and valued pelts and hatchets. It's odd I'd think of gambling on a day when my daughter testifies, perhaps gambling away the peace we've worked so hard for her to seize.)

Mr. S was at his very best that evening as well he should be. In such a short time he could boast (though he didn't) a home for us, with a meeting place at one end large enough to house over one hundred Nimíipuu who came to hear him speak while one of the Nimíipuu criers translated. Fields of corn and potatoes and wheat surrounded our mission, and beyond were rings of tipis set like praying hands pointing to the sky. It was Mr. S's belief that the Indians needed to be domesticated and be less wandering by seasons not only so they could consistently hear the Word and learn the Lord's ways but because he worried there would be more white people coming into our country and they would overrun The People.

Mr. S described them as "Children. Such kind people, the Nimíipuu, while many of our 'white tribe' are not." I agreed with the latter but not the former. They were not children. But they were curious, questioning, intelligent, caring people, non-judging. As for the white tribe? I cringed when I heard that the missionaries at The Dalles would not send supplies to those on a wagon train who'd taken a wrong route in 1845. Did that demonstrate mercy? They claimed the people had made a mistake and must live with the consequences, but the Samaritan didn't ask the injured man why he'd taken a route known to be peopled by thieves. He simply helped him. My husband and I saw it as our mission to bring such mercy. To bring Jesus to their souls and prepare them for the changes that would come. Changes we brought about by our making it over the mountains with my father's little wagon. If two white women could survive the trip, then before long there would be many others, not just missionaries caring for their souls, but those who would want their land: this hot, majestic, verdant, tree-barren hill country cut by sparkling streams. Were we wrong?

I sometimes feel guilty for my part in bringing about such change.

Mr. S and I had worked on the language together. I count it one of the most joyous experiences we shared, this effort to translate important biblical stories and songs into Sahaptin, their language. That I have that memory of the two of us pursuing a purpose together gives me peace on difficult days when we no longer have a mission. Dr. Whitman insisted the Cayuse learn English, and I equate that demand to some of the unrest we heard of among the missionaries themselves, the Whitmans and Eells, even those early years. I had been concerned when it was decided that we would not all remain together as one mission. But later, I was grateful my husband had decided—along with Dr. Whitman—that we would do more good to go where we'd been invited by the Nez Perce than try to convince another tribe that they wanted us.

But I digress from telling of a day of such joy when the press arrived. It confounds me how difficult it is to hold happy memories, how much easier to remember trouble. Perhaps the painful memories are ways to try to restore the time before the tragedy, and yet suffering arrives when one longs for what is not and can never be again. We did celebrate that evening, and for several days the Indians staged dancing and horse races, their skinny-tailed dogs sniffing and panting in and out of the tipis. The People baked salmon on sticks angled close to the fires, roasting the fillets as long as Mr. S's arm, so that we could chew on the savory flesh in the morning, even when the fish had cooled. The dried slabs of fillet would keep for months. Eliza thrived on the meat, and we all had fishy breaths despite the liberal use of tooth powder.

During the afternoon respites when the Indians slept in the heat, we missionaries bent over the typeface and the press. Mr. S and Joseph had built a small building to house it, with windows to bring in good light, and there the men worked to put the parts together. Mr. Hall, tall and willowy, had an ease about him, and he was gentle with his wife as few men I've ever seen be. He joked, too, and I found it a delight to laugh. Mr. S is a serious soul, purposeful. He told me laughter takes up space better spent in work. Once, in seminary, he wrote a treatise on how to win six hundred million souls worldwide to Christ in twenty-one years. He had much to accomplish and I took it as no small gift that he had chosen me—no, God chose me for him—to do such work. Of course that was before I knew that Henry had asked someone else first to share his life with him and she had declined. Imagine my surprise to meet that very woman one day and share a seven-month journey across the continent with her and her husband. Later my child would be taught by her in far-off Waiilatpu. It was good I had the focus of the language to put into typeface and to print, keeping my own sinful, envious thoughts at bay.

Once the Sahaptin primer was complete, we intended to translate the book of Matthew into their language. They would be the first books printed west of the Rocky Mountains—a language primer and the gospel. They would exist because of Mr. S. And yes, in no small part because of me. I hope I am not being prideful.

Martha Jane, we call her, and Millie, my two youngest, play together today while Eliza and Mr. S are at the trial. Henry Hart, our one son, chops wood. I hear the distant chink-chink of the axe fall. He should be in school and would be if we had remained at Forest Grove. I sometimes wonder what tribe we displaced with the forming of a school and town, so many missionaries arriving on those plains at once. Maybe it too is sacred ground, as where the Whitmans chose their "place of the rye grass," a field with meaning to those Cayuse people. I never took that love of landscape as a sacrilege as Dr.

Whitman did. He recognized no sacred places of The People.

But I felt God close in certain landscapes, heard him whisper to me in the wind, felt his warmth at an evening fire, in the blood red of the sun setting over the hills at Lapwai. The land gave up so much to sustain us there: shelter, food, clothing, even the skin pants I learned to make, the carrying of guns and riding horseback lethal to cloth pantaloons once worn by my husband. And later sheep my husband introduced to the region brought wool and spinning and weaving dresses and shirts that actually fit and hadn't arrived inside a wooden barrel smelling of whiskey or the sea sent two years previous by the Mission Board. It gave us memories worthy of the telling, which Mr. S did in lengthy letters to the Mission Board that were printed in their newsletters, helping raise finances to support our work here. There.

We are no longer there.

Later, Mr. S wrote pleading letters, but that is for another day. In that land of rivers and rounded hills we were allowed a successful ministry with many souls seeing Jesus and accepting both his love for each of them and forgiveness, too. Our Nimíipuu believers at last held language in their hands. Books. It was a miracle of no small measure. That's what I must hang on to, not what happened after.

⇒ 4 ⇐

SECRETS

My parents had shared a passion in their mission work. I doubt they had any secrets between them. Mr. Warren and I held nothing noble between us, though we did have a common goal of receiving my father's permission for marriage. That challenge could bind us together like blackberry juice ink to paper, rarely fading.

Nancy and I shared a bond like that, she who also survived the killings. She knew my secrets, too, of meeting with Mr. Warren when I ought to have been making soap. We also shared the secret of how we healed or tried to. We talked of it while she held a skein of yarn around her thin arms as I rolled it into a knitting ball. I remembered few survivors, except for Nancy and the Sager girl. She had once stayed with us in Forest Grove when orphans from the wagon trains and tragedy flooded onto that Tualatin Plain. Nancy had been there that day in November when our world changed forever.

I barely knew Nancy then. She'd come overland in '45 and stopped at Waiilatpu as so many immigrants did. But they rolled on into the Willamette Valley and returned in '47 when Dr. Whitman needed a millwright. The Cayuse had burned his mill in that place of sweet grass where the Whitmans' graves lie. Mr. Osborne, a big man with red hair that he gave to all his children, was a millwright, and so the family left their cattle and pigs in the valley and came back east across the mountains. "Going backwards" was how Nancy said her father spoke of their journey, but it promised to pay well and he had a contract for two years. And in his own way he hoped to contribute to the mission work by allowing Dr. Whitman more time to do what he was trained to do—treat people and share the gospel. Though my father once let slip that Dr. Whitman was never trained to deliver souls as my father had been.

As she holds the yarn, Nancy sits in a precise way. Every time. Feet together, her seat forward on the rocking chair that she does not let rock her into comfort. When she enters, she touches the back of the chair three times, looks out each window, straightens the curtains I've sewn, returns to the chair to sit. Only that chair. When I ask her why she does those things, she laughs and says, "You know." And so I do.

I have my own rituals. I must say the Lord's Prayer three times each morning and each evening before I fall asleep. If I fall asleep mid-prayer, when I wake I must begin again and add a fourth time. In the morning, I must lie awake going over all the terrible things that might happen in the day. If I do, I believe that the Lord will have heard me planning, taking care of my sisters and my brother, preventing their deaths by drowning in the Calapooia or from standing too close to a fire. If I hear the chop of the axe outside the window, I quickly imagine my brother's death so that it might not occur. I imagine a difficult crossing on Kirk's Ferry that my father takes daily to act as post-master. That I survive each death of those I love gives me confidence to join the day. When I see Nancy, my heart beats steadily instead of the racing as it often does, for we are kindred spirits.

She was in the white children's school with me, taught by Mr. Rogers, and together we attended the Sunday school class taught by Mrs. Whitman. A tiny woman, sweet as honey with hair the same color. She began each fall class of Sunday school with the Twenty-Third Psalm, and I wished that Mrs. Whitman and dear Nancy had been with me during the hostage time, as we could have recited together "Yea, though I walk through the valley of the shadow of death, thou art with me, thy rod and thy staff they comfort me." We were all in the valley of the shadow of death but in different places that November day of 1847. No one who wasn't a part of that terror really understands the nightmares or the moments of searing loss that return unexpected. I think now they are memories of our powerlessness and betrayal, when our world went from being safe and protected and adventurous to the day we began wearing fear and uncertainty like a too-heavy cloak. To take it off exposed us to a fearsome vulnerability, but wearing that cloak slowed us, kept us from moving forward into a life God planned for us.

Nancy and I lost touch after that terrible November. The Osbornes escaped after spending a perilous night under the floor at the Whitman mission, breathing shallow as a bat so that the Cayuse stomping over their heads, all full of blood lust from their killings, didn't find them huddling there. Mrs. Osborne had the measles with a terrible fever, and a week or so before they'd buried their baby who died of that disease. But her illness was the only reason they had been close enough to that safe room with time for Mr. Osborne to pull the boards up and shove his family and himself under to safety.

It seemed a miracle that her family appeared in South Brownsville not long after we did, attending my father's church. Her father occupied half the bench in our little congregation and he'd snore and fall off the backless seat, making a racket. No one uttered a word, as my father insisted on absolute attention and a strict code of silence but for his words that often pelted me like hail. I confess I did not hear much of what he spoke of. I had no fear of hell, really. I'd already been there. And some days I wasn't certain but that I lingered at that gate again.

The real secret Nancy and I shared was in how we tried to resolve the nightmares and anxieties, which we did that spring day after her rituals and our winding the yarn into balls. "If you weren't there, there isn't much another can really tell us about what to do, isn't that right, Eliza?"

"Absolutely. Mama used to tell me that we did the best we could, that the Lord looked out for us, but I still wonder why he didn't look out for the others. I mean, what did we do that we deserved to live when they didn't?"

We sat in that main room of our log home pondering that question that seemed as tangled in my mind as the knitting yarn could get. I noted a hole in the chinking between the logs and told myself to remember to tell Father. Or likely attend to it myself. He took any mention by me of a household need as a criticism of himself.

"Did you want to go to the trial?" Nancy posed the question. My answer was interrupted by my sister needing her knee looked at. Millie bounded to me, trusting I would do my best to make her feel better.

"I fell."

"So I see." I dabbed at the wound with my apron edge. "What were you doing exactly?"

"A . . . a rabbit came by and Yaka chased it and I ran after it through the garden and stumbled at the rocks you put there to mark it. I'm sorry. Rabbits don't notice fences."

"Apparently you don't either."

"Are you mad at me, 'Liza?"

"No, of course not." I sounded cross but it wasn't at my sister: it was at myself, that I'd failed to imagine that anyone might stumble on the rocks I'd carefully lined up to mark the perimeter of the garden, hoping to keep the grasses from encroaching. Lacking a spiderweb to put across the wound, I poured a splotch of my father's elixirs to clean and stop the bleeding.

"Ouch! Ouch! Ouch!" She danced from foot to foot.

"I'm sorry it has to hurt to feel better." I kissed her knee above the cleaned wound and she was off on another adventure.

I fixed tea for Nancy, watched her center my mother's ironstone cup on the saucer, didn't answer her question about the trial, didn't comment on her orderly ways. Changing the subject always proved a good way to avoid uncomfortable things. I did that instead.

"Did you notice? I didn't get upset over Amelia's bloody wound."

"Now that you say that, I do. Maybe one day we'll be normal again."

It was a hope, though without my mother to model wisdom in uncertain times, I wasn't sure I'd recognize what healing really was.

●●●

Later that day, feeling braver after Nancy left, I went in search of my mother's wisdom inside those missing diaries. I thought she might speak to me from beyond the grave, bring me comfort if I saw some similarity in how we faced our days. So like a mouse sneaking beside a sleeping cat, I secreted my way scratching through my father's things—their things in a trunk stowed in the barn loft. An old leather pouch he once carried gave up nothing but its scent. I moved aside a stack of clothing of my mother's with her lavender scent still wisping in the folds. A tattered wool jacket rolled against the side. Cedar bark chips fell out when I lifted it up. My father might have worn it when they wed. No, at her funeral. I heard the horse stomp below me in its stall. Listened for my father's or siblings' footsteps. All was quiet. But still, no diaries. *Were they left behind in Lapwai?* I found books, lots of books, including one I remembered my mother reading to me. *Fables for My ABC Book.* Then my hand touched a velvet bag and I thought at first it was a neck collar with a gold clasp on it. I reached inside and there it was: my mother's wedding ring. I fingered it, imagined her wearing it. I couldn't hold back the tears.

Time drifted and I knew I must put things back before my father returned. I wiped my face with my apron, slipped the ring on a leather twine, and tucked it around my neck like a hidden necklace beneath the blouse I wore. He would never see it and he wouldn't marry without it, I was certain. I stepped over the small shame I carried with it as I put things back into the trunk.

Nancy had wondered aloud one day why she often did things she later felt so sorry for, things she couldn't seem to keep herself from doing. I pressed the ring beneath my chemise and changed the subject.

⇒ 5 ⇐
SACRIFICES

My father was a bear the next evening just before I put potatoes, venison jerky, and spring greens on the table. "Where is it? Who intruded into my trunk?"

"Henry! Did you take your mother's ring?"

"I didn't. No, sir. I didn't." My brother shook as Father stood over him, a Goliath to a failed David. The look on his face ought to have told my father that he didn't do it.

My sisters huddled in the corner, Millie with her thumb in her mouth, a habit given up long before, I'd thought. My own heart pounded like the butter churn.

"How could you, Henry Hart?" I stepped between my brother and my father as he raised his fist against my brother. "Now I won't have it when I marry."

My father turned me toward him, his fingers digging into my shoulder. "You're worried about your marriage? That's of no merit." He pushed me aside. "Who among my children, my very own flesh and blood, has stolen from me?"

"Maybe someone else took it. People do come and go here," I reminded him.

"Henry Hart! Do you confess?"

Why didn't my father accuse me? It was as though he knew but wasn't sure what he'd do with me if he found the truth. I think he thought me fragile. And yet I wanted him to accuse me, I'm not sure why. Maybe to recognize that I existed outside of the aftermath of loss. Nor was I only his helper.

"You will go to bed without supper for a week, Henry, or until you confess. Do you understand, boy?"

"I didn't take it, Papa, I didn't." Tears welled up in his eyes. Shame clouded mine.

"Go!"

And I let my brother climb the ladder to the loft and take the blame.

There'd been no confession, of course. And a week later, mid-May, Father told us he had to travel to Fort Vancouver on business, a journey of five days. He left and Henry was reprieved from his lack of supper. He scowled at me.

"What?" I said.

"You took it."

"I saved you from being beaten," I reminded him. "He was going to hit you."

"But I didn't take the ring. You did. Slipping me food each night doesn't make up for your lie, Sister. You took it."

"I did."

"I knew it!" He slammed his palm on the table. "Why didn't you say?"

"Because as long as he has no ring, he won't remarry."

My brother blinked and stepped back. "Remarry? He'd never do that. Mama's only been gone two years. You should tell him. Still, it was wrong of you to let me take the blame." He pouted, his lower lip pooching out, his fingers circling a wood knot in the table.

"Men tend to need wives." I ignored the truth of his statement. "They put away pain that way, I suppose. If I'm widowed, I'll never remarry."

"Who would marry you anyway? Not that Warren."

"You might be surprised."

"I wonder what business Father has at Fort Vancouver."

"He didn't say. Do you want to eat at the table with us tonight?"

"I guess."

I was grateful we'd crossed an impasse, changed the subject. I loved my brother, but to my shame, I was willing to sacrifice him to hold near my heart something precious from my mother and to degrade myself to do it.

Four days later my father's "business" stood beside him in our house. Rachel Johonet "Jane" Smith arrived in May 1853, barely two years after my mother's death. She came around the Horn, as they say, by ship, looking like a woman at once elegant by her posture and choice of hat and dress—and yet frumpy, with stitching pulled out across her wide girth and the feather on her hat leaning over her forehead. When she let out her breath, the feather lifted and then settled. She gripped the arm of my father.

"Meet Rachel, your new mother. We married at Forest Grove."

I stared, then finding my voice corrected, "That would be stepmother." *When had this courtship ensued?*

"Welcome." My brother, as always, spoke the right word.

Apparently one of those long foolscap letters my father sent off wasn't to the Foreign Mission Board but to Rachel in Boston, asking for marriage. My father filled us in, chattering like a schoolboy. She'd been a teacher. Did he imagine she'd be one like my mother was: gifted, a facility with languages seldom equaled, a creative artist? I was glad I had her ring even though it didn't stop this . . . this defacement of my mother's memory.

"She's come to tend my home." He smiled at her. "So you can have more time to study, Eliza. I've done this for you and the children more than for me—though every man needs a woman to walk beside him. And I must say I am chagrined to have misplaced your mother's wedding ring."

He glared at Henry. I waited to see if Henry would expose me but he didn't. "Rachel has graciously accepted that there is no ring," Father continued. "At least until I find it . . ." His eyes scanned us. "Or can afford another."

"My name is Rachel Johonet Jane Smith. Well, I guess Spalding too. But you may call me Mother if you wish." Her voice was clear as a mountain stream. I wanted to muddy it.

"And if I don't wish?"

"Eliza. Don't be rude."

Rachel pressed her gloved hands on my father's arm as she turned to him. "No, no, that's fine. I appreciate a child who speaks her mind." That won her one check for good with me. "Then Rachel would be preferable. I do understand your reluctance."

She had kind words for each child, noting Millie's new front teeth and Martha's arched brows. Henry, nearly as tall as Rachel, nodded formally to her. To me Rachel said, "Your father speaks so highly of you, Eliza, of such a help-mate you've been to him. And of your . . . tragedy. I'm so sorry."

"There's no need for you to be sorry," I said. "You had nothing to do with it."

My father cleared his throat. "Good, good. Let's get settled in then, shall we, Rachel, dear?" He lifted the carpetbag he'd carried, pausing to walk with it to his bed . . . their bed.

Her eyes gazed around our simple home and I saw it as she did: a plank table with two benches on either side and one chair at the end. My father's. The rocking chair on the rag rug I'd made. Our beds were stuffed with bedstraw, a plant that grew beside the river in the moist areas. Henry and I slept in the loft; the little girls on mats nearest my father's bed. Rachel pushed down on that pad with a flattened hand. "It feels so . . . different."

"You're accustomed to feather ticks, I suspect." This, from my father. "We have fewer amenities here. I tried to explain the conditions to you, Rachel." She'd arched her eyebrow. "Mrs. Spalding." His correction brought a smile to her wide face.

"Something to order then. A person's sleep is paramount to good health. *Godey's Lady's Magazine* affirms it. I'll be subscribing to that, as well. The magazine is excellent training material for young girls. I'm sure you'll like it." She smiled at Martha, who curtsied. I'd never seen my sister curtsy nor grin as huge as the one she gave Rachel when the woman lifted Martha's chin in her gloved hands and whispered, "Such beautiful features."

"My mother corresponded with the editor of *Godey's*," I said. "We have copies here."

"Did she, now? How glorious for you all."

"Just old ones," Martha said. "Old copies."

"Well, my, that's unexpected. And excellent." She removed her yellow gloves. Both dress and gloves had brown accent piping. Her crinolines swirled as she surveyed beyond our faces and filled the small space further. "A quilt will form as a divider until we can add a room for the children's beds, don't you think, Henry?" My brother opened his mouth. "I don't think I can . . ." then closed it. We'd never heard a woman call my father "Henry." He'd always been "Mr. S" from my mother and "Reverend Spalding" or "Postmaster" from other men and women in our town. Or Father.

"He didn't know to whom you were speaking." My father expressed an awkward chuckle. "We call him Henry Hart. His mother's maiden name."

"You'll be plain Henry then, Husband," Rachel clarified. "That way there'll be no confusion. Isn't that right, Henry Hart? And we'll keep your mother's name. Ever in our presence. Henry Hart. That's lovely."

She won another point from me as my father nodded. He certainly couldn't be besotted with her, could he? It was a marriage of convenience, and at that moment I found myself less troubled by her presence than by the surprise of it, that I had failed to see any signs. Still, it would be good to have an extra hand at fixing meals, making soap and candles, carrying water buckets, milking cows, weeding the garden, drying fish and berries, letting out the hems of little dresses. I might even have more time with Mr. Warren. Despite the trepidations, the possibilities suddenly sounded delicious.

"Now then, let's rustle up some grub." My father used a phrase I'd only heard spoken by men tending sheep back at our mission in Lapwai. He rubbed his hands together too, a gesture foreign to him. He acted . . . giddy.

Five pairs of eyes turned to Rachel Johonet Jane Smith Spalding.

Her blue eyes wide, her mouth a perfect *O*, she said, "Surely you don't expect me . . . ?"

After a moment's pause, my father spoke. "No. Of course not. You've traveled far today and must be tired. Eliza, please prepare our supper."

I turned toward the cupboard where we kept the flour, soda, salt, and blackberry syrup to stir up syrup bread.

"Dear Henry. Didn't I tell you? Didn't my dear brother-in-law explain?" Rachel removed the hat pins while she spoke. "I don't cook. I'm a professional woman. I've never even boiled an egg."

The Diary of Eliza Spalding

1850

I am ill now, not even able to be up and boil eggs for my children. Henry Hart prepares them as Mr. S and Eliza spend time and money in Oregon City at the trial. I hear the chatter of my children being nurtured in the kitchen.

Today I found a letter to my brother Horace among his things stored here in Brownsville. In March 1846 I had written to him:

"I thank God, whom I serve from my forefathers with pure conscience, that without ceasing I have remembrance of thee in my prayers night and day; Greatly desiring to see thee, being mindful of thy tears, that I may be filled with joy." Paul writes these words to Timothy and me to you, my dear brother Horace. I thank you for sending me the message of our father's death. He was a good man, though how I wish he had found his way to the Lord's blessings. But we cannot know these things. At the last moment, my prayers for him may have been answered and I will see him again in a better place. I pray too that our dear mother awaits him with open arms and that one day you will be there with my sisters and all of us as well.

It is of great joy that you will come west and bring my inheritance such as it is. Our father had said quite clearly that upon his death I must return to New York to secure my land as my siblings acquired, which is of course impossible. Even though things are more settled than in '42 with Mr. S no longer being considered for dismissal, we lack both funds and the will to make such a lengthy trip, and heaven knows what would happen to our work here in our absence. Your plans to come by ship to Vancouver are wise. Send us word upon your departure and we will prepare to bring you here from the Fort at Vancouver. If you can make your way to Fort Walla Walla, that would mean a much less arduous trip for Mr. S to meet you and bring you to our Lapwai mission. What a joy it will be to hold you again, dear brother. My regards please to my sisters whom I hold in my heart.

Ever your faithful sister,
Eliza

While Henry Hart prepares our eggs, three-year-old Millie and five-year-old Martha speak together in a language almost their own, their leaving dolls making a happy family—the dolls made of leftover cloth, a cotton ball for a head, and yarn to mark the sleeves as arms. They appear cheerful, not stricken by all that happened, not scarred as Eliza is. She endured so much. I worry that she is too stalwart, too strong. Even a tree must bend in the wind or it will break, have its roots exposed. I fear her breaking and my not being here to tend to her healing.

I awaited Horace's arrival that day with such joy the year before everything happened. I was eager for his companionship. The tensions between us and the other missionaries, the Smiths and the Whitmans, grew ever worse. Dr. Whitman sometimes refused to act as the mission doctor, which was his responsibility. He would not come when I gave birth to Eliza, until it was almost too late. The child nearly died. Other times he told Mr. S what he must and must not do in bringing the faith to our Nimíipuu. He seemed jealous—such a childish emotion—when Timothy, Joseph, and a white man, Connor, asked for baptism. We had not brought the Indians to the faith "in English." Such a petty thought. We were not forced to learn Greek or Hebrew before we found the faith. We learned in English, our language. Why not teach in Nez Perce?

Marcus Whitman's intrusions troubled us and

things only got worse with the arrival of the Smiths. Marcus was not trained as a minister of the word. Mr. S was. He felt we should not be teaching in the Nez Perce language, that our Indians should learn English. Yet the Whitmans rejoiced with the printing press and the publication of our primer and the book of Matthew, both in Nez Perce language called Sahaptin. At least outwardly they rejoiced. The Halls did celebrate. They taught Hawaiian at their mission. Like us, they did not require English for their converts and they too were successful in bringing people to experience love. I miss Sarah Hall immensely.

And what good was English, just to speak to us? We could easily speak their language after a time, even little Eliza. We taught the scriptures to the young men who did know English, and as criers, they taught their people. I drew pictures to describe Noah's ark and God's provision and rainbow promise. And they did a splendid job of reteaching the women and children, the braves and the elders. Yes, they may have missed some nuance of the faith but what they needed to know—that Jesus loved them as they were and would greet them in Heaven—they understood. To my thinking, is there a greater message?

All the missionaries, wives, and children had a meeting at Waiilatpu, all of them, in '42. I refused to attend. I didn't want to hear the bickering nor their unkind words about Mr. S—and me, I suppose. My teacher training allowed me to draw, sing, play harmonica music, hymn-sing, and do every handiwork I could imagine, giving experience to words, using head, heart, and hands. Our Nez Perce learned quickly! I drew the Bible stories of the woman with the lost coin, using bones from their stick games for currency —or did I paint dentalia, the small round mollusk shells used as currency? My memory fades. I painted David and Goliath, drawing an Indian boy and man. A river stone and slingshot caught their interest, easily. I painted pictures using inks I made from red berries and black berries and the sunny flowers that sprang forth in spring. All ages loved the colorful stories and I felt useful, as though the talents given me had found a place of investment.

I think the Whitmans and the Smiths were envious. So I remained at home with the children while the others went off and met in '42 at Waiilatpu and did the business of sending reports to the Mission Board. I knew something wasn't right when Mr. S returned early. He claimed it had been a contentious time but they'd resolved hard issues. Later, as we lay side by side on the bird-feather mattress, he whispered what had happened. A letter from the Board awaited him at the meeting. It was full of complaints lodged by other missionaries against us! Because of these unfounded complaints, Mr. S and Dr. Whitman, too, had been dismissed.

"Dismissed? That can't be! Why?" I edged up on my elbow, brushed my long braid aside.

"They say we've lost our way, not brought sufficient heathens to the Lord." It was how they counted success, by numbers rather than by how people changed their lives.

"Well, maybe not Marcus but you have. We have."

He lay with his hands as in prayer across his stomach. "Perhaps we have focused too much on getting the Indians to settle near the mission. We did it for a good reason, to protect them, especially since Marcus invites the immigrants, makes them feel welcome so they'll stay and we'll have a state one day. That appeals to him more than saving souls. But maybe we spend too much time in plowing furrows rather than in planting seeds of faith." In the moonlight I could see him blink rapidly. "I may have failed us, Eliza. I may have failed us."

I reminded him of Young Timothy coming to the Lord. Of Joseph, seeking baptism, giving up the ways of the medicine doctors and the strange spirits. How could he speak of failure? "Are we abandoned here, then? All our work we're to forget ever happened? And go where? How? We have nothing but the clothes on our backs. Or is even my nightdress the property of the Mission Board?" I felt a panic new to me, greater than when I almost died coming here across the continent. Was it shame, a fear of failure? Anger at whom? I inhaled, slowed my heartbeat, resolved to remind myself we were in God's hands. I kept my voice calm. I could see Mr. S was distressed beyond words. "Who lodged these complaints?"

"Smiths, I imagine. Maybe the Eells."

I rose from our bed. The moon shone full through the single window casting a square shadow onto the puncheon floor. I paced. I knew Narcissa and Marcus still grieved the drowning of their little Alice, born not long before our Eliza. Perhaps that's what brought on all the chaos, the complaints. Grief is a shape shifter. Narcissa could be demanding and they complained that they were not well treated by their Cayuse Indians. When they came here, they could see that we had friends among The People. Matilda and I laughed together as sisters, shared stories in a language Narcissa didn't understand. We saw the Nez Perce as people, not just heathens needing our Savior. We were willing to let them teach us things about them, about living here. At that time, it seemed to me the Whitmans had abandoned their efforts to bring the Book of Heaven to their Indians, whom they dismissed as stubborn, demanding money for the use of their land. Instead the Whitmans focused on the emigrants who came, more each year. The Whitmans prepared for settlement, for the arrival of new pioneers who would take even more prime land from the Indians, and spent their time selling goods to those on wagon trains while we spent our love on the Nez Perce and their souls.

I heard Narcissa say once she had no interest in teaching the Cayuse, that they were too "hardheaded" to be taught. I did not find that so. But she would not have complained to the Board. Marcus had been dismissed too in the letter campaign.

To this day I remain confused. I heard later that everyone agreed that "our" differences had been settled, that complaints against various families would cease (meaning Mr. Smith would stop sending his letters of concern to the Board) and I was relieved. But then Mr. S let it slip that part of what made things settle was Marcus chose to head east to plead our case to the Board and explain the difficulties with Asa Smith and his haughty ways (God forgive my using unkind thoughts about that man) and that Mr. Smith would head to Hawaii. Oh the poor Halls will have to deal with him now!

And then the blow that night, as the moon cast glitter over the Clearwater River. Mr. S told me he agreed that we would stop teaching in Sahaptin, use only English.

The very thing that made our work thrive he agreed to throw out, to have my students repeat things in English by rote, words they neither understood nor took into their hearts. I was ready to write a letter of complaint to the Board myself for the foolishness of men!

❧ 6 ❧

COOKSTOVE WISDOM

Men can be so foolish! Why would my father marry a woman who knew nothing of cooking and couldn't even boil eggs? It became *my* duty to teach her. "Dry kindling starts the fire in the fireplace. Then we bring in green wood because dry wood burns too quickly. We need at least an hour to make coals."

"You just burn it up?"

"Coals. We cook over coals, not open fire. Did you never watch anyone cook?"

"We had coal stoves in Boston." She smiled. "Perhaps I'll ask your father to have one shipped here."

"Can you cook on it? I'd support the expenditure."

"I can't cook on it, but you could." She had a little-girl voice when she was caught in an insufficiency. "Maybe you could teach me."

"When the coals are just right, died down a bit, we start adding wood, to maintain the temperature we need." I showed her how to swing the bar that held the iron *S*, how to use the tongs to lift the bale on the smaller cast-iron pots to hang them on the *S*, then swing it back over the coals.

"If the stew gets too hot, you can swing it out and stir." I handed her the tongs so she could try, and to her credit, she did all right. I imagined her getting burned and knew she'd be alarmed at my treatment: layering on the scrapings of a raw potato instead of medicine. "Careful you don't burn yourself."

"Oh, honey, let's not talk about possible problems." She patted my hand. "That's what brings them on."

Her comment was so foreign to how I controlled my world that I stood speechless.

I finished my instruction, cutting pieces of venison into the stew, giving her dried carrots to slip into the water. I don't remember much of what else I told her that morning. Rachel had handed me a pondering that sent me walking. I spent my days conjuring up concerns, believing that would keep them from happening; poor Rachel seemed to think such thoughts just gave trouble an invitation.

"That woman will kill you. Neither she nor your dad seem capable of seeing how hard you work." Mr. Warren and I rode our horses side by side up the Territorial Road north of Brownsville in the fall after Rachel's arrival. I'd removed my shoes that hung on either side of Nellie's neck, let the air cool my toes. Our rides happened infrequently, as Mr. Warren worked to raise money for his herd.

"No, I shouldn't complain to you so much. She's really all right. Just so unlike my mother, from her bulk to her sense of fashion to her lack of skills. My mother could do anything and she did it with a gracious heart."

"And so can you." He leaned across the space between us and put his hand over mine.

"I'm not so sure about that gracious heart part," I said.

I rode bareback on Nellie, my dress pulled up above my calves to reveal bare feet and a touch more skin than was really proper for a young lady. His hand felt like warm butter, quelling the small uncertainty I sometimes felt around him. He would appear out of nowhere while I hung pumpkin slices to dry in the barn rafters, or while I strung beans in the shade at the side of the house. Like a slow sunrise he'd be there, sometimes not even coming near the house, but close enough for me to see him staring. The uneasiness of surprise lessened when we rode together.

"Rachel's good with the little ones. Martha loves looking at *Godey's* with her, and she plays dolls with Millie—"

"While you're stitching up your father's pants, I suspect."

He was right about that.

"They love to have her read to them. She's reading Washington Irving's *Life and Voyages of Christopher Columbus*. Millie loves adventures."

I enjoyed the stories too, while I stirred the stews that would feed us. I missed reading to the girls.

"I read a Washington Irving book once."

"*Rip Van Winkle*?"

He shook his head. "No, ma'am. That's a short story. I read *Astoria*! It's about settling this country. I brought it with me from Missouri. I'll lend it to you, if you like."

"I would like that." His sweet offer surprised me, as did his knowledge of a short story versus a book. "I wasn't aware that you liked to read so much, Mr. Warren."

"I figured reading is something that matters to you. I bet your father has never asked you what you like to read, now has he?"

"No. It's a given that I do read and inform my mind and study Scripture."

"But reading's a pleasure and you deserve such, Eliza. You really do." His voice was honey to a bitter tea. After a pause, he changed the subject. "I've been listening to your father. In church, I have." I raised my eyebrows at this news. "He doesn't speak much of getting what we deserve except for the disasters that befall us." He inhaled as though speaking out of turn. "I interpret the Scripture he reads differently. Isn't it sayin' that we're all worthy just by being loved by God? Even though we mess up?"

Good enough just by being born? That hardly

95

seemed likely but it was an intriguing thought, made more so coming from Mr. Warren.

We'd ridden north, skirting Brown and Blakely's where my father postmastered. Rachel thought me out bringing in the cows, but since she had no idea of how long it took to round them up or milk our two, I took the chance when Mr. Warren rode out of the shade of the oak looking like a man who saw me as beautiful despite the darkness that dwelled inside. We dismounted. I spread the blanket I'd rolled in front of me. We lay back beneath the trees, me with arms crossed over my chest, he up on his elbow, his other arm stroking my wrists. The scent of horse from the blanket tickled my nose and I sneezed.

"I'm ready to commit," he said. "I'll let your father pray upon my head and say whatever words he wants of me, to show you that I love you with all my heart."

I swallowed. "It's not me you're to love with all your heart." But oh, I so wanted him to love me fully, even though I knew it was a greater love that would bind us if it was meant to be. I had conjured a terrible life with him, his drinking being some-thing serious, his kindness to me a ploy to get me to give myself to him, heart and soul and body. I imagined him injured by a runaway horse and being an invalid I'd need to care for. These thoughts contained my world, made it livable especially when chaos threatened as it did with Mr. Warren's breath blushed sweet against my neck. My own breathing shortened, his whiskers rough against my chin. I imagined my father being outraged at our marriage. I imagined Mr. Warren's drinking—if the rumors were true—interfering with our happiness. I imagined I could never please him. Yet my heartbeat quickened.

"If I do, will you marry me?"

"Oh, Mr. Warren, yes."

"When?" He was so close I could see the pores in his skin where whiskers threatened.

"December, next year." I breathed fast. "After I turn seventeen. Rachel will have learned enough by then to keep my father and his children fed. Christmas is a lovely time to wed." I searched his eyes. *Is he serious, truly?*

"It is. But must we wait until a year and a half?"

"Where will we live?" A sudden practicality raised its head.

"I've found a place. A donation land claim the owner wants to sell. It's up in the hills a little ways. Lots of trees we can cut and take to the mill. Some meadow land for the small herd I've accumulated. There's already a cabin. Want to see it?"

I did. But I also didn't want to leave this place of safety, lying beneath the trees, the sound of the Calapooia River gurgling, Mr. Warren's warmth beside me. Could this be God's blessing, this pleasant respite from my fears? His breath sweet upon me. Despite what Rachel subscribed to, I must not let myself think of happier things, for surely then they'd disappear like birds flying into sunset. Thoughts beset the future.

I told him I didn't want to see the cabin. Yet.

"I asked Mrs. Brown how she made such good coffee and she said she added an egg." Rachel leaned over the coffeepot on the stove my father had purchased for her that fall. We were learning together how to cook on it. I still preferred placing the pot inside the fireplace coals, but we were being "modern" with Rachel the kitchen head.

"I think they meant to crack the egg and put it in raw."

"Oh, do you think so?" With a long-handled spoon she reached into the grounds, pulling out a stained, shell-intact egg.

I shook my head. How could one woman be so ignorant? That was uncharitable of me, but these incidents occurred several times a week. She lacked common sense, as Nancy called it—everyday wisdom. I tried to be kind, I really did, but her efforts always meant more work for me until I decided it was better if I just did it myself, leaving her the more pleasurable task of reading to the girls. She would be "teacher" and tell stories of her privileged life in Boston where paid maids and cooks provided the common in her common sense.

She was even worse with the cookstove. I still had Henry cut green wood as well as dried wood, but now he had to chop to fit the firebox on the stove. It was easier for me to simply start the fire with coals from the fireplace, so that meant we kept two fires going. Rachel liked the extra heat while the rest of us sweat cracklings. Our stove had six eyes with handles, six places for pots to boil, eggs to fry on, coffee to bubble up even with a whole egg plopped inside. The stove needed watching, but Rachel would start a pan and then wander away much like Martha did but she was only seven. I expected *her* to have a flighty mind; not Rachel.

And my father. He tolerated all sorts of uncommon sense from Rachel, things he'd have raised his voice about if I had done it. She left the gate to the garden open and the hogs rooted their way in. During butchering she fainted, actually swooned into a heap of crinoline-covered linens when my father made his first cut into the abdomen of the hog whose leg she held. The limb flopped onto the back of my father's neck, splattering blood on him, on her. She sank away and that day I . . . I disappeared too.

I'm at Waiilatpu again. Blood streaks across the face of Dr. Whitman, who falls victim to a hatchet, then a gun. I jerk at the sounds. Frank Sager had run away days before, but he is back, then shot by the Indian Joe Lewis. He falls dead at my feet. We're in the house. My limbs feel cold and numb. I hear the Indians' muffled calls to Mrs. Whitman, promising they will harm her no more. Mr. Rogers, our beloved teacher, holds her by the elbow as they come into this room and I see that she's been shot; his arm hangs loose with blood pouring. The smell suffocates. She sees her husband dead and falls, nearly pulls Mr. Rogers down. I cannot move. A Cayuse, maybe one who shot her, lifts then walks her to the chaise lounge. So strange—to aid the one you've injured. Then another raises his hatchet against our teacher, who shouts out, "Oh God, no!" Mr. Rogers falls. Blood arcs onto his murderer's face as the man turns toward me. A dozen others whooping like cranes singing of their victory rush past him, pulling him toward others who have come from the barns to see what the noise is about. The smell is thick in my throat. The sounds deafening yet muffled like I am underwater. The curious are struck down in seconds; the chunk of blade to bone, a sound so fiercely final. I pull my apron starched with bluing over my face, inhale the scent wet with blood. I push away the sounds, and stand frozen while all around me I hear the heart-cries of death. We children from the school stay silent, await our end. I hear horses, more shouts, then in a language I can understand, Chinookan mixed with Cayuse and Sahaptin, we are told to "Go! There!" I turn to the children, tell them to move, and like cattle we are herded to a room with immigrants, poor people merely stopping on their way west. It's cold, evening now, as we huddle. A man shot in the belly groans, begs to be finished. He dies in the night but I do not remember that. Nor did I hear Mr. Canfield, wounded, slip away toward Lapwai. I sleep, blessed sleep protecting me, as later imagining all the awfuls in the world would become a way to contain the uncertainties in my life.

"Eliza! Get smelling salts." My father shook me. "Help now. Poor Rachel." His voice pulled me back into this present moment. He didn't notice where I'd gone or that I shivered. "This is too much for Rachel's sensitive nature. But she so wanted to help with butchering. Go on. Get the salts, Daughter. You're all right."

I stumbled to our cabin, slowly back into this place of autumn leaves, the sound of geese calling to each other high above. For a moment their calls were cranes above Waiilatpu, but the dog's nose against my hand as I walked kept me here. "Yaka. Good boy." I let him come inside while I pulled the smelling salts from the box, my hands shaking. I checked on the stove, made sure the damper was closed so we didn't have to tend to it for now. My ritual of safety completed, I headed back out, the molding leaves of autumn musking the air. I put my arms beneath Rachel, and she sat up as I swept the salts beneath her nose. With my father, we half carried her to the cabin where she rested all day, and my father and I—with the help of Henry Hart and the little ones—finished the slaughter of the hog. My mother would have helped without fainting. And she would have seen me disappear and brought me back to warming arms to stop my shaking. My father defiled our mother's memory with his marriage, even if Rachel did her best. She would never be as good as my mother's worst.

The Diary of Eliza Spalding

1850

I fail my husband, not being able to care for my household. Horace my dear brother has agreed to remain with me during the trial. I am so grateful, as I have three children to care for and my own health has deteriorated. Do I repeat myself? I should look back in this diary and see if I speak overly much of my trials. Long hours I spend in bed, praying through a persistent cough that tires me more than when I taught school, sewed, dried foods, picked berries, and yes, rode horses, the latter for pure joy and the feel of the wind in my hair, the sun on my face.

Gracious God in heaven, be with my family, me. Help me to set aside these thoughts of anger and betrayal directed at the Mission Board, my husband's insistence to expose Eliza to yet more pain. Help me see that you are in all places, light and darkness, that we can better see the light because we have wandered in the shadows. With gratitude for the lives you spared I remain your humble servant. Amen.

I was strong on our journey west, though more

than once I asked Mr. S to leave me behind. It was a genuine request to hasten a death I thought could not be avoided. I did not wish to be responsible for the deterioration of the work we'd been set to do. I didn't complain. It was a practical matter. I was with child and, merciful God, may I one day understand—I lost the infant. And if this was God's provision for me, an early death to bring me to his Presence, I was prepared for it. But my dear husband would set our tent at night, cook over our fire, settle me in, bring me tea. And by morning, I would be better. Praise God.

I suppose a part of me did not wish to let my husband go on without me, traveling with Narcissa Whitman, a woman Mr. Spalding had once proposed to, though she had declined. We were near the fort at Laramie when Mr. Spalding once confided to me that he wondered if we ought to have come with the Whitmans. "I question her judgment," he whispered. "She wasn't wise enough to accept my offer of marriage so I'm not sure I have confidence in her ability to truly teach the Gospel."

I confess I'd been surprised to hear him speak that way. I found her cheery and lovely to behold, as the fur trapping party we traveled with demonstrated daily, tipping their beaver hats to her, leaning in when she lifted her tinkling voice, chasing after her bonnet when the wind caught it and it sailed away. A simple neck string would have solved that problem.

I hope he will remarry, my dear Mr. S. I would pray that he would find a helpmate for him, someone to carry on the work away from Lapwai, though I pray he might one day return there. I never will. My days are numbered.

Mr. S waited on me on that journey. Tended me after we escaped to the Forest Grove, and I improved enough to teach at the little academy. Today my dear brother waits on me, brings me tea. Like Mr. S, he can cook. And we speak easily together (through my coughing) about New York and Ohio where I attended classes beside my husband, how I ran a boardinghouse for students to pay for Mr. S's schooling. "You could do that here," Horace offers. "You love to teach."

"I do. But I have a feeling that I won't be long in this world."

"Oh, don't even say such a thing. You're what, forty?"

"Forty-two. I'll be forty-three in August. If I live that long."

"You've a babe to raise."

Dear Millie. She is an active child.

"Matilda helped raise my others. And dear Eliza." There Eliza sits with her father at the trial of those Cayuse, caught, confessed. They will be hung, no doubt. The trial feeds the people who hunger for actions that take them from their powerlessness. They seek revenge more than truth or justice. Eliza should not have to be there, but my words to Mr. Spalding fall on deaf ears. A deaf mind as well. He has been so different since those days following the tragedy. And now, two years later, there is this trial and Eliza attends because her father insists she will be the best reporter, calmly telling of what happened, how she was the only one who could understand the hostage-holders' language and thus commu-nicated with them, expressed their desires to the hostages and then to British messengers negotiating their release. We'll never know the terrors she experienced while under siege. She will never know ours, believing she was dead, fearing for our lives.

Horace cut into my memory. "Don't be absurd. Matilda is a lovely Indian woman but she certainly did not instill in your children the love of God you tout so strongly. You're needed."

"I wish you knew the Lord, Horace." I patted his hand, strong, with liver spots.

"I know of him well." He grinned at me, then removed the rag from my forehead and prepared another mustard paste to grab the fever that came and went like bad dreams.

"You would find in him a kindred spirit of kindness and gentleness."

"Maybe I know him through you."

"It's not the same," I told him. "Think what joy it would bring to me to have one more soul to anticipate seeing in heaven."

"Enjoy the soul you have before you," he said. "And appreciate my cooking."

Have I told him how much his presence meant to me when we learned of the assault? Or how grateful I was that he did not panic but cautioned us to wait to see what the word truly was, whether Mr. S and our Eliza were actually gone from this world? I doubt I've told him. I will do so before I die. Let him know that his arrival was God-sent, to be there when I grieved my daughter and husband's death; to be there when Mr. S arrived emaciated and in shock as we learned there were hostages as well as deaths and prayed that Eliza was alive. Then the Nez Perce came and whisked us farther up the canyon, for our safety, they said. For all we knew, we were being held hostage too, awaiting our own demise.

⇒ 7 ⇐

HELD HOSTAGE

My memories weave a complex web. They hold me hostage one day so I can't act; other days they send me toward plans that might not be the best for me. No words would ever make my father consent to our marriage, even if I approached contrite, even if Mr. Warren was baptized a believer. So long as my siblings needed tending and Rachel gained few house husbandry skills, and I was stuck at home, I'd remain his true assistant in his work. Rachel had begun teaching school. Henry Hart cooked when I traveled with my father. But a year from now, I had decided, Andrew and I would marry. Wouldn't my mother want that for me? Happiness with a good man?

Christmas was a lovely time that year, 1853. The school became a vision of the party and feast in *A Christmas Carol*, a book by Mr. Dickens that Rachel had shipped from Boston and read to the little girls. I eavesdropped as I mashed potatoes. It was the only time I ever saw my father lose his temper with Rachel, yelling at her for bringing fiction into the house, for tainting our minds with untruths. But the story spoke of memories, of experiences gone that could still touch us. The ghost of the future was a crooked finger beckoning us to make the future different, to somehow learn from what had happened in the past and make the present a more comforting, kind, and, yes, safe place.

"God can use anything," Rachel told him. "Don't you remember the biblical Nathan who told a story to David that changed David's heart?"

My father relented then and let her read it to us more than once. I loved the rendering of the feast on Christmas morning when Scrooge has blended past with future into present, willing to change while he still had the chance, to let the past transform him rather than define him. I thought how lovely it would be to decorate the school with greens and berries and mistletoe for the Christmas program, hoping to capture the joys of the season that we'd all known when my mother was alive.

I garnered my sisters and Nancy Osborne and a few others to string popped corn and berries on the tree my father chopped to put inside the schoolhouse that winter. Small candles we made ourselves decorated the tree, and Mr. Warren offered to be one of the guards to douse any branch that might catch fire. My father could hardly refuse him. We arched greens over the few windows, hung them with mistletoe given up by the oaks. My father said Meriwether Lewis called it the Great Grape of the Columbia during the Corps of Discovery that opened up the West. Small apples with more red than brown high-lighted the greens upon the mantel as they surrounded the large candle I'd made and placed in the center.

For additional decoration we hung our quilts created by the women of Brownsville. Carpenter's Wheel. Crown of Thorns. Barn Raising with Prairie Points. We encouraged scrap quilts with reds and greens and whites and hung one or two by wealthier women whose work was made of only those three colors. They could afford the material while the rest of us used bits and pieces. The evening flickered with candles and the voices of neighbors grateful to have survived another year, feeling blessed to have a teacher and a pastor in my father and his new wife.

He didn't preach that evening. Instead a bit of the former man appeared, smiling, patting chil-dren on their heads, laughing out loud at Mr. Blakely's joke. Rachel beamed. I think she took credit for his transformation—and he did look upon her with affectionate eyes. My stomach gnawed as I watched them, wanted to say some-thing. I chose to eat a pastry Nancy had made instead. We sang carols, the room warmed by the fire and friends. When the children opened their meager presents that Mr. Warren and the other guard handed out from beneath the tree, I caught

Mr. Warren's gaze. He wiggled his eyebrows, grinned, then tended back to his task.

Yes, Christmas would be a lovely time to marry.

After the church service while men and women chatted in the cool rain before stepping into their buggies and wagons, Mr. Warren pulled me behind the log building. A steady rain misted and we ducked under an umbrella Rachel had brought with her that I raised.

"You can push it onto a belt," he suggested, "and wear it when we're riding, to put precious things into." He'd gifted me with a small leather pocket purse with my initials worked into it.

"I don't wear belts. You just began wearing one yourself."

"I'll make you one."

"I didn't make you anything." I should have thought of something for him. I wondered at my lack of generosity, but Mr. Warren interrupted my shame.

"You'll still marry me next year. That's your present to me."

"If you have my father baptize you, yes."

He kissed me then and would have done so again, but my father shouted my name and I slipped away into the night, shaking the rain from the umbrella. I couldn't show his leather gift to anyone except Nancy, but I treasured it. That night, I put my mother's golden wedding ring inside.

• • •

The winter had its way with us, sending rain in shapes: drizzle, downpour, fog, and once or twice a freeze. We even woke one morning to snow, a rarity. Rivers rose, and yet that spring of 1854 I traveled with Father south to start a church at Spencer Butte not far from Eugene City where he'd also worked to begin a Presbyterian church. We rode through spring drizzle to Grand Prairie where Father preached and then on to Albany where he began a Congregational church. Both were closer villages, but still it meant much riding and no time to mix with Mr. Warren. It wasn't like the old times, when my father and I had ridden and he taught Scripture along the way, spoke of the high hills that placed their arms around us all at Lapwai, breathed in the hot, dry air. Here, moisture was our companion, low fogs in the morning, high streams we crossed with trepidation. And a man obsessed. He talked incessantly of Lapwai, of getting the Mission Board to approve his and Rachel's return. Ours, too, I imagined, if I still lived with him.

"Why go back there?" I gave my horse her rein, so she stopped and tore at grass.

"Lapwai? Why, it's my life. Your mother's life. We did such good work there, Eliza. Such good work. The People need me."

"They betrayed us."

"What? What a thing to say! They saved our

lives, your mother's and mine and your sisters and brother. It wasn't Timothy's fault he couldn't rescue you and the others. Don't even think such a thing."

But I did.

I changed the subject. "You often left Mama behind in Lapwai." I kept judgment from my voice.

"She did fine. She had Matilda. We did the Lord's work there, Eliza. Just as we do here, bringing the Lord to people to light up their darkness. Someone always has to remain behind."

I trusted we were doing the Lord's work when I traveled with him as a child. I wasn't sure we still were. I believe he took me with him because I could sing all the hymns and he knew that our hearts are turned through music. But it concerned me that my mother had remained behind so often with no one but Nez Perce to look after her, her husband far away in case of trouble. She must have felt abandoned. I knew I would.

The hills in this Willamette Valley were all referred to as buttes and grew out of the lush, flat landscape like those blemishes that appeared on my chin or forehead during my monthlies. We dismounted to give our legs a stretch and relieve the horses too. "So you think one day I'll marry?" I posed the question to my father as we watered our horses at a small stream not far

113

from Spencer Butte. "I'll have a husband to look after as Mama looked after you."

"Marry? Well. One day. But you're just sixteen, Eliza. A girl. You have much promise before you, and thankfully, there are no young men panting at my door for your hand. That's all I'd need." He grumbled that last under his breath, but I heard it. "One day you'll go to the Tualatin Academy, and when you do, you might meet a young man worthy of you. I see none in Brownsville. There were no mates for me here either. A friend found Rachel for me."

Something you ought not to have done. I picked at the horse's rein. "There are some young men of interest." The horses tugged at new grass. We'd have to be careful or they'd collick with the tender shoots. My Nellie twisted her head to nip at a fly, jangling the bit.

"We'd best be riding." He helped me mount Nellie sidesaddle, then eased himself onto his bigger gelding.

"There is Mr. Warren, of Missouri. He came to classes for a time."

"Warren?" My father jerked his head around to look at me, his hand resting on the rump of his horse. He scowled. "He's a drunk. I thought you'd followed my orders about not seeing him. You have, haven't you?"

"Why do you say he's a drunk?"

"Everyone says it." He turned back, shouted

114

over his shoulder. "God will find the man for you in due time. Don't you worry."

His certainty of Mr. Warren's fallen nature caused my face to burn hot. But I'd already imagined the worst, so I knew it couldn't happen. I just had to find a way to make my father accept what God had already ordained.

"Andrew! You frightened me." He'd entered the cold smokehouse and stood behind me so when I turned I stared into his face and gasped. I struck his chest. "Don't ever do that, don't surprise me like that." Wiping an errant hair from the bun at my neck, I stepped back.

"Got you to call me Andrew 'stead of Mr. Warren."

"Mr. Warren is proper. My mother never used my father's Christian name, and you, well, for you, Mr. Warren is fitting." I gathered my skirts and knitted shawl to slip around him. I didn't like him just showing up, pressing his luck against my father seeing us. Our breaths were puffs of white against the crisp air. Lately we'd agreed to meet away from here, when my father was at the post office.

"As it happens, I haven't come to see you." He grabbed my elbow, gentle but with purpose. He leaned in to kiss me and I let him. "I've come to see your pa about that baptism. Need to get that out of the way if we're to wed when you turn seventeen. You haven't changed your mind."

"I haven't. Neither have I told my father." I paused. "Are you really going to ask for a baptism?"

"I am."

The horses stomped in their stalls. I could hear the crunch of their teeth grinding at the rye grass in their mangers. "I wonder if going forward on Sunday might be . . . better." My father wouldn't refuse him then. Who knew how he'd respond to a "drunk" with the two of them alone. I'm not sure why I thought my father would deny anyone, but Mr. Warren might be different in his eyes as I'd mentioned him again.

"In front of everyone? Naw. I'll have enough to stand for on Saturday nights with my card partners teasing that I must have done something religious to get you to marry me at last."

It was the first time I realized that cards might be a part of his thinking after we married, after he chose the faith.

"You won't be seeking such things once you have the spirit of the Lord inside you. He meets all needs."

Mr. Warren put his arm around my waist, pulled me to him. "Not all a man's needs. Even your father has a second wife with spit and fire to her and surely there's no finer man of God than him."

I hadn't thought about my father's "needs" in that way nor that Rachel had both spit and fire.

She was comely and the harsher life here had required taking in and hemming her dresses. But my father had married Rachel to take care of us. He had married her the very day she'd stepped off the ship in Vancouver, took her to Forest Grove, then spent the night somewhere. He brought her home already his wife so there'd be no "talk" of impropriety. No, he married her for us and it was his bad fortune that she had so few abilities to care for herself, let alone four children. But then why did he keep her? It was a question I would ponder later, after I convinced Mr. Warren to wait. I needed more weeks to prepare my father.

In May, I overheard Mr. Blakely ask my father my question at Brown and Blakely's store. I stood as in a pool of still water between the aisles of crockery and tin candleholders, certain that the men weren't aware that I was there. A slender Kalapuya Indian man carried fish in to Mr. Blakely, and after he left Mr. Blakely asked my father, "Can you make things work, then, Reverend?"

I wasn't sure at first what they talked of.

"Rachel's a good woman."

So Rachel's lack of domestic skills was food for gossipy tongues. She was so unbeguiling, expressing her lacks through comments about how strange it is that "bluing turns sheets white" or wondering aloud "why people sing songs to the butter churn." She didn't know that the chant tells the churner when the dasher should go up or down. No one wished her ill will, but Mr. Blakely's question while my father sorted mail was one I had asked of myself.

"Can I make things work?" My father repeated his friend's question, the *shif-shif* of letters being posted a backdrop to my beating heart. "I have to make things work. That's what marriage vows mean. I made my bed, now I'm meant to sleep in it. Even if Rachel has no knowledge of how to clean the cords or pluck ducks for feathers or even sew the tick up."

Mr. Blakely laughed. "Well, I imagine she warms that bed good."

My father coughed. "She's learning domestic skills. Eliza's teaching her. It's good training for Eliza's own house one day. I once thought I'd send Eliza for more schooling. Her mother wanted that. To go back East or back to Tualatin Academy. But Rachel's not ready yet to handle what needs doing. Oh, I can leave her alone enough to take Eliza with me to start that new church south of here. Not sure when Rachel will be ready for that. Travel's hard on her. So—" He must have leaned across the counter as his voice got louder and I heard the slap of a post. "Can't let Eliza go until there's someone to take over, and until then, I can make it work."

"Makes sense."

Neither man spoke after that, each returned to his labor. Birds chirped and I heard the swooshing sound of Mr. Blakely winding string onto the roll he'd later use to wrap paper around the dry goods bought by the women of Brownsville. It was 1854, spring. My mother'd been gone three and one-half years.

It came to me that what my father wanted in this second marriage was someone to care for his children, not a workmate as my mother had been, not a companion. He had me for that. He wanted a mother for us, a noble cause. But when he saw his new wife couldn't be that, he was willing to sacrifice my future education, my mother's dream for me, willing to say to himself it was fine to keep me home until his children were raised, to keep my life as his companion in the work. There'd be no path for him to give his consent to marriage for me, not to Mr. Warren or any young man. Not until Millie and Martha Jane were old enough to be married and on their own and that was ten years away, at least. Millie, the youngest, was only seven.

I shivered, standing in the aisles. My gloved fingers turned cold.

My father might have thought that Rachel would learn how to wash the bed ropes every spring or how to gather straw for the tick or how to get that stove temperature right to boil eggs and pay attention long enough the eggshells didn't burn on one side and pop out on the other in a scorched and waterless pan. No, this was as it would be, whether by Rachel's stubborn design not to learn new things or the privileged life she had before when someone else did everything for her. I saw my future laid out before me, a hostage to my father's wishes.

A drunkard, my father had called Mr. Warren. Well, I could handle that. I too could "make things work."

8

MAKING THINGS WORK

I sought him out. Mr. Warren no longer worked at the docks in Oregon City. Instead he'd begun repairing the log house on the donation land claim he'd purchased for us or was paying on, at least. We'd spoken of a December wedding, but that was too long to wait. I imagined him being injured. Maybe falling from the roof he patched with new shakes. There were rattlesnakes in the hills behind the farmstead. One might creep in at night and strike. Measles. Had he been exposed to measles? I certainly had, at Waiilatpu that year. I imagined him getting the speckled disease and then like the Indians sweating in their lodges before plunging into cold rivers and their deaths. I remembered how Dr. Whitman had tried to warn the Cayuse about not sweating, not jumping in the rivers. They had not listened and blamed him for killing their own while the "whites" survived. If I imagined Mr. Warren taking such a cure, then he would not do it. It made perfect sense to me. Imagine the worst; control the future.

"Mr. Warren!" I shouted, not seeing him on the roof as I rode up. "Are you about?"

I waited in the quiet, slipped off Nellie, and

led her to the hitching post. Moss covered the overhang on the wooden porch I stepped up on. "Mr. Warren? Are you here?" The quiet left unease. Inside, the house was empty but for a small table, two chairs, a cot, and some empty bottles in the corner. Beer? Whiskey? More likely elixirs. My foot caught on a raised portion of the floor. *Creak, creak . . .*

I am back at Waiilatpu, back seeing the floor where Nancy Osborne and her family hid, that place they snuck out from when they escaped that night. I see shadows move in the darkness and much later hear a Cayuse say, "Spalding's dead." My body is numb. I hear nothing; all is quiet. I don't remember anything after slipping to the floor and falling asleep. Hands touch my shoulders and I scream.

"Whoa! It's just me. A nice surprise having you here."

"Andrew? Oh! I . . . yes, I thought I'd see your progress." My heart pounded and my breathing turned shallow. "Please, please don't do that. Don't startle me."

"Sorry. Are you checking up on me? I'll be ready by Christmas. Don't you worry."

I looked into his brown eyes the color of soft fur. Could I find safety there? I wasn't certain. I plunged in anyway. "Let's not wait until

Christmas. I think we should go this month, this day even, to the judge in Oregon City. Speak our vows and claim each other forever."

"Not a church weddin'? Don't think your father would approve of that, darlin'." His Missouri history sometimes showed up in his words. "Besides, I haven't spoken my promise to you yet, about the faith."

"Do you believe in God?"

"I guess I do. But 'Liza, you wanted everything correct and proper and I'm willing. We can do this in the church—"

"Belief is enough. You are a part of the faith. Baptism can come any time after, by a minister in Oregon City if need be." I'd just thought of that.

"Your pa would want you to wait."

"Yes, until forever."

"That's true. Very true." He stroked my arm.

"He wants me to look after the girls. And teach Rachel Jane all about keeping house, cooking, raising children." I fiddled with the ties on his shirt. "We can bring my sisters here, after we're married, Henry too, can't we? Let my father cook for her. Rachel can go with him to hand out paper tracts when he speaks at churches here and there. That's the life he wants." She couldn't carry a tune in a butter churn but so be it. I took a breath.

"Wait, 'Liza. Eliza." He held my shoulders at arm's length, bent down to look at my eyes beneath my bonnet. He pushed my poke off, untied the ribbon at my throat, then tossed it with one hand onto the cot. Beside another pile of bottles. I turned my attention back to him.

"Are you backing out, Mr. Warren?" I hadn't imagined him doing that. Why hadn't I imagined that, to keep it from happening?

"No, no." He took me into his arms then, kissed the top of my head. "No. I'm grateful as a man can be that you would want to hurry our promises along. The house isn't ready but if you are, we can make do. We could have Hugh Brown marry us, right here. He's a JP."

"No. Away from here. And about the children? My brother and sisters? You told me they could come live with us."

"We can cross that bridge after we've crossed this river. Let's plan for tomorrow. Will you tell your father?"

"Not until after I'm Mrs. Andrew Warren."

We made arrangements to meet the following day and I rode home. I sliced ham from our smokehouse, remembering that Mr. Warren said that's where he'd been when I rode up, in a smokehouse; so we'd have pork at least, and smoked salmon when the fish made their run up the Calapooia. I didn't hear any chickens, so maybe my father would eventually give me the loan of one or two laying hens or Nancy's family might let us buy one. I thought of Nancy, wished I could include her on this special day, but it wouldn't be wise to tell anyone. While I organized in my mind what I could pack and take with me, I cut up last year's potatoes into grease I put in the spider, then set the three-legged skillet on one of the stove's eyes to heat. Millie and Martha played with the stocking dolls Rachel had knitted them. I had one too, stuffed with duck feathers inside a tiny sack, a miniature bed tick with arms and legs attached. The limbs flapped around, but the center, like my resolve, was firm. I touched the leather purse at my waist. The ring was in there. Did I dare to use it?

In that lull before my father stopped his lesson preparation and I served supper, I carried a bag of my clothing wrapped inside one of my mother's quilts out into the barn. Nellie nickered and I spoke softly to her of my plans. Horses know how to keep secrets.

That evening, everyone ate well and seemed especially jovial. My brother even commented on the great taste of the dumplings, something he rarely did. I wondered if he knew, but didn't see how he could. I listened with attentive ears to the conversations: Rachel's nasal Boston tone, my father's clipped responses to simple questions followed by lengthy answers when an issue of principle or justice or the Indians or the legal status of colored people in Oregon came up. The little girls giggled when I told them of a rabbit

Yaka had chased and how the dog's tongue hung off to the side of his mouth. I breathed my family in, aware that this was the last evening I would have as Eliza Spalding, their older sister. After this I would be forever Mrs. Andrew Warren. I would make things work.

That night, I whispered the Lord's Prayer three times as I crawled onto my straw-filled tick, slipped under the quilt, pushing Martha a little from the middle. She sprawled in her sleep. I wondered if Mr. Warren slept face up or down, feet straight or curled against the cool. The last thing I did that evening before I tried to sleep was imagine the terrible things that might happen in the morning: Andrew changes his mind. My father discovers my quilted bag in the barn. Millie, Martha, and Henry come down with fevers. Rachel has a stomach complaint I couldn't cure with asafetida or valerian. Nellie gets loose. Yaka dies. Andrew isn't there when I arrive in the morning.

My eyes flew open, wide awake. A full moon shone through the window. A rushing in my head and heart pressed my eyes as though someone had thrown cold water on my face. A need to do this now, before it could be stopped. I wondered why I waited.

So I didn't.

Nellie nickered when I entered the barn, the moon beaming streams of pale light through the cracks in the barn wall. The smell of hay comforted. "We're going for a night ride." I whispered the words. I knew the river would be fordable and I wouldn't need to wake Kirk's ferryman. I also didn't want to take the new covered bridge, as Nellie's hooves echoed in the structure. She didn't like it either. The plodding of Nellie through the stream might wake the ferryman, but I doubted it. Even if he heard it he'd have no reason for alarm. And the moon would light my path.

I saddled Nellie, tied the quilt rolled up behind the saddle, found the stump I used to mount, slipped my leg onto the knee brace of the sidesaddle, leaned down to push the door open, rode through. I eased the door closed, though couldn't reach to hook it shut. I hoped the wind wouldn't blow it open or my father would see it early and notice Nellie—and then me—gone. I wanted as much lead time as I could manage.

"Whatcha doing?"

I twisted my head. "Henry Hart. What are you doing out of bed?"

"I guess I'm old enough to be up before sunrise."

"It's a long way 'til then. Go back to bed."

"Heading to Andrew's, are you? I could ride with you, keep you company."

"Oh Henry Hart, I'd love your company, but this time, this is, well, it's a secret, but I'll share it with you. Promise you won't tell Father for at least a week. Promise?"

He nodded his head. "You're getting married."

"How did you know that?" I hadn't imagined Henry interfering. He pointed his chin toward the bedroll. "I didn't figure you'd spend the night 'less you were proper married."

"We will be soon enough. And I'll be back. We're going to live north of here, but a little ways, and I can see you often."

"I'd like that." His next words startled. "I'm lonely, 'Liza. I miss our trips, you and Father and I, to Fort Vancouver and Spokane. I miss Mama and Timothy and Matilda and Joseph and even sneaky Mr. Craig. I miss them all." His voice broke. "And I miss you, even though you're here."

In that moment I knew I missed that Lapwai life too. All those people who had been so much a part of what we did, all the Nez Perce who welcomed my parents and the Jesus books, who sang the songs we loved. I missed them all despite their betrayal. And oh, how I missed our mother.

I dismounted and took my brother in my arms. "I'm not abandoning you, I'm not. I'll be back." I held him as a puppy clings to comfort.

"It won't be the same, it won't. Everything's changed." He'd had no part in either the massacre or the hostage stalemate that went on for four weeks and I'd thought him unscathed by the ordeal. But he'd seen my father arrive, feet bloodied, near death; he'd been there when

128

Mr. Cranfield brought the original news of all the Whitmans' deaths, and my own, in error; he'd been rushed upriver by the Nez Perce, then to Spokane, and then on to Fort Vancouver where they waited while the British negotiated the release of the captives, then overland to Tualatin Plains and finally to Brownsville, disrupted like an acorn bounced along by grazing hogs or cattle. He'd suffered too.

"You're right, it won't be the same. But we can make something new between us, new memories that aren't hurtful and all wrapped up in Mama's dying and Rachel coming and all that sadness . . . before." I felt him sob against me, swallowed grief that shook his shoulders. "Shh, shh now, it will be all right." I held him away, looked into his tear-spilled eyes. "We'll be all right. All of us. I'll see to that. You can come and live with us, Mr. Warren and me. Would you like that?" I hadn't gotten Mr. Warren's approval for the offer, but I hoped it would bring small comfort to my brother at this moment.

He thumbed his eyes. "He's all right, I guess. But I'm not sure Father will be all right without you here."

"Father will do fine." I said the words to convince myself as much as Henry.

He nodded, wiped his nose with the back of his hand. "I'd better go back in."

"Yes. I wouldn't want the others to come trotting out here. I'd never get off. Lend me your hand, will you?"

My brother formed a cup of his palms and I stepped in as he lifted me upward toward Nellie's saddle. He stepped back as thunder rumbled.

"I won't forget you, Henry. I won't."

"I'll close the barn door for you."

I waved good-bye and pressed the reins against Nellie's neck. Leaving Henry was the only hesitation I experienced in the questionable move forward I began that night. I was committed. I had to make it work. That's what I repeated as the first drops of rain began to pelt.

The Diary of Eliza Spalding

1850

Rain falls like sheets of pewter, so hard sometimes I cannot see the oak trees across the yard.
I'm grateful my husband and daughter stay in
Oregon City and aren't out riding in this weather.
I'm glad Horace is here for company and for the
care of my children. The one regret I had of our
marriage in Ohio was that none of my family
could be there: not Horace, not my five sisters,
not my parents. It was good that before we left
for the mission field we did travel back as
husband and wife then, and my father gave us
his blessings and one hundred dollars and a
wagon that we took with us all the way to
Lapwai. But the wedding was lonely for me. I
had committed my life to the Lord and he had
provided for me a good man, a reverend who
had studied beside me, allowed me to learn
Greek and Hebrew with him, and never minded
that the languages came more easily to me
than to himself. And he was a good husband,
writing to my family, asking their permission for
our not returning to New York to marry, though I
wonder what he would have done if my father

had forbade it. I was twenty-five years old when I married, a spinster. But still, I was surprised when he told me he'd written to my parents asking for my hand. I didn't speak out or up. It was not my place. I lived with people who had taken me under their wing to allow me to be close to my intended with full expression of propriety. And we were proper, always.

Even on our wedding night I was not flummoxed, as my husband is a tender lover, a good man despite his temper, a temper never thrown to me. And I can calm him. I just can't ever change his mind once he has it set. As with insisting Eliza go to the trial, to be deposed and testify. I wonder what state I'll find her in and how long it will take for me to have her speak in normal childlike tones again, if ever I'll hear her voice laced with laughter rather than despair? The nightmares grew more intense when Mr. S began speaking of the trial. I wonder how she fares. It's not right that she is out of my sight, away from arms I might wrap around her in protection. Mr. S will not coddle her, but I think walking beside a child carrying legitimate fears is not a coddle but a balm, an act of mercy, and are we not compelled to love mercy? Mr. S uses the same Scripture from Micah 6:8 to remind me that "to do justice" comes before loving mercy, and Eliza's presence at the trial is part of acting justly. But

I grieve for the child that was and wonder if I abandon her when I submit to my husband's will. I entrust her care to you, God—a mother's constant prayer.

❧ 9 ❧
ANXIETY SHIFTING

I longed for Mr. Warren's loving arms to surround me with protection. I knocked on the door but no one came to answer. Wasn't Mr. Warren staying there, at "our home"? I knocked again. The rain had lessened and a moon promised light enough to capture the beads of moisture on my cape. He must have gone to his parents' with plans to meet me here in the morning. I shivered. *Have I miscalculated?* With Nellie unsaddled and cooled down, I spent the rest of that night alone in the dark cabin, my bedroll enough cover in the morning chill to bring me blessed sleep. It was the first night I'd spent all alone without a sister sharing quilts or a parent in another bed across the room. I awoke in the morning to the face of my soon-to-be husband.

"I guess you're anxious." He grinned. I smelled a sweetness on his breath, new to me. His eyes looked fevered.

"It seemed easier to get an early start. I couldn't sleep. Where were you?"

"I couldn't sleep either, darlin'." He paused. "I stayed with my parents, told them of our plans."

"You warned them not to say anything until after we're gone?"

He nodded. "They're happy to have a Spalding in the family. My pa thinks some of your smarts will rub off on me."

I didn't know what to do with that compliment, at least it seemed like one though a backhanded slap at his own son.

"You're smart enough." I spread my hand in an arc to take in the room. I noted the bottles were missing. "You have your own home and a place for your wife."

"And family."

"Yes. A family." I swallowed. It was a subject we'd never discussed. "But not right away maybe."

"Best we be on our way, little lady." He pulled me up from my pallet, kissed me despite my having no tooth powder with me. He ran his hand up my back. "Hmm, hmm. I'm going to like having this to wake up to every morning." He bundled up my quilt bag, tied it tightly with the hemp rope, and carried it out to put behind the saddle he'd already put on top of Nellie. "Glad you have your own horse."

"She's not really mine." I stroked the mare's soft nose, felt the soft bristles. "Millie rides her as much as I do." My father would miss the horse when he awoke, probably more than me. For a moment I wondered if my father would come riding down the lane to grab Nellie back, if not me. I imagined him doing so; so of course, he wouldn't.

Mr. Warren helped me mount, then threw his long leg over his own saddle with bedroll already attached. And we set off.

I heard afterward that my father rode through Brownsville shouting, "My daughter is dead to me! My daughter is dead to me!" Had he spoken those anguished words the night of the massacre as he made his way nearly ninety miles from where he'd been thrown by his horse, traveling by foot to tell my mother what she already knew, that the Whitmans had been attacked, many women and children taken hostage? Mr. Cranfield had preceded my father's return to Lapwai, so my mother knew and waited only for word of the fate of her husband and her child. Together—if he lived—they'd have to decide whether to seek refuge at the Spokane mission or stay where they were among the Nez Perce.

But while he was riding through town shouting of my demise, news of my disappearance being explained by Mr. Warren's parents, that I'd willingly gone with him with the intent to take marriage vows, I was happily riding beside my soon-to-be husband welcoming the balmy spring, pleased that our two-day ride to Oregon City would likely take us to a wedding day of May 11, 1854, the middle of a lovely month. It was an outing beneath a honeyed moon—as they call those special times after a marriage. We had our honeyed moon to guide us before the ceremony, without the intimacy of such an occasion. We chatted as friends until Mr. Warren added, "A few of my dock mates will raise a cup with us afterwards. A celebration."

"They will? How do they know of our wedding?"

"I'll tell 'em when we have our supper in the inn. They'll be resting in the saloon side, I'm sure."

Are those hoofbeats following? Is my father chasing us? A part of me wanted him to care enough about me to come after me. "Maybe we should camp early," I said, ambivalence dancing in my head.

He set the tent beneath oak trees near where a group of Germans worked to construct a town they called Aurora. We'd followed the lazy Pudding River, so we still had the familiar stream to camp by when I watched as Mr. Warren took a flask from his saddlebag and drank.

"Medicinal?"

"Absolutely. Want some?" He offered the flask to me.

I shook my head, didn't protest his drinking from it, one swallow then two before he put it in the saddle pack. He was clear and calm with me, found dry pine needles, urging the fire to take, and we boiled soup in a tin pot he'd brought. A man was entitled to his medicine. Nothing Mr. Warren handed me could flummox me. Father wasn't following. I saw myself as one of those brave heroines serialized in *Godey's Magazine*, women who rose above difficult situations during the Revolutionary War, women who saved their husbands and family after bankruptcy. I'd even read *Jack Tier*, a raucous story of a woman deserted by her husband who followed him to sea, dressed as a man, making her way for years without him realizing she was there, watching out for him. I could do whatever had to be done. I could look out for myself.

"You're screamin' loud enough to wake Washington and he's been dead for years." Mr. Warren shook me awake. It was the dark before the sunrise.

"I . . . they come sometimes." I slowed my breathing, swallowed. I hadn't ever told him of Waiilatpu, but he'd heard the general stories. "I'll be all right. I . . . I don't have them often. I'm sorry." I lifted the damp bun from my neck. Changed the subject. "Are the horses still hobbled?"

"Animals are fine. It's you I worry over." His brown eyes looked marble-glassy. "Your screams woke me like a bullet."

"I'll be fine. Once we're married I bet I never have another."

"What are they about?"

How much do I tell him, one who has never known of such a trial? "Suffocation, mostly." I turned away. "I can't breathe and danger lurks in various forms."

He held me then, asked no more questions, rocking me as though I were a child, using his wide thumb to brush away nightmare-tears.

We could see dawn rising. "Do you want to just get on?"

I nodded and we made an early start, breaking our fast with hardtack and dried apples I'd brought along. The countryside dressed in dawn was awash in dew, full of wild iris, meadows with spring grasses, and in the distance, east, a snowcapped mountain named Hood beckoned. We rode through such verdant country, crossing streams and eventually hearing the roar of a sound-deafening waterfall. "That'll be Willamette Falls," Mr. Warren raised his voice. "And beside it Oregon City, capital of the Territory, where we'll speak our vows."

And where I'd last visited with my father for the trial.

⇒ 10 ⇐
VOWS

Mr. Warren and I started up the steps of the courthouse where the trial had been held. A buzzing started in my head. I couldn't catch my breath. I stopped, grabbed Mr. Warren's arm. Spots danced before my eyes.

"You all right?"

"Yes. It's just . . . could we rest first? Have a canteen of water?"

He pulled out his pocket watch. "Sure, but they might close and we'd have to wait until tomorrow. I hate to pay for two rooms at the hotel. We need to get the license here."

"Oh. Yes. Financially it would be better."

He took my elbow, eased me to sit on the steps. "Put your head between your legs. My ma says that helps with fainting."

My single crinoline puffed out as I lifted my skirts and sat, then put my head between my knees. He sat beside me, waved his hat for a breeze. "Must be the heat of the day." I panted like a dog, something my mother suggested could stave off nausea. "Why don't you go in and get things started. I'll join you."

"Well . . . all right. If you're sure. You aren't changin' your mind, are you?"

I shook my head, no.

"I'll be back quick as a dog's wag." He leapt up, causing a brush of air to cool my face.

I kept myself aware of the steps against my legs, the breeze on my hot face. *I'm here. It's a different time.* I remembered, without going away, my father looking disgusted if I said anything to the lawyers—in depositions, they called my telling—about a kindness one of our captors offered, that they gave us water or shared a dried carrot, keeping us alive. Were they not showing us a mercy? Was I not supposed to tell? Then witnesses, the young woman who was taken every night by Five Crows, a Umatilla chief telling the priests we were huddled with that he intended her for his wife. She'd begged us, pleaded in wails as horrifying as the screams we'd heard the night the Whitmans died, to not let them take her. But the priests knew that resisting meant certain death. Her death she probably prayed for, but it did not come.

I remembered the five Cayuse who sat before us at the trial, dressed in white men's suits, their hair cut, not looking fierce. I didn't recognize them as those who killed anyone. Maybe they'd given themselves up so the ransom could be paid, the money, arms, and trade goods? When I heard them speak, my ears closed and I heard nothing, just watched their mouths move in silence. I couldn't tell if they had been the ones asking me to trans-late, to tell Lorinda she must go. I would have recognized their throaty voices' demanding for Five Crows, words like coal cutting hard and black.

I hardly noticed that I'd sat upright on the steps. I tried to stay present at the trial, but I could not. Even their faces faded away. Then I was no longer in that hot stuffy courtroom nor even waiting for Mr. Warren. I'd gone back to Waiilatpu.

"Tell her she must come," an Indian demands. "She will be wife."

The snake Five Crows wants Lorinda Bewley, sends a guard to bring her. She is lovely, twice my age. I translate the guard's order and she sobs, runs to the priests newly arrived in the Territory. Why are they even hostages, so new to this place? They know only about the deaths of the Whitmans and likely worry over their own. She is dragged away . . . And each night for a week I am told to tell her "You must go" and hear her wails. One time I add, "You are keeping us alive. If you don't go, they'll kill us. They say that. You are giving up your life for ours. Like Jesus did." I wasn't sure she knew how her sacrifice—that whatever they did to make her wail and sob so— was saving us, keeping us from having the same fate speared through us. "God will be with you." Words my mother prayed when my father and brother and I left on our journeys leaving her behind. I am an empty vessel. No one to comfort me, everyone like sleepwalkers. Daily I send Lorinda to her pain.

The wind shifts and I hear the thundering falls and breathe easier. I'm in Oregon City, waiting on Mr. Warren. At the trial I had heard words of all that happened over again. Who died in which building. Who escaped. Who met their death by bullets or by hatchet. How Mr. Himble made it over the fence only to have an Indian shoot him and say, "Oh, see how I can make the white man tumble." His daughter saw him fall.

Timothy, a Nez Perce and early convert of my father's, and his friend are sent by my mother to Waiilatpu to get word of us once Mr. Canfield arrived to tell of the massacre. The bodies still lie unburied when Timothy comes into the room where some of the fifty-nine hostages cower. Oh, how my heart sings at the sight of him, a friendly face, come to take me home. I send an arrow prayer of thanks.

But he bends down to me and says, "Eliza Spalding." His eyes are kind. "The Cayuse will not let us free you. If I try to take even you or any of the captives, they will 'scour the country' until they find and kill us all."

I remember the word "scour," such a kitchen word carrying grating certainty, cleaning up a mess, debris. We are that mess. Timothy does not apologize. The Nez Perce do not say those English words "I'm sorry." They give a gift instead. One day he will give a gift.

At that moment I begin to cry. I'd held myself together, weaving threads of faith and hope. But Timothy's words bring down my tears. We are all powerless and betrayed, by everyone: the Cayuse who killed; the Umatilla people who took advantage; the Nez Perce who let them do it and force me to remain. Outside my body I do not plead, but inside, my whole being begs him to rescue me, us. He squats down beside me, lifts my bloody apron to wipe away my tears. His voice cracks when he says, "Poor Eliza, don't cry. You shall see your mother again."

I think he means in heaven.

But I never talked at the trial. I keep my then twelve-year-old eyes staring straight ahead at the judge, only briefly glancing at the accused and the others who'd been held with me. A French interpreter, Jean Toupin, relayed what happened once the British arrived to negotiate. I sank into the background at the courthouse, tried to forget what happened at Waiilatpu. I think making me attend the trial was more for my father than me. As was our being witness to the hangings, all night hearing the construction of the gallows, the hammer blows like bullets against bone. When the day came, I held my apron up before my eyes just as I'd held it when it seemed we all would die, the scent of starch still brimming with the memories.

"Here." Mr. Warren placed a cool handkerchief to my hot face, the wet bringing me back. "You all right? Wasn't sure you'd still be here." He smiled his relief. "You better?"

I stared, then nodded.

"Good. Hey, you cryin'? What's that about?"

"I'm all right."

"Let's get this signed." He showed me a paper. "You have to come inside. Then if you want to marry somewhere else, there's a JP just down the street."

I let him pull me up, hold me just a moment. We entered and I clutched Mr. Warren's arm. We signed the three-folded document they kept, received a second document just like it to take with us to show the justice of the peace. The walls closed in but I stayed there, in that place, made myself feel the cut log counter, experience the heat of the day, smell tobacco smoke clinging to the clerk's coat. I stood beside my future husband, then let the sunshine flood my face outside.

It took few minutes to change my status in the Territory and, yes, within my heart. I was a wife now, as my mother had been. *I did it, Mama!* My husband's first insistence was that I call him Andrew.

"My mother always called my father Mr. Spalding or Mr. S. It's a moniker of respect. He called her Mrs. Spalding."

"I don't know a moniker over a molehill. I just know I'd like to hear my name when I'm with my wife. You can call me Mr. Warren when you're with your friends but at least with me, I'm Andrew, that understood? And you, Mrs. Warren—" he bent to kiss me as we stood outside the log house of the justice of the peace— "you I'll be calling Eliza, wife, beautiful one, little lady, sweet pea, darlin', and whatever else comes to mind. Oh, and Mrs. Warren too." He had half a dozen names for me. I took them as a gift. He was kind about his request, but insistent. I vowed to work on what he wanted. He'd keep me safe in case my own imaginings failed me.

The vows we spoke had been followed by words of Scripture and I was grateful. We signed that paper folded three ways and while I knew the folding aided in the filing system, I still liked the idea that the Trinity showed up that day. We walked the town and Mr. Warren showed me where he'd worked. I suspect he looked for some of his mates but didn't find them. I didn't recognize any of the streets so saw them as though for the first time. I didn't even remember the boardinghouse where my father and I had stayed during the trial.

"That's where I worked on the steamboat."

"You build boats?"

"Just the one."

"Must have been quite a great day at the launch." Men crawled over a hull, hammering.

"Must have been. They'd let me go. Too many late arrivals, they told me, as if showing up late is a reason to let a man go." He patted my hand linked within his elbow. "I always stayed long after to finish up what was started."

"I'm sure they were sorry later to be without your skills."

"Yes, ma'am. I'm sure they were. Let's stop here." He opened the door to a mercantile. "Darlin', what do you think about this?" He held up a golden ring, the twin of my mother's. "Spare and elegant, just as you are."

His voice was a baritone, deep and resonant. He held my hand then, tugged at my gloves, one finger at a time, staring into my eyes as he did. I felt my face grow warm. My hands free of their binding, he slipped it on my finger.

"We're bound now, you and me."

I hadn't told him I already had a ring. And secretly, I was pleased I didn't have to show my mother's ring to the world. It was something of my mother's I could cling to privately. Still, I wondered how Mr. Warren could afford such a ring when my father hadn't afforded one for Rachel. I didn't ask. "We were bound by the vows and God's words read aloud."

"That's so." He pulled me to him. My straw hat, worn for the occasion, brushed his cheek. My face grew hot with his public affection but I stood up straight when two women buying bakery goods looked at us and frowned.

"You'll have to forgive my husband," I said. "We've just married." I held up the back of my palm to show the ring.

"Oh, well, congratulations."

Mr. Warren squeezed my shoulder. "That's my girl." His whispers warmed my ear.

We stayed the night in a hotel built up against rock walls, overlooking the falls. I could see building going on above us on the rocks that rose up from the river like paintings I'd seen of castle walls. This was a burgeoning town and Mr. Warren—Andrew—could find work here easily should the farm and his cattle business not prosper.

Andrew was a tender husband, kind and patient with his young bride. *Godey's* had failed to give me fair warning of both the strangeness and the joy and I had no mother to ask. Once there'd been an article about preparing for one's wedding night, and the admonition to not wear a short-sleeved dress with long-sleeved underwear. Actually, I knew little of emotional connection either, but that evening I didn't imagine all the awfuls and terribles I could have. While my husband slept beside me, I remembered Timothy, his stature, the gentleness with which he'd wiped my eyes and ears of tears when he had to tell me he could not bring me home, fear and sorrow like a buffalo robe weighing on my shoulders as he abandoned me. But he'd made a promise that day that I would see my mother again and so I did. All in due time, that's what he was saying.

That night I rested in the comfort that I was not alone. I had no nightmares and in the morning I vowed that I would stay with this man I loved through thick and thin and weather the storms any marriage faced. I'd treat my marriage like Rachel's woodstove, working hard to keep the fire going, not too hot and not too cold, making sure the damper was closed so no outside winds could buffet or send a flame across the floor to burn things up.

➤ 11 ➤

TO MAKE A BED AND LIE IN IT

It didn't take long for me to acknowledge that despite the difficulties, my father had provided well for his family. He set the standard. At Mr. Warren's home, we too had dishes and bowls and cups, pans aplenty. Hogs and sheep for food and wool and a spinning wheel Andrew's mother gave me. Venison too. I'd taken needles and thread with me, buttons and a few female necessities; my dresses, underdrawers, and books. Just a few books. But nothing to cook with. For the first weeks, we used the tin pot and ate a lot of rabbit stew, rabbit soup, rabbit chopped and fried on a new wood cookstove Andrew bought me.

"I can't thank you enough for this laying hen," I told Nancy. She'd made her way to our small farmstead two weeks after our wedding. I'd told Henry Hart I'd be back within the week, but we hadn't made it yet. I wasn't looking forward to facing my father again.

"Your dad's still pretty upset." She handed me the cage with a hen and a rooster too. I'd have to keep them in the barn, let them out each morning, until Andrew fixed up a chicken yard where the hawks wouldn't swoop down and get them or any chicks, and the raccoons could be discouraged.

"So I've heard. He came and got Nellie."

"Do you have any sassafras tea?" Her red hair glistened in the sun that also brought out her freckles. We walked back from the barn.

"I do. Let's drink it on the porch where it's cool and we can see the meadow. I love this view, so long and wide, and not broken up by trees."

I'd let her change the subject from my father, but I wanted someone to tell. "He got here late afternoon and had Millie with him. She was sure happy to see me but acted a little mad too. Wanted to know when I was coming home. I told her I'd come visit as soon as Father invited me."

"What did your dad say?" Nancy sat beside me on the porch steps, the hen cackling beside us in her cage.

"Nothing. He acted as though I wasn't even there. Then, just before he mounted up he said, 'When things get tough with the drunk you married, don't look at me for any invitation. You are dead to me.' "

"He said that in town too." She reached for my hand, patted it. "How awful for you. Was Andrew here?"

"I expected worse. And no, Mr. Warren was out back still planting. We got behind with our wedding trip to Oregon City." I sipped my tea.

"I've only been there once. Did you take a meal near those falls?"

I needed to tell her about my father's visit and she kept going off on another trail. "My father accused me of stealing the horse."

"That's just silly. You only borrowed it."

I nodded. "Here was the worst, for me anyway. He said, 'I've put a lot of time and money into you and this is how you repay me?' Not a word about what I'd done for him without payment of any kind. Not one word about all the 'love' he hadn't put into me, I guess. At least he wasn't claiming he'd wasted his love on me."

"Maybe he meant his love would always be there."

I shook my head. "If you could have seen his eyes, heard the tone of his voice. There was spittle at the corners of his mouth and his face was all red. His hands were fists. And then he said again, 'You are dead to me.' "

"I'm so sorry. We don't have to talk about this."

"Millie started to cry at his loud voice, and in truth, Nancy, I felt myself get sleepy! Can you imagine? I just wanted to go inside, lie down, and sleep. Like when . . . well, you know."

"I never could understand how in a time of fright you could fall asleep." She tugged at her red curls. "But maybe that's God's way of giving you strength. You weren't going to change your father's mind and his words pelted like hail, I suspect."

"You think so?" What had discomfited me was that I'd imagined my father's outrage and assumed by doing so it wouldn't happen. It didn't happen as I imagined: it had been worse, his visit leaving a hollow place in my stomach.

"I just get all persnickety when I'm frightened now." She took a drink of her tea.

"I wasn't frightened, just mad, I think."

"Oh? Well, I get scared just like I did when we hid under the floor and heard the Cayuse stomping and howling. I just have to get everything in place, not let one little dish be out of order in the cabinet. Takes so much time sometimes I barely get supper on for us. We're always late for church with me straightening this or that."

"Frightened? That's not it exactly." I tried to grasp the feeling. "I think when my father railed against me, I just knew that he was wrong and I felt righteous in disagreeing. But then I got so sleepy and went inside. I didn't even hug Millie good-bye."

Nancy spent the afternoon and we picked wild strawberries, cutting them up to dry in the sun. Afterward, we worked on a log cabin quilt, the pieces meant to be jumbled up.

"I think a quilt is almost human." Nancy held the material to her face, as I was prone to do with my apron, and inhaled.

"That's what a good friend is too, like a quilt, as comforting as a mother's arms."

"Especially one who has been through the trials with you. No one else can truly understand, right, Eliza?"

I nodded. Things got better with Nancy around. I'd need to keep her close at hand.

Andrew and I got through those first months. I discovered that we had money, though he proved very strict about how I spent any coins and reticent whenever I asked where it came from. My father had given me much more responsibility for buying our supplies than Andrew did. Within a few months Andrew brought a nice horse home after an evening in town. He'd gotten a good price on it. She was a trim little grey mare with black spots on her rump like the Nez Perce horses. Her coloring reminded me of spring snow, when the dark ground thaws up through the white. I called her Maka, the Nez Perce word for *snow,* wishing I had someone to speak Sahaptin with and then caught myself for the wish. The Nez Perce—Timothy especially—had failed us, despite my father's defense of them.

Andrew finished the rope bed and I filled the tick with straw. He could tease and be loving, then sometimes in a flash his eyes would narrow, his mouth firm up, and his fists clench on either side of his waist. He did that one day when I returned home on Maka, late.

"What did I tell you about visiting your family? I want you here."

"You were gone, off until who knows when? I tended the chickens and the hog, weeded, milked the cow. I had time and the weather promised to be good."

"You weren't here when I got back."

"You came home unexpected."

"Unexpected was I? Your husband, unexpected?"

I removed my straw hat while he talked, began supper preparations. "I had every intention of being here for you. I always am. You changed your plans." I smiled, to lighten the moment that had become as hot as an untended woodstove fed too much green fuel.

"Don't sass me, Eliza."

I turned to him, spoon in hand. "I had no intention of it. Just speaking my words and trying to calm yours."

"I don't need calming, I need someone who listens and does what I tell her to do."

I didn't add fuel to his fire but instead returned to stirring the biscuits. I licked a bit of the batter from my fingers.

It had been the first trip I'd made back to my father's, uninvited. Rachel had opened the door to me and hugged me before stepping outside. The little ones had rushed to me shouting how they missed me. Martha Jane cried and asked, "When are you coming back? I stepped on my dress hem and see, it drags." I looked around for needle and thread and saw that my set had not been replaced by Father. I told her I'd bring needles for her and show her how to do it herself. Then Henry started out from the field when he saw the strange horse. I walked out to meet him, little girls on either side of me. They left me, heading toward Yaka, who barked near the split-rail fence.

He smiled, facing me. "I'm leaving for Tualatin Academy later this month."

I felt a pang of envy, of wishing my father had made such a provision for me.

"You'll like it." I only vaguely remembered Forest Grove. I wondered if he did.

"It'll be fun." Henry straightened a split rail.

"Fun, well, I'm not so sure about studies being fun, but what a great change it will be. Rachel's learned to cook then?" Rachel sat in the sunshine on a bench at the side of the house, fanning herself, out of earshot.

"Not well. But Father does it and he seems to enjoy it. We've all gone on his forays to Spencer Butte where he started that church. Then sometimes it's just us here, without him, and Martha fixes the fried potatoes. We eat a lot of stew. Father says he'll come back for Sunday service here twice a month. And he's still trying to get the mission in Lapwai back."

I shook my head at the futility of his efforts. "I can't see that ever happening." Yaka bumped my hand then. "I missed you too, you little bear." I scratched his head. "Andrew doesn't want dogs around, at least ones not trained to work with cattle." He'd heard about a kelpie, from New Zealand, a breed that worked with sheep, and hoped it would train to herd cattle. We had a herd of thirty head and a ready beef market to people headed south into California looking for gold. "We're supposed to get a special breed of dog off a ship before long. I'm looking forward to that. Give me someone to talk with when Mr. Warren is off doing what he does."

"I hear rumors, Sister." Henry looked at me. "He—"

"Don't tell me." I raised my hand up in protest. "He's good to me, I'm provided for, and for the first time in my life I'm putting on a little weight because he does the heavy work and I'm not racing after you all." I punched him in the shoulder with affection.

"Maybe you're . . . with child."

My face grew warm. "I'm not. No, I'm just happy, though I miss you, Martha and Millie and Yaka." I tapped an invisible head with each name. "And Father too, though he doesn't care one way or the other."

"He thinks you've lied to yourself about Andrew."

"Well, he's wrong. And I didn't come here to defend myself or my husband. I came to say hello. I've done that so I'll go." The little girls returned, clung to me, begged me to stay, and my leaving proved difficult. I could see their powerlessness, knew what that was.

When I got back home, I found myself defending my having gone at all. Andrew's upset took away the small joy I'd found in seeing my brother and sisters again. I placed the biscuits on the sheet and stuck it in the oven. This marriage and family had its challenges but I'd chosen it. I'd have to shape it as I could.

We did attend my father's church the August after we married. I didn't know whether to tell my father ahead of time or just appear. We decided on the latter. We joined the throng carrying baskets and tying up buggies and patting horses twitching their muscles at flies. I looked for my family who lived next door and didn't have to ride anywhere. I didn't see them. I waved at Nancy Osborne toward the front as we entered the cooler room. Andrew removed his hat, stomped his boots on the step, knocking off any wayward dirt, and we took a seat near the entrance.

My father's back was turned, and by the time he faced forward, the benches in front of us were filled and I don't think he saw us. Andrew's dark hair was slicked down and had that little indentation formed from wearing a hat.

He fidgeted and I leaned over. "Are you nervous? We don't have to do this."

He shook his head. "I'm ready."

I was so proud of him, asking about baptism and belief. A part of me understood as I never had before how my mother must have felt bringing someone to that peace. I hadn't pressed him after we married. After all, I was the one who rushed us, the one who worried about what my father would say and truly, that he might forbid our marriage. But he didn't and we were husband and wife now.

My father began to sing—he had a fine voice—and we joined in, familiar words to me sung from memory, as there were few hymnals. I noticed Andrew didn't raise his voice. My father preached then, going on for over two hours. The room grew warm, and around noon, bees worked their way through open doors. Mr. Osborne, Nancy's father, fell off his bench near the front, but no one spoke. It was a common occurrence, and it proved enough for my father to actually look out at the condition of his congregation fanning ourselves with hankies and gloves, our backs and bottoms sore from the hard benches. It was when he scanned the crowd that he saw me. I watched his face pale. But then he seemed to see Andrew too, and a small frown formed on his forehead. "We will sing 'Rock of Ages' and then we'll take a respite for lunch, resuming after." I thought it strange he would pick a Methodist hymn, and people around looked a little befuddled, but we all knew the words, just hadn't sung them for a long time.

"Wait up, Warren," my father boomed.

We waited for others to leave as my father strode up the short aisle.

"What are you doing here?" My father's scowl announced a storm approaching.

"Attending church." I spoke for us, though he had asked Andrew. "There aren't many churches around and I've heard there is a fine preacher at this one."

He harrumphed. "You are here to . . . ?" He lifted his palms out, directed his words at Andrew.

"He wants to be baptized." I blurted it, fearful that Andrew might change his mind, might not say it.

"He can speak for himself. He certainly does in town."

I opened my mouth to ask about that when Andrew spoke. "Sir. I've come to repent of my ways and ask forgiveness."

"I'm not a priest."

"Sir?"

"I don't grant forgiveness. God does. Just ask and it shall be granted."

"And you'll sprinkle me then?"

"After some instruction. It's not magical, you understand. This is a serious undertaking, one that says you're committed to a new way, the only way. And consequences are greater to backsliders than to those who never choose the faith."

Was he trying to talk Andrew out of it? And what was it my husband wanted to confess?

"I understand, sir. Shall we do this?"

My father nodded once and we returned to the front of the church that was also the schoolhouse and the meeting room for civic discussion. I picked up the bronze baptismal bowl, and as I'd done a hundred times when traveling with my father, I went outside to fill it with water. Martha saw me and came over.

"I'll be finished in a minute," I said. "We can talk then."

She nodded, recognizing the baptismal bowl. I turned from her and went inside.

Andrew already knelt on the hard floor and my father was saying things over him. I saw my husband nod and heard a sob, I thought. *Is he crying?* I set the bowl down. My father still had not looked directly at me, but he dipped his fingers into the water and spoke the words he'd prayed over Timothy and Joseph at Lapwai and hundreds of others; over me and my siblings, as babies; and in Brownsville, over men and women alike. My father finally turned to me. "Will you work to help this man keep his vows, grow his faith?" It was a question with direction, that those present committed to the new congregant to nurture their faith. "Yes," I said. "With God's help."

My father nodded. He wrote Andrew's name into a book and we walked outside. In the oddest way, I felt more married than I had the day in Oregon City when we'd said our vows.

But my father had spoken to me only as a member of the faith asked to do my duty. He moved away from me, and when I called out to him, he kept walking, stopping to talk with Mr. Osborne, others cooling themselves with their hats or paper fans in the shade.

"That wasn't so bad." Andrew pushed his hat back off his forehead.

"What was it you confessed?"

"Things." He looked away—ashamed? "You needn't be bothered. I'll be better now." He pulled my shoulder into his, held me while I stared at my father's back.

Within the week, while the bloom of his baptism and my father's tolerance of my marriage was still fresh, Andrew told me he'd be going to Vancouver to get the new dog and that from there he was going to make inquiries about buying more cattle. He'd be gone several days.

"Where do you get the money? I just wonder." I darned one of his socks, bit off the thread. "You're so frugal with what you allow me for household things."

"Don't you be worrying over money."

"I have a good head for figures. We could map things out together."

He turned with that glaring look he could get. "Don't you have everything you need? More than most, I'd say. Got whole sections of one color cloth for your quilting, don't ask you to piece things, now do I."

He was generous about my quilting supplies. And about my sewing things for his mother and my sisters. I'd even bought needles and given them to Martha and showed her how to stitch repairs. "I didn't mean to upset you." I stood, brushed a smudge from his new duck pants. "I wondered if when you're back I might take that basket to Henry Hart. I'd have to be gone a few days. Nancy and I could go together. It would be a nice outing riding my new horse."

"Who'd take care of things here? No. I'll arrange for it to be taken to him. You have a home to tend to, Eliza. Best you give up childish ways of riding off into the sunset."

While he was gone, I arranged for his mother to look after the chickens and the hog and weed the garden for a day or two. She was happy to do it. "You'll return the favor, child." And I would. "Woman's got to get her feet on other soil once in a while. I'll like coming here. Quiet and cool and I make do for myself."

She made it sound so nice I wondered why I didn't just stay home. But I did want to see Henry, so I rode off, not with Nancy, but by myself.

Daniel Methany's ferry crossed the Willamette, the view taking my breath away. The current was swift, the breeze cooling on the hot August day. I liked wondering what would happen along the next mile.

It was still some distance to Forest Grove, but the landscape rolled with a copse of trees interspersed with wild roses and the sounds of summering geese chattering along the Tualatin River. Maka was a steady mount and I loved just being with this animal/companion. After the hostages were released, this landscape is where we'd come to, in rainy winter though, and my thoughts and feelings then were jumbled as the dog's food and heavy with despair. This summer day nurtured. I spent one night at a boardinghouse and left early in the morning where an imposing clapboard building with a cupola rose in the distance. It was part of the Academy, where my mother had last taught. I found Henry sitting on a stump in a shaft of light beneath big fir trees. He sat still as a statue and the green around him looked like pictures of Eastern parks. He looked up when I called to him, stood, smiled, and gave me a long hug.

"You came all alone?"

"Yes. Alone. To bring you this." From my saddlebag I handed Henry a cloth filled with fresh-baked goods, cheeses, a new shirt I'd sewn him.

"Andrew had a basket sent down too."

"Did he?" *He followed up on his word.* "I wanted to bring something myself. And see the school. They've built new buildings." I turned around. "I remember the old log one."

"Everything changes." He picked through the basket, pulled out a hunk of cheese that he broke, handing me a piece. "You should be here instead of me. You'd shine."

"It would have been nice if we were both studying here," I said.

We walked the tree-lined campus of one brick building and then outbuildings where the students stayed. This place had been one of my mother's hopes for me. Attending again would honor her legacy, but my father had changed his mind about furthering my education and then I'd married instead. "You can stay over at Mrs. Brown's boardinghouse. You remember her?"

"My intention."

I didn't remember our old teacher well. But I remember after the hostages were ransomed and we were whisked to this place, she was a kind presence while I stayed close to my mother, clinging, really. This place had been a refuge. I'd attended classes; Mama taught one. Then Mama had taken ill with her coughing; my father moved us to Brownsville where we knew no one. I'd endured the trial, and my mother had died. Maybe that's why I'd wanted to see Henry Hart at Forest Grove where we'd all been together, safe. "We're all just spokes in a wheel," I told my brother. "A wheel that keeps moving along."

I had a new wheel and Mr. Warren was its hub.

I circled around his needs, just as I once had for my father. I wasn't certain I liked the direction this wheel moved. By coming to Forest Grove on my own, I'd taken it a new direction.

The Diary of Eliza Spalding

1850

They are back, my daughter and husband. Praise God. Eliza looks as though she is in another place, her eyes distant. She is changed again. She follows orders but answers only in one or two simple words. Mr. S assures me she did not need to testify, that her answers to the lawyers were too "sympathetic" to the Indians. What strangeness is that? Mr. S tells me the Indians never confessed, that they never claimed to be the ones who committed the deeds but were found guilty just the same. All Oregon City was on edge, fearing reprisals from other tribes if the death sentence was imposed. He prayed for that, he told me. Prayed for death. Dr. McLaughlin, once head of all Hudson's Bay and the Northwest Territory, testified he tried to warn Marcus to move, that their lives at Waiilatpu with the Cayuse were not like what we had at Lapwai with the Nez Perce, but they had waited too long to change, Mr. S reports. Waited too long.

There being no jail, Sheriff Joe Meeks held the convicted men in a locked shed. His own daughter was one of those who died of measles at the Whitman site and was never buried because of what happened afterwards. In the aftermath, he found his own child's body and I think of this more often than is wise. How I feared for Eliza all that time.

Mr. S says the convicted Indians were visited by two Catholic priests who baptized and confirmed them before their deaths by hanging. S should have offered that forgiveness, especially if they claim to be sacrificial lambs to those actually committing the crimes. Does not our Lord promise redemption for every soul no matter how dark? S tells me he and my Eliza stayed for this "carrying out of justice." Hanging. Oh how I disagreed with him! Both that he announces that justice was served and that he brought my child to witness such. Has she not seen enough death? Where is the Reverend Spalding I fell in love with, the compassionate man who understood humanity, our vileness and yet our ability to be turned around? God forgive S that he seems to gloat in this tragic outcome where death begets more death and the Catholic priests are there to offer comfort while my husband rails against them as new enemies.

I must find a way to comfort Eliza. Maybe Horace can. I've failed so greatly in the protection of her spirit.

I must seek forgiveness for my admonishment

of my husband in this entry. A wife must defer to her husband except when physical pain is obvious. S has never hurt me—though my mind and heart at times are wounded. Our lives were blessed with friends and good work and a joy in each other. His ordination was a day of celebration and we applied for the Osage mission field shortly after. Our life's pursuit moving forward as Presbyterian missionaries. I wonder what might have happened if we had gone to work among the Osage instead of the Nez Perce. But I was with child and the Osage option went to other missionaries. Then, I lost the child, and Marcus Whitman found S and within the year we were on our way to the Nez Perce, a choice that changed everything. God gave us the greatest blessings and brought us to the greatest despair. But perhaps that is what change entails, the lofty and the low of living.

✵ 12 ✵

A Full House

Everything changed the afternoon Andrew came home and told me he sold Maka.

"Why? She's a good horse. Sure-footed. She doesn't startle at birds or flying debris. Why would you—"

"You ride off too often. You're needed here."

"You're gone half the time."

"I'm making a life for us."

He was doing that. I shouldn't complain. There was ample supply of meat. The garden had produced well, and I'd dried fruit and strung up beans, and he'd even brought me a box of apples from the Aurora colonists just north. The apples were smallish, but I sliced them and dried them and they'd be good in pies this winter. I'd hoped I might be with child by now, but I wasn't, a good year and a half into our marriage. One of the joys I had was riding Maka. And he'd just taken that from me.

"If I promise not to ride without your permission, could I please keep her? I miss Nellie and you were so good to buy her for me in the first place."

"I won her. Then lost her."

"You . . . won her? At cards?"

"What else? You think I know how to play your Indian stick games?"

When had I even mentioned the stick games to him? Maybe when I talked of the early years at Lapwai, before The People let my family down. Maybe I spoke too often and too freely of those times watching the games, riding on fast horses, letting my hair blow free in the wind. My childhood had begun and ended there among The People. But I hadn't imagined Andrew would find resentment in those comments. I'd thought with the smell of liquor no longer on his breath, all was well. Yes, there was another sweet smell but not whiskey.

"But cards? Gambling, with the gift you gave me?"

"It was that or one of my good beef cows, and frankly, those are more valuable than your horse. I'll get you another. Maybe even win her back. What's for supper?"

He was so cavalier about it, so abrasive in his ability to simply say, this is how things will be. Was that what happened in a marriage? That men set all tones and women must either play their tune or the instrument of their partnering would be taken away?

"Can there be no discussion of this? I could perhaps sew in exchange for what you owe for the horse. Or trade some of my dried vegetables and fruit; agree to make pies each week for the winner."

"No one cares about that kind of trade. He wants the horse. It's what I put up, and now, a man of my word, I'll deliver. We'll talk no more of it." He patted the dog and I had a moment's ire burn like a too-hot stove. He might have offered the dog. For what he'd paid for the cattle dog, the horse would still be mine.

Andrew wanted no part of the proposal I gave to him the day after he lost Maka.

"But I could teach school then, earn extra money."

"We're fine, I tell you, just fine. No, you need to be here." He kissed me. "A married woman go to the Academy? Of course not."

"My mother attended college after she was married. She sat beside my father. You could go too. We could sell the farm and you could become a businessman, a lawyer maybe. One day a judge."

He pulled me to him. "And one day, hopefully before too long, we'll have a child. I wouldn't want you working so hard you're too tired for tryin'."

I let him hold me. Truth was I liked the quiet talking that followed our intimate time, especially when he shared his plans with me, his hopes, just as he had when we'd first met, about doing something big one day. He still wanted that ranch, but I thought of other things for him. He was a smart man, and up until this gambling away my horse, I'd always thought him wise with his money.

But I had hopes and dreams too. If I wouldn't be allowed to go to school as my mother had always hoped for, then I had another plan. It was what I wanted more than schooling; I'd offered the Academy up first as a diversion, a chance for Andrew to say no, making it more likely he might later say yes.

"If not being trained to teach school, if that's not going to be permitted, then I want to bring my sisters to live with us."

"What? Where did that come from?" He held me at arm's length. I was tall enough I almost looked directly into his eyes.

Abby, the kelpie dog we'd acquired, barked outside, and he stepped out to see what bothered her. Apparently he couldn't see anything so he stepped back in, bringing the dog by her collar with him. "Your sisters?"

"Henry Hart's gone and Rachel, well, you know about her abilities. My sisters miss me, and if they were here, my father and Rachel could travel together more easily. And there'd be fewer people for him to look after. It would assist."

"I wonder if he sees it that way."

"I'm not sure. But I'd like to talk with him about it. If he'll talk to me." I might still be dead to him. "He surely wouldn't allow it unless he knew that you approved." It had struck me somewhere along these marriage months that my father, while still hostile to me, acted pleasant toward my husband. He'd forgiven him. Not me.

He shrugged then. "That Millie takes a lot of chances. Runs everywhere."

"She falls down a lot, it's true. But she gets back up. That latter, by the way, is a Spalding trait."

He harrumphed. "They'll have to go back home when school's in session. Too far to take them every day."

"Maybe by next term there'll be a new teacher at the north end."

I had to walk south through North Brownsville, across the covered bridge, and then a mile or so farther southeast to my father's home. I decided not to rile the girls with my offer before my father consented. He'd be angry if I went around him, but I hoped he'd see the practicality of it.

He worked at the small table in the front of the church/school, his Bible open and foolscap paper filled with notes beside him. It looked as though he wrote a letter. Probably to the Mission

Board. He was nothing if not persistent. He looked up when I came in, then put his head back down. I could hear Millie and Martha talking briefly on the back steps.

"You can't ignore me forever," I said. "I did not die, though you would have me so. Am I so horrid a person because I chose a man to marry you find unworthy?"

A long silence followed. I let it. Flies buzzed. I swatted at them. Finally, into the months of distance, he spoke. "I had hopes for you. One day you'd teach with me, as your mother did. We'd go back to the Nez Perce. The Board will succumb eventually. How can they deny the work we did? After all we did, Eliza."

He is speaking to my mother.

"Father."

He turned back to me with eyes glistening. "We worked so hard. She had so much grief. Losing the baby. And then a second and then you almost dying that first month. You were so sick and Marcus so long in coming to bring medicines. So frail."

"There were other babies?"

"You were so weak, couldn't hold down your mother's milk. We thought you'd die, but you lived and with such promise." He lowered his head to his hands. "And then you married."

"It didn't remove my promise, Papa." I knelt beside him, looked up at him. "I'm still capable."

"But not to travel with me to do the Lord's work."

"Rachel supports you."

He sighed. "She does as best she can, but not what you accomplished with me."

"Perhaps if I had the little girls with me, she could be of more assistance."

He looked at me then. "What?" Would he be affronted or see it as a gift? *So unpredictable. So like Andrew.* "You would do that? Take them?"

"If you'd allow." Anticipation like a butterfly lifted my spirit.

"Warren, he is . . ."

I didn't end his sentence but repeated its beginning. "He is . . ."

"Stable?"

"I see no evidence of drink." I didn't mention the gambling.

My father tapped his cheek with his finger. "Then yes, it would be of great help for you to take the girls with you. I'm certain they would like that. But I'll miss them, both of them. Henry's gone to school."

"I know."

"You could have gone too."

"When?" I bristled. *Don't ruin this.*

"If only your mother hadn't died."

"Yes, our lives would have been greatly different if Mother hadn't died."

But she had died, her last days as vivid in my

mind as the sounds of the sheep bleating in the distance. Her hands so cold, her eyes growing glassy, breathing rattling like wind against a broken gate. I'd prayed that she'd be well, prayed aloud. Then to myself, prayed that she'd die, be at peace. She clasped my hand, lifted a finger to answer my childish pleas, tapped it gently. "It will be well," she said. "All will be well." I claimed it as a promise yet unfulfilled. Perhaps my father's permission for me to have my sisters near was the beginning of all being well.

The girls were with me when I discovered a few months later that I was pregnant. It was February 1856. I'd gone into Brownsville to see the new doctor there. I knew already from the stoppage of my monthlies I must be with child. I wasn't frightened, though learning that my mother had a stillborn baby while they lived in Ohio and then lost another on the journey overland to Lapwai did cause me pause.

"You're going to have a niece or nephew," I told my sisters. They were close enough in age and stature they reminded me of twins. Miraculously, Andrew had acquired Maka back again, so the girls had a horse to ride and so did I. He'd purchased a buggy too, and we discovered Maka was trained to the harness. I'd driven with the two girls as we traveled along the frozen, snow-less road into town. Upon leaving the doctor's,

Millie begged to go on to Father's, to see if he was there. They saw him each Sunday, Rachel as well, but I could tell they missed them. When Father was at home and feeling tender, he often read them stories, Rachel having convinced him of a novel's merits, and was his old self, the way he'd been sometimes with me and Henry before everything changed.

"Can we name it?" Their enthusiasm took away the doctor's somber comments about the importance of taking care of myself, of not straining over heavy things, especially with my mother's history.

"I think the baby's father and mother might like the honor of naming this child, but I'll take suggestions."

"I say we call it Nubia." This from Millie. She dragged out the word so it sounded like "neeeew-bee-aaah."

"Nubia? Where did you hear that word?"

"Rachel says there's a country in Africa with that name," Millie answered. "I like how it sounds. It's like a new bay-bee-ya."

"Well, sort of," I said. "It does have a pretty ring to it. Nubia. But we don't live in Africa."

"Name it America."

I actually liked that name. "America Jane," Martha Jane said. "After me."

"I want her named after me."

"Amelia?"

Millie crossed her arms, holding but one hand in the rabbit fur muff I'd made for each girl and given to them at Christmas.

"You'll freeze your fingers off being petulant."

"I don't care. You should name it after me too."

Sorry I'd even honored their wishes by discussing it, I said, "Andrew and I will decide. But if we do choose America, Millie, it will be because you came up with the idea of naming a child for a country, our country. And if we choose Jane, it'll be for Martha, so really, America will stand out even more than Jane's name. Are we settled?"

They both pouted, but at least Millie put her hands back in her muff and the rest of the ride home was silent, offering me time to consider that I was going to be a mother. I figured in my head. My mother had been thirty years old when she had me. A hard pregnancy from the few comments she'd made. I wished for her to have had a friend that she could have shared her journey with, someone whom now I could ask about my mother's life. But she'd been isolated of women friends except for Nez Perce women. Maybe they were enough for her. I wondered about Matilda and if she still lived. How I would mine her memory for stories of my mother—if I ever saw her again. But even she had betrayed us . . . sending us away.

I'd be nineteen if this baby came when expected and wondered if being younger than my mother's motherhood would be better in the end. I couldn't know. I was powerless to control the outcome, but there were some things I could do, the doctor said. And getting good rest and pacing myself in the garden or at spinning and not chasing after cattle or chopping wood would be at the top of the list. I could still ride a horse but no galloping.

When I told Andrew later that same day that he would become a father in November, he swung me around the room and held me close as my crinolines continued to sway. "I'm as happy as a man holding a full house in my hands," he crowed.

"I'd hoped you'd be that happy . . . but also I hope a full house is a rare occasion, something you seldom see?"

"I don't see it much, that's sure."

"I meant—"

"I know what you meant. It's an occasional thing, Eliza. A man needs his distractions." He twisted my wedding ring, then held my hand.

I was torn by having the privileges his gambling offered—the return of the horse, clothes he purchased store-bought for me and sometimes for the girls too. Compared to some, I lived a treasured life, one others might even envy. He was happy about the baby and so was I. What more could I ask for on an otherwise crisp February day?

Andrew went out that evening. He rode his horse. The night was colder than usual for our mild-climate Willamette Valley. I heard him slip out and didn't ask where he was going. I suppose I should have. I might have prevented what happened. At the very least I could have revised my imaginings of thinking troubled thoughts in the hopes of preventing them. But Nancy says I couldn't have stopped it. Some things just happen.

The Diary of Eliza Spalding

1850

I never recovered my full resources after Amelia's birth. My little Millie. Tiny though she was, her arrival in this world caused much distress, and even now, when she has just turned four, I still strain to sit for any length of time. I pray she never becomes an invalid like this. Perhaps because I was already thirty-nine when she was born, perhaps it is my own fault to be with child at such an advanced age. But these things are ordained by God, this birth and death, and I defy his sovereignty when I question the why of it. But question I do, ever since we were forced by the Mission Board to leave Lapwai.

When Mr. Canfield came to warn us, I sent Timothy off to see if he could find S and Eliza, a last act before those gracious Nez Perce people—for our protection—packed us out our door and far into the valley, away from the mission in case the Cayuse came. We stayed in Matilda's family tipis, warm as toast. Martha Jane made the trip well. But Amelia, our little Millie, not yet one year old, fussed, receiving my own grieving through my milk. Matilda wrapped her in a baby board, the swaddling comforted and I could rest. I was at the mercy of the Nez Perce and I wondered through my fevered prayers what I would do if something happened to my husband. Where would I go? What place was safe? If they would have me, I decided I would stay with these people who were more family to me than my own sisters. I even wondered what might happen if the Cayuse came demanding me or any of the few white persons we employed. Would they turn us over? I looked at Joseph and at Peter, two Nez Perce who not only claimed Jesus but learned English well enough to teach the gospel to those as yet unformed in the faith. They were good young men. They had always been kind to us. They were different from the Cayuse. I had to remember that. I had to trust that God knew where we were and what our future held.

It is 9:00 a.m. This was the hour when I, Narcissa, Mary Walker, and Sarah and the other missionary wives all ceased our work and prayed for our children. Our Maternal Society, we called it. Narcissa wrote of it and the Mission Board published our extended giving of support through prayer in their newsletter. A part of me was a bit envious that her words were published, but she captured our hopes for the society well, and after her dear Alice drowned, I was grateful she had experienced some small joy in the publication. She lost so much. The death made me more vigilant and I had S build a fence around our house-garden and small yard so that Eliza didn't waddle off to the Clearwater River. And she never did, but I remember with such sorrow that the Littlejohns' boy did. They were people called by God too, who came west to support us. Their little boy met death on our river. Eliza came inside and asked where he had gone and we ran outside, his mother and me—we had no Matilda then—called out to him, and then we saw the hole in the rope webbing S had woven to serve as a fence. The boy had crawled through. Had Eliza seen him go? I hoped she had no memory of his disappearance and the Lord offered me solace in that regard by the purity of her question when she came in, wondering where he'd gone. At three, she was too young to be responsible for watching him. Somehow they'd both gone outside without us mothers noting. S was gone. Mrs. Littlejohn bereft. Hugging my Eliza I still felt so alone.

Another alone time, me with baby Eliza, and over a thousand Nez Perce came in to the mission for lessons I taught, to hear S preach the gospel, to work the land and plant wheat. A day when trepidation came upon me like an angry mountain storm, quick and fierce for my husband's abandonment of us. He insisted he must go to Waiilatpu to work out some permission with the Whitmans. I understood then what it meant that we at Lapwai were but a branch of the larger mission that included both our sites. And then later with the arrival of others, that the "site" encompassed land beyond mountains among different tribes of Indians.

These thoughts discomfort. My back aches more.

Maybe S wanted the distance from the woman he'd once asked to marry. Maybe he liked doing what he wished without Marcus looking over his shoulder. But Marcus was the doctor for all our "missions' sites" and he was 120 miles away! Meetings always seemed to happen at M's site, forcing S to go there and leave me at Lapwai. And that day, he left, and while Eliza slept I took out my paints and drew the story in Luke of the woman and the lost coin, though I show it as her having many strings of mollusk shells used for adornment and in trade. *Dentalia*, the Nez Perce called it, and then I paint her having lost one precious strand and how she scours her tipi to find it. I make her face with the high cheekbones of the Nez Perce, give her long black hair I color with blackberry ink, put a touch of strawberry juice on her cheek. She carries a lamp with expensive oil she burns in her search, an investment in seeking that lost treasure. And in the last panel she is rejoicing and I show her dancing on soft moccasins, hands to the sky, offering up the shells. I put knitting needles and yarn in the corner behind her and told the Nez Perce students that her joy is because she has found what was lost, but more, that her dance is that of God's when we allow ourselves to be found and we knit him into our hearts. I wish I could have taken those panels with me. We left in such a hurry.

On that day as I painted I heard the thunder of hooves, enough to wake Eliza. I stood at the door and watched as dust came up the valley, hoof-powder of a hundred horses. I saw myself in the valley of the shadow of death. My heart pounded as I held my child to me and waited what fate the Lord had set before us. I did not even pray, a fact that astounds me still. But perhaps I knew at that moment my small words would come in human time. God already knew and had us in his hands. I felt my heartbeat slow, thought of S and how after all we'd been through this was now the climax of a life's work. We were ended. He would go on alone and I asked then for prayers for him as I knew he would blame himself for leaving us, his guilt compounding his grief. And I felt a lifting of my spirit, that death had no fear for me in this valley. My child would be taken with me and never know fear nor sorrow in her life. How wrong I was about that.

When the dust settled, a man I called Joseph came forward, his son beside him, on magnificent horses, both of them. The boy had a presence about him exuding confidence even in his youth. Old Joseph, as I came to know him, in a mix of Sahaptin, English, and Chinookan, all which I could understand, said he hoped they had not frightened us. I think I laughed in my relief. They came to welcome. They would summer near us, and work as S had asked them. When I told them he had gone for a time but would be back, Old Joseph smiled. They had met him on the trail. "He says to look after his family," the younger Joseph said. "It is The People's way to also look after strangers until they are as family." I thought of a Scripture, about living honorably among strangers.

They set about making their camp as I wondered at how my great fear had dissipated before I even knew of their friendly intent. I showed young Joseph the panels and he said, "The woman, she is strong. Like our women."

"Yes," I told him. "And in this story she is God seeking what is valuable, our hearts and souls. See how she rejoices when she lets God in?" He held the last panel of the celebrating woman with such a light upon his face I asked if he would like to take it with him. He declined, said he already had it in his heart and it belonged with the other panels to be shared with everyone.

That night more than one hundred fires flickered, their lights like bright knots among the knitted fabric of this wide country and our place within it. I imagined God weaving all threads of us living for him. Old Joseph was our first convert, his son not long after. Young Joseph I felt would follow his father's authority granted by The People as their chief. Such promise we saw in our foreign efforts among strangers, turned to such disaster, and all must have passed through our Lord's hands. I will one day soon ask of him, why.

⇒ 13 ⇐
LOST AND FOUND

Strangers brought Andrew in the next morning. With frost on his whiskers, he would have died if not for the alcohol in his system, or so one of his comrades said. And he'd have complained of more pain with his broken leg, the bone piercing against but not through the skin if not for their ministrations. "Like an icicle thrust upward," this stranger in my home described. It was bandaged tightly around a board to "push it back in its channel, Missus." And to hold his leg steady. I could smell alcohol on their breaths, though they said their drinking had ceased long before dawn. They'd taken all that time to get Andrew treated at the doctor and then home.

"That's what friends are for," Andrew said, his eyes glassy with laudanum—or more. The rescuers were in much better shape, laughing as they hauled him into our cabin and laid him onto the bed.

"Fix them vittles, woman." Andrew waved his hand like a hat circled overhead.

The girls awoke and I sent Martha to the henhouse for eggs while I stepped behind the divider quilt to change from my nightdress into a wrapper and fresh apron. I jabbed at the fire and added water to the coffee kettle, then nestled it in among the now glowing coals.

His friends, with Irish accents, began waxing on about their evening, about how Andrew arrived at the saloon with words of "happiness about your impending kin." I frowned. "Your wee one coming. Sure and he's a happy lad."

"Happy, yes indeedy."

"Uncle burped," Millie said. "And he didn't say sorry."

"That's the least of his social lapses. Get the syrup from the larder and put it on the table, would you, Millie? Thank you, child." I loved it when she did as she was asked without a protest.

Eggs arrived. I grabbed striped meat (as Andrew called bacon), mixed up johnnycakes, spread them on the round griddle as soon as the woodstove heated. With my other ear I heard the story of the night, how they played cards and Andrew had lost. (Which explained his friends' great "kindness" to him, taking him to the doctor, bringing him home. If he'd won they likely would have left him to the cold and wolves, a just recompense for having taken all their funds that night.)

"He usually holds his liquor well, Missus, but he was harborin' visions of grandeur with a son beside him on that cattle ranch he's always talking 'bout." These men were no strangers to Andrew; only to me.

"Needs riding lessons. Man's got to both hold his liquor and his seat." This from the skinny one, slender as a bacon strip, his comment causing all three men to howl with laughter. Both of my husband's comrades sported broken blood vessels across their noses, and for the first time I noticed my husband's face in a new way. At that moment, his cheeks were scraped but there was that telltale sign of liquor consumption. Over time. I'd never acknowledged it before.

"How did his face get so scraped up?"

"He fell into a pile of rocks, slipped right off the horse and then whooped so that the gelding pulled back and his leg was still in the stirrup. He got dragged a ways."

"Right into a boulder where his horse deposited him and left him with an arrow-looking thing pushing against his leg. Took us a bit through his wailing to see that it was bone trying to break free." This so-called friend had reached into the cupboard and handed cups around, poured hot coffee from the kettle he'd grabbed. I must have frowned at his intruding in my kitchen. "Just being helpful, Missus. You got your hands full there."

"Almost lost my supper." The skinny one continued. "Never seen bone like that come up."

"So we took him to the doctor. What are friends for?"

"Doc weren't none too happy to be woke up at that hour. He patched it, pushed it back, and wrapped it good, but he says infection's likely. Said he'd be by later today to take another peek. Gave us laudanum to give you to numb his pain when he starts to really come out of it." The helpful coffee-serving friend pulled a bottle from his pocket. "Laudanum."

"Thank you." I grabbed it from him with more vigor than intended, plopped it on the table. "Don't mistake it for syrup," I said. "Breakfast's ready."

The men pulled up chairs and ate, quiet for a moment. Andrew moaned once or twice but no longer participated in any part of the discussion. I eavesdropped, learned of how regularly these men saw my husband, how much they knew about us, and how only when they let others join their games had the friendliness waned into real distress. A favorite horse lost. A promissory note written, giving up future profits when a beef was sold. How grateful the men were when Andrew played, as "he always brings the best whiskey."

The stories were told with too much detail. They were still under the influence themselves, I decided, or they never would have been so open with their words. They were in the enemy's camp sharing secrets and they didn't even know it.

My sisters sat wide-eyed, listening, patting a leavings doll. I'd have to explain later what all those stories meant and ask that they not repeat any of this to our father or Rachel or they'd be whisked from my care in a second.

Andrew's friends left after eating their fill, glad to see "Warren's in the tender hands of such a lassie." I fed the girls and myself then, checking on Andrew, whose snores rumbled like water over river rocks. I attacked my own chores, cleaning the griddle, heating the irons. Cooled, the iron's weight might keep the bone pressed so it would mend. I thought I'd seen my mother do that once with a young Nez Perce boy. I chopped wood for the fireplace, brought in an armload to put in the firebox beside the woodstove. At least we'd be warm.

Together the girls and I slopped the hogs, fed our two sheep, opened the paddock so the oxen could meander in the fenced pasture. Back in the barn, I filled the manger with loose hay for the horses.

That's when I noticed I'd lost my wedding ring.

Frantic, I pushed back grass hay, dug into the manger. Nothing. I might have lost it anywhere. I stomped back into the house to heat water for our Saturday baths. Abby sat on the porch, brown eyes pleading.

"Dogs aren't allowed in the house," I told her.

But when I opened the door and smelled the liquor and the laudanum, thought about my ring lost to the hard labor, I turned back. "Dogs might not be allowed in the house, but if drunks are, then you are too."

In the afternoon, Andrew roused. I wasn't aware he had wakened until he moaned. "What have I done, 'Liza? What have I done?" His faced flushed red, chin dropped to his chest. His shame pricked my heart toward softness. It didn't last.

" 'Liza, darlin'—"

"Don't you 'darlin'' me! You, you've lied to me, misled me, you've been drink—"

"I have not." His voice rose. "Last night, the first time in a long time and I am sorry. I am real sorry." He rubbed his forehead with his fingers.

I wasn't ready for apologies. "Sorry? Sorry that you'll be laid up for weeks, if not months? Sorry that you brought men into our home and asked me to feed them, also drunk, I might add, in front of my sisters? Sorry that you what, aren't free to do what you want without a little . . . guilt?"

"You'll always best me with words, 'Liza. Mine are small. Just, I'm sorry, for everything."

"Everything? For marrying me?" I jabbed at him. "You were baptized. You took a vow."

"I don't need you to tell me."

"But why? You're smart. You're inventive. You're a hard worker. Why?" I paced, paused to look at him and saw tears pooling in his eyes.

"What is it? I want to know . . . even my . . . my part in this."

"You have no part. Well, you're in the hope I had for healing an old wound, but I seem to keep opening it with liquor and the rush of card playin'. Or maybe I'm trying to drown it." He looked away. *Embarrassment.* That's what I saw in my husband's eyes.

"Tell me." I sat beside him on the feather tick and he winced. His physical wound demanding we remember. *Is it the laudanum speaking?* I didn't know. "Just tell me why you do this. Do you even know?"

His shallow breathing filled the silence. Then, "The same reason you try to control the world, 'Liza, or disappear inside your mind where no one can reach you. I do it to stop the pain. And so do you."

"What pain?"

But all the wishing and probing brought nothing. Instead of relieving his burden, he returned to sleeping, the bridge to our healing broken. No laudanum could remedy that.

❧ 14 ❧

LEARNING THE LANGUAGE OF MARRIAGE

We managed the summer, neighbors helping as they could. The O'Donnell brothers—I'd learned their names—showed up, sheepish but willing to haul in water, chop wood, while Andrew healed. The doctor said it was my nursing that accounted for his progress; nursing and taking on the tasks my husband simply couldn't do. Oddly, once I let go of my anger, accepted the challenge before me, we became a family, of sorts. Andrew said I was happy because I controlled the household and him, knew where he was each moment. He said it with a smile, but I heard truth in that.

In the evening we read Scripture and the dictionary, too, learning new words together. *Extenuate. Lassitude. Fortuitous.* My sisters giggled and didn't even realize they were learning too. We made the best of our turmoil.

"You do what you have to." That's what I told Nancy when she brought me a wooden box of staples from the dry goods store. I didn't get to town much now. "Remember when I wondered how Andrew spent his time? Well, he rode, trying to keep the cattle close where he could see how they fared, pushed them through trees, hoped to keep them from a wildness gained from never seeing humans."

"And kept wolves away? I hear them howl, even in town."

"Yes, especially during calving. I'm suddenly an expert in cattle-raising though I'm not very good at it. There are wolf signs. I wonder if I should carry a gun."

"You're riding astride?" Nancy placed the bolted flour in the bin, wiping up the slightest dust of it before she took the salt from the box and put it in the cupboard. "Would you mind if I straightened up your shelf?"

"Mind? No. I just haven't had time. And yes, astride. I can't believe my mother rode sidesaddle all across the continent. Of course she wasn't riding while carrying a child, but still." My father's mention of "babies" before I arrived made me wonder if what I'd just said was true.

Nancy chattered on about her brother's latest love, how her mother had pneumonia but had recovered with the summer heat. Her father said there was talk of bringing a woolen mill to the area. "They'd employ a lot of people, girls too. I might get a job there." Nancy was sixteen and pretty with that flaming red hair. I said as much to her as she finished up organizing my shelves.

"Oh, maybe I am." Then, "I've met a lad." She blushed.

"Of course you have. It was only a matter of time."

"His name is Andrew too. Andrew Kees. He came from Pennsylvania. I told him about what happened and how I absolutely seem to take so long to do things. He said he didn't mind 'a-tall.' That's how he says 'at all.' A-tall." She looked wistful, her busy hands stopped as she spread the words out with her fingers as though writing them in the sky. "He's a cooper. A good one. He has contracts for barrels with the store and blacksmith too. The only thing is . . . he's nearly forty."

"Forty years old?"

"Next year." She fiddled with her red curls. "But he's really good to me. And when I told him what happened, how frightened I'd been and how we survived, he said I was very brave to keep on living, to not let that past tragedy hold me like the hostages we were, that life happens and we have to move on." She sat down, straightened the chair pillow, but this time let our teacups rule the table without intervention. "He says sometimes, after a bad time, we form new habits. That's what my organizing is." Her fingers reached to turn the teacup handle toward her, but she stopped, put her hands on her lap. "It's just a way to fit things into tight places, when I'm not sure I can. So I look for things I *can* do. That's what my Andrew says."

"He sounds very wise. And kind. Absolutely kind." I grasped her hand, squeezed it, let it go. I wondered if I might find another way to control my life besides imagining terrible things, being a shrew to my husband. My efforts to control the world weren't really working anymore. And being self-righteous with Andrew didn't advance our marriage either.

"When you lose things, kindness fills the spaces, he says," Nancy continued. "He lost a wife and child already. And his farm back in Pennsylvania." She straightened the handle on the sugar pot. "We have nice conversations. He hasn't said anything of marriage. I mean, we're just friends."

"Friends make the best marriages." I knew I sounded wistful.

"Any more sassafras tea, darlin'?" Andrew shouted from the front porch where I'd helped him hobble, placed his leg up on a pillowed chair, and handed him his leather-working tools and the saddlebag he worked on, stamping roses in the leather with his mallet while Nancy and I tended to things inside.

"I'll get it for you!" This was Martha Jane who swooped in and brought him a cup of the cooled tea I'd taken from the spring just before

Nancy arrived. The best thing about Andrew's recuperating was that the girls entertained him, scurried to get him water when he was thirsty, made him sandwiches when I was out for the day on horseback, even stewed a hen we'd have for supper. Andrew was good with them, complimenting their cooking and baking. He didn't bark at them the way he did at me.

"Can you feel the baby move?" Nancy brushed away crumbs from the tablecloth. I nodded. "Isn't it funny? We were just girls not so long ago and soon you'll be a mother. Your mama would be proud."

"I could never be the kind of mother she was, so loving and a good wife too."

"Sure you could. She was your model. You'll do good, I know it."

"I'll do well." I laughed when she frowned. "Ignore me, Nancy. Grammar is a specialty of mine. And forgive me. I just have to correct, fix things whether they matter or not."

"I've been in that horse race." She grinned.

Nancy rose to leave and I hugged her, grateful to have a friend who didn't need explaining to. After she left, I sat for a moment on the porch beside Andrew. The girls and I had picked blackberries in the late July morning, and I could smell their ripeness even though the branches we'd plucked were well beyond the barn. I kept them chopped closer to the buildings, as they took over a place. I wished more than once that the Molalla and Kalapuya Indians, who had been on this land first, still burned the underbrush. But with split rail fences marking "territory," the settlers forbade it. Instead, we chopped vines and shrubs, working twice as hard than if we'd monitored flames doing that work for us.

The doctor came and I rose to bring him coffee.

"Andrew's bone's healing well, thanks to you. First signs of civilization are healed bones, I always say. Someone had to bring food and water so that bone could rebuild. Kindness. Had it back in ancient times when we still lived in caves. A good thing our ancestors brought with us. You remember that, Andrew Warren." He nodded toward me. "Be kind to your wife here. She's got her hands full."

"And I gave her most of that full house she's holding."

A fire hit my face, hot with his reference to gambling and his claim that all we had was what *he'd* brought about rather than my having any part to it.

"And I'm sorry I did that to you, Eliza. Sorry for this happening and truly grateful for how you're keeping me from . . . bad things."

I frowned, realizing he hadn't meant that the good things I held had come from him but rather that these challenges that consumed my daily efforts were his fault: his wound, my need to care for him, bringing in wandering cattle. Maybe even him wanting my full attention whenever he came back to the house. He gave me great power, maybe too much. *Does he think it's me who keeps his lips from liquor instead of Who it really is?*

The doctor left, and Andrew and I sat together, the girls with their little leavings dolls playing in the dirt in front of the porch. My belly swelled and the baby kicked. I placed Andrew's hand on my abdomen. "Feel that?" He nodded. "New life. We'll get you through this, and we'll have a new life to care for. As his *papo* you'll do him proud."

"You're sure it'll be a boy?"

"Some things can't be known nor planned for. They just are."

He patted my belly. "It's been five months. Maybe I'm done with drink for good."

"You've been counting too?"

He nodded. I thought maybe in this closer moment he'd tell me of that pain he carried. But he didn't and this time I wisely didn't try to force it from him. I kept my counsel and enjoyed the present moment, another part of the language of marriage I was learning.

We named the baby America Jane. She was born November 7, just a week before my nineteenth birthday, in 1856. How I wish my mother could have met her! That same dark hair, those brown eyes wide to the world, taking in the lantern light, my face. I had sent Martha riding on Maka for Nancy and the doctor on that unusually mild November morning. Nancy arrived first. By the time the doctor arrived America Jane was waiting.

"I named her," Millie told Nancy. "America."

"America Jane," I added. "We'll use her full name as it's so lovely."

"Rachel calls herself Jane too," Martha noted.

"That she does. So our little girl's name will represent many good girls."

I gasped as Nancy handed my baby to me.

"What?"

"I . . . I just saw my mother's hands through my own on this child's chest." A grandchild for my mother. And my father. "He would have wanted her named Eliza, and if a boy, Andrew." But I wanted each of what I hoped was many children to have their own name, make their own way. A flood of warmth filled me as I let those tiny fingers like butterfly kisses brush my palm. My child. My very own child.

"I'll bake a cake for her." Martha was our little baker, and though she was but eleven she was handy with the cookstove.

"I'm pleased the delivery went well. You helped so much, Nancy." To share this moment with a friend brought our Savior's love to the occasion.

"All that riding and chopping wood, doing Andrew's work, kept you healthy. It's no wonder this baby took little time to get here." Nancy beamed with our success as she cut the cord. "She knew you had things to do and didn't want to keep you from it!"

I was once again so grateful to have a close woman friend. Was Matilda a friend like that to my mother? Did she midwife and cut my youngest sister's cord as Nancy did?

The Nez Perce kept the umbilical cord, put it in a pouch. I remembered then that Matilda had said it would keep a baby close to its mother for life whether in a pouch at the baby's throat or with the mother.

I put my child's cord in the leather pouch that Andrew had given me years before, feeling a twinge of guilt with my mother's wedding ring still there too. I wasn't sure why I kept the Nez Perce ways in some things. Nancy took the afterbirth outside and buried it deep enough that the animals wouldn't dig it up, upsetting Abby who had trotted after her. Millie brought the dog back inside.

Nancy had relegated Andrew to the porch, but he'd come inside when Millie skipped past him with Abby in tow. He laid his cane beside the chair and reached out for our baby. I handed America Jane to him, swaddled in a quilt. He held the child in his arms.

"She has your chin," I said. "Firm."

"I hope she has your strength."

"Mine? No, more like her grandmother's. She was the strong one who kept things going." She and my father worked so closely together. I suspect they never had a moment of doubt in their lives about their ability to raise a child, make a life, or of God's place in a challenge or even about how to live with uncertainty or the lack of ability to influence one's own life. She was solid, through and through. Firm. I believed that about her and their marriage and how things were supposed to work. I wanted to be like her, her family and faith giving meaning to her life. I had a purpose: raising a child, making a marriage work. Of course, marriage is like a language, and as with any language, it was easy to misinterpret.

The Diary of Eliza Spalding

1850

My children give meaning to my life. I imagine
Eliza working with her father who one day
might get our mission back. He writes such
passionate letters to the Mission Board, makes
such a strong case to continue the work we did
there. We should just return. The trial is over
and there've been no new uprisings. My
thoughts toward the Board are full of disappointment. The "shoulds" of what they should
have done are weights around my heart. I
remember a letter S showed me, one of
recommendation when we sought the mission
field. His professor had said S was an "average
student," in fact lacked "common sense," but
that I was an "exceptional student who would
make the most superb missionary wife." S
wasn't fazed by this affront to his abilities. He
said he knew God was with him by bringing
me to his side, to fill in his "lackings," and I
should be proud to know our professors saw
such gifts in me.

He also said common sense was overvalued.

It was his passion for a cause, a dream—
that's what saved those who might act in ways

others thought lacked common sense. He reminded me we would not be here, would not have had the many souls brought to Christ, would not have printed those gospel books in Sahaptin, the Nez Perce language, if we'd listened to the "common sense" of those who said women couldn't cross the continent and survive. We'd survived and thrived. I was glad S told me that. I could see purpose in our work and know that Eliza working with him after I am gone will continue to bring meaning to my life, long after. And I forgive S for the slights, the times he left me behind. It grew my character, those times of dark uncertainty.

I wish Matilda was with me so we could talk about those days. She learned English so quickly and then Scripture, speaking Psalms in English and then in that lilt of clicks and swooshes that marked the language of The People, as though the very earth with its waterfalls and wind-swept ridges had given up its secrets to create the language of Nez Perce. I miss her counsel about children. I miss her brokering our lives, being that go-between for when S did something that offended or when I did. Once I held a Nez Perce toddler in my lap and pointed to her image in a slice of mirror, hearing the gasp of her mother as she whisked the child from my arms. It was Matilda who told me that a Nez Perce child is not permitted to see her own reflection until her soul is fully formed for fear if she sees that image she will search forever for that other self. "We even swirl the bath water," Matilda told me. Such is not our belief, of course, but how to explain the nature of the soul with no way to lose it but by action or behavior. More importantly, she aided my understanding that the way I saw the world was not the only way to see it. I put away the mirror and once again was so grateful for her presence. She taught me use of local herbs, of plants that gave up inks and healing. And when once I was nauseated from my being pregnant, she held my head and told me to "pant like dog." I laughed but did it and it worked. I so wish she could have come with us. But she would have been reviled here, even though her people kept us safe, were like family to me and always will be. Like the Mission Board, people here have trouble distinguishing between the many tribes.

Martha Jane comes to sit with me. She brings her doll, the one I made for her. The baby, oh, the baby "Millie" my last, who talks a streak at four and who thinks horses are big dogs meant for her to grab a tail and even walk beneath them. She has her ways. I think she is her father's favorite as she is our last. My last. Before I am taken home. How I wish I could have been buried in Lapwai! But this Brownsville will do. Where our earthly bodies are planted is of no matter. We go where we are led by God and men whom God has placed in our lives. It's where our souls soar to, a path of grace broken for me a long time ago. I am so grateful to have heeded the call. Grateful for my children. Grateful for Matilda too. When S was gone, it was Matilda who reminded me I was not alone.

☞ 15 ☜

STRETCHING THROUGH THE DARKNESS

A year after the night when Andrew was returned by his friends, he did something lacking common sense. He'd been so faithful! But he left our cabin, left me alone, went out and "found himself at a game," as though his body simply took control of his mind and his limbs. "Man has to have a little entertainment after being cooped up in a cabin with four women all year."

Four women. Me, my sisters, and our America Jane holding her head up for just seconds while lying on her tummy. The kelpie stands beside her, vigilant, watching over the child. The dog takes on cattle at their noses, pushing them back, but with children, she is a guard dog, soft yet making sure that all is well. I seek a Kelpie for my marriage.

That Andrew would choose on his first outing on a late February day to be with his "friends" astounded me. What was the draw that led him to make a decision of such un-common sense? Doing what he wished. Making his way regardless of the impact on others.

He came home without liquor on his breath, so my ire was not as fueled as it might have been. Maybe he did need a small diversion. He had no money with him though, so I hoped the game was but a friendly one, the exchange of jokes and stories more than coins. We still had cattle and the horses when he returned, and he'd arranged for drovers to round them up for branding in the spring. Perhaps as my mother often said, all will be well.

In time, Andrew worked back into his former tasks while I took on baking goods Martha Jane and I whipped up for the "Rachels" of the region. The new enterprise brought in revenue, and I found satisfaction in contributing income to the family. I discovered there were a number of women lacking yeast bread skills. They welcomed the chance to purchase or trade for baked goods already prepared. Each year more people crossed the continent and came farther south from Oregon City, seeking land not already spoken for. October and November were the most difficult times for new arrivals, and I found I could put some coins or other trade goods aside by bringing baked goods into town to sell at Brown and Blakely's. Andrew watched me put money in the tin bucket I kept in the back of the cupboard. I had another stash, too, one Andrew didn't know about—for a crisis if one happened. Planning for how to respond to a disaster was not the same as "imagining" one in hopes of keeping it from happening. Was it? As a young mother I had moved on from that bad habit, one Rachel had said invited trouble. Not imagining a dreadful future gave me room to see happier possibilities: America Jane growing strong, walking and jabbering sometimes recognizable words.

Once while delivering the doughnuts alone, Martha and Millie at home chasing after America Jane, I came upon a camp of Kalapuya Indians filleting fish taken from the river. Their features did not startle me, but the fish blood did. For a moment I looked at the fish and people, smelling the fire, the wind in my face. And then I wasn't.

What I remembered next was the touch of someone stroking my hair saying, *"Yok-sa. Klose."*

"Good hair." The words were Chinookan jargon, the hand touching the hair at my forehead cool and smelling of water and earth and smoked salmon. Brown eyes looked down at me, concern on their faces. They were not the tall-stature people like the Nez Perce or Cayuse but they loomed large over me. I tried to sit up, swooned again, but stayed with them, listening to my breathing. Maka tugged at grass off to the side. One sat behind me and I leaned against her. They were a quiet group in their movements, a beaten people, no longer staked by their land, clinging to a present history.

"You go away?" One spoke in English.

"Yes. I . . ." I looked around. I was in the middle of a group of women, maybe five. I smelled fish and saw the blood on their hands. My straw hat lay beside me. I swallowed, but I didn't go away. "Thank you," I said, seeking the Chinookan word but not finding it. I'd lost the language of the people who had left me behind at Waiilatpu.

"You fall. You hurt?"

I didn't think I was. Apparently I'd slumped off Maka and landed in the tall grasses beside the river. Maka stood waiting, pulling at weeds. "I'm fine. *Klose.*"

They helped me up. One brought Maka around, then formed a stirrup of her palms, and I stepped inside, mounted sidesaddle, the way I rode in public.

"Fish?" one woman said. She squinted, looking up at me, holding the salmon. In that moment I remembered how the Nez Perce brought salmon to my family. Fish, sustenance; fish, a gift, salmon given up in season.

"I'd love some. Here." I dug in my purse for coins, but she shook her head, nodding with her chin toward the baked goods we could all smell.

"Of course." I opened the white towel covering three loaves of bread and handed them to her. The Brownsville Rachels would be short. She took but one loaf, returning the rest to me.

"Is enough."

I tried to memorize their faces filled with smiles. They did not look like the Cayuse and I was grateful. In the distance, at the river's edge, I heard a man shout, come up from the bank with another fish and a spear. They weren't paying him attention. I knew the women were to be close to the water to take the catch and fillet them, set them at the fire to smoke while men speared or tended nets or traps. Torches lay beside the place where the women worked and I suspected they'd light them in the dark and continue both fishing and working through the night. Another woman wrapped my fish fillet with big leaves and I opened my pack for her to place it inside the leather. It must have weighed three times my loaf of bread and one end stuck out it was so long. "Dried by *hatia*." The word popped into my head. I touched the part of the fish that stuck out. "Wind." She looked confused, then must have made the translation from the Nez Perce.

"Aaaaah," she said with a smile and I was reminded of Millie and her "I looooove that" as she dragged the word of happiness out.

"Aaaaah," I said back.

Later that day when I returned from Blakely's, they were still busy at it and I waved. They lifted their chins in recognition. Neighbors. Not strangers. I saw the fish blood but stayed in Brownsville on a spring day. Maybe in the future when I saw fish blood I would remember their kindnesses instead of the massacre when I was ten. This Brownsville was a *klose* place, even though it was where I lost my mother.

My father ignored me after church, but he did permit the girls to remain with us even after America Jane was born. I saw then how much my mother must have needed Matilda. She had four children and worked hard to paint Bible stories, teach, manage my father, learn Sahaptin—for all the good any of it did her. I taught the girls and I took it as a compliment that my father permitted me to be their teacher, given that I was "dead" to him. He liked seeing them twice a month at the Sabbath service. Especially Millie. She was his favorite, allowing her to interrupt when he spoke, giving in to requests for treats at the store. She was a fine young horsewoman, staying astride even riding bareback at a fast run. "I'm an eagle, flying," she told me once. Her frame was slender as a pullet's wishbone. She was a charmer too. I think all youngest children are, while oldest children are meant to always strive to be their parents, protecting even when young ones name it an intrusion. I could see how my father adored her. Still, I vowed I wouldn't let that happen, let one child worm her way deeper into my heart than another.

Andrew was happy with his brood, or so I thought. He limped a bit but had resumed all duties, rode with his cattle for days at a time. When he returned, we nestled down with a good meal, a reading from the Word, something I'd begun after Andrew's last trip to town. I taught the girls to spin and weave. We had a good life.

Yet in our cabin, Andrew chafed. He barked at the girls if their chattering got too loud for him. Didn't look at me when I spoke.

"Would you like a berry pie tonight? It's your favorite."

"No."

"We washed sheets yesterday. They smell so good. Did you notice? You always do."

"No." His hands worked a set of leather reins, softening them. He resisted my attempts to soften him.

"America Jane learned a little poem I taught her. Would you like to hear her recite?"

A deep sigh. "I need to check the barn latch. I'm not sure I closed it."

Maybe having to be away from us for a few days at a time gave him something that being around all the women in his house didn't. He said his more frequent separation was because he had to take the herd higher into the hills and away, what with the valley being "fenced up" as he put it and the longhorns gotten from California needed wider range than our beef cows. "Same species, different needs," he said. Not unlike us humans, I thought then.

At one point that fall of 1858 he said he'd be gone a month. "I need to find more land. Don't worry. I've got drovers checking the cattle."

"Where are you headed? Could we go with you? Make an adventure of it?"

He looked at my burgeoning belly. "No." He held me then. "I'll be back." He kissed my ringless knuckles.

"I never thought you wouldn't."

Andrew returned in the fall, not sharing much about his journey.

"Did you find the land you were looking for?"

He scratched at his neck and started that lip chewing he hadn't done for years.

"I looked. Still looking. All this talk about Oregon becoming a state, free or slave, raises the stakes about staying here."

I swallowed, treaded like a mother not wanting to wake a sleeping child. "Move?"

"What did you think it would mean if I found land somewhere else?"

"I . . . I guess I thought the cattle would move but not us. And statehood, that makes a difference?"

"Rules and regulations come with statehood. My pa came from Missouri to avoid all that."

"Well, hmm, I hadn't thought someone wouldn't want to be part of America." Our citizenry confused me, and it was true, the

Spectator newspaper was full of letters and columns about slavery, free blacks, taxing authority, and the like.

Our talking of such things grew more intense until he pounded his fist on the table, shouting "Silence! Can't a man have a moment of peace?" He'd shoved the chair back, then stomped away, leaving my sisters with startled looks and America Jane in tears. Something was amiss but I didn't know what.

Our second child, Martha Elizabeth, arrived in January 1859. We called her Lizzie from the start. On February 14, Oregon became a free state and entered the Union. But we also included in the constitution an exclusion clause keeping free blacks out. Our new state harbored ambivalent-voting men. I wondered how Andrew voted. My sisters burst into lovely young ladies at the new state's festivities on Valentine's Day, and I took some credit for Millie's knitting and sewing skills, and Martha's imaginative baking. My sisters were twelve and fourteen already and of great aid to me with two children. Our baked goods continued to allow purchases for cloth and needles, ribbons for the girls' hair and bonnets, catalog orders for crinolines and clocks made in France. I found myself chatting with Rachel about what Eastern women wore and spoke to her more as a friend than an intruder to my mother's memory. I sang as I worked and rarely visited Waiilatpu in my nightmares or my thoughts. Except for Andrew's reticence about his discovery of new land or not, I thought we'd settled into a rhythm as predictable as a rocking chair.

Then Andrew came home drunk.

The O'Donnell brothers brought him in again, and he demanded I fix them a meal though the clock chimed three, but I declined this time, incensed at him and annoyed at myself for not anticipating, for having given up my "thoughts of preparation," imagining the worst. I had failed to notice signs. I'm not sure what they were, but I must have missed them. Or maybe I misinterpreted what I observed. My prayers for his giving up drink had been answered for so long and then . . .

"You. Get out!" I pushed at the O'Donnells, who stumbled against each other and giggled like schoolboys as they headed out the door. They were happy drunks, not mean ones. Lizzie's breath caught in her sleep as I hissed at my husband, "How dare you come into my home in this state."

"Your home? Our home." He didn't really slur his words, but his eyes were like warbled glass windows at Blakely's store. And he swayed, leaning toward me. "Oh, 'Liza, come here now. I'll be good." He tried to hold me when I straightened him, but I'd have none of that sloppy charm.

"You defile our home and me with your . . . your actions."

Abby shook in the corner, her ears lowered as though she'd done something wrong, and my sisters, awakened by the ruckus, sat wide-eyed on their pallets. Thank goodness my babies slept through it. My long night braid lay across my breast and I tossed it back over my shoulder. "You diminish us with your betrayal, your disregard for your children, my sisters, for me. Have you no shame?"

His dark eyes widened in surprise. "No shame? Shame is all I have, woman. It's all I have."

"You have so much! A home. Family who loves you. You're an intelligent man. Kind. We have a good life. Why would you throw it away? I don't want our daughters growing up with their father who's a d—like this." I couldn't call him a drunk, I couldn't. It had been my father's word and I refused to say it. But Mr. Warren did.

"I'm a drunk."

I pressed my hands against my ears. "No. Yes. You drink. Something happens to make you drink. You said once it covered your pain. What pain? Tell me. Please."

He'd plopped onto the bed—maybe the force of my words pushing him there—and sat up, swaying. "I'm going to be sick."

Martha Jane came out from her huddle in the corner with a wash basin. He took it from her, lowered his head.

"Pant like a dog." I gave him the instruction my mother had once given me to stave off nausea.

In a moment he looked up, pale. "I'm not sure you can hear the truth, Eliza, of who your husband really is."

What shame could he possibly carry that was as great as mine? "Just tell me."

"Ah, 'Liza." He leaned back onto the bed and then . . . fell asleep.

I had all I could do not to throw a basin of cold water in his face. Instead, I tried to imagine what he carried like heavy stones or what had happened to make him turn from the path he'd been on, being a good father, looking after the cattle, being kind to me, not drinking or gambling. Had I done something earlier in the evening to upset him? I thought back and couldn't name a thing.

It was evening when he awoke. I'd fed the girls and they'd gone to bed and slept. I nursed Lizzie. The fire crackled in the fireplace sending heat to our fronts while the woodstove warmed our backs. I heard him start to talk.

"In Missouri. I had a friend, a good friend, though he was a slave. My pa gave him to me when we were boys. Jeremiah. That was his name."

I turned my head. "Your parents owned slaves?"

"Just a few. We had a hemp farm. Couldn't have made it without them, my pa always said. They worked hard." He grew silent.

I kicked myself that I'd interrupted his telling. "Go on." I drew the rocker closer to hear him better and give him the privacy I could tell he needed.

"When we got ready to leave Missouri for Oregon . . ." He paused, his eyes looking upward. "My pa told me that since I was seventeen I needed to make 'big boy' choices. Jeremiah could come west with us and I'd have to pay his way since he belonged to me. He might be free in Oregon Territory, we couldn't be sure. Or, I could give him his freedom in Missouri and not take him along. Or I could sell him—he was my property—and keep the money to cover my own expenses coming west."

"What did you do?"

"None of those." He leaned his head back against the duck-feather pillow. His handsome face wore weary lines against the pillow slip stained with baby goo that starching hadn't gotten free. "I lost him in a game of cards."

"You put Jeremiah up as collateral?"

"You're right to judge me, Eliza."

"I didn't, I was—"

"Your tone of voice did."

I kept my counsel, letting him continue.

"What kind of man would do such a thing,

Eliza? That's what you're asking yourself, isn't it? What kind of man would betray his best friend; treat him as though he was worth only what I could get for him?" His voice caught. "Every time I see a colored man here, I look twice, to see if it might be Jeremiah. I saw a colored man tonight. A free black, I imagine. He drove a freighter. He looked me in the eye and smiled. I couldn't look back."

"Did you . . . did you try to buy him back, Jeremiah?"

"I wish I had. I told my pa I'd set him free and he'd left us, just like that." Andrew snapped his fingers. "My pa thought Jeremiah ungrateful. I didn't correct him, compounding the evil that I am." His voice caught again.

For only a moment did I wonder if he was telling a tale to trick me into seeing him with forgiving eyes, his anguish palpable. I reached over Lizzie to brush the tears from my husband's stubbled cheeks. I'd never seen him weep. "I'm so sorry you had to make that choice when you were so young."

He snorted. "I was seventeen. I thought I could win him back, before we left. I thought . . . I don't know what I thought." He ran his fingers through his hair. "I gambled because it was fun and I figured I could get money to start here, in Oregon, with Jeremiah, free. God forgive me." He choked on those words; inhaled regret. "When later I did win big and I went to look for him, his new owner had already sold him to someone heading west to California." He fingered tears from the corners of his eyes. "So now you know. No shame, you said once? My shame. I can't even describe it."

I reached out and touched his arm, a psalm coming to mind about a hand stretching out in the darkness without wearying. I stroked his wrist. "You've punished yourself enough." I whispered the words. "You have sought forgiveness; now the task is to receive it, every day. You are not evil, Andrew. You are a good man who made a bad choice. You've made better ones. With God's help, you will again."

"With your help too, 'Liza." He reached for my hand, squeezed it, then turned his face into the pillow, his back to me, his shoulders shaking. I put Lizzie in her cradle, the one her father had made for her. Then I crawled onto the bed beside my husband, stretched the length of myself against his back, my apron catching on the brads of his duck pants. I pulled the wedding ring quilt up over us, and reached around and held him to me. He gripped my forearm like a lifeline.

"We are all wretches, lost like the biblical woman with the missing coin. Lost until we knit God into the fabric of our lives," I whispered. For the first time I truly believed it.

Part Two

☞ 16 ☜
UNPREDICTABLE

The winter rains and mild weather of 1858–59 with no hard freeze had doused the ground in springtime, making squishy everywhere, walking to the smokehouse, gathering chicken eggs, feeding the hogs. The neat cows stood in muck while I milked them, and the bottom of my skirts and the girls' caked with mud, straining the threads at the hemlines. I'd put the milk bucket into the spring and had just returned to the house to skim the cream from another pan. Lizzie would be ready to nurse. It was but a month or so after Andrew's revelation about Jeremiah and I'd noticed his pacing had returned. Irritable, restless in the evenings when I urged him to whittle something for America Jane, hoping that might distract his thoughts. Still, his announcement was totally unexpected. "We're moving."

"What?" I turned to him, spoon in hand. "Moving? Where is it you plan to go and why?"

"Washington Territory—on the Touchet River."

I barely had a breath. "Near . . . Waiilatpu?"

"No interfering state rules there. It's still a territory. Man can do what he thinks best for his family. No taxes. Fewer regulations."

"If I'm remembering, our Oregon Territory didn't even have money to fund an army to send for our hostage rescue after the Whitmans died nor put down the uprising with the Yakima. A tax might have been a good thing."

"They got you back."

"The British got us back. They paid the ransom."

"It's about time you put those memories to rest, Eliza. Life goes on. Are you going with it is the question."

"But this is our home." Why was he upsetting our lives like this? He paced, the slight limp a reminder of his earlier choices. My sisters listened but offered no commentary.

"I want land where cattle don't have to stand in muck more days out of the year than I care to count. There's free land east of the Cascades and few people to populate it so we can have that cattle spread I've always wanted. You're familiar with the terrain. Hillsides with grass to their bellies. Treed areas near the streams and then, gracious goodness, almost no rain in the winter. Snow, but no constant drizzle for weeks at a time. Don't you miss that high dry country, darlin'?"

I didn't. And I didn't want to leave what we had in Brownsville. Why hadn't I imagined it might have come to this?

A few nights later, as memories mixed with prayers kept me from sleep, an odd sound brought me to the porch where Martha Jane stood, dressed for travel, a small satchel in hand.

"Martha? What are you doing up at this hour?"

She looked startled in the moonlight, her wolf-fur hat wisping around her heart-shaped face. She was fourteen years old with brows that framed deep brown eyes.

"What are you doing with your bag?"

"Oh please don't try to stop us. Bill and I, we're eloping."

"Bill?" *Am I really awake?*

"Wigle." She whispered it and what followed. "He's a good man. He's twenty-four, and when he turns twenty-five he comes into some money. We thought we could wait but we just can't."

"But how? I mean, I've never seen him around. When?" Then the important question: "Does Father know?"

"That we're in love? Of course not. He'll have me signed up to cook and clean for him and Rachel and Millie for the rest of my life now that you're leaving!"

"I haven't decided yet whether I'm going with Andrew or not."

"Oh, you'll go. And Father won't let us join you. I can't go back to Father and Rachel, Eliza. Don't make me."

"But you've only turned fourteen this week. It's too . . . early."

"You did it. Barely older than what I am now."

"I was seventeen."

"Be happy for me. Here's Bill."

She skipped off the porch as Bill Wigle dismounted. He tipped his hat at me, then made a stirrup with his hand so she could mount the horse he'd led in for her. He tied her satchel behind the saddle. I stood like a lump, unable to do or say anything to stop them.

"Where will you go?"

"Eugene City. No one here would ever marry us, not with Father around. Wish us well, Sister."

I pulled my shawl closer to me.

"What's going on?" This from Millie, her eyes full of sleep though. She carried a lantern from behind me, held it high. Her eyes grew wide. To Martha she said, "You're going to do it?"

I turned to my youngest sister. "You knew about this?"

"Of course. You're so preoccupied with the babies and Andrew—"

"And work, keeping the two of you in fine style."

"I'll take good care of her," Bill said. He was tall and lanky and wore a silly lover's grin. "We're going to live with my brother Jacob, in Harrisburg."

"Father will—"

"Not be happy. But he'll never approve anyone I choose." Martha leaned into Bill. "Just as he wasn't with your Andrew. He wants to keep us close, doing things his way."

"Don't you worry. I'll look after her, Mrs. Warren." No longer grinning, Bill seemed bent on assuring me of his good intentions, but the man was going to marry a child! He sat straighter on the horse, tipped his hat at Millie and me, then reined his mount down our lane, Martha Jane riding close beside him.

If they were going toward Eugene City, they'd have to go through the Gap on the Territorial Road. I hurried back inside and dressed, told Andrew I had to make a quick trip, that Millie would watch America Jane when she woke. "I'll take the baby with me."

"What are you doing, darlin'?" Sleepiness, not worry, threaded through his words.

"Saving a life."

"I'm going with you." Millie leapt from the porch heading toward the barn. "I'll get horses."

"No! You stay right here, young lady, and look after America Jane." Lizzie awoke to all the commotion then. I thrust the baby at Millie. "I'll saddle Maka myself."

My horse ready, I jammed a rain hat on my head, hung a slicker on my back, and mounted. Millie patted the baby in comfort, then handed her to me already swaddled in a blanket. "I could help," she said. Like a sling, I tied Lizzie to my breast, the sling knot thick against the back of

231

my neck, the hat wide enough to keep her dry. I pulled my oil slicker over us against the March chill and drizzle and rode hard, the leather reins wet in my hands. It's what my mother would have done, rescue a child.

"Bill Wigle. That snake. I thought he was a good man." My father pulled his pants on over his long johns, outrage pushing at him as he grabbed a worn shirt, one I'd sewed for him some years back, yanked it over his head. "He paid attention in church." He narrowed his eyes. "All he wanted was Martha Jane's attention."

"I don't think he's a bad person. But she's so young."

"Your opinion is not welcome. It was a mistake for you to marry Warren." His jaw clenched. "She's off copying you, eloping. I never should have let her live with you!"

"It wasn't a mistake," I defended. "It's just that she's not ready and I hoped she'd go to the Academy next year, like Henry Hart did. I hate to see her throwing away her chance."

"She's not getting out of my sight after this, I can tell you that." His Rachel handed him his boots. "You were too lax with her, Eliza. Or this never would have happened."

I did wonder when they'd formed this union, but should I say . . . "She was fearful she'd have to come back here."

"Fearful?" He stopped, stared at me.

"When we move. To the Touchet country. If I go with Mr. Warren." I looked away, patting Lizzie's back, warm and safe against me as she slept in my arms.

His face grew red. "I'll deal with that later. I've got to see if I can stop them. Oh, what did I let you do to my Martha Jane!"

Rachel watched the ruckus happening in her kitchen. "Don't forget this." She handed my father his hat as he stormed out the door. She turned to me then. "Tea? I can boil water now." She nodded toward the wet spot at my breast. "You best feed that little one."

"I can't believe she did that," I told Andrew.

"Millie's the wild one." He nodded at my sister eating porridge. She grinned. "I thought Martha had more sense."

"She didn't want to go back to Papa's. Me either, really. But I suppose I'll have to." Millie stirred her breakfast.

"So you've decided to go with me," Andrew asked. "Good."

"I haven't decided one way or the other whether I'm going to Touchet."

"Where is that anyway?" Millie looked at us both.

"In Washington Territory in the best grassland and grazing country a man could ever wish to see.

Water from a blue river. No one around to speak of. Indians are all settled with the Yakima war over and the Cayuse sent packing."

"It's . . . it's not far from where I went to school once, at the Whitman Mission." My fingers felt cold as I picked up the porridge bowls.

"Oh, gosh, why would you want to go back there? I've heard all the stories." Millie shivered her shoulders.

I looked at Andrew. "I don't know that I do."

Two days later in the evening Martha Jane and my father arrived back at our cabin.

"Traitor." She stomped past me.

"You'll thank me one day, you will," I called after her. "You're too young, Martha." I put Lizzie on my hip. She could hold her head up well. To my father I said, "Where did you find them?"

"At his brother's. I chased them through the Gap, but they had too much of a head start. Gave Wigle's brother a piece of my mind, too, harboring a child-stealer."

"Bill's no stealer! He's my future husband!"

I joined Martha behind the dividing blanket where the girls slept. Millie sat up and yawned. "Marriage is a big choice," I said.

"One you made without meddling from anyone else. How dare you interfere in my life!" She turned, threw her small bag on her pallet, crossed her arms over her breast.

"I only did it because I care about you."

"You just want me around to work, so you can be bossy. You're not my mother. You never were. You, you act like you're such a saint having survived a terrible ordeal." She wiggled her hands by her ears, mocking my experience. "Well, I survived it too. I remember being huddled up with Mama wondering if Father was dead or alive, if you were dead, if we were all going to die."

"You couldn't have. You were too young to remember."

"I remember," she shouted. "But *I* didn't let it shape every single thing I've done since, lording it over the rest of the world."

I struck her across her face. Gasped at what I'd done.

Martha put her fingers to her cheek. Lizzie cried, buried her head in my breast.

"I'm . . . I'm so sorry." I backed away. "I never should have—"

"No. You should not have." She returned to stuffing more clothes into her carpetbag.

"You'll break the seams."

"I don't care if I tear them to shreds! At least I'll have done it myself without the . . . the . . . obstruction of a self-righteous sister."

Tears streamed down her face and I approached to hug her.

"Don't. Touch. Me." She turned her back to me.

"I'm glad Father doesn't want me staying here. Anywhere near you is the last place I want to be."

I spent the next day pondering my actions. Why had I interrupted Martha Jane's marriage to Bill Wigle? I had nothing against the man. I barely knew him. But she barely knew him either. Yes, he was much older but that was common in these parts. A married man could claim twice the land and a woman could have her half in her own name if she chose. But there was really no need for Martha to claim land. My father had divided his property when my mother died, giving Martha Jane and Millie and Henry Hart parcels while he remained on one himself. As the eldest, I imagined I'd receive that piece when he died, but he'd designated a plot in the hills for me. Why was I so adamant about how other people lived their lives?

Andrew had left to care for the cattle while I was at Father's, giving me plenty of time to stew and ponder. Lizzie fussed and I fed her while Millie moped about missing Martha. America Jane squirmed too, asking after her *papo*. My sisters were an integral part of our lives and now, here we were, split open like too-ripe melons. I hadn't seen this schism coming, not a bit of it. My telling my father hadn't brought me into his good graces either, the elopement affirming for him that I wasn't a good influence on her. Martha acted like

I was tainted meat, and Millie might well decide she didn't want to be around me either. Or my father would reclaim Millie and they'd all be back looking after him and Rachel too. Yes, she could boil water. What a transformation. I shouldn't worry.

But there was more to this, I knew it. That morning, we read from Matthew and the words that stood out for me were these: "Go ye and learn what that meaneth. I will have mercy, and not sacrifice." *Learn what this means.* I didn't know how. I hadn't been merciful toward Martha, though I intended that. I did think she was too young. I did hope she could go on to the Academy next year. And maybe there was a part of me that wanted to keep her from not seeing the shadow side of Bill in the way I'd missed seeing some of Mr. Warren's darker ways. I wanted time to investigate Bill. I didn't want her to sacrifice her life looking after an unpredictable man—even though back with my father she'd be doing just that. *What have I done?*

I couldn't go with Andrew to Touchet, not with the family splintered like kindling. We'd have to resolve those issues before we could go. Or perhaps this was God's way of telling me not to go. *Oh Mama, how I wish you were here to teach me what this means.*

The Diary of Eliza Spalding

1850

We are charged by God to discover meaning in everyday life, to ponder and explore. God gave me the Nimíipuu who helped me, us. They were in my dark places and stayed there with me, did not simply push me through. I learned so much from the darkness. Learn what this means, Scripture tells us. I learned to lean on the Lord more in times of peril.

I write of a time when the Methodist Reverend Lee visited Lapwai for several days. I thought S impulsive when he suggested staging an Indian battle for the Reverend to witness. Our Nez Perce had attended Sabbath services with close to one thousand worshiping together, listening to S's words. Reverend Lee was well impressed and then S suggested the sham display. Our Nez Perce came dressed with face paint and marked their horses too with much red and colorful ribbons and cloths tied into the horses' manes and flowing from their staffs. Intricate beadwork shielded the animals' chests, the sunlight glinting against the highly prized cut beads. The men carried guns and hatchets and long knives and rode their horses hard back and forth in front of us, stirring up powdery dirt. Some men were tapped to "die" at the point of a gun, falling from their horses. I held Henry Hart, who was not yet three, while Eliza clung to my dress through the spectacle of dust and noise and fearsome faces. Henry had insisted that we watch.

The actions frightened Eliza, as she'd never seen the fierce war paint, the howling, men falling from their mounts as though dead. And then, to my horror, their "murderer" would leap down and remove their scalp! Fake scalps placed there to be sure, but the swiftness of their knives around the "dead" comrade brought screams from Eliza that I could not stop. I handed Henry to his startled father and glared at him as I grabbed Eliza and carried her into the house. It took me hours to calm her. What had S been thinking to stage such a sight? I had words with him of this and he claimed naively that while such a display could have upset Eliza, Reverend Lee was fascinated by both the fierceness and the piety of the Nimíipuu, so different from his gentle Kalapuya in the Willamette Valley. "He'll tell the Mission Board about how well our Indians are doing, how they like to perform to satisfy us."

Reverend Lee's Indians were but few and not fierce at all, simply surviving from the diseases he said were brought by the British on their ships. I thought then a man's mind was surely different from a woman's. Did they not know that at any moment that fake battle might not have been sham? That we might be the real dead whose scalps were taken? And for a child to witness this! I shiver. Thank God nothing bad came of it. Still, it was but five years later our Eliza did witness such atrocities. I wonder if she remembers that sham battle now that she is almost thirteen.

Almost thirteen. And she will become that young woman who must care for her brother and sisters and her father most of all, after I am gone. I must speak to her of duty. We women are required to recognize and keep to our commitments. I did. I did more than I imagined I could do, endured the isolation, the worry over my husband and children when they traveled far, the inexplicable acts of my husband at times. I wrestled with my questioning but found the Lord could withstand my inquiries. And while I didn't always get answers, I got peace. That was enough. I might never have sought or found it in that way if I hadn't had those times of danger. "I can do all things through Christ which strengtheneth me." Philippians 4:13. That's the message I must give my children.

And that the Lord goes with them, into whatever darkness or light they walk, especially if they go in reply to his call. And he does call them to amazing things if they allow. I think S has taught me that, living out his dreams, bigger than either of us. He didn't convert everyone as he once proposed in those years we were at school, but he brought more than six hundred Nimíipuu to the Lord. Imagine! And the Mission Board whisked it all away. My heart aches to go back to Lapwai.

❧ 17 ☙

THE CHOICE

"I never want to go back to Waiilatpu, ever. Or to Lapwai. Or your Touchet dream. I want to stay right here in Brownsville, where Mama is buried. Do you hear that, Mr. Warren?" That familiar "Andrew" would not fall across my tongue again. He'd be Mr. Warren, the "man of the house." He Who Decides, as the Nez Perce might put it. And he would father no more children, at least not with me.

"I hear you, darlin'. And you don't have to go. Stay rooted if you want. I've got a plan to do and be something bigger. I thought you'd like to be a part of it, keep your family together, but it's your doin'." We sat at the table. He picked at candle wax drippings I'd failed to scrape up.

"You say I can't go alone with the children through the mountains. You'd need to take us."

He'd stood, taken a bun from the warming oven of the stove. "You've had plenty of time to prepare, 'Liza." He downed a large glass of milk, wiped his mustache of the foam. "If you'd made up your mind earlier I would have helped, but I've got drovers lined up and we need to head over the Cascades while the weather is good."

242

Warren Creek rose, marking snowmelt in the mountains. I heard it gurgle.

"Why can't I take the wagon and just follow you? If we were to go, I mean."

"For the tenth time, because there is no route through the mountains for wagons." He brushed bread crumbs from his duck pants.

"Barlow built a road where people said none could go."

"We're going straight east from here, 'Liza, across the Cascades, then up through the high desert, making our own trail. Daniel Waldo says there's an Indian route to follow, that he's taken it. No one believes him except Wiley and me. Wiley says he's crossed it, but he'll say anything to get investors to make a road."

"You invested in a road?"

"I also put $100 toward the mill plans here."

"Did you?" *A change of subject.* "Then we should stay here, look over your investment."

He shook his head, a smile that said he knew what I was doing. " 'Liza, I'm going." He'd finished his milk and now a fly buzzed around him. He swatted at it, and when it landed he whisked his hand and caught it and grinned. It wasn't the first time. I marveled at his swiftness. "I want you along, but if you won't go, that's your choice." He softened. "I need to do this. I . . . I don't want to live an ordinary life, 'Liza, where every day's predictable and I have no challenges to see how I'll wrangle my way through. I . . . I owe it . . . to others, to you and my children to live a good life but to live it with, I don't know the word. Gusto? Abundance, maybe? That's a word in Scripture, right?"

I sensed that he laid bare his soul in those few words, perhaps more insight into who he was than I'd ever heard before. I might have envied a bit that clarity of passion.

"Look, 'Liza. You always said you missed the stories of overland travel in a wagon the way so many others came west, like Nancy Osborne and my family. Your parents. This is a way to get a . . . feel for it, something you were deprived of, you being born in Oregon Country. Think of it as an adventure."

"I didn't think I'd have to experience it alone!"

"I can't wait for you. The passes won't be open for long. We'll meet up at the Columbia River, near The Dalles and head east together from there. That is, if you decide to come."

"My mother took a wagon where they said none could go. She and my father. And the Whitmans. I bet we could get a wagon over the Cascades."

He sighed. "They didn't have much of a wagon left though, did they? And they traveled with a trapping party for a good part of that way so they weren't alone. You cannot follow me and the herd. If you're coming, you could take Barlow's trail or head farther north to Portland and take the river route. Either way, meet me in The Dalles. But I won't wait for you. I'll have to keep the stock moving."

"It's inhumane to leave without these things settled," I wailed. "What kind of husband and father would do such a thing?"

"Your father, for one. Things weren't all that settled before they left to come west, as I recall him saying more than once in his preaching, reminding us all that God's in control. They 'happened' onto the last steamship heading upriver. They 'happened' onto that trapping party. 'The Lord was with us.' So he'll be with you too. Things don't always get settled in your good timing, Eliza. You can't control the stream. And—" He lifted my chin, his brown eyes soft and loving. "You don't have to go."

His words stunned me. I'd been trying to make him do things. Make him stay. Make him let us take the wagon and follow him. I liked him better when he accommodated because of his guilt. He wasn't feeling guilty now, and was much surer of himself. Whether I followed him or not was of less concern than that he be on his way as soon as the mountain thaws happened. He really would go without us.

"Touchet will be a new start for us." His warm fingers pushed errant hair from my damp forehead. "Better grazing for the cattle, wider vistas, fewer people encroaching, less harping about cows getting through fences. And no state bearing down saying 'do this or that.' No taxes in Touchet."

"It's two-sea."

He lifted his eyebrows.

"The pronunciation. It's not French."

He shook his head, a smile on his face, then pulled me to him. Though my arms were stiff beside my body, he still held me, his voice like low strains on a violin. "I want you with me, you and the girls. I want you there. But I'm going. Has to be this way. It's a better life for us. And who is to say this isn't the Lord working his way in our lives. I haven't had a drop to drink since I told you about Jeremiah and claimed the land."

"You won the land in a card game."

"No, I didn't, Eliza. My cattle business has been successful. In Touchet—two-sea—I'll be free of 'bad friends,' as you call them. We'll start over. I'll keep my promise not to drink."

"I didn't hear that promise."

"It wasn't made to you."

I cried then, hiccuping sobs. He patted my back. "I don't want to go. I don't want you to go. There's no one there I can count on. I'll be alone with the children. My sisters, left here. Nancy . . ." I understood for the first time how Matilda Sager must have felt when my parents sent her away but a few months after the massacre she'd survived with me. She was just a child and she had cried so hard, begged to stay with us. Her tears brought nothing, no change to my father's mind about her leaving. My tears had no effect on Mr. Warren either.

"And then there's the closeness to Waiilatpu, to all that . . . what happened. I can't go back there."

"Maybe this is the Lord's way of helping you put all that behind you. Behind us."

Could that be? I felt myself lean into him, soften my stiff bed-board resistance.

"Life is uncertain. You can't line it up the way Nancy does."

"I know."

"And memories aren't real, 'Liza. We mix them with who we are now." He held me away from him, hands on my shoulders, his brown eyes gazing into mine, that shock of dark hair pulling forward as he spoke with kindness laced with resolution. "You can do this, Eliza. You're strong, smart, enterprising. You've been good for me. You've helped your sisters, your dad. Use some of that stashed cash you've got and buy a solid wagon. Our oxen are seasoned."

"You know about my stash?"

"My mama didn't raise no dumb kids." He grinned.

Can I do this? He believed I could. A zest surged through me. A possibility. "I might need you to sweeten the pot with a little cash," I said. "I'll have to find someone willing to abandon ship here and head east with me."

"Now you're talking. Leave the stove here, though. Too heavy to cart. I'll get one brought for you. If you get an offer on the farm that sounds good, take it." He wiped my eyes with his thumbs, his calloused hands warm against my chin. "You always said you wished you had stories to tell of coming along the trail, overland. Here's your chance. Our chance."

"Only I'm going in the opposite direction of your coming from Missouri."

"You're doing it the Spalding way. Contrary."

I actually laughed at that. I blew my nose. Was that what I was being? I didn't want stubborn to be the legacy I gave my girls or my sisters. I wanted them to see strength in their heritage, to learn that they could grow from challenges they faced. Yes, I could tell a travel story, of my escape from terrible harm. But was that the only story I wanted to be remembered for? No, I wanted them to remember their grandmother's courage, and see a bit of that inside of me and themselves. This time I had the option of choosing to go. And we weren't running from an uprising, worrying even as we hostages were taken downriver with our British rescuer, abandoned by the Nez Perce. Rain pummeled our shake roof. I disappeared back . . .

Tap-tap. Is it gunfire? No, hail dropping against the tent canvas covering our bateau. We're huddled together, we hostages. I startle at each unfamiliar sound. For more than four weeks we wondered day by day if we would see the next. One of the children, I can't remember who, swings her arms like a windmill and stands up, clawing for air, pushes her face out, lifting the bateau cover. Along the shore, Indians ride! Someone shouts, "Heathens!" Captain Ogden orders, "Get your head down!" I know then we aren't yet safe, might still die at the hands of angry Indians chasing after, the Columbia River be our wet grave. I burrow beneath the Hudson's Bay blanket, covet safety as I shiver.

"Eliza? You all right?" Mr. Warren squeezed my shoulders, took a stumbled step to hold me, a residual from his injury.

"Yes. I'm fine."

"You went away again." He kept one hand on me while he reached for a jug of water, giving me a drink. "Maybe you'll do that less when we're in Touchet." He took the handkerchief from my hands and dabbed at the edge of my eyes. "Take what you need from my purse," he said then. "You'll be fair about it. Get the best wagon you can and load. I'll see you in a few months." He kissed me hard then, almost skipped out the door.

• • •

If I joined him, left familiar fields and streams, I'd be alone often in Touchet while he rode with the cattle. If I didn't join him, my marriage would be over. I remembered my mother speaking of the times when she'd be left behind with four children, for days, while my father was off at meetings or arranging for shipments at the fort. I have only two to contend with, but my youngest is a baby only four months old. Little Lizzie. America Jane won't be three for months, each needing tending while I work. How would I manage walking beside an ox team celebrating my fifth anniversary alone with two babies? I shivered. I wasn't skilled enough to take them safely to Touchet nor stable enough to make sure my mind didn't drift leaving them in danger and alone.

Mr. Warren left that morning, and watching him ride away I felt as I did when Timothy of the Nez Perce abandoned me and I feared I'd never see my mother again. I shouted after Mr. Warren, running out onto the porch, seeing him as he rode from around the barn to the lane. "Don't you want to know my decision?"

He brought up the horse, twisted in the saddle. "I'll see you soon." He whooped and twirled his hat, upsetting his horse, which pranced, switched its tail, then took Mr. Warren away.

How did he know that watching him disappear brought on a compulsion to pack and follow, to seek the safety of my life with him and not as a woman left behind? I'd be taking a different route to join him but hadn't I always? God willing, I would find him, his cattle, and his dream. Maybe I'd find myself. The fear lifted.

"Let's get started," I told Millie. "We have a journey to make!"

I missed my sister Martha as I packed. She was fun to have around, made me laugh as she tossed flour on my nose and with Millie would insist we ride bareback in the hills behind the house. She reminded me that I'm not a matron with two children but a girl still, at twenty-one. "You never outgrow the need for adventure," she told me once, a twinkle in her eye. "Without it, how will you fill your heart?"

"My heart is full with my children. I have the Scriptures to sustain me."

"And your children will draw from you so you must find ways to keep the well filled. Yes, the Scriptures. But even they speak of music and dancing and laughter. Papa doesn't preach much on those sections, but they are there. I've read them. And if it were written in our time they would have added riding on fast horses with the wind in your face." She spoke with that certainty I was seeing as a Spalding trait. And I had thwarted that by betraying her attempt to fill her heart with Bill Wigle. So had my father.

I placed the mirror and pedestal in the trunk, catching a glimpse of myself: a drawn look with hollow cheeks and a straight ink line for lips. I ought to smile more.

"Look at baby Lizzie." America Jane pointed at a different mirror she sat at with her sister. "She sees herself."

I snatched my daughter, turned her baby face into my chest, my hand pushing her head into me. "What's wrong, Mama?"

"Nothing. Let's just get things ready so we can follow *Papo*." I didn't know why I'd swept my infant from the mirror. *Something my mother once told me?*

"Mr. Warren might have waited, helped a little," I said to the children.

"At least you have me," Millie said. She entered from the chicken house, brought in eggs she'd fix for our breakfast. She placed her hands on her low back, sighed. She'd already carried in a heavy bucket of water we'd use to wash with when we finished packing.

The sun had been up for hours and I needed good strength to tell my father we were leaving. After breakfast, I harnessed the horse to the wagon, put the girls in. Millie held Lizzie steady while Maka pulled our rig, trotting us toward what I knew would be disaster. It would happen even though I anticipated it. This time I wasn't wrong.

My father paced around, waving his arms as though preaching. "I forbid it! You cannot take your children to that country. You cannot."

"Mr. Warren and I will decide for me and our family, Father."

"You never should have married him. He's unpredictable, lacks common sense, and this move is but another example."

I remained calm, as my mother would have done.

"You're disappointed, Father. But a wife is duty-bound to go with her husband. As my mother did, even resisting your telling her that long trip from New York would be too hard with her illness. But she came anyway."

"Yes. She came anyway because she felt God telling her to come with me and I agreed. After a time. Thank goodness. Whatever would I have done without her?" His eyes got that faraway look that consumed him when my mother's memory was invoked. I was glad Rachel was out in the washhouse, though what she did there I couldn't imagine. Millie had gone out to assist her, so she wasn't there to hear what my father said next. "You will do what you will. You always did. But you will not take Amelia, and Martha Jane has no will to be with you."

"She'd be far from Bill Wigle."

"I'll monitor that. They are my responsibility and I will not allow them to go there among the Indians that are not our Nimíipuu. They are the only Indians I trust. I can't believe Warren is taking you so close to the Cayuse. And with the Yakima Wars just ended."

"Why you trust the Nez Perce I don't understand. They forced me to stay at Waiilatpu. They held you and Mama hostage, then sent us all away and—"

"They sustained us, Eliza. They kept us alive."

I shook my head. His memory was twisted as a rope.

"It was the Mission Board that insisted we all leave."

"That's not what Mama thought. Timothy, the Nez Perce, they failed us, can't you see? They invited you to come, then sent you away." My stomach clenched, inviting a subject change. "The land is good that Mr. Warren claims."

"Pshaw! What does he know of land? Or hard work. Or beginning a life in a harsh landscape. No, I ought to insist you leave your daughters with us here along with Millie and Martha."

"I'm not staying, Papa. I'm going with Eliza."

Father turned to Millie who had come back inside. I wondered where Martha was. Probably off with Bill Wigle!

"No. I decide. You stay here."

"She needs help, Father. Two small children, driving an ox team by herself? You would sentence her to that?" A voice of support: my sister Martha Jane who had just entered. "You're aware of the trials. You've talked of them." She appealed to the compassionate side of him. I nodded to her, hoping she could see my gratitude.

"Your choices are mine to make. Let her hire a driver if her Warren is so flush he can leave without selling his property here. Let her hire another wagon to take everything with them. Everything except my girls. And may the Lord forgive me for not retaining custody of my granddaughters, as their parents lack common sense, are loony, and put them in harm's way."

The furies found me. "You speak of harm's way? What of the times you left my mother alone with these two?" I nodded to my sisters. "What about the times you took Henry and me miles from home, risking our lives? We nearly froze to death when we crossed the flooded Snake and you wouldn't let us build a fire. Or the time you took us to the Pacific. If we hadn't been taken in by that mixed-blood Indian when we crossed the Cascades, we might have been lost forever in the mountains, never seen the ocean. What of the time you ran the Indians into acting out death and dying before our eyes? Do you remember that?"

I recalled in great detail the foreshadowing of

death at Waiilatpu. How terrified I was when the hair came off at the end of a knife held by men I recognized and, yes, loved. I thought Timothy was dead, that Raymond had killed him. The screams and shouts and horses as fired up as the portrayers, prancing, twisting, dust rising with a hundred hooves while those along the sidelines cheered them on. Thank God that my mother took us inside.

"I remember strong children who weren't all that cold in the last miles. You never complained. And God provided that Indian in the Cascades. I remember a fine display of horsemanship, which is what I hoped Reverend Lee would see." Father's gaze took him to the past. "And the contrast between their devotion to God and what they'd once been."

"Some still are 'what they'd once been.' " I'd heard rumors of converts returning to old ways.

"Not the Nimíipuu, no. Cayuse, yes. Some Umatilla, too, which is why I will not allow your sisters to travel with you to their country. Millie will return with you and get her things. I'll come fetch her in the morning. It's decided."

"What's decided?" Rachel stepped through the door, her round face dripping with laundry room sweat. Maybe she had learned how to heat the water and blue the whites.

"Millie is coming home."

"Lovely," Rachel said and plopped onto the

hickory rocker, fanning her face with her apron. I marveled at the ease with which she accepted whatever surprises life offered.

We two were silent on the way back. At the cabin, we put the little ones down to sleep, fixed a light supper. We were finishing when Millie said, "I'll defy him."

"No. He's right. There is a danger in that country." The memory of the spectacle just reinforced what I already knew. We weren't that far out from the finish of the Yakima uprising and we headed where disgruntled Cayuse roamed. Land of the Umatilla, of Chief Five Crows, the one who had tortured Lorinda. And maybe, in a season, there'd be Nez Perce, and who was to say if they still kept Christian ways or in the twelve years since we'd left Lapwai if they too were now "what they'd once been." At any rate, I didn't want to find out.

"But you'll need help, Sister."

I nodded, then reached for her hand as we sat at the table. "I'll find someone. I'll see if I can get another couple to join us, bring their wagon and possibly have room for some of our things too. Maybe a woman to assist with the children. I can walk beside the ox team, but I'll need muscle for the yokes. I don't know who to hire, but I will pray for the right person and trust that if this is my call then God knows what I need."

✦ 18 ✦
THAT WHICH SUSTAINS

Father came the following day and took my sister away. I wept after they left. "We'll see each other again," I told Millie, who looked every bit her almost thirteen years. I thanked her for what she'd given me and thought then I needed to thank Martha too. They'd been my companions when Mr. Warren wandered away. It made me wonder how my mother ever said good-bye to Matilda or if she'd had the chance to do so once we were all sent from Lapwai.

"Are you busy?"

Nancy Osborne put her head in the door. I wiped my eyes with my apron.

"Is a mother of two ever not busy?" I said it with a light voice. Nancy had that fragile look on her face she got sometimes. I never wanted to say anything that might push her into silence.

"I suppose not." She came through the door and stood beside me, closer than I would normally prefer, but she did that, too, on her "bad days." She found safety in being close to taller bodies. I wanted a wide berth, didn't even like people standing behind me at the mercantile. I'd step aside and allow others to go first rather than imagine them hovering there behind me, no telling what they might do to harm me.

I handed her Lizzie and pumped water from the spring into the teapot and set it to brew on the woodstove. Mr. Warren had said he'd purchase a stove for me once we were in Touchet. I wasn't to bring this one.

I had the use of this old woodstove I'd come to love until we left and the farm sold. At least we had a farm to sell. I feared when he told me we were moving that he'd lost it in a card game. When I questioned him about the area being closed to non-Indians, something provided for in last year's treaty, he waved his hand at me, dismissive.

Having a stove go with our farmstead would be a selling point, he'd said. I just hoped he didn't forget his promise.

Nancy sat with my daughter on her lap. She wiped the edge of Lizzie's mouth with her apron. "I'm feeling sad about your going, I guess. Brings back memories, dark ones."

Nancy dropped her chin close to the baby's head. America Jane toddled over and lifted the baby's fingers, up and down, like a metronome. "Any kind of change bothers me, Eliza. Having the table just an inch or so from where it's supposed to be flutters me. I've tried to ignore it, like you said to do, but I'll get up in the night and move the table because I can't sleep. Then

I'll lie back down and I'm still wide awake and get back up and move it again. It's been more than ten years, Eliza. The strangeness, it's related to what happened then."

I put the tea leaves in the caddy, poured the hot water through them. "It takes time."

"But you're having no problems, not a bit."

"Oh, I have my problems. I just figure they're from Mr. Warren, not from the Cayuse." I laughed and she smiled with me. I didn't tell about the row with my father or of my interference with Martha's future.

"You don't ever wonder if you might have done something differently?"

All the time. "Of course I do. But we don't get to do it over. We only get to learn from it."

"I think God was punishing me because I didn't pay good attention."

"Attention to what? Nonsense. You were younger than me. And you endured worse. God doesn't punish in that way. You were a power-less child lying there under that floor at the Mission. And you escaped. Your father hid you well among the rushes. You didn't cry out when you heard the Cayuse searching. Your father found you. And even when at first they wouldn't let you in at the fort for fear of Indian reprisals, God was with you. And here you are. It's a happy-ending story."

"You don't really think that, do you? I'm almost

twenty. I'll never have a life with another if I can't sleep, can't let things be. Who besides brothers and sisters and parents would put up with a woman prowling through the nights, rearranging tables?"

"It will serve you well at the mill." I kept my voice light, straining not to return to Waiilatpu.

She snorted. "I guess carding and working a loom require precision."

"Would you like this dish towel I embroidered? I have too many to take." She nodded. "Have you told your Andrew Kees? You spoke of his kindness."

"I have. But I'm not sure even he can put up with my lining up tin cups while people are still drinking from them." She pulled her hands back, started straightening my dishes, one hand on Lizzie, the other fussing like a mother hen. "I'm sorry, so sorry. I just—"

"I don't mind if you organize my world." I took Lizzie from her and began to nurse.

"But that's just it. With you moving, who will be safe?"

I began singing a lullaby. My daughter nursed greedily and then soothed to the music. America Jane leaned her head against my side as I sang while Nancy wiped her hands on her skirts, stood to fold sheets and clothing, placing them in the trunk. She refilled her tea cup and drank.

When I finished, Nancy said, "Thank you. Tea and singing does make me feel better."

"You'll keep yourself safe. You'll reach out a hand to God and accept the comfort he sends."

"Is that what you do?"

"Not as much as I could." I'd considered asking Nancy to join me, to look after my girls. But I suspected she wouldn't come, and being honest or maybe selfish, I wondered if looking after her might take as much time as caring for my children.

"That's what you'll do after we've moved. You'll fix yourself tea. You'll garden. You'll work at the mill. You'll spend time with Mr. Kees and be warmed by his patience and kindness. And maybe," I continued, "day by day, you'll see a table out of place or a cup with the handle turned the wrong way and you'll let God arrange it as he would."

"It's nice of you to imagine that."

"You'll come visit us. We'll have a fine time. You can play with the children." America Jane hummed as she put her doll to bed.

"You'd let me?"

"Of course." What horrors did Nancy harbor about her ability to give and love?

"I don't understand it. I wasn't even a hostage. After three days we were safe. But you had—"

"A different experience. But each of us was powerless for a time." I wiped Lizzie's chin of my milk, put her on my shoulder to burp, then placed her in her cradle. "It was unique for each of us. I'm finding a way to live with it. I can talk about it even. Sometimes. I still try to make the world conform to my pattern. Maybe I'll always have that. We survived, and that's what we must hang onto. Survival shows our strength."

"And I rise in the night with nightmares and horrors, believing my father is already dead."

"We did share that experience," I said. And just as suddenly I was back . . .

"Spalding dead. Tell them." The Cayuse pushed me forward, spoke in their language. I must tell the others my father is dead? To scare us. No one will rescue us. That's my horse the Cayuse is riding. Or is it Tashe? I fall onto my knees. He must be dead. A child sobs.

Lizzie's cries woke me. I wiped at my face, reached for my child. America Jane lay on a quilt on the cabin floor sound asleep while dear Lizzie mewed her discontent in Nancy's arms, reaching for me.

"I don't wonder you can doze at the drop of a spoon." She gazed about the room. "You've done an awful lot of work getting ready."

"And more to come."

Nancy rose to leave then and I held her, one arm around her shoulder and my past; the other holding Lizzie and my future. I drank in the history we shared but stayed with this place we found ourselves in now. "You'll visit."

"It's a long way away."

"Maybe we'll come back to see Father and my sisters. And we'll write."

"I'll just imagine you talking to me when I get to fretting." She wiped tears from her cheeks.

"And I'll do likewise."

I gulped then, grief like claws closed my throat. We shared so much and we were separating. My mother's death came back to me.

Nancy's tears wet my cheeks and then I stepped away from her. "You're a strong woman, Nancy. You're a good woman. Mr. Kees sees that. Don't be afraid to let him love you and just love him right back."

She smiled. "I will do my best to straighten him out as though he were a cup and saucer."

We both laughed then and we walked arm in arm out to the porch, leaving Lizzie cooing beside her sister. "I don't know what to say." She nodded. "I love you, Nancy, like a sister."

"And I you."

She untied the reins from the hitching post and I waved as she mounted her horse and rode away. I wondered when our paths would cross again.

After a supper of beans and gravy over a loaf of my soda bread, I read to the children from one of my mother's books she'd drawn and painted. I used to love watching her mix the colors from the wildflowers we picked together. We gathered berries, too, that we later pressed into ink. I wonder how she found time for all that while feeding us and teaching. When we had paper to spare, my friends would draw their horses or their dogs or the feathers handed down from their fathers. What I had loved the most about the books though was that the words were in Sahaptin, words the Nez Perce used. My mother wrote how the Creator made the *Hisamtucks*, the sun, and the willows, *Tahs*, the wind and the rain (*Hatia* and *Hiwakasha*). With sleepy eyes, my girls listened to the swoosh and rhythm of those Nez Perce words, words I once hoped I'd never forget. Some things stayed in my memory while others drifted away like duck's feathers out of a poorly stitched mattress tick. My father said she'd had to stop teaching in Sahaptin. How it must have galled my mother to be told by the Whitmans and Smiths and the Mission Board that she must not use the language of The People. I wonder if then, long before our last year in Lapwai, she hadn't already begun to die.

No terrible memories rose up to grab me in the night. But in the morning I remembered my lapse with Nancy the day before. If she hadn't been here, would my girls have been all right? I was in danger, my memories pulling me backwards. Would they come more often as I returned to the shadow of Waiilatpu? Or was following my husband less about obedience and more about God's guidance that I face my demons and put the past to rest.

❧ 19 ❧

CHANGING PLANS

My anxiety threatened to bubble over and burn as a stew on a too-hot stove. I was at my father's home.

"We could have time together, all of us. We'll go together, as a family."

"I'll not have you steal them into that country, not with that unpredictable Warren. That 'pass' he supposedly knows of, dangerous, if it even exists. He won't even make it. You'll arrive in The Dalles and find no one waiting. No. You should just stay here. He'll be back with his tail between his legs."

He hadn't seen Mr. Warren's resolve. He hadn't heard the excitement in his voice when he spoke of the impending cattle drive, the thrill of starting anew. Some men, like my father, celebrated the building up of things over time. Mr. Warren was of the other sort, men who longed for new beginnings, for whom a finished thing was less exciting.

"We want to go, Father." Martha spoke. Had she forgiven me? Gotten over Bill to see the wisdom in what I'd done? What our father had done?

"I don't." Millie expressed herself. "I want to

stay with Eliza and the babies but not in some faraway place. It'll be a lot of work too."

"Good luck finding someone to drive the team. At least he left you oxen to pull the wagon. He did do that much, didn't he?"

"Yes. I just have to find someone responsible, for a few months."

"There's no help here." My father left the house then, Martha tailing after him still talking, pleading? If she came, maybe the two of us could handle things ourselves. Millie held America Jane on her hip.

"Why don't you hire one of those poor Indians I see fishing?" Rachel spoke. "They could use the money no doubt and perhaps having one with you would ward off other Indians you might encounter. I mean, if you must do this alone—I can't believe your husband has abandoned you like this, why not—"

"He didn't abandon me! He's taking a different route and he had to leave. I'll join him."

"Well, yes, of course." She leaned into me and the baby in my arms. "Are you frightened?"

"Yes." I was, all the more in my having to make new routines with my sisters no longer there to look after America Jane and Lizzie. "But courage is doing what must be done despite the fear, it's going on even when you want to quit."

"My exact thoughts when I boarded the ship to come meet your father. He needed support; I could give it. So my fears were of little matter to the higher duty." Rachel continued. "Have you considered hiring an Indian to drive, offer protection, what with you going into Cayuse country again?"

"You might have a good idea, Rachel."

"Do I? "

"About hiring a native. One of the Kalapuya people maybe. Or Molalla. But where to find one."

"The Lord will provide." Rachel patted my arm, bent to kiss the baby's head.

I said good-bye to my sisters then. I had no idea when or if we'd be together again. More than three hundred miles would separate us. They'd be older, wiser, when I saw them again. Rachel and my father were nowhere around. "Tell them good-bye for me, all right?"

On the way home, I stopped at Brown and Blakely's and asked Mr. Brown's son, John, if he knew of a Kalapuya whom I might hire.

"To do what?"

At thirty, John Brown managed his father's store and he looked strong enough to be a driver, arms like twisted rope, hair the color of wheat. "To drive my wagon to the Touchet River, Washington Territory."

"Heard Warren had headed out. Too bad I can't leave the store, I'd do it myself. I like exploring new things." He smiled at Millie and she blushed. *What's that about?*

"And I'd hire you. But do you know of someone I might get? I thought an Indian might be good, as escort going back into Indian country."

He was thoughtful. "I do. He brings in fish," John Brown said. "Stands up to those Klickitat that moved in giving the Kalapuya a hard time about taking salmon from 'their tributaries.' Always fair with me, though. Lives on the Grand Ronde reservation but gets papers to leave to fish old sites. Good judgment and good English too. Don't know if he has a wife." He told me where I might find him that time of year, fishing season just beginning this far south along the Willamette River's streams.

His name was Little Shoot and I found him where Mr. Brown said I would, near a certain place on the Pudding River. He said he'd learned his English from a colored woman and his grandmother, the latter dead and the black woman moved to southern Oregon with her children, though "I see them some. They visit at Soap Creek."

"I'm looking for someone who can drive my ox team and soon, within the week." I still needed to find another couple to come with me in their own wagon that had room for more of our things. But I could leave if I had to, so long as I had one driver. "I'll have these two little ones with me."

America Jane hid her face behind my waist in the buggy I drove. Lizzie slept in a quilt at my feet. The man smiled at America Jane and she pulled back into me but kept an eye on him.

"Where is your man?"

"He left with several drovers and three hundred head of cattle, heading to Walla Walla country over the Cascades." I pointed east toward the little-used route. "Have you heard of that passage?"

He lifted his chin up and down once. A yes. "I know of journey stories that way. From Santiam People. It follows a river through mountains. Good grasses on the other side." Maybe Mr. Warren had gotten good advice after all.

Lizzie woke and I put her on my lap. Little Shoot grinned, teased Lizzie then, hiding his face with his hands, then jerking them away. She giggled, her pudgy hands and feet kicking out together with a vigor that nearly took her from my lap. *This man has been around children.*

"We'll go by way of Portland, take a boat and meet at The Dalles. And then on toward Walla Walla. If my husband has already moved on through, I'll have to try to follow him and your help would be welcomed all that way. If you're willing." Little Shoot was taller than me, with strong arms. The Yakima Indian wars just across the Columbia had ended the year before, but he could pass as Yakima should we encounter trouble on either side of the river. I thought him a good choice.

He was thoughtful. "I can go. I will need to tell my woman, my wife."

"Would she come along?" If she did, I might go with just our wagon, forget the other couple.

"It is near her time. But she has people to care for her and the new child while I am gone."

He was already a father, finding ways to provide for his family. I suspected the reservation didn't offer much in the way of improving his lot.

We talked of payment and agreed on a price. His long black hair shone in the April sun, and he brushed it from his face before reaching to shake my hand. "I've never been asked to shake my hand as a man."

"The colored woman, Letitia Carson. I work with her making cheese. She shakes hands to say we have a trust. I would smoke instead." He grinned.

"I can shake a hand, but smoking is out."

He lifted my fingers, soft, delicate almost, with one quick up and down and then release. I'd say it was feminine but it might also have meant respect instead of contest, not palm to palm in challenge. I took respect as my interpretation.

I'd made a good bargain. The sense of satisfaction for having made a contract surprised me. Now all I had to do was find a couple willing to pull up roots and travel with me.

To travel with total strangers, to not know if they saw a sunrise as an interruption or a joy; to wonder if they liked a quiet meal or conversation;

to not be certain how they disciplined a child who meant no harm or where they thought a dog belonged: these were all things I had no real time to discover. While I changed Lizzie's napkin, grateful she tolerated my milk well and didn't suffer from chronic diarrhea as apparently I had as a baby, a young couple pulled up in a mostly empty wagon drawn by two mules. The canvas covering lay folded in the wagon bed beneath the metal bows. It was two days after I'd hired Little Shoot and nearly a month since Mr. Warren had left.

"So. We hear you head east, *ja*." He had an accent, German maybe or Swiss.

"Yes. I am."

"This is my sister, Hannah. We are the Ruckers, brother and sister. I am Charles." They weren't much older than me. "Mr. Brown tells us of your need."

"Yes, please come inside. Can you tell me something about yourselves?"

"We are with the colony north of here."

"Aurora?" It was a scatter of buildings lived in by hardworking people who had come from Missouri a few years before, who shared their income and needs communally. They were fine cabinetmakers and they'd started a mill and played musical instruments, or so I'd heard. They followed a leader but were said to be Christians.

"Yes. Aurora. We are free to work elsewhere."

The girl spoke, emphasizing the last two words. Else. Where. She spoke less-accented English than his but clear. She had blond braids wrapped around her head, eyes blue as lupine. She had one sleepy eye. Charles on the other hand was shorter than his sister, rounder, and he wore a floppy black hat as from Missouri. "I work with oxen. I manage your wagon."

"And who would drive yours?"

"Hannah would. She's quite good, *ja*. Not a problem for her."

"I have an ox man, as it happens. But it's good to know there will be four of us capable of managing our teams. I will welcome your hands with my children. Are you willing to provide care for them too?"

"I can do this." She said "dis," but I knew what she meant. She had a wide, somber face and didn't smile as we spoke of their life in the colony and how they needed to branch out and earn money they'd bring back to the community. I wondered what criteria my mother used to find Matilda, how she knew to trust her to take me to Waiilatpu that last time.

The Ruckers drove a harder bargain than Little Shoot had. They charged for their labor as well as the wagon even though they intended to return with it to their colony after we reached the Touchet River. For now, it would be filled with Warren household goods. I was renting space. Our negotiations complete, I asked them if they had any difficulty traveling with an Indian.

Hannah's eyes grew large. "We hear tales. Yakima, Modocs. It's not one of them?"

"No, a quiet Kalapuya man who has permission to leave the reservation."

"He might prove as protection for us, *ja*?"

"That was part of my thinking, too, Mr. Rucker. So I hired him, as he came recommended." I thought I ought to ask these two for someone to recommend them, but as my mother might say, beggars can't be choosers "Tomorrow we leave," I said.

"Grateful I am," Charles said. A phrase he used often. "We stay the night."

"Oh, well, of course. Best you come in for some supper then. We can load until dark, wait for Little Shoot to come in the morning to finish up."

"*Ja*, that's good. Come, Hannah. You take that end and we load the bedstead first."

"No. I mean, I plan to sleep on it one more time. We'll load it in the morning."

"Best to load the heavy bedstead on the bottom, Frau Warren. Maybe you could sleep in the wagon, *ja*?"

"I don't think so. No. Please, let's just get an early start loading. Little Shoot will be here to help."

"Grateful I am dat you are clear with your orders." Charles tipped his hat.

I sighed relief. They were no-nonsense people. They set a task and did it. It would be an adventure with four such people having certain ways of doing things venturing into unknown territories. Maybe I'd learn how to live better with my husband after dealing with strong-willed people on this trip.

Mr. Warren's path would take him east of Brownsville and along Wiley Creek. Wiley had told Mr. Warren he'd made the crossing last year and intended to do it again, hunting on the little-used Indian land—public land, Wiley had called it—on the eastern side of the Cascades. A large rock outcropping skirted the pass both east and south and he was certain cattle could be brought through single file, moved north to The Dalles to rolling, high grass country. But there could be no wagons. Mr. Warren would take a different path from me, not for the first time in our marriage.

He'd been gone a month when we finished loading our two wagons with household goods, grain for the horses, chickens in their cages. One of the Rucker pair would also have the two sheep trotting behind their wagon. Mr. Warren had been insistent that we needed the sheep, but he didn't want to be traveling with them. My father loved his sheep. He'd built up a huge herd while at Lapwai with sheep the Hawaiian Halls brought with them along with the printing press from the

Sandwich Islands. Once, one of the rare times my mother insisted that all of us go to the annual gathering at Waiilatpu, my father drove his herd of twelve sheep the 120 miles from Lapwai, let them graze on the lush grass near the mission, and when the meeting was over, we all rode back, my father bringing up the rear behind his flock. At least no wolves got them, which he was sure would happen if he'd left them unattended. I always wondered why he didn't think the Nez Perce would watch them, but perhaps it was that time of year when the Indians camped in places farther from Lapwai. Otherwise there'd have been a dozen families near us, people more than willing, as they always were, to help my father, including watch his sheep.

But they had changed, those Nez Perce. They no longer wanted us there.

We made good progress and Little Shoot got on well with the determined Ruckers. He simply eased his way doing as they asked, only once or twice gently suggesting an alternative in such a way the pair weren't offended. I needed to watch that young man to see just exactly how he did that.

Just before we left, I took a final tour of what had been my home since marrying Mr. Warren. How soon would the mice claim it, make nests in my woodstove? I ran the stories in my head: where I'd dropped a knife and barely missed my barefoot toes. The incision still jabbed the floor.

Where the O'Donnell brothers had deposited him with his broken leg; where he'd shared his deepest shame with me; where I'd given birth to our two girls.

"Mama, someone comes." I turned to America Jane's words.

"We couldn't let you go without saying good-bye," Rachel said.

"I knew you wouldn't come to us." This from Martha as she dismounted.

"But I said my good-byes. I . . . I don't know if I can ache that much again."

My father scowled, but Rachel beamed, whether out of her success at getting him to do something he didn't want to or because all of us were together—except for Henry Hart who'd gone off to Washington somewhere. "You missed telling me and your father adieu."

I hugged Rachel then. My father stood by the wagon while my sisters cuddled their nieces.

"I might have visited you, but as you can see I still have more things to load." Here before me stood my family. And I was leaving them. Perhaps always had been. At least I could recall a dozen long good-byes. This one would be short. I had to get on my way.

"Don't fret," my father told me. Such an odd admonition.

"I don't."

"Ah, but you do. That's what's happening when

you turn back to that sad time. You scold your-self, rebuke what happened to you there that was not your fault. None of it. No one's fault. Except those Cayuse. And the Catholics, of course."

Maybe it wasn't the Cayuses' fault either as they defended what had been taken from them. Losing things doesn't always bring about a kinder, more grateful heart, appreciative of what one still had; sometimes loss hardened it. But perhaps there was a choice in that.

"Your concern is noted." I kissed him on his whiskered cheek. "Thanks for coming to say good-bye. All of you." He stood stiff, but he didn't turn his back or brush his cheek of my touch.

I didn't want tears to puddle in my eyes, but they did. I feared then I would go to sobbing or, worse, change my mind.

I inhaled, stepped up onto the wagon. Little Shoot handed my baby to me. America Jane sat beside me. Little Shoot moved to the oxen's head. He'd walk beside the oxen, carrying a stick to guide them. Charles Rucker checked the ties on the bleating sheep and the butter churn hanging from the bow. We had one milk cow and my horse tied behind our wagon. I turned to wave and shouted, "You'll see us again, God willing." It was similar to what Timothy had told me about seeing my mother when he couldn't take me from the murderers. I prayed it would be in this life and not the next.

"You'll see us again, God willing. The exact words your mother said to her parents when we left New York!" He shook his head in wonder.

I saw tears on my father's cheeks and turned north to our new beginning.

❧ 20 ❧

HEADING BACKWARD

Our first evening stop developed our routines. We'd packed grain for the oxen and mules to supplement grasses that grew beside the road. We didn't want them wandering off onto people's property, something overland emigrants didn't have to worry over. Everything was still free range in the eastern part of the territory. That's what had appealed to Mr. Warren. After Charles built a fire and Little Shoot set up tents, the Kalapuya and Hannah picked berries into a twine basket Little Shoot brought with him. Later he washed up the dishes and I commented on his doing women's work.

"Work does not know who does it. It just wants to be done."

I smiled. "Someone taught you how to do what is typical of women's work, though."

"My grandmother. She feared I would not find a woman to accept my ugly face so made certain I could feed myself."

"A wise woman. I'll remember that if I ever have a son." I surprised myself by thinking I might want another child with Mr. Warren. My annoyance and anger at him was waning even then.

Despite my trepidation at going it without my husband, I found myself sleeping deeply, waking to the sunrise and the sweet smells of summer.

Our third night north, we heard wolves howl and we huddled the sheep close to our wagons. I was pleased for my helpers even more. In the morning, the trail took us near the Aurora community, so the Ruckers asked if they could stop at the *gross haus* where their leader and several families lived, to let them know they'd hired out for a time. As it was a Sunday and we'd stopped for the Sabbath, I agreed. We heard music coming from the long two-story house with a wide veranda, and Charles explained that worship began on Saturday afternoon and ended at Sunday noon, followed by music and food and "talking. It is when girls and boys can be together."

"Otherwise women do what women do and men what they do," Hannah added, "unless it is time to butcher or stack hay or pick hops. We do all together, those."

Little Shoot and the girls and I remained with the wagon, but we could hear the festivities and I wondered if the Ruckers might change their minds about going with us. I thought of what I'd do if they did. Turn back and wait until I found others to go with us? But they returned and my imaginations once again resulted in the fears not coming forward. Perhaps making the commitment brought on the peace not found in all the ruminating about whether to go or stay.

We headed north toward Oregon City the following morning and the Ruckers commented on how many more houses there were. "Coming across the trail we saw not so many people. It grows fast here."

"Imagine if you will how much it's changed since when I was young," I said.

"You came across when?"

"I never did. I was the first white child to live born west of the Shining Mountains."

"Aaahh," Little Shoot said. "You are long time here."

"Not so long as your people."

We had our evening rest not far from the Willamette Falls.

"You are grandma, a *kasa*?" Little Shoot grinned. "You tell stories of your growing."

"Not old as a grandma, but when I was little we lived in Lapwai on the Clearwater River, and every year dozens of white people came our way when I was old enough to remember. I haven't been back. I imagine it's changed greatly." I didn't say I had no desire to return.

"Where my people dug roots and hunted deer, already people live there, make it different."

"I imagine they do." All our Lapwai buildings had been built on someone else's land, not even "owned" land, as my mother explained to me. The

Nez Perce didn't see the hills and rivers as belonging to anyone. It was there for use, given by the Creator, in order for all his people to survive and thrive. Everyone was charged with caring for it, being wise.

"Grateful I am that Dr. Kiel purchased the acres our colony has," Charles said.

"From Kalapuya?" Little Shoot asked.

"No. Others already claimed it. A man named White."

Little Shoot nodded as though that made perfect sense. Charles looked away. The Cayuse claim that the Whitmans had stolen their land came to mind. Could the violence really have been about that? About who had the power to give and take what they so desperately loved? Who is to say what made them do it? Taking back power could be a vehement thing. Was that why our Lord had encouraged us to do things a different way, grant forgiveness?

Lizzie fussed and I moved away from the wagon end where Hannah had placed hardtack and beef jerky for our light supper. The Ruckers had brought back sausage with a perfect blend of spices. I fed my baby and listened to Charles play his harmonica while I tucked America Jane into her bedroll in the wagon, knelt beside her to hear her simple prayers, then crawled in and spoke my own. I wasn't certain what forgiveness really was, but it had come to me in the context of the Cayuse. I asked for clarity in my prayers that night, direction. *Grateful I am.* I echoed Charles's words. I hoped that by the time we reached Touchet country I might have found a better way to look at what had happened to me not far from there and forgive my husband for taking me to a place of memory fraught with harm.

We passed through Oregon City quickly. I didn't need to go anywhere near the scaffoldings, though surely they'd been torn down. People had lost their taste for hangings and a jail had been built after the trial. But I could still see the faces of the men: Tiloukaikt. Tomahas. Kiamasumpkin. Isiaachsheluckas. Clokomas. The Cayuse (and the Umatilla people too) had claimed at the trial that their actions were required as revenge on medicine men who gave poor medicine. Dr. Whitman had not cured their measles and many had died. His medicine was no good and justice meant he must die too. But the jury disagreed. More than Dr. Whitman died, they said. Some women and children too. And all were not killed in the heat of that one horrible day. Several were slaughtered over a week later. I'd forgotten that until I heard it at the trial. Perhaps to keep us hostages meek and frightened and willing to do whatever they said. I remember watching little Mary Marsh knit a long stocking for one of the Cayuse who grabbed her chicken-leg arm, pinched it into pain, and told her to "Knit" or he would kill her. I had to translate but his ferocious face told her as much. He boxed her ears when she failed to knit fast enough for her captor. They kept water scarce as a baby's whiskers. They decided when we would drink. One Sager boy died trying to get us water. They shot him with the canteen in his hands, two days after the initial assault.

"Mrs. Warren. You are ill?" Little Shoot spoke to me, his hand shaking the guiding stick keeping the oxen on their path. I walked beside him. "You do not answer me."

"What? No, I'm fine." My heartbeat slowed. This day, I heard the thundering falls as falls and not the hooves of horses from my past. I stayed with my children, here.

We camped the next day outside Portland, and I took Charles with me to the Oregon Steam Navigation company to secure passage on the middle river to The Dalles. Gold discovered in the Washington Territory the previous year spurred new craft-building, so I hoped we'd find a ship. Lizzie rode with me, her not being able to be far from her food source, and I didn't know how long our negotiations would take. America Jane was content with Hannah and didn't pout when I left her—a good sign, I thought. I had no fear of leaving her behind.

We had little trouble finding a vessel but were

told we'd have to wait a day, miners paying to go first. There were stories of Paiute raids on miners who ignored their rights to the land, searching for gold in some "blue bucket" mine an immigrant claimed to have left behind. Danger lurked there on my husband's journey.

How long Mr. Warren's crossing would take was an unknown. But I felt a pressure to be on that steamship, as I'd taken so long to decide. We hurried back to bring the others and camped near the Company to load first thing in the morning.

The sway of the craft on the water reminded me that I did not like boat travel. America Jane stood beside Little Shoot, smiling while I lost my breakfast despite my panting like a dog and found myself shaking as Hannah took Lizzie from my arms. "I watch her, *ja*." Lizzie didn't protest and I was grateful, as my stomach did. Even when the water was smooth, the chug of the engines, the smell of the wood that fired them, the sounds of water pouring over the wheels, all worked to keep me off balance even when I focused on the timbered horizon.

The constant wind in my face tired my eyes, irritated the girls. We reached a rapids and a falls and had to portage east around it and board another boat. I welcomed the walking respite. When we reached The Dalles, we disembarked again and this time we took the wagons on our own.

I remembered this little town from when I'd been so ill after Father, Henry Hart, and I traveled to the ocean. I'd gotten sick on a boat then too. But here I'd had some other ailment that didn't want to let me go. I remember feeling weak and frail, barely hearing conversations between my father and Mr. Walker and Mr. Brewer, both missionaries to the round-faced Indians who fished there. The falls thundered like the Willamette's and perhaps the noise kept me from hearing as well.

"I have been to this place," Little Shoot said. "My *kasa* takes me long years ago."

"Those men look different, Mama," America Jane said. I shushed her, though she was right. The Indians who fished here were rounder and not just on their faces. I didn't see many horses tearing at grass either. The town smelled of fish and bustled with river traffic and a mercantile and even a hotel with the name Umatilla House across the front. Every business stood ready to sell goods to the trains of wagons arriving from the east later in the year and to miners heading east. Dragoons in uniform stood in small clusters away from their fort for the day, reminding us that we were only a year beyond the latest Indian Wars.

Arriving toward evening as we did, I took a room at the Umatilla House, leaving my wagon with Little Shoot, who would not have been given a room even if I'd rented it for him. He said he'd tend the two sheep too. The Ruckers stayed with the wagons as well, though I offered them a place. "We take cost of rooms as add-on to contract, *ja*. We stay with goods."

In the morning I sought to find out whether my husband had arrived. Surely someone appearing from the south with three hundred head would be remembered. If not, then I could assume he had yet to appear.

"Nothing like that's been this way." This answer from the hotel manager named Graves when I questioned him. "Sure we'd hear about it, though he wouldn't come into town I wouldn't guess. Where's he headed with them? I might buy one or two from him."

"Touchet River, in Walla Walla country."

"What's there? If you don't mind me asking."

"Grass and missing fences. And a drier climate than in Brownsville."

"It's that, all right. Well, if I hear anything I'll send word."

The old worries began. Might Mr. Warren simply bypass this landing and cross upriver and I never know? Would he believe that I had come and send word? Maybe he'd think me contrary and decide I'd remained behind. What if something had happened and he wasn't even alive? Had I lived weeks as a widow and didn't even know?

"Mama, when's *Papo* coming?"

"I don't know, America. We just have to be patient."

"What's a patient?"

"Not what is a patient, but we have to be patient, to keep our thoughts calm, find things to occupy ourselves until we receive what we're waiting for."

"Are you a patient?"

"Am I patient? I'm trying to be. I miss your *papo* too. Let's walk out to the wagons and see how Hannah and Mr. Rucker and Little Shoot fare."

"I'm a good patient," she chirped.

I didn't correct her word usage a second time and for a moment did wonder if all my imaginings of the worst did make me a kind of "patient," ill in my thinking while my body was sound. I shook myself and sent up a prayer for advice about how to proceed, something I ought to do more of. It's what my mother would have done.

Back at the hotel Mr. Graves said, "I've been thinking about you heading east. Going the wrong way with those wagons. Everyone else is heading west."

"We've been there," I said. "Been east, too, but going back that way."

"How far? Virginia? New York?"

I shook my head. "Back to the beginning." He puzzled at that and I let him. I walked near the water, waiting. I was without my husband and who knew for how long?

The Diary of Eliza Spalding

1850

I write of a time after Millie was born, Martha still just a baby and I was without my husband. S decided to take Eliza and Henry Hart across the Cascades to the Pacific Ocean. How I would have loved to have seen those waters! They were gone for several weeks while Matilda looked after us. S had once left an old Indian in charge to run the grist mill. He'd done it before, but the older man had also been pushed aside by a group of rowdy, younger Nimíipuu one day. They pushed the old man down. S ran out to stop the ruckus and one young Indian struck S, crushed him on the hard ground, choked him. I ran screaming from the house, pounding on the back of S's attacker. It was the first time I ever lost my composure, and my blows were of little effect. Several other Indians who had brought their grain to be ground saw the trouble and pulled S's attacker off.

"Do you not know that we would never let anything happen to our Spalding," the Nimíipuu told me later while S rubbed his throat. Their words were reassuring, but what if they had not been there at that providential time? Henry might have died. And I, left alone with the children. What would I do? The answer to that question was never more far away nor as real as at that moment when he was almost choked to death. I told S he'd been foolish to intervene but he admonished me with words of our Lord, that what is a greater love than to lay down one's life for a friend. The old Indian had befriended us and he had given his life in service to the Lord. S knew he had to do whatever he must to defend him. His words shamed me and I never again complained about his impulsive actions. With enough thought I could see that all he did was in service.

It took me a time to see how that long trip to the ocean was in service, though. S told me they'd gotten lost in the mountains, rescued by an Indian. Eliza came back ill with the flux, and though eight years old and riding her own horse, she had made the return trek, S said, sitting in front of him on his horse as she was too ill to ride her beloved Tashe alone. They'd stayed extra days at The Dalles mission because of her frailty, conversing with the missionaries there, I suppose. Perhaps that was the Lord's design, as S and those ministers shared the strains of their work as well as their joys. I had Matilda to share my days with, but a man does need to have other men to acknowledge his efforts, can learn from a time away from the strains of family demands. A wife's words are often not enough to bolster.

⇒ 21 ⇐

LEAVINGS

Men needed times away from the responsibility of family, I supposed. I imagined Mr. Warren and his drovers enjoying their nights beneath the moon, telling stories of the day. But so did mothers need such respite, if only for a few moments. My sisters had given me that and I hadn't really acknowledged how important they had been.

Walking the streets of The Dalles, I admonished myself to be patient. But by the second day, I couldn't find patience in me if it had been a cow mooing in the corral. Hannah and Charles determined they needed to get back and no cajoling would change their minds, though grateful I was for what they'd done. We loaded all the household goods we could into my wagon and I asked that they take what was not as essential as I'd once thought when I had room to take it. They would return it to my father's house—or mine—in Brownsville, without a fee as they had stopped before we arrived near Touchet. "Tell my father that we're fine. Please don't tell him that you did not see the cattle yet. I don't want him to worry."

I watched them roll their wagon on board the steamship and head west. Hannah waved and America Jane sniffed. "Just like the aunties," she said. "Always good-bye."

Little Shoot stood beside me.

"Do you need to return to your family?"

"I am here."

"Yes, I know, but tell me now if you can't wait." It occurred to me that I should set a time to wait for myself. Did I go forward with Little Shoot and hope I'd find my husband who didn't have the decency to send word for me if he'd already gone through? Or should I send Little Shoot south to see if they were still on their way? I must have said some of those thoughts out loud.

"I could do that, ride south. There is reservation there, Warm Springs, and Wasco people are placed there. These Celilo Indians are relatives." He nodded toward the round-faced Indians standing on scaffoldings with ropes around their bellies while they speared the big salmon jumping upriver above the roaring falls. The June sun glistened against his damp body. "One might ride with me who knows the route."

"You've asked?"

"Watching sheep does not take much time. They are like big dogs."

"I suppose I have spoiled them. They like biscuits too much to wander far. So yes, please. See if you can get word about my husband."

We stayed at the wagon, alone. I washed out Lizzie's napkins; took care of my own intimate apparel, hemmed America Jane's dress, then spot-washed it, looking at my sun-browned hands, gloves being impractical except leather ones to handle oxen yokes and harness. We looked like vagabonds more than a "cared for" family. But money grew scarcer and my two nights of luxury on a bed served to annoy that I couldn't really afford to stay there again. What would I do if we failed to make our rendezvous?

Had my mother ever allowed herself to get into this position? She couldn't get immediate help from the other missionaries, but as her husband was employed by the Mission Board, without him in service, she'd be asked to leave Lapwai and find another life. With four children. Maybe my uncle Horace would have assisted. He would have helped me, too, if he hadn't moved away after her death. My mother had her faith to sustain her so she wasn't really alone. Maybe I wasn't either. It did no good to imagine the worst. Better to sing songs to my children, gaze at the stars.

I bedded the girls down under the tent and pulled my bedroll up to my chin. Little Shoot had told me of the woman he'd worked for, a colored woman. "She is left alone with two children," he told me. "When her husband dies, they come, take all things from her, candlesticks and dishes. Sell them."

"How could they?"

He had shrugged his shoulders. "She is the color of charred wood. White faces do what they want." He'd gone on to say she delivered babies, raised her children, worked land. That woman, Letitia Carson he called her, had a skill. Perhaps I'd discover my own skill if Mr. Warren had indeed gone on without me, by his choice—or not.

Stars twinkled in the wide sky unbroken by tall timber or small oaks. It was a Lapwai sky, wide open from round hill to round hill, a river rushing in the background. The sky was a blanket of blackness dotted with silver brads. I felt so small, so powerless. Yet I felt less alone than I had in years.

I drove the ox team into the town the next morning as I could figure no other way to manage the two girls and still go into the Umatilla House to see if Mr. Warren had sent word. I took it as no small accomplishment that I lifted the heavy oxen yokes and managed the harness while America Jane looked after Lizzie on a quilt. "Grateful I was," as Charles would say, that my youngest couldn't yet walk.

And grateful I was when Little Shoot caught up with me as I lifted Lizzie from the wagon bed in front of the hotel. The sheep bleated at the sight of him. "He comes!" Little Shoot shouted as he dismounted Maka, breathless, dust brushing his fine face. "A day behind. You are to resupply flour, salt, sugar. He comes for you. Drives the herd east."

"Papo's coming!" I swung my daughter in a dance. America Jane grabbed my skirts, grinning as she hugged.

I spoke a prayer of gratitude. I could be flexible. I could adapt. "Both skills," I told the girls, whose blue eyes sparkled, reflecting my joy. More adjustments would be called for, but for this moment, I felt the anticipation of the unknown instead of its dread.

"There you are!" Mr. Warren leapt from his horse and danced me around. "You're a sight for trail-dusted eyes."

"Mr. Warren, Andrew, welcome."

He kissed me then, that thrill of flutter like the first time. My face felt hot when he released me. We were back at the site where we'd had the wagons, Little Shoot advising my husband where he could find us. I'd washed the girls' dresses— with Little Shoot's help—and put a clean one on myself. My hair was less a tangled mess than usual, pushed up into a thick netted twist at the top of my head, an ivory stick Rachel had given me pushed through it.

"You bet I'm welcomed. What a beautiful sight after six weeks with those drovers and the back end of cows. It's a doable pass. It is."

"Grateful I am that you find us more attractive than that." I curtsied.

He laughed with me, kissed me soundly again, then looked me in the eye, causing yet another thrill from toes to head. "I have missed you."

"You didn't wonder if I'd come or not?"

"I prayed you would. That you'd get everything organized to be here together."

"I'm rather pleased with myself that I managed. I discovered having an important task needing to be accomplished and bringing all the resources to bear to make it happen is quite—"

He lifted his eyebrows.

"Powerful."

"A fine word." He swung Lizzie from the blanket where she'd been lying on her tummy, pressed his hand on America Jane's head as she waited patiently beside him. "It's so good to have you all here."

"Where are your cows?"

"They'll be along in a day or so." He looked around. "Where are your sisters?"

"Father wouldn't let them come."

"Didn't want them in Indian country, I'll wager."

"I guess that was it." I didn't want to tell him what my father had said about him and his lack of common sense. Sometimes doing what others think is insanity is actually impetus toward significance. *Go and learn what this means*. In truth, taking a risk had led to meaning for Father and his work; my mother too. And now, perhaps for me. "Little Shoot's been a good escort. You knew he came from me when you saw him riding Maka." I didn't see the young man now, decided he was on the other side of the wagon giving us our privacy.

"Little Shoot. That Indian? He served you well?"

"He did. And he found you."

"We've really no need of him anymore."

I hadn't thought that far ahead. "I . . . I guess you're right, though he's been good with the children. And the sheep."

"You and I will trade off driving the oxen."

"I have the children—"

"I'll send a drover when I'm on horseback."

"Yes, of course. Well, he has a wife waiting for a baby, so I imagine he'll be happy to return. I'll just express my thanks and pay him."

"I already did. He's gone."

"No! I didn't get to thank him. I thought he'd stay on until we got to Touchet." A niggle of fear wormed its way into my throat. Going back to Cayuse country, I had counted on Little Shoot acting as intercessor if we needed.

"He said he was happy to serve you."

"*Papo! Papo!*"

America Jane hopped up and down, and Mr.

Warren handed me Lizzie as he lifted his oldest daughter and rubbed his whiskered face against hers. America Jane giggled as she tugged on his beard.

"He did well with the children. They'll miss him." I sighed. "I keep having to explain where people go."

"Good practice. Living is all about the different ways we say good-bye."

"I can't believe he left without saying anything to me."

"He didn't abandon you, 'Liza. People leave because they've finished their business. It isn't about your business."

"Well, I prefer hellos."

"Me too. Hello, Mrs. Warren. Are you free for supper tonight?"

Oh, how I was!

Before Little Shoot found my husband, bringing him to me, I had written and posted a letter to my father telling him that we'd arrived, that all was well, and that he ought to consider bringing cattle and coming too. It was not too late in the season. It was an impulsive act taken within my waiting. I hadn't known when I wrote it whether Mr. Warren had gone on ahead, if something had happened to him, or what Touchet would offer, but I felt a confidence that we could make it through if we needed to. And having my sisters near would be a pleasure as well as a help.

The cattle caught up with us, bellowing and shaking their bovine heads of flies. We followed them, continuing our journey east. For most of the trip, we trudged beside the oxen away from the river to ridges high above the Columbia. The views were majestic. Copses of timber dotted the horizon, fading to rounded hills, the grasses turning brown from the hot sun but still majestic, like waves of amber. Then down steep, rocky trails, back toward water, crossing the Deschutes and then the John Day flowing into the Columbia. "John Day's River." Mr. Warren chewed on a long grass as he nodded toward the slow-moving stream. "Named by the Astor party. I guess the Virginian had gone mad on the passage west. They had a hard time. Got here in January and he was nearly skinned alive by In—" He stopped himself. "Never mind. It's a pretty river, isn't it?"

"Is the Touchet as large?"

He shook his head. "But it'll be good for transport. Feeds into the Walla Walla River and that into the Columbia. And the grasses, see how tall they are on either side of the John Day? We'll have that kind of grass at Touchet."

A wheel broke on the wagon while the faithful oxen pulled us up rolling ridges high above the Columbia. Timber, green, didn't make a good repair, but we managed, getting ourselves moving again. Often, I carried the goading stick, Lizzie in a quilt on my back, America Jane on a long rope to keep her from wandering away. I walked beside the wagon, and Mr. Warren rode ahead to be with the drovers, keeping us far enough back to be out of the cattle dust but close enough to be of help if they should get spooked and stampede.

None of that happened and grateful I was.

When we rolled down and crossed the Walla Walla to arrive at the fort, I was ready for a night on a bed of feathers instead of on the ground. I had not been to the fort since we'd been taken there first after the hostage negotiations were completed. I heard the iron hinges grate as the gate opened.

Clunk! Gates close behind us. We are safe. A woman, not a hostage, an Indian, comes to me and I shrink until her soft words are spoken in Sahaptin. I stare at her, tell her my name.

"Spalding," she says and claps her hands together, the movement and sound a startle. "Your father, here."

"*Papo*?"

My father steps out of the guardhouse, his eyes searching until he finds mine. "Spalding!" the Nimíipuu woman says then and she reaches for my hand to lead me toward him, but I run, run into his arms. "*Papo, Papo*, you are safe. You are safe."

His tears mingle with mine as he bends to hold

me. "Eliza, oh, my child. We are all safe. We are all well. Your mother, she will be better when she sees your face. Thank God, thank God."

"She is alive?" *My mother lives!* I search the adult faces looking at us, their eyes glassy with tears at the sight of our arrival.

"She's at Fort Vancouver. Your brother and sisters. We'll join them."

"We won't go back to Lapwai?" My dolls, my books, all left behind.

"We can't." His words falter. "We'll be together. Just not in Lapwai. We are here. Safe. At this fort." The happy sounds of other reunions, the cries of joy begin the disheveling of terror.

" 'Liza, are you all right?" Mr. Warren sounds concerned, his voice pulls me back.

"What? Yes. I . . . I think so." Twelve years later, I'm facing old, cold memories as hard as the iron on the fort's gate.

"Everything is so strange. It's as though it's a different fort."

"I suspect it is." Mr. Warren removed his hat and rubbed his forearm to his sweaty brow. A red rim marked the hat's residence. "This fort was built in '56, for soldiers in the Indian Wars. The one you remember, it was abandoned. We're downriver from where that one stood. Don't you remember?"

"I—how could I forget?" My limbs shook and I

reached for the oxen, steadying myself against the warm body. I'd been anticipating how I'd feel about that fort, all its memories. But the physical space of it was no more. We'd traveled right past it. My memory kept secrets from me.

"We'll let the soldiers know we're in the territory but move on. Not far from Touchet now."

I nodded, gathering my thoughts. I had returned to a time, a reunion, that didn't happen where I'd thought. I was discovering that the past I remembered wasn't always the past that was.

The Diary of Eliza Spalding

1850

Between the stories I remember of Lapwai and the facts of how it really was lies memory. How to separate one from the other? In my fading I remember the good times. Matilda speaking in English about Jesus. Eliza laughing as Mustups, a Nimíipuu boy, pulls her in a cart made of a fir round. Henry Hart catching frogs along the Clearwater. My little girls born healthy. A day before my daughter went off to school when we rode alone. She found an iris. Or was it some other bloom? Oh how I wish to return.

Before we were invited to Kirk's Ferry, known as Brownsville now, and S became obsessed with the trial, I thought we could have just gone back to Lapwai. Things had settled down there and I missed The People so. Matilda could have nursed me back to health, taken care of the children. That place of the butterflies was where we'd been called to by God. But Henry insisted we could not return without the sanction of the Mission Board. "Why not?" I asked. "The Board don't understand that the Indians are different in different places. Our Nimíipuu want us back. We could return and do our work without the Mission's support, show them what we can still accomplish there. Take the remnants of what was left and build something new with them. Be as homesteaders are, building up a claim with our neighbor's help."

"We accepted a call from the Board," S insisted. "Your logic does not enter in."

"We accepted a call from God. And circumstances have changed. Aren't we compelled to change with them?"

"You do not remember the difficulties we had there. And without the Board's support, there would be grave tensions. Not all want us back. Some have lost the faith."

I remembered our lives as good there, full of challenges but rich in present moments, small gifts of living. "Are we not meant to forget past difficulties except to learn from them, to take more informed stands to better serve? Do you not remember Philippians 4:8?" I quoted for him, "Finally, brethren, whatsoever things are true, whatsoever things are honest, whatsoever things are just, whatsoever things are pure, whatsoever things are lovely, whatsoever things are of good report; if there be any virtue, and if there be any praise, think on these things."

He shook his head. "I will write another letter."

I remembered then just how stubborn S

could be. Henry ranted about the Catholics, then, about their part in the uprising, which to my way of thinking was nothing, they'd only just arrived. He raved about justice that seemed of vengeance to me. And I wondered then if this man had broken his mind, if all the trauma of the years had taken him from me, this man who was so far from the man I had married. I hope I live long enough to learn from our trials, to gain from past lessons.

❧ 22 ❧

SEGMENTS OF THE PAST

How, when I was so grateful to have seen my father after the rescue, could such dissension live between us? Had my father always been so stubborn? How did my mother handle that? I had made overtures to him. Yet I had willingly gone away while our disagreement broiled. He'd say I am the cause of our separation, having left my home to marry Mr. Warren those years before. But aren't children allowed to make their own way without their parents always hovering? How would I learn from my mistakes if I made none? I didn't think my marrying was a mistake, though there had been moments. Maybe my mother had those moments too. I wondered how she wove them into the gracious, loving woman I so missed.

Another thirty miles beyond the fort and we entered the Touchet River valley. And oh, the grass! It was just as Mr. Warren had described. We watched as the cattle meandered down the ridge to the river, then disappeared in the meadow, their beige backs like raw potato slices among a sea of mustard greens. Their big heads and long horns pushed the grasses aside, the sun spattering across the horns like flickering firelight. They spread out, the nearly three hundred he'd begun with. "No small feat," he told me. "If I ever need a job, I can drive cattle across the mountains."

"You have employment," I said. "Taking care of your family."

"And my cows."

I was happy to see him happy.

Near the river, the land flattened out more, and in the shade of cottonwood trees and with a view of willow bushes, we set our tent. Our life began anew.

"In years to come," Mr. Warren dreamed aloud for me, "the cattle will graze on the upper hills that rise one thousand feet above us, I'd guess. We'll plant wheat there. Here, the grass will sustain those beeves and us as well."

We had the river for water and the bounty of the land on which to build his dream.

And we had each other.

We stayed in the tent for several weeks while the drovers constructed the log house we would eventually move into. A lean-to off the main cabin would one day be a bunk room for the three drovers, from California, they said. They had worked cattle before the Catholic missions closed there. They spoke another language among the three of them, Spanish. I thought I'd learn it too.

The building came slowly, as the men rode out every few days to keep the cattle from wandering into the next territory. I was alone with my daughters then. I found time to write, hoping for a wagon to take my letter west to family. I hadn't heard back from my father after telling him the cattle had made it over the pass nor of my invitation for them to join us. I knew that not far away, about eleven miles, were the remains of Waiilatpu, and I knew that one day I would go there. Perhaps at last to say good-bye to the teacher, Mr. Rogers, whom we all loved; to the Whitmans, whom I adored as well, especially Mrs. Whitman. Mrs. Whitman had treated us white children with such care.

I'd gotten the drovers—Jose, Romano, and a man we called "Pet" to build a willow fence around the yard that the sheep kept clipped but also to keep the children away from the river. Mrs. Whitman's grief began when her little Alice drowned living close to a rushing stream. I didn't want to lose a child to the Touchet. I remembered at Lapwai looking for the Littlejohns' boy and hearing horrified screams as his mother and mine searched for him along the Clearwater; crying as the Nez Perce divers pulled his body out in the late afternoon. We'd had a fence at Lapwai. I made sure this one would keep my girls in.

It didn't keep the rattlesnakes out, however. And each morning before I let America Jane run outdoors chasing the Kelpie when the dog wasn't otherwise "employed" with cows, I'd beat the grasses, shout to them to head on away, to look for mice another day. I didn't want them killed. They had their work to do. I wanted them to do that work away from those I loved. Lizzie crawled and pulled herself up on me when I sat in the rocker under the tree and knitted winter socks.

On a day in early August with the cabin half finished, Mr. Warren and the drovers left to go into the hills to check the cows' pasture again. In the evening dusk, I took out my leather tools and worked a strip of hide that might one day become a belt. It wasn't like baking, where my efforts were quickly eaten; tooling leather was a lasting art. One that soothed.

The men had been gone a day when a family heading east stopped at our site. I wasn't wary. From a long distance I could see the rider make his way with a pack animal. A second rider followed him. The sheep bleated at his arrival and I recognized him then as the mixed-blood man we'd followed with his family the year my father and brother and I went to the ocean. He carried a letter from my father. I waited until I'd fed them and they'd moved on before reading it.

The letter told of news, that Nancy and her Andrew had set a wedding date for the following year.

On yet a more important note, Rachel and I have taken your advice. We are buying cattle.

We will drive them over Wiley's pass and run them with yours. Expect me and the girls in August. Rachel will come when the school term ends in October. Your sisters are looking forward to being with you again.

I hadn't told Mr. Warren I'd invited him! That might have been a mistake, but I saw it as the road to reconciliation for them and for me when I'd sent my letter. I never expected my father to actually do it. Make a visit, that's what I'd suggested. Or had I offered more? Mr. Warren had planned for this journey for years and my father impulsively listens to me after one missive? I'd invited him to visit, but he buys cattle and joins us? What would Mr. Warren think? I spent that evening tossing in my bed. America Jane kicked off the light cover over us as the heat of August stayed the night. I saw the sun come up. "Grateful I am," I told my girls.

I'd finished my daily Bible reading in the morning and written a congratulatory letter to Nancy when I stepped outside the tent and saw the road filled with dust. Maybe thirty Indian horses with riders came over the ridge and down the trail, their hooves like the thunder of the waterfalls; like the sham spectacle my father had asked the Nez Perce to display. Were they Yakima? Cayuse? Umatilla? Nez Perce? Enemy or friend?

"Quick, girls, stay inside." America Jane stood rooted, staring at the dust. "We'll play a game. America Jane, you hide under the tick, pretend you're playing in snow." *Had she ever seen deep snow?* "Pretend you are a mouse hiding under the quilt. Take Lizzie with you. Try to keep her quiet." My heart pounded. "Don't come out no matter what you see or hear."

I grabbed the varmint rifle next to the door while their eyes bore into me like dark stones inside the whites. Lizzie began to whimper.

"No." I hissed. "No sounds. America Jane, hold her close. You are mice hiding from the hawk. Not a sound. Go. Now."

My throat felt parched as the chicken house floor. My hands shook and I felt sweat dripping down my ribs. There were too many riders, but I could hit a few perhaps, let them know I was in control. Keep bullets enough to shoot my children and myself, if necessary.

I stood beside my rocker, heart hammering as a butter churn, my fingers feeling fat and sluggish near the trigger as I held the rifle at my side. When the dust settled around them, the lead man said, "The Nimíipuu bring greetings. There is no need for weapons."

The voice was soothing and in some odd way familiar.

"What do you want?"

"We camp here." He wore a head band around

straight black hair that rested on his shoulders. He spread his arms out wide to take in our tent and beginning cabin, the river and the land. We'd taken their place just as the Whitmans had done, settled; uninvited.

"Each year," he continued, "but not all year."

He spoke in English, but I responded in Sahaptin, the language slipping from my tongue as though I were ten. "My husband and I were unaware."

He frowned. "Eliza Spalding?"

"Yes. But how do you know that?"

He sang out my name again, dismounted. "It is Timothy. We hear that you have come to this country."

I put the rifle stock to the ground, held the barrel with my hand.

"You are frightened? Do you not remember your old friend?"

From far away his voice carried across the years. "The one who left me behind at Waiilatpu."

His eyes softened. "Yes. That Timothy."

"I . . . I . . ."

He opened his arms to me then and I found myself dropping the rifle and, like a grateful ten-year-old child, running into them.

I cannot describe the joy, the reunion. A few of the others I also knew. I asked after Matilda, learned she had died, but Timothy said Old

313

Joseph, my father's first convert, spent winters near Lapwai as before and worshiped in the old building. "We keep the old ways but your father's Jesus ways too. Sometimes. Some do not understand why he left us, you and your father and mother."

"Why we left you? But you didn't prevent what happened. The Cayuse are your relatives, you could have stopped it. Then you sent us away and chased the hostage bateau to make sure we left."

"You believe this?" He pushed back strands of long hair the wind teased.

"I do. You took my family up the canyon and held them hostage there. Isn't that why my father couldn't come to save me?"

"This is a false story you tell yourself. He could not come because his presence would have risked all the hostages, maybe your family and all those with white skin. Blood filled the air and made men foolish. But your father chose wisely, though he hated to let you be there at Waiilatpu. We had to hold him back. Your mother, too, had to hold him back. And at the end, we escort the bateau, for safety, happy the ransom was paid. We could not prevent what one tribe chose to do, but we could protect the agreement made to release you. That is what we did."

"But I thought . . ." How had I confused their intent? "You didn't force us from Lapwai?

Prevent us from taking our clothes and books?"

"We thought it safer for you to go to those white towns for a time, but we wondered why Spaldings didn't come back to us."

For a time. My mind swirled like a river eddy. My father blamed the Catholics and the Mission Board. I blamed the Nez Perce. Who did my mother blame, or did she?

He looked around. "I do not see your mother or father. They have gone to heaven?"

"My mother."

He spoke in Sahaptin to those who had dismounted, telling them of my mother's passing. "Your mother was loved."

"I know."

"Your father too. We did not understand why he did not come back once you were free."

I frowned. *They wanted us back?* "My father writes to the Mission Board every month, beg=ging those men to allow him to return. But you do not want us."

"Who tells you this?"

"You sent us away. My father . . . he tries to tell them that you are not warring Cayuse or Yakima, but all Indians are the same to the Board."

"As some of my people see all white people too."

"My father is coming here. You will come back when he visits?"

His face broke into a wide smile. "We will stay. We stay to see Father Spalding."

"And us? My family and I. We are intruding, I know, but can we remain?"

"It is your way," he said. "But we know a daughter is like her father: faithful, caring of The People and the land. Planting." He nodded toward my small garden patch, one of the first things I'd completed after we arrived. *Am I like my father in other ways too? Strident. Forceful. Stubborn. Unwilling to forgive or see other possibilities.*

"Yes, planting." That's what my parents had done: planted wheat and potatoes but more, planted the love of God into the hearts of many.

The Nez Perce set up their camp a short distance beyond our tent, dogs sniffing history at old haunts. I thought then of how easily The People accommodated our intrusion. I brought my girls out and introduced America Jane, who curtsied her respect, then ever curious, eased her way into the throng of children who were part of the Nez Perce party. I held Lizzie on my hip, bouncing her as I listened to the sounds of people laughing as they worked, watched the horses be unloaded of their travois packs and be set free to tear at grasses. Skin-covered tipis rose up like white asters, dotting the landscape along the river. Timothy introduced me then to his wife and children. I served them dried beef and knew when Mr. Warren returned we would slaughter a cow and serve fresh meat. We'd have a feast of welcome. Maybe they had tried to keep us safe and protect my parents and siblings. At least today my girls would experience the pleasure of these people before Waiilatpu, as I once had. There'd be so much to tell Mr. Warren when he returned, to ask my father when he arrived. Evening settled on us like a knitted shawl. And in the quiet I organized my thoughts. Timothy squatted on his heels before the small fire I'd built outside the tent to keep the coffee hot.

"We aren't far from that place where I last saw you," I told Timothy. "Do you remember that day?"

Timothy drank the grain coffee I'd prepared. I sat on the rocking chair just outside my tent, holding Lizzie on my lap. Dogs barked in the distance and thin threads of smoke rose up into the red sunset sky. The sun felt warm against my face, heat bristled beneath my collar.

"I remember. We go by that place when we return to Lapwai, and I speak a prayer to the Great Spirit and to the Jesus God that their souls rest. I would take you there?"

"All that sadness? No. I couldn't."

"Sadness. Yes, this is a good way to say what happened there." He took another sip from the tin cup and Lizzie fussed so I put her down to crawl on the blanket beside me, handed her a wooden toy I kept in my apron so she'd sit. She wasn't yet strong enough to stand alone nor pull up without help. I wasn't sure I was either.

"You were a sad child at that place." Fire

sparks flitted up into the sky. "I wished to rescue you but could not. It is a lesson I have learned often since. Some things cannot be changed. We must fill the vessel we are given."

I stroked my daughter's dark hair. "Someday, maybe."

"When you are ready, I will take you there, Eliza Spalding, so you can put bad memories to sleep forever."

"It's Eliza Spalding Warren. And maybe one day I'll go with you." I still had another to forgive—myself. I had not acted as I might have to blunt the pain so many felt at Waiilatpu.

❧ 23 ❧

KNITTING LIVES

"They're friendly Indians?"

"Yes, of course. Timothy was an early convert of my parents."

Mr. Warren had returned, leaving the drovers with the cattle, and his welcome to the Nez Perce was a wary one as we stood outside the tent. "How'd they find us?"

"Timothy said he heard I was here. From someone in The Dalles, I imagine."

"Will they stay the winter? They're consuming grass here and some of those tipis are set right where I hope to build the barn."

I hadn't been aware of my husband's animosity toward the Indian people. I wondered if Little Shoot had left so abruptly on his own. "They'll likely leave as soon as Father gets here and they can see him."

"Your father is coming? When did that happen?"

"He wrote." I picked at a button on his vest. "He's bought cattle and he and my sisters are bringing them through, the way you came, and heading to the Touchet River. They're . . . it looks like they'd like to settle here, too, run their cows with ours."

"What? The whole Spalding spawn is coming here?"

"Spawn. What a terrible thing to say of my family."

"You're right. I love your sisters like the ones I never had." He brushed my hand away. "You organized this, I know it. You can't just let things unfold on their own."

"I have been like that, I know. And it's brought you a consternation. But I sent the invitation *to visit,* really that's all I suggested." *Hadn't I?* "I would like to have a bridge between my father and me. Between the two of you too. My father took on the rest. You know how impulsive he can be. You're like him in that way."

Had I married in part to get away from my father and found a man not all that much different from him? If that was so, then God must have a sense of humor.

"I don't think I'm anything like your pa." He cleared his throat of the dust and spat.

"Let's just see what happens. He may not even come." Timothy and several men approached then and I put my hand on Mr. Warren's arm. "Be pleasant."

He snorted, tossed what was left of his coffee onto the trampled grass, the beads of moisture sparkling in the morning sunlight.

"We would finish your cabin. If you would seek this."

Mr. Warren didn't say anything at all. I nudged him.

"My father helped build Father Spalding's house," Timothy continued.

"That was a very large building." I remembered it. "Eighteen by forty-eight feet. Mother taught school at one end and sometimes she had two hundred students. Father held church at the other end."

"We studied outside often."

"Mr. Warren, will you accept the offer of his help?"

"Yeah? Well, sure. Having extra hands to build would be a good thing. Especially if your father's coming. I want a separate house."

And so as with my parents, the Nez Perce people worked to construct our home along another river. The logs they dragged from the copses of trees that dotted the rounded hills, and the work was made so much easier with their many hands. One day two other pairs of hands arrived to assist. The O'Donnell brothers, James and John, with their Irish accents and a "bit of the thirst" they thought needed quenching. I recognized them. They were Mr. Warren's gaming friends.

"So I'm not the only one who sent invitations."

"I didn't think they'd come." Mr. Warren dropped his eyes, found his boot toe needed concentration. Later that evening he added, "They wouldn't help with the cattle drive, so I figured . . ." I felt him shrug his shoulders as we curled beneath the light blanket in the tent. Tomorrow we'd set the ridge line on the cabin. Adobe built the fireplace, though I still hoped for that stove that Mr. Warren had promised.

"You made a promise, you said. Not to me, you said."

"I didn't take their offer to imbibe, did I?" He turned away from me.

I pressed my hand against his shirtless back. "No. You didn't. And I'm grateful. And I'll treat them as your friends. After all, they brought you home one night and probably saved your leg."

Quick as a snake strike he turned to me. "Don't bring up old things, 'Liza. It does no good and it angers me."

I pulled away, startled by the intensity.

"I . . . I was only saying I'd treat them well. As I hope you'll treat my family when they arrive."

"Good. Just do what you're going to do without telling me about all my past sins and omissions, all right?"

"Yes. All right."

I lay awake long after I heard his heavy sleep-filled breathing. I wasn't sure I knew how to have a conversation with my husband that wasn't laced with the poisonous past. I'd worn that path so soundly I didn't see there were other trails that I could take. With both him and my father I needed to make some change or I'd be doing what

I'd always done, and that hadn't taken me where I wanted to go.

What did I want then? To be full again, as I had been when I was ten before I lost all semblance of a normal life. To be safe. I didn't want to imagine disasters or whine. I wanted a happy marriage. I wanted my children to know their father and enjoy his company. I wanted to see my father bounce his granddaughters on his knees. I even wanted to have a different life with Rachel, to stop comparing her to my mother. And I wanted my mother's legacy to be remembered. Not only of her love for us but for her life's work cut short. I could see how the Nez Perce still loved her and the stories. And The People loved me too. If I could forgive what I thought had happened, I might let their kindnesses fill up my hollow place.

Late August and the heat sweltered as I tugged at garden weeds. I could smell the fish baking at the low fires and knew we'd have a feast that night. The salmon run, as they called it, had reached the Walla Walla and the Touchet River too. We'd have slabs of dried fish to feed us through the winter.

"Mama, look!" America Jane pointed at a slender man wearing a wide-brimmed hat. He looked familiar and I recognized his walk. Joy rose up.

"Henry Hart, what are you doing here? I thought you were freighting somewhere." My brother hugged me, his back carrying no fat beneath my fingers.

"I was. Still am in a way. I've a place, on the Snake River. I supply travelers and work with the army to bring food to the new reservations."

"But how did you know we were here?"

"Word travels on Indian smoke." He grinned. He was tall and bronzed as an Indian, handsome, my little brother. "And these are my nieces." He held each girl. I wondered if there was a woman in his life and asked. "Nope. Still a bachelor and that's all right. I'd like to have something to offer a wife and at present I'm still pretty . . . well, let's just say I'm glad the Yakima wars are over and they're letting some folks come this way looking for gold. Things should pick up then."

"Are the strikes near here?"

"North," he said. "They're prospecting and a few nuggets have been found. Word will get out and then I'll be in better shape. I'll freight into the mines." I hoped Mr. Warren wouldn't take it in his head to search for gold.

"You're here now and I couldn't be happier. Guess who else is here?" We walked toward the tipis and my brother clasped the forearm of Timothy, a sign of respectful greeting between friends.

My father arrived shortly after. About twenty

head of cattle, their long horns glistening in the sun, came shrouded in dust. "Stay away, America Jane. They're not friendly like our milk cows. Let your grandfather push them along."

But it wasn't my father pushing them at all, it was Millie and Martha Jane, both girls riding astride. My father drove the wagon drawn by two fine-looking mules. Another man sat beside him. I'd hoped it might be Little Shoot but it wasn't. I could see that from a distance, as the man was shorter. My sisters shouted and waved ropes over their heads keeping the cattle moving away from the cabin area and where the Indians camped. Several Nez Perce mounted bareback horses and kept the herd in check until they fanned out beyond us into the tall grasses turning brown away from the water. We hadn't had any rain since the day we'd arrived.

Behind the herd and in front of my father's wagon came two shoats. I hadn't seen the pigs in the cattle dust. No sheep, but pigs. And there were chickens in cages hung along the wagon side. He was definitely here to stay.

Mr. Warren may not have welcomed my father with open arms but the Nez Perce did. Tears filled my eyes as I saw my father grow taller in their company, wrapped in their praises. Their happy chatter was a music chime. And then real music rose up, old hymns my mother had taught them in Sahaptin and English, sung with vigor. They all remembered the words and I did too. Even my brother stumbled through some of the Nez Perce versions. "I was never as good at languages as you, Eliza." If I didn't think about the language, in the music, it just came, like grace, without me doing anything to make it happen. They repeated the song in English and I so wished my mother could have been there to hear it all, to see that much remained after we left our life at Lapwai.

At the evening feast prepared in my father's honor, my sisters and I danced with Timothy's wife and the other women, toe-heel, toe-heel in a circle while the drums pounded. For a brief moment I heard the drums at Waiilatpu, but I made myself stay safely with my sisters, dancing beside the Touchet River. Mr. Welch, the driver who'd come with my father, let himself be pulled up into the throng while giggling Nez Perce women showed him how to circle dance. He laughed. Soon my brother joined them, his lean body as tall as Timothy's. He smiled into the eyes of a Nez Perce girl. I looked over at Mr. Warren standing beside the cabin, thinking I'd invite him to dance, too, but he wasn't smiling.

"Join us," I said, walking toward him.

"Welch has two left feet and I'd have two right feet." He scuffed the dirt with his boot, the brim of his hat hid his eyes. "Your brother's pretty light on his toes, though." He pulled me to him then, kissed the top of my head as he put his arm over my shoulder. He wore a sheepish grin, so he hadn't been upset, just feeling awkward.

"But see, it's just a simple step repeated. You'll get the hang of it." He made no move to join me so I stood beside him, watching.

"They love my father. And look at him. He's smiling in ways I've never seen, at least not since that day when I returned from Waiilatpu. I'd forgotten how happy he can look."

"He'd be a lot happier if you hadn't married me."

I refused to pick up his bait. "But I did marry you." I kissed his cheek. "And I have no regrets."

"You don't?"

"Do you?"

"You can be a hard woman to please, Eliza. But no, I've no regrets. And I'm glad you came along." He turned to me then. "I'm a difficult man. I've made mistakes. But this cattle thing, I think we're set with this."

"They look to thrive."

"And so will we. I guess your father's coming with a few head more won't make much difference. And he brought pigs."

"Yes. Ham and bacon for Christmas, assuming that shoat's pregnant."

"But his bringing cattle means he sees the merit in this too. My own pa didn't. He thought I was crazy. Like you did, I suspect."

"Not crazy. Just a dreamer. I guess I'd lost my dreaming ways when Mama died."

"I know you wanted to go to school."

I shrugged, but his sensitivity to that loss of mine was warm water soothing my soul. "I did. But I've good books to read. And I can teach my girls. And more people will come here, when they see how fruitful the land is. The Whitmans did pick a beautiful country. If only they hadn't chosen a field the Cayuse claimed as sacred."

"What's done is done."

"Yes. And we are here ready to start a new life."

But then every day is a day that starts a new life, that requires knitting and going back to pick up lost stitches.

⇝ 24 ⇜
PICKING UP
LOST STITCHES

I greeted the O'Donnell brothers respectfully, fed them, watched as my husband joined in their banter, each of them drinking only my grain coffee. But the brothers weren't here to stay. "We're seekin' a sheep herding job, don't ye know."

"We have two sheep," Mr. Warren said.

"Aye, but they're herded by the Kelpie. No need of us."

I packed a lunch for them, patted the saddlebag as I pulled the leather down. It surprised me that resentment seemed to leave with them.

Henry made ready to leave, too, but saying good-bye didn't seem as final as when I'd last seen him at the Academy.

"You left without ever telling me," I said. "It seemed forever before Father told me where you'd gone."

"I didn't see a future in Brownsville. Father and Rachel were settled and there I was with them, the girls having moved in with you." He shrugged. "And maybe I was still a little mad at you that you didn't find a way to go to school."

"And then there was that incident with the ring, your taking the blame."

He frowned. "Oh, pshaw, I'd forgotten about that. You should too. Do you still have it?" I nodded. "Maybe it's time to give it back to Father."

I shook my head. "No, Mother wouldn't have wanted him to marry again as he did. She wouldn't want that ring on Rachel's finger."

"You can't be certain."

"A daughter knows those sorts of things without being told."

"Huh. That intuition thing is beyond me."

"At least now you're within a week's ride of us."

"If you ever need anything, send word."

"By . . . ?"

"The Indians, of course. They travel here and there and everywhere, even ones supposed to be on reservations. They'll help you, too, if you treat them square." We hugged and then went out to talk with our father, working in my garden. Together they walked over to Timothy's camp.

My father and sisters had other plans too. They had no intention of remaining with us, or at least my father didn't want to stay. Millie would have joined us. Even Martha mellowed.

"You have a roof over your head and a fireplace," Martha said. "We've got a leaky tent."

Father approached as she whined.

"You have a cookstove," I pointed out, wishing my father had brought mine. Mr. Warren had not kept that promise, at least not yet.

"But when it rains—"

"With Nimíipuu hands we'll have our own cabin before snow flies."

Mr. Welch, my father's driver, had moved on before my father's cabin was even built, seeking work at a settlement growing upriver they now called Walla Walla.

My father spoke his ruling as law and Martha stomped away, defeated.

"Any letters you want to send, best get them ready." My father cinched the horse Millie would be riding. I thought again that the girl would cinch her own horse, but my father just liked doing things for her, his "little invalid," he sometimes called her to her rolling eyes, though she did complain about her aching back after she rode. "I'll take them when I go to meet the steamship and bring Rachel here in October. Meanwhile, my girls are staying with me."

"Here though," I clarified. "With us. You'll build a cabin on this site."

"No, not here. Why would you think that? There's nice acreage south, just a few miles. We'll build there. Starting tomorrow. Henry's going to help before he leaves. I told him that was the least he could do after deserting us like he did all those years ago."

I didn't ask for the story. There were things that had happened under my father's roof that I had no knowledge of. I'd thought my brother finding an occupation was my father's wish. Apparently not. There were so many issues never discussed in our family. I wanted to talk with him about Timothy's offer to take me to Waiilatpu, but now didn't seem the time.

I'd have to travel a bit to bring that subject up.

Martha Jane was not happy about them heading south. I wasn't sure why she was so adamant about staying with us, especially since our alter-cation when I foiled her wedding. I would have welcomed her assistance. That's what I told my father.

"She's fourteen," he growled. "I will decide where she lives and where she doesn't. Until Rachel gets here, I need her more than you do. Millie, bless her, can't cook up vittles like her sister."

"Maybe she'd learn if Martha wasn't there to do it for you all." I pulled the iron bale from the sidewall near the fireplace and stirred the potato stew I brewed. Sweat beaded on my forehead. The August heat sweltered.

"I've spoiled her, but she's sickly."

I'd seen her riding that horse like she was born to it. She danced with the Nez Perce girls without a hitch and giggled with the Nez Perce boys. "Sickly?"

"You don't see it, but I do. She has her discomforts."

Her monthlies. Yes, those could be troublesome. "But only for a few days a month."

"It goes on longer. She needs rest and not cooking for an old man, his wife, and her sister."

I didn't say that he'd never granted me that luxury when my heart was breaking over Mama's death, those lost times after Waiilatpu. And what about Martha Jane? She had taken my place in looking after them all.

"Millie can stay here with you if you like. Just until the baby gets a little older."

Millie would whine about doing the work. I thought of Martha Jane who would likely grow more morose if her sister got to remain and she didn't. "No, you know Millie best. When Rachel arrives we can talk again."

"Sensible girl. I see you've matured some, despite choosing Warren against my will."

I sighed, then walked outside to tell Martha Jane what had transpired.

"I want to stay with you. They're like children sometimes, Papa and Rachel and Millie too. They seem so needy."

"I'd be asking you to work here, too, if you stay."

"Yes, but if I did, then I could see Bill when he arrives." She clasped her hand over her mouth.

I lifted my eyebrows. Then, "I won't say anything. You're fourteen. I never should have interfered. I thought I could prevent heartache from hitting you. But I can't. Any more than 'saving' you from disgrace—"

"It's not a disgrace to marry someone you love!"

"Keep your voice down. Father will hear you. I meant that I had no right to say anything. I was trying to protect you, to keep you from making a mistake."

"As you did with Andrew?"

"No." I struggled to find words. "My shame is living when so many didn't."

" 'Liza, you don't have to—"

"For not saving them, the ones who died, the ones like Lorinda who were used up. Even having Father send Matilda Sager off because seeing her made me go away in my thoughts. Those were mistakes. Marrying Andrew wasn't."

"I don't remember Matilda Sager."

"But you do remember some of it."

She nodded. "I remember Mama's eyes filled with terror and I didn't know why. What was I, three? What I said to you the night after Papa followed Bill and me, about all I remembered, I really didn't. It was just stories other people told me later. I think that happens sometimes, our memories get tangled up with other people's. But I could still tell there was trouble. And the Indians rushed us away, upriver, and we waited. Mama prayed and prayed."

"She always did."

"Not like then, though." Martha sighed. "I wish I was more like her."

I looked at her. "That's a hope of mine as well. Maybe we could do what she and the other missionary women did—pray each morning between 8:00 a.m. and 9:00 a.m."

"We could try that."

"I'm not sure we're meant to be as good as Mother was, but knowing you're thinking of me at the same time would bring a comfort."

"She figured out how to live with Father."

I laughed. "She did. Can you forgive me for keeping you from Bill?" I'd asked around after the attempted elopement, and people said it was too bad because Bill was a good man.

"Only if you don't do it again," she whispered. "He's coming here next spring. I'll be fifteen in March and Father won't be able to stop me then."

"I'll keep your secret."

And I would, my silence knitting a thread of closeness to my sister.

I sent letters with my father when he rode to pick up Rachel at The Dalles that October. Nancy would receive one from me, and Matilda Sager who had moved just south of Weston, a town only a couple of days' ride from Touchet. My father knew that Matilda had married a year after Mr. Warren and me. She already had three children.

I hoped she had a happy life and wanted to tell her of my sorrow that, when she lived with us, I had become so inward my parents sent her away. I was glad she'd found someone to love with the courage to receive it back. That was the greatest healing balm, I decided. Someone to love and, if fortunate, to love you back.

Mr. Warren was gone often that fall, and after the Nez Perce moved on, I was alone with my girls. I was almost glad then that the Ruckers and even Little Shoot hadn't remained. Each day I could read the Scriptures and pray at our allotted time, thinking of my sisters. I kept my children safe, put up my garden harvest, carded and spun and tended the sheep and the two piglets my father sent over for us. Meadowlarks serenaded, their slender bodies weaving on a single blade of grass. The smells—dry earth, the cook fire, my laundry soap—pieced the morning. I drew strength from this landscape, strength I didn't know I needed.

The winter turned out to be mild with only a few dustings of snow, and grass aplenty fed the herd. Rain fell in sheets in November, gouged the ridges, but lasted only days, not weeks as in Brownsville. Without mishap, we rode to my father's for Christmas that year, celebrated the New Year in our own cabin with the drovers eating at our table before heading back into the hills. After we rounded the cattle up and branded them—something Mr. Warren insisted we'd need to do—they'd drive a portion of the herd into The Dalles in the spring and sell them. At least, that was the plan.

Spring came on balmy and early. I planted my garden seeds inside potato skins and squash hulls, kept them by the hearth, waiting to see if we'd have a spring freeze. In March we all rode over to my father's to celebrate Martha Jane's fifteenth birthday on the twentieth. Bill Wigle had already arrived. I recognized his sorrel horse as we rode up.

There wasn't much of an argument, which surprised me. Bill was firm and clear about his intentions. Martha Jane was old enough to decide things for herself. "You, sir," he told my father, "need to accept her choice as well."

"He's right." Rachel patted my father's arm. "They can make it work. We made it work."

"We had experience, years on us. She's so young. Too young." He opened and closed his fists at his side.

"Martha's had her share of living as well. Frankly," Rachel nodded to Martha Jane, "I'd like to protest the marriage because she takes such good care of us. But I must not be selfish. You must not be either, Husband."

His fists sank into open palms he raised, begging, something I'd never seen him do. "At least do it officially. Don't go running off like your sister. Let God be the primary witness and the rest of us too."

Martha kissed his cheek. "Thank you, Father."

"What would you say about you officiating?" Bill had a baritone voice that carried authority with it.

"That's a wonderful idea," I said. "Then you can go to The Dalles and repeat the ceremony officially. Traveling a hard thirty miles a day, it would take us five, maybe six days to make The Dalles. The same distance back."

"You'll repeat the ceremony in The Dalles?"

"Absolutely, sir."

"Fine. Might as well do it today. After you plant the garden. I'll see then how hard you work."

Martha Jane's pink cheeks set off the sparkle in her eyes as she stood before our father twenty days after her birthday, Bill at her side. I felt all teary, almost as though a daughter of my own was marrying. I had helped raise her and I wanted to believe the bigness of her heart—loving and forgiving me for interfering—were also traits I passed on. They also came from our mother; and yes, I was beginning to see, from our father too.

✺ 25 ✺

A STUDIED CHANGE

The dry summer heat visited all season, without a drop of rain for more than sixty days. The girls played inside, out of the hot sun, as the willows offered little shade. We were wary of snakes making their way from the foothills to the river and keeping the girls inside prevented my being constantly on patrol. Still, a coiled rattler might appear on the doorstep where the porch offered cool. Or in the privy. Or anywhere in between. The ground proved hard and drier than was good for a garden, so I hauled more water than I had the year before. And the herd's grasses sprouted early too, but without the rain nor a preceding season of snow, the grass didn't grow to the heights that welcomed us the previous summer. At this rate, there'd be little feed for the cattle without pushing them far. If even then. But maybe inland things were better. Rain did fall, but in hard bursts, too fast to soak the earth and discharge its life-sustaining force little by little.

In September, Mr. Warren drove one hundred head to The Dalles where they were purchased, slaughtered, dried, and sold, much of the beef shipped downriver to the Willamette Valley, where Martha and Bill lived. They stayed with his brother, farming on fertile land. Our house in Brownsville stood empty. I hoped my woodstove was still there and more than a nest for mice.

My brother bought several head for butchering and sale at his post and to freight in to the miners, more coming in to look for gold.

"Didn't get the price I really wanted." Mr. Warren pulled his gloves off upon his return from The Dalles. "Seems lots of people are selling out because the feed's so poor. We need a good, wet winter to keep the price up."

"And if we don't get it?" I put tooth powder on Lizzie's brush.

"That's the gamble, darlin'. Ranching is all about the gamble."

"And trying to decide what we control and what we don't."

We didn't get the wet winter we wanted. Never had I prayed for the rainy season as I did that year. I hoped something would sell—our home— or we should sell more cows. The wheat we planted looked neglected. Without rain, it was. When I wasn't tending my family, piecing quilts, scaring off raccoons from the chicken yard, and considering our future, I had time to think about the future and the past. About what Timothy had said, and my father. And how I might have mixed up what happened at Waiilatpu and Lapwai all those years before.

• • •

In the spring of '61, I raised the issue of the dry winter and my concern about the cattle surviving this new year. My husband frowned.

"This isn't any problem, Eliza. A fellow has to weather the ups and downs of the market. We still have a large herd, and yes, we drive them farther to get them feed, but we find it. And no one's told us we can't be where we are. Where would we go with two hundred fifty head of cattle?"

"But you risk danger, being on Indian lands."

"From who?"

"Whom," I corrected. "From the government if they find out we've been using the land set aside for Indians."

"They adjusted usage for the miners. They'll do it for cattlemen too."

"But they haven't yet. And what if we don't get the rain again? Or we have a hard winter, what then? I think we should sell out and go back to Brownsville." There, I'd said it. Blunt and pushy.

"What's your father say?"

It surprised me he would ask. "I haven't talked with him about it."

"See what he says. I bet he'll argue for staying."

"Timothy thinks it wise to sell and leave."

"He would. He'd be happy to have us *So-ya-po* gone."

"Maybe he would, but he would be honest with me of his assessment."

"What? Are you crazy?" This from my father when I told him of my concerns. "Sell out? No. Why, we had hard times, your mother and me, and we stuck it out."

"But you had no choices."

"We did. We could have gone to Waiilatpu or Fort Vancouver and rode out the season, returned when the weather improved. But we'd have left behind all the Nimíipuu and our sheep and the orchard. No, we had to stay and God gave us a way."

"You didn't have two hundred fifty head of cattle to feed."

"I don't have that many now. My small herd can find feed through the winter. No, you're mistaken and you do your husband a disservice insisting that he leave. Doesn't she, Rachel?"

"A wife must share her concerns, Husband. She would be derelict in her duty if she did not."

"Eliza's stubborn. A wife needs to defer to her husband when she's wrong."

My sister Millie expressed no opinion verbally, but as I left, she raised her eyebrows and showed me clapped hands barely lifted above the waistband of her apron.

I did caution myself, to see if I was pushing Mr. Warren because I'd been left out of the decision-making; or if I was trying to think the worst, as prevention. Or if I didn't like him being gone so much chasing after cattle. But I didn't believe I filtered this solution through fears or old patterns. I could see signs. The cattle hadn't gained as much weight as the previous year. The grass had not grown back in all its flourish. The kelpie walked as though on coals in response to the hot ground that never cooled. My own garden even well-watered couldn't resist the hot sun that stayed warm even when it was near ten o'clock in the evening. The land needed respite, too, and would achieve it however it must.

"I'm concerned enough that I will move back to the valley. Without you, if need be." I told him this in late summer of '61. He'd been back less than a day after being gone with the herd for two weeks.

"What?"

"Not as a threat, Mr. Warren. But to prepare, as I believe you'll come to my thinking by next year. But it may be too late then."

"You would just leave me, take the girls, and poof?" He snapped his fingers.

"We'd just be waiting for you 'down the lane,' so to speak."

"A couple of months down the lane." He paced, his agitation a surprise. Then, "I need to imagine you're waiting here. It's part of what keeps me going."

"Does it?"

"Oh, Eliza, if you only knew how much I need

you. And I do respect what you have to say, more than ever since we've been here. Something changed." He scraped his hand through his thick hair.

"It did. I think it's been finding a way to make it on my own, not blaming Father—or you—so much. That's why I believe we need to make this move. Sell, now. Even if Father resists it. If I'm right, we can rebuild the herd when the weather is better. We can start again. But if we wait, we could lose it all, not be able to restart."

"I . . . Let me think on it."

We lay awake side by side that night, a hot breeze blowing. They'd brought the herd in closer and would take the cows upriver seeking untouched grass. They bellowed their discontent. "You really think we should quit?"

"I believe their cries will only get worse."

I'd almost found sleep when he said, "All right. We'll sell. Move back. You win."

I wanted to correct him, say this wasn't a competition, but I didn't. "You will?"

"Yes. I've been trying to think what to do. I can see them skinny as rails, some of them. The grass isn't feeding them like it did, even when there seems to be a lot of it. And wandering so far for feed takes pounds off them too. I . . . wanted to talk with you about it, but I . . . was ashamed."

I blinked. "What on earth do you think is shaming?"

"Bringing you here only to have to turn back."

"We made the decision to come here together. At least, we both wanted it. In the end."

"But then how can we turn our back on it?"

"We have new information. There's nothing to be ashamed of in changing one's mind in a thoughtful, prayerful way. We're doing that. I haven't 'won' anything, Andrew." I stroked his whiskered face.

But I had won something. I'd won a way to speak clearly what I wanted without cajoling him or threatening him or making him feel worse. I'd put out my wishes and I suspect it was that clarity of purpose shown with respect that "won" that day when we decided we would leave.

The Diary of Eliza Spalding

1850, December

Before leaving the States to answer the
Nimíipuu call to bring the Book of Heaven,
we had ruminated about whether to travel with
the Whitmans. How we whispered in our shared
tent, S and I, deciding together as good
marriage partners do. We had buried our first
child before leaving, a grief that joined us rather
than caused a split; I carried with me the pain
of that child's loss. It rode beside my joy in
having a shared life with S.

I rode sidesaddle across the continent with
only one major mishap. My horse startled at a
snake or hornets nested in the ground and I
was thrown except my foot hung up in the
stirrup. I remember Mr. S shouting to a marksman to shoot the horse while my back scraped
against rocks and vines and mountain shrubs,
dust clogged my throat and I thought I would die
and then I lay still when my foot broke free. I
thanked God that I didn't hear the marksman.
Couldn't have, because the horse was caught
and rescued. As was I. But ever after that, my
back pained me. And for just a short time, I
believed I should return with a trapping party

heading east, for I had lost another child. I feared my health would interfere with God's call. S would have nothing of it. He promised to remain with me for as long as needed and the Whitmans too. I was forever grateful, as going back would have been the hardest journey I would ever have had to make. It would have been a disappointment, but turning back doesn't mean one has failed, does it? It can be a needed new direction.

✺ 26 ✺

GRATEFUL I AM

We chose a new direction. It's not easy turning back. We heard of people on the wagon trains who changed their minds. I doubt my parents ever had to make such a choice. I remembered the Exodus of the Bible and how those people wanted to turn back because things got hard. And oh what horror there would have been if they had done so, gone back into bondage, into slavery. But we were not merely selling out; we were starting over even though we'd been in Touchet country less than two years. It takes courage to risk, to quit on one's own terms, taking what you have as the humus for new growth.

"May I go back with you?"

Millie cornered me after I'd told my father we were selling out, taking the herd to market to get what we could get. He was welcome to put his cattle in with ours. He declined.

"I don't think Father will let you."

"I'm nearly sixteen. I can make up my own mind about things."

"I won't pamper you the way Father does."

"Pamper me? I'm doing the cooking and cleaning and laundry and—"

"I've seen Rachel doing laundry. And every second time I come to visit, you're off riding Nellie, so I know you have some time not spent in slavery."

"There's no future here for me. I want to be where people are. I heard a war has started between North and South. It could come here and I'd have lived my short little life without ever knowing true love or true trials or true hope for the future."

She was being dramatic, but then, she always was. Still, I could see how she longed for something more.

"If Father allows it, I'll agree too."

Of course, he didn't. "I need her here. Besides, you've talked Warren into this crazy decision to sell out when you've barely gotten here, so I don't think I trust your judgment. We had hard winters in Lapwai too. We got by. The Lord always provided."

"I fully accept manna from heaven. But he also admonished us to learn what this means. And what this means is that we need to sell and make alternate plans."

"Well, do that without us. Millie included."

I'd packed the wagon yet again, this time secure that I could manage it with the girls, knowing that Mr. Warren would be not far ahead. We had decided to replicate our journey of two years previous. We'd travel together leaving this Touchet country as far as The Dalles. I'd board the steamboat into Portland with the girls. Mr. Warren would sell what he could there, then he and the drovers would head south through the Warm Springs reservation, maybe selling beef to the Indian agency, then through the meadow and across the Cascades coming into the Willamette Valley just east of Brownsville.

We separated at The Dalles and Mr. Warren kissed me beside the wagon before we parted. "Pray the market's better in the Valley."

"I'll pray for a safe journey. For both of us." I kept my anxieties wrapped in prayer.

"See you in a few weeks." Then, "Oh, I have something for you." He pulled a small box from his pocket. "I noticed awhile back that you took off the wedding ring I gave you. I didn't blame you, after my, well, my lapse." He cleared his throat. "These two years in Touchet with you, I've felt more married than I ever did before." He took out a gold ring and slipped it on my finger.

"Can we afford—?"

"It's less than the price of a cow, darlin', and you deserve it."

"It's lovely. I really didn't remove the other one. I lost it. In the manger the night the O'Donnell brothers brought you home."

"Fortuitous."

I punched his shoulder. "You and your big words. Oh, I have a gift for you too."

"You do?"

"I planned to give it to you on your birthday but so much happened in August. Mama had an August birthday too." My mind wandered. "Wait. It's in the trunk."

I handed him a leather belt tooled with his initials in it. *AJW*. "To go with our brand," I said. I'd worked the leather myself in those long hours when Andrew was away. He rubbed his thumbs over the raised letters.

"It's a good gift, 'Liza. No more suspenders." He smiled. "We're not turning back, darlin'. We're startin' everything new. Even how I hold up my pants."

The next morning I headed west on the trail so many other immigrants were taking west, bone weary from their journeys as they embarked on one last section of the trip. Wagons could take the Barlow Trail, a roadway made in 1845, with each new traveler gradually chopping out the overgrowth of trees and shrubs, paying a toll at the other end. A terrible mountain crossing called Laurel Hill took three hours per wagon to lower with ropes down over the rocky ridge. We would take the boat, portage as we needed, then I'd drive the oxen the four days it would take to pull up in front of our old home. I felt strong, stronger than I ever had. The thundering falls of The Dalles a backdrop to my confidence.

"Sister! Pull up!"

I turned and squinted. *Millie?* What was she doing here? And did Father know?

"Millie? What's happened? Are Father and Rachel all right?"

"They're fine. I'm going back to Brownsville with you."

"Father allowed it?"

"Never." She leaned forward, patted her animal's sweaty neck. "Please don't send me back. In the end, he'll know I found you. We'll write him a letter."

She didn't look disheveled even after what had to have been a two-day hard ride. The horse looked winded though. "You slept out alone?"

"I stayed far enough behind you that you couldn't see but I knew where you were. 'Just find Eliza and you'll be fine.' That's what I told my horse." She smiled. "And Timothy rode with me for a ways so I was safe. He headed back several miles ago."

It was all a game to her. I envied her.

"And here we are. I looove adventure." She dismounted and whisked Lizzie into her arms, snuggling her toddler neck.

"Auntie Millie!" America Jane scampered from around the wagon, hugged my sister. Yaka trotted up then, distracted by a rabbit, I guessed.

"You brought Father's dog too?"

"He followed me." Millie shrugged.

My hands gripped the goad used to keep the oxen on a steady trail and I squinted at her. I'd given myself the task of making my way alone with my girls, to test myself. Her presence interrupted it. I had to decide if the responsible thing to do was to make her go back, take her back, or let her come with us. I weighed the options.

"You'll write him a letter." I couldn't take the time to go back.

"I will. But don't you think it's providential that I caught up with you?"

"Providential? I was just thinking it was an inconvenience having to decide whether to send you back or take you back."

"And you've decided well." She grinned, dimples deepening. "Sometimes providential masquerades as inconvenience, but it all works out in the end."

Millie proved to be an expert with the animals as well as with the children. The oxen were like pets to her, standing on the barge we took down the Columbia, letting her hobble them each evening so we wouldn't have to chase them in the morning. And her chatter made the miles go easier as she filled me in on news of life in Brownsville after we had left. "And John Brown, the one who directed you to your Indian driver, he's very nice to me. He remembers I like hard candies and always gives me one when I come into the store."

"He's a bit older than you are."

"Boys my age don't interest me. John likes nice things and he has money to get them."

"And Father's aware of your interest in Mr. Brown?"

"I never told him, of course. I saw what happened with Martha and Bill. No, I just keep it to myself."

He'd be furious with her for leaving Touchet. I looked back several times expecting him to be riding on a raft behind us. He'd have words for me whenever he did catch up and I knew he would. He'd never let his favorite be away from him for long.

Pulling up in front of our old cabin, grateful I was that it had never sold. Grass had grown up around the steps and a portion of the porch roof looked like an old man needing a cane. America Jane jumped down and Lizzie, two and a half, squirmed until I lifted her down to Millie already standing beside the wagon.

"No one's been here for a while."

Inside, the only thing left was the wood cookstove. It had waited for me, that metaphor of my marriage. Solid, holding heat when tended.

I didn't even mind that Mr. Warren had taken

another route and wasn't yet home. I could make it on my own, be a partner to him. I didn't just respond to what he presented; I could initiate and we could work together. Our time in Touchet brought me that. A certain scent told me there was a packrat somewhere near, and when I bent down to close the open oven door I saw the nest. Such flotsam would have sent me railing before Touchet. Now, it seemed perfectly understandable. Ignore what matters and scratchy things take over.

"Eew," Millie said. She'd just bent to the oven.

"We'll have cleaning to do before we do much else. Go get the broom from the wagon. We'll unload that first." She groaned. "And I guess you were right, Millie." I was as cheerful as she'd been when she caught up with me in The Dalles. "Your chasing us and inconveniencing me was definitely providential."

Mr. Warren sold the cattle. We saw old friends those first weeks back and it was a bit like a honeymoon with my being less demanding of my husband and him being home and attentive with his daughters. I saw Nancy and congratulated her and Andrew Kees on their marriage. From travelers, I picked up news about the widening war back East. Things seemed calm enough in Brownsville, the weather mild. I took new interest in my mother's seeds and drove for cuttings at my father's old house. It had not sold either, so I made a point of keeping it swept of spiders. They might come back one day. I planted the lilac starts at the corners of our cabin. Mr. Warren purchased pigs we butchered and hung in the old smoke-house, the scent of cedar strong to my nose. He bought a couple of sheep for me, to replace the others we'd left with father and Rachel. And we had plenty of beef jerked and kept a few animals should we wish one day to start another herd. I couldn't imagine that, but Mr. Warren was insistent and it was an easy compromise for me.

It was November and the chill mixed with the season's steady drizzle. I'd just returned from a visit with the doctor telling me what I already knew, that we'd have a baby in the summer. We'd be closer to medical care even if Millie could midwife.

As I entered the cabin I heard my name shouted from behind me. I pulled my coat around me against the wind and turned. "There's been an accident. Millie asked I come get you." It was John Brown. He wasn't riding really fast, but he did say there'd been an accident.

"Did you ride to the doctor first?"

"No, she said come here. She's just down your lane."

I shouted to Mr. Warren what had happened and for him to get the doctor. "Put the children in the buggy."

"Best bring a wagon if you got it," John said. "She's in a terrible pain and isn't getting up."

"Bring the wagon instead," I directed. I thought about having America Jane look after her sister but decided against it. "Bring a quilt for the girls."

I ran down the lane behind him. The wind had turned and snow threatened. In the distance, I saw my sister's form on the ground, her horse standing beside her.

"What happened?" I knelt beside her, wiped mud and rain from her face.

"It's not the horse's fault. Nor John's. It's not. She stepped in a mole hole and threw me, then rolled over on me, trying to get her balance." Her face was white as oyster shells. "I can't feel my legs. I can't feel my legs, 'Liza." She grabbed at my arms.

"Just be still." I threw my coat over her as she began to shake. Ice pelted down, turning to snow. "Mr. Warren will be along any minute." I wanted to send John for the doctor but thought we'd need him to lift Millie into the wagon. To John I said, "What happened here?"

"It's like she said. We were riding along, well, racing along, and her horse tripped and tossed her, then stumbled right over her. Poor little thing." He looked at the horse, not my sister, when he said that. Then back at Millie.

"Do you have a slicker you can tent over her? She's getting soaked."

"Oh. Sure enough." He unrolled a slicker from behind his saddle and ambled over to us as though he headed toward a bill collector rather than a crisis. "This is sure awful. I had an aunt once who was laid up for life after a horse fall. She never walked again, poor thing."

"I'm not sure we need to hear about that right this minute. Can you hold that slicker wider? She's getting soaked. She'll go into shock."

He maneuvered himself to be more helpful. Asked Millie how she was doing.

"Not so good."

"Sure hope Warren gets here fast. My arms are getting tired holding this up."

"Well, poor you," I snapped. "My sister's lying here injured and all you can think about is your aching arms?"

"Don't, Eliza. He's helping."

She was right. We were all doing the best we could.

The wagon came into sight and Andrew had thought to put a loose board into the back. He pulled it out and as gentle as we could we rolled Millie to her side, trying not to hear her sobs. We pushed the board under her. I saw no blood, but her scream of pain when we touched her back told me more than I wanted to know. The three of us lifted her into the wagon bed. John tied his horse to the rig, then climbed in and continued to hold the slicker over us. The girls were huddled inside quilts at the front of the wagon. They looked like baby birds sticking their heads out from a nest. Andrew pulled his hat down against the sticking snow and drove into Brownsville.

I prayed over my sister then, for her recovery, for this injury to not be as bad as it looked, for it not to be permanent. And I prayed for myself. For when I'd have to tell my father that once again one of his daughters had come unto harm while under my tender care.

That storm began the worst winter we'd known since living on this side of the mountains. By mid-December nearly three feet of snow blanketed the Brownsville ground. One morning the sun shone and a thaw melted the top, but the next night, the temperature dropped below zero, leaving a sheet of hard ice covering everything like a frozen lake. We axed trails to the privy, chopped wood twice a day to keep the wood-stove burning, sawed through ice at the spring to get water. The temperature plummeted to below zero and then stayed there for more than forty days. It had never happened before.

"What does that mean, *Papo*?" America Jane asked as we all hovered around the round tin holding the thermometer every morning.

"Dang cold!" her father said.

The animals could not break through the ice to brush away the snow and eat the grass. We had no hay put up—people didn't do that in the Valley, grass usually growing year-round—so daily Mr. Warren went out in the cold and chopped through ice to water the oxen, the five cows we'd kept, our milk cow, horses, and the sheep. Chickens roosted in the smokehouse. I didn't say it out loud, but I know he wondered too if the cold and snow was even deeper in the Touchet country where my father and Rachel remained. If it was, the cattle would be dead come spring. I prayed my family wouldn't be.

We fell exhausted into bed each night, sometimes entertained ourselves after the outside chores were finished by sitting around the cookstove coming up with "as cold as . . ." similes. As cold as a woman scorned. As cold as a tongue frozen to an icicle. America Jane offered that. "As cold as my feet, but at least I can feel them, Mama." Millie lay on a raised pallet John and Andrew had made for her, recovering. As cold as death did not count for any points. In years to come we would say "As cold as '62," as the year set the standard against which we pioneers compared whatever winter we were in. None were ever as cold and snow-drifted and destructive to cattle and sheep as the winter of '61–'62.

The temperature was hard on Millie, too, her bones shivering. John Brown visited often, bringing treats and treasures from the store. Maple sugar candies. A tin of sweet milk. We discovered the two had been "stepping out" before the accident. She'd gotten some feeling back in her legs for which we praised God. But she needed my arms to sit, use a thunder bucket, and lift her dress off over her head. She was an invalid; something my father had always imagined her to be, fragile and frail. Now she truly was.

He'd be furious when he learned of her condition.

I did not carry the weight that it was my fault. Yes, I could have sent her back to Father when she caught up with us in The Dalles. But he could have come after her and he didn't. And yes, I could have watched her more closely, but I had small children to look after, and Millie's slipping out to ride didn't alarm me as a disaster: it was her pleasure. And she didn't have to always ride as though a fire burned behind her. She could have loped along beside her John. The weather might have been better; the mole hole could have been bored somewhere besides the middle of our lane. There was blame enough to go around but also none to claim. Tragedies happened. People suffered. I was learning that it was what one did with the suffering that mattered.

We did not get news of my father until he and Rachel arrived in the summer of '62 a few weeks after I gave birth to Amelia, named for her now invalid aunt. "She's Minnie," I said. "We can't confuse all the Amelias."

"Millie and Minnie are easy enough to confuse," Andrew told me, but he liked the nickname "sure enough."

We listened to Father's sad story, of how the grass burned to a crisp after we left and how snow started in December and they had six feet by Christmas. The same phenomenon of melting snow turned to ice kept the cattle from the feed. "Snow was chest high and the cattle all died. I . . . It was the saddest thing to hear their moans and not be able to do a thing about it but shoot them out of their misery. Some died before I could get to them, like the air was sucked right out of them, one blizzard came so fast. Sun came out and you'd have thought it a fairy land of sparkle but for the dark blots of carcass, mostly their heads visible above the wintry grave." Tears formed in his eyes, mine too, with the picture of tragedy he painted.

"He cut up some of the dead and we made a meat soup to feed them but they kept dying." Rachel wiped her own tears at the memory. "The temperature dropped to thirty-two degrees below zero and stayed there for forty days. I've never been in such a cold." I noticed three of her fingers were whiter than the rest of her hand and she rubbed them near the fire.

"I hadn't put up any hay. The grass was so

abundant." Father chided himself for not thinking ahead. I could hear it in his voice. But he wasn't alone. No one had.

His grief so raw, he barely flinched when I showed him Millie, his precious one, lying on a settee we'd purchased for her. "I'm getting better, *Papo*. Eliza's taking good care of me. And John is too."

That perked my father up. "John? John who?"

"John Brown. Your friend's son."

"Why, the man's thirty-some years old."

"And able to take care of me. As soon as I can walk again. He's already had canes made for me. And one day, we'll marry."

"I forbid you to marry—until you can walk again."

"That'll be incentive."

I thought of how powerless parents really are to define their children's lives. Thinking of Martha and Bill and even me and my Andrew, it was clear parents often didn't know what was best for their children in the end. My mother had defied her parents before receiving a modicum of support in the form of a wagon, $100, and her father's com-pany for the first hundred miles on their missionary journey to the Nez Perce. After that, she never saw him or her mother again.

I knew nothing of my father's parents, but he certainly challenged the Mission Board, the authority in his life, and still was. He hoped to go back to Lapwai and begin his mission again but wouldn't without consent. If my mother had lived, I had no doubt she'd want to go back with him. That still bothered me. I couldn't shake the truth that The People had deserted us even with what Timothy had said. Even Henry Hart suggested the Nez Perce had been kind. One day, long ago, Father had said as much. Truth was, I didn't want to affirm that I'd wasted time carrying false memories since the time that I was ten. Who would I blame for all the tragedy my family had faced after Waiilatpu if what I remembered was false? Didn't someone need to be blamed?

My father moped that year, had difficulty finding his way. He continued to travel and preach, to write his letters to the newspaper or the Mission Board, any who would listen. Rachel's teaching salary made it possible for them to live frugally in their cabin. But like my husband, I could see my father grow restive. I didn't know how to fix it. Maybe I wasn't supposed to.

⇒ 27 ⇐

NEW SIGHT

"I'm going back." My father spoke as I stopped by to bring fresh bread for him, Rachel, and my sister, Millie, whom Father insisted move back in with them. It was summer. Millie had improved, walked often without her canes, still favored her sore back. My father still cooked but Rachel managed the laundry and the garden. Dried beans hung from the rafters. Millie even rode her horse again, saying that being astride was the best medicine she could have to renew her strength. I admired her spunk and told her so. She and John planned a wedding in November. She lay on the settee we'd sent with her with my youngest, Minnie, playing patty-cake on her lap.

"Where are you going back to? Ohio? New York? Touchet?"

"Lapwai. Timothy and another convert, Raymond, invited me to visit last year but I don't want to go just to visit. I want to stay there, to do my work again. Mission Board be d—" He stopped himself from swearing.

"Rachel, what do you think of that?"

"If that will make him happy, then of course, I'll go with him. But I'm teaching here this year again. He'll have to make the trip alone."

"Maybe I'd go with you, Father." It was an impulsive act, the kind my father would make.

"To stay? To do your mother's work there?"

"No. To make the journey with you. To keep you company. To ride back here later on my own." And make new memories.

We took pack animals as we had when my father took me and Henry Hart on our journeys leaving Mother behind. No wagon. I didn't worry about the two older girls; they were staying with "Granma Rachel" and Millie. Minnie I had with me, the child nursing and never far from the fill. I did sew up the sack where she could ride on the side of the horse, juggled by a rope on the saddle horn. She slept to the rhythm of old Maka's gait.

Along the way the land was littered with cattle carcasses. So many had not survived.

"I should have listened to you and Warren." My father shook his head.

"You weren't alone. Judging by all the sun-bleached bones. We were fortunate. You thought differently."

He wiped his nose. "I wasn't meant to be a cattleman. Preaching, that's my calling. Maybe teaching, though that was your mother's gift, among many. And farming."

"Why didn't you go back earlier, as you're

doing now?" We'd swum the horses and pack mules across the Deschutes River and the John Day and continued to ride beside the Columbia on a well-worn trail, the horses' hooves dusting up puffs despite the rocky path. The hills and lava rock cliffs to our right brought thin but blessed shade.

"I didn't think I could go back without your mother. Oh, she wanted to go, but I had it in my head for the Mission Board to bless this work, to know I was doing it . . . not only for myself." I let the silence sit. "I wasn't certain I was strong enough to return without the Board's blessing. Trying to sort out what's God's will and what's the Reverend Henry Spalding's." He punctuated that last with an awkward chuckle.

"You never doubted that you were called to be there, did you?"

"No. Never. But the politics, the arguments." He sighed, pulled up on the reins to let his horse tear at grass. "And there was a meeting at Whitmans'. Your mother didn't go. I didn't want her to come. I told myself it was so she could continue to do the good work at Lapwai, but I had another reason. The other missionaries, they grumbled about our winning souls in Sahaptin rather than in English. None of the others worked to learn the native languages."

"I remember Mother saying that. I've lost the language, too, mostly."

"Without use it disappears. She was such a great teacher. A better student in Greek and Hebrew than I ever was. I didn't want her to have to hear the hostility toward us from the others. I didn't want her to wonder about what God was having us do there. So I went alone. Oh, I know they talked about me, the missionaries, as this 'distempered man,' but I had to be abrasive to get things done when the authority was so far away. We were all on our own, really. Our gatherings were the only checks we had on each other. And when the recruits arrived, especially the Smiths, there were letters sent back condemning our efforts. Mostly because we taught in Sahaptin and not in English. If only they could have seen the converts, their faithful hearts."

He tugged on the reins and we rode on. After a while he started talking again. This was the most my father had ever shared with me about his work, speaking to me as though I was an adult, not someone he had to teach or preach to, but just be with, to share his failings.

"Whitman was never trained as a preacher. He was to be our doctor and then, there we were, so far away from him, at his insistence choosing Waiilatpu. Or maybe Narcissa's. She could be strong-willed, that one.

"Anyway, I asked myself, what was the point of our coming to start a mission 'together' if our partners were far away? I don't think the Mission

Board could imagine the vastness, or the number of distinctive tribes." My father continued. "The Nimíipuu invited us, not the Cayuse." He shook his head again. "Things got so bad we were dismissed by the Board. I never wanted your mother to know that. And part of the complaint was that she spent too much time teaching in their language and I spent too much time showing them how to make a living in a changing world. It . . . it was a strange time."

"And then Waiilatpu happened."

"And then Waiilatpu happened."

We rode in silence for a time, the breeze warm beside the river. We made a camp and Father shot a deer. After a supper by a fire, he said, "I brought along your mother's diaries." A coyote howled and the horses stomped at their hobbles. "I read them now and then, to remember her. She still tells me what to do." He looked sheepish. He walked to his saddlebags and pulled them out. "It's time you read them."

I held them as though they were gold. No, manna, food to nourish.

We stayed two days to dry the meat beside our fire. And I read. Read of my mother's thoughts those first years, her words as she faded away. And of how she loved The People who became her family more than the missionaries or other whites who visited or stayed. I inhaled her longing to have my father return and even saw that she *wanted* him to remarry. She spoke of Matilda like family, not someone who only worked for her.

"Mother loved Lapwai, the way I once did."

"It was her life. Leaving it killed her."

"She didn't feel they'd deserted you."

"Deserted us? The Nimíipuu? No, no, no. They kept us safe. Good heavens, if they hadn't whisked your mother and the children upriver to a site they could defend, well, I hate to think what might have happened."

"But they knew some of the Cayuse. Couldn't they have stopped it? Don't you blame them just a little for that?"

"People tried to warn Marcus. Even John McLaughlin. You remember. He testified to that. So there were signs but none the Nez Perce could have interrupted."

"Until I spoke with Timothy, I thought they tried to take us back, when we were in the bateau."

"They rode to act as guard so no Cayuse followed."

"That's what he said."

"You carried around these false beliefs all this time? Why didn't you speak to me about them? I'd have set you straight."

I snorted. "Speaking to you had its own challenges. We never could carry on a conversation without leaving tufts of turf dug up. Not like we are today."

He pursed his lips but he didn't disagree.

"I was so alone after Waiilatpu." Minnie fussed and I let her suck my finger.

"I know. Timothy would have brought you back, but he couldn't. He grieved that."

"I thought that you were dead. All of you." I swallowed back memory tears.

"It must have been a terrible time for you. I'm sorry that happened to you, Eliza."

I blinked. *He understands. He does.*

"She . . . she wanted you to go back to Lapwai?"

"She did. Even without the Board's blessing, but I just couldn't. I regret that. But I've decided: I'm going no matter what the Board says."

"There've been so many things I didn't understand. In her diaries . . . she wanted you to find a Rachel?"

"Of course she did. I wouldn't do anything to mar your mother's memory. Rachel's a teacher. Not like your mother was, but a teacher nonetheless who shares my passion for our work. She's a good partner, Eliza. Always was."

"Yes. Yes, I see that now." Those diaries were a gift, though one that contradicted so much of what I'd believed I knew. The past is but a puzzle with pieces missing and misplaced.

When we moved on in the morning, we met a wagon train heading west. We bypassed the "Place of Rye Grass," Waiilatpu, the main trail to

371

Lapwai a few miles south. I wondered if I ought to ask my father to go by there, with his help to face one last shame, but I didn't. And then we left the route and followed the road up into the hills, crossing the Snake, riding beside the Clearwater River to Lapwai Creek where I'd discover what it was that I'd been missing—what my mother had missed too.

Sensing the presence of other horses, our mounts quickened their pace. We rounded a bend and there it stood—the log home and church my parents had lived and worked in, built by the Nez Perce, for them. A few tipis dotted the river's edge. Horses whinnied back to ours. Minnie made noises and I took her from the carrying sack and fed her, sitting beneath an old apple tree in the orchard my father had planted. Quiet like wet earth settled around me and I felt a sacredness in the silence. I didn't know what brought the peace but it was there.

My father hobbled our horses and walked toward me, bent a bit with his aging.

"What will you do here, alone?"

"Oh, if I am meant to be here, I won't be alone," my father said. "All right if I walk to the tipis? They'll have seen us and be sending people our way. I'll be close enough to hear your call if you need me."

"We'll be fine."

I watched him leave us and had a momentary imagining of something terrible happening: a rattler waiting to strike; one of the dissonant tribal members who resented my parents' intrusion coming out to argue with him. I remembered my mother's diary story of him being choked and the first and only time she said she'd become flummoxed. I should call out to him, remind him to be careful. But I remembered Timothy's words and Paul the Apostle's words too: "Finally, brethren, whatsoever things are true, whatsoever things are just, whatsoever things are pure, whatsoever things are lovely . . ." I'd think on those things. My mother had quoted the entire verse in a diary section I'd read the night before.

After Minnie ate, she dozed on my shoulder and I stepped inside the house, that place that had nurtured me those ten years, expecting it to be empty. But someone was kneeling at the far end, kindling the fire. I walked, my feet echoing, but the person did not turn. Then I was in front of him and he looked up. His face registered confusion and then a smile that started at his mouth and spread across his face onto his eyes.

"Do you remember me?"

He shook his head, tapped his ears and mouth. A flash of memory warmed my face. This man had lived with us for a time, helping Mother, pulling me in that little wagon with fir rounds for wheels. His name was Mustups.

"He doesn't speak. And cannot hear you." I turned to a Nez Perce man and my father who'd entered behind me.

"Ask if he knows me?"

The two made signs and then I was told that Mustups rocked my cradle when I was a baby and kept me safely from the river. "He says all these things are yours. All the trees. Seeds your mother planted."

"Which plants?"

He took me outside to a small bed, still maintained, of asters.

"I thought she only planted garden seeds and the lilac bush."

"Your mother loved flowers." My father had his hand on my shoulder. "She had little time for them, but this little plot was special. Didn't you remember?"

"No, I don't."

"Mustups has kept it, it seems. Perhaps he'll keep my grave one day. Bury me here, Daughter." His friend signed, asking if Mustup tended the plot and he nodded. The blooms were gone but I could tell they'd come back in the spring.

I walked around the house then, over to the fence that kept me from the river. I saw where Henry Hart and I had raced each other on our Indian ponies along the water, our hair flying like our horses' manes. The hills were a blanket of brown around me. The quiet of this place vanquished the clashing memories of Waiilatpu. This was a place of peace.

Then near a clearing I drifted in my mind, but felt a tightening in my stomach, and must have clenched Minnie as she stirred on my hip. "Did I press you, little one?" Holding her kept me in Lapwai, though I saw a memory unfold before me. The sham battle, but this time, older now, I watched a child watching men performing as though dancing to the drums. Nothing frightening. Nothing bad happened with that battle except the lingering fear it sent the small child. I heard birds singing, not the screams and howls of men in paint. Beyond, I watched the horses graze by the camp, black tails flicking against white rumps. One raised its head. Maka whinnied back. I was restful. Peaceful. Calm. That child found comfort.

I turned around slowly to take in what my mother would have seen each day: the comfort of the hills, the chattering water, a lone raven overhead, the faces of the people she had come to love. A breeze brushing tendrils of her hair. I could see my mother here, and with a sigh of understanding I knew then what had been missing. Her rest. Her peace. Her calm. One day, I would bring her here to be buried in Lapwai, "the valley of the butterflies," where her life truly began. And where it ended.

"Timothy is expected later," Father said. "And there are others who still worship and hold the faith. Not Old Joseph, I hear. He has separated into another band that resisted the treaty signing. He was my first convert, the first I sprinkled in baptism." He sighed, then brightened. "We'll have worship this Sabbath."

And so we did. It was a marvel to see both familiar faces and many new. Eyes bright with recognition of "our Spalding" and looks of sadness when told of my mother's death. Timothy knew, of course. I'd told him. They sang hymns my mother had taught them, haltingly. "We have not sung them for many years," Timothy told us. I thought my father would be upset, but he patted Timothy's shoulder in understanding, his eyes filled with a kind of joy I hadn't seen for a long time.

"They've forgotten." I held Minnie on my lap while my father picked up the hymnals he'd brought with him. I didn't think they'd done much good. People sang with their eyes closed, from memory, if they sang at all.

"Of course they've forgotten. Unless one nurtures the faith, it disappears."

Blunt as he said it, his words carried no heat to them nor did the message that followed. "It's how I know I belong here. Ours is a God close by as well as far away. Jeremiah 23:23. I bring the message to them of a God who is in all places and who gives them tools to take him with them when they go." His face brightened. "I'm to ensure the watering hole is here and keep the water clear and quenching." He held the stack of hymnals against his vest. "That's how your mother thought of her work—as a mother. To keep the lives of her children clear and quenching."

He whistled then, tapping my daughter's chin as he walked out into the sunshine. She rocked in happiness upon my knees.

Before Minnie and I left, Timothy took me to his stick house. It was up the valley a little way, the smallish structure with a black stove, not a cookstove, but a little heating device. He patted it like a good dog when he walked by and beamed as he pointed to a picture on his wall framed in wood, wobbling glass covering it. It was a painting of blind Bartimaeus, a man healed by Jesus. Beneath it were the words "Presented to Timothy by Mrs. Spalding."

"It is my greatest earthly possession. I love the story. Jesus asked the blind man what he wanted, he did not assume to read his heart. This is your mother. She came and listened. She did not assume to know. She asked in our language what we wanted and I said I wanted to see Jesus. She said it would be so, by merely asking."

I could ask for new things too. And so I did.

❧ 28 ❧

FILLING HOLLOW PLACES

My father remained in Lapwai while I began my journey home with my daughter. I felt a little skip of anxiety going such a distance yet found my father's reference to Jeremiah comforting. God is a God both near and far away. My mother would say I wasn't without guidance. I had the experience of so many journeys, memories I knew were not always trustworthy but that, when they appeared in my days as I rode home, I could transform them, wrap them into the wife, mother, daughter, woman I'd become and hoped to be.

I rode old Maka and had one pack animal I led, and for quite a distance, beyond Lapwai, my escort, Timothy, rode beside us. Because the Nez Perce always traveled with many families together, others followed us, but they stayed back beyond our dust so as not to intrude. Minnie with her dimpled cheeks got handed all around at our campfire that night, and I was grateful that at least one of my children would have a memory perhaps of being loved by Indians as I had been.

As we approached Waiilatpu, I knew what I would do.

"You said you would take me."

Timothy nodded. "I wondered if you would want to make the journey now that your father has found his peace again."

"Maybe there I can find mine."

In the morning, we rode toward that place, Minnie with me, riding the ten or so miles through hills beginning to turn brown from the hot sun. Near the river it was cool and the horses drank at the stream, their bits jangling as they slurped. I held Minnie in front of me, wishing for one of the baby boards the Nez Perce used. I wasn't sure why I hadn't brought the sack. Maybe to keep the heartbeat of my child close that I might use it to steady my own. She liked riding and patted the saddle horn, sitting now outside of my body where months earlier she'd been inside. At least I wasn't riding sidesaddle as my mother always had. How she managed a child while on that precarious seat always remained a mystery, and grateful I was, once again, that we girls were allowed to ride astride. I sewed split skirts for all of us.

With the sway of the horse's gait, my mind wandered to other journeys made through this landscape in which so much had changed and yet remained the same. Memories of that last ride with my mother. Memories of Matilda taking me to this place that fall of '47, taking me to Waiilatpu, that meadow we now came upon. My mouth turned dry and I tried to say something but couldn't get the words out as we entered the perimeter of what had once been the Whitman Mission. "Place of the Rye Grass." I spoke it out loud. The grass grew tall against my horse's withers and it swished against her flesh. It was the only sound I heard as we rode slowly into my past.

There, the adobe mission house stood, transformed by heat and time. Beyond crumbled another such house that emigrants often stayed at, deciding whether to winter with the Whitmans or continue on to The Dalles or race the snow, crossing the mountains into the Willamette Valley. Some had chosen to stay that fateful November and never left this place. I saw charred remains of the grist mill with grass growing through the blackened beams lying like sticks on the ground. Nothing left of the chicken house, smokehouse, or barn. My heart beat in my ears. My father said there were seventy-four people there that November day. Eleven died then; two more of the children later when held as captives. I could hear their cries. My fingers felt cold, sluggish on my reins, slowed by old visions. I could see the chaos, the shallow grave. The sounds were deafening, and I put my hands to my ears, buried my face in the sweet-smelling hair of my child.

Timothy touched my hand still holding a rein. "You are here. It is not then."

I gasped for breath. Looked up at him. "Yes. I know."

"Birds sing, there, near the pond. You can hear them?" He moved his horse closer to the water's edge and Maka followed, taking us with him without my effort, past a lifetime.

"The mill pond," I whispered.

"It remains."

"But the mill is gone, burned. How . . . ? I remembered it still standing that day."

"No. It was taken before you came here that last time. The burning, it was an early sign of trouble. You do not remember it correctly."

What else did I not remember correctly?

"Yet it's part of my memory still intact. How can that be? And the orchard. I thought it was on the other end." I remembered then a kindness, a Cayuse splitting wood and carrying it for me to the fireplace, building a fire to warm us. *Were there other small gifts of compassion?* "Mr. Osborne escaped through there." I pointed to a falling-down rail fence. "John Sager went for water for us after three days. He was so ill. Shot there." He'd sacrificed himself for us.

I spoke a silent prayer for him and all the others. The site confused me. It was all so much smaller than I remembered. "The pictures are sharp in my mind but they're fuzzy here."

"What we remember is not always a true arrow. Memories fall short or range too far."

"My mother told me once that the Hebrew word for *sin* could be translated as 'missed the mark.' As with an arrow."

"Your mother taught that grace covers such thoughts, Eliza Spalding Warren. There is no sin in remembering in error."

But in that moment I felt there was. "Timothy, I'm so sorry. I remembered wrong and blamed you." How brave he'd been to step into the danger to let us know we were not forgotten. It must have hurt him as much as me to leave. When we cannot offer sustenance to those we care about, especially to a child, the weight of our reliance on faith bears heavy. "Can you forgive me for believing your people had abandoned us, that the Nimíipuu had betrayed me?" At last I used their preferred name, Nimíipuu, as my mother would have.

"It is not mine to forgive."

"But you didn't mean to leave me. I . . . I thought you could have taken me away, but I understand that all the choices were horrible ones. You made the ones that kept people alive. The People didn't send us away; you let us go to the safety of Forest Grove. And I blamed you for that. I'm sorry. So sorry." I touched his forearm in respect; felt a shifting in my chest.

He put his hand over mine. "Your mother showed us about forgiveness. You must forgive yourself now. It is so."

"Forgive myself?"

The past swirled back. I saw the priest baptizing the murderers. No, I couldn't have seen that. It wasn't done in front of me. We had huddled inside, pushed together into a room awaiting our fate, strangled by the smell of sweat and fear, of moans from those injured whom we could not save. My father told me the priests had done that, baptized the Cayuse who held us. *He can't know that.* I breathed faster and Minnie whimpered. I patted her small hand, inhaled the lavender scent of her hair.

Our captors forced us outside then, demanded we carry on, feed chickens, milk cows, make bags for the dead. With Matilda Sager—who was younger than me—we two tugged at the weight on sheets we'd stitched, ignoring blood stains, dragging bodies to a shallow place in the ground. She cried throughout. I moved stiff as a hatchet. Stack after stack of white bags held those we'd loved. My arms and legs ached and still they goaded us to continue. Here in Waiilatpu, years later, my palms sweat. My fingers twitched in memory. "Matilda Sager lived with us for a time but I could not talk to her. To anyone. When I saw her I saw the sheets of bodies and the needles we used to sew them up. She cried so when they came to take her from my parents' home in Forest Grove." I felt a sob well up. "I sent her from my family. I abandoned her."

"Your mother was ill, Eliza. It was better for that child to be where you did not remind her of this place and she did not remind you."

Maybe that was so, but it was also cruel of me to want her gone, unforgiveable.

A raven circled overhead and in his call I heard the cries of Lorinda Bewley, begging me to tell the hostage takers—pleading—to let her be. "She was a beautiful girl," I said out loud. "Lorinda. I failed her too."

Timothy shook his head. "You could not keep her here when Five Crows sent for her. Just as I could not take you with me when I came. You did what you could. She did what she could. We must forgive ourselves the rest."

Had I done all I could?

Timothy led us toward a structure, weeds grabbing like old fingers at its side, roots growing through adobe. "In that building or where that building stood we cooked for them," I said. "And they made me taste all the food first in case we'd poisoned it. There was little food for us." *Is that true?* "No, after the first few days there was plenty of food on tables. I couldn't eat. Couldn't eat." I gasped, a memory clutched my throat. "The priests told the Cayuse to kill the two wounded men we'd been caring for. I . . . Could they have said that? Did I get it wrong when I interpreted their words? The Cayuse made me tell them what the priests had told me." Minnie fussed. "Shu-shu." I calmed her as I tried to calm myself.

"You cannot know. You saw through a child's eyes, remembered through a child's heart."

"Lorinda's brother and Mr. Sails died because of my words." I heard the panic in my own voice. "Did I misunderstand, did I translate it wrong? Oh Timothy!" I turned to him. "I caused their deaths!"

"Your words did not carry the clubs that killed them." He dismounted and lifted Minnie from my arms but stood close; I could still feel their presence. The grass waved chest deep. It tickled Minnie's feet as he held her and she giggled, a glorious sound. "Are you certain you and the priests shared the room?"

Hadn't I been asked to translate their commands? My father said that's how it happened, but he wasn't ever there. All I remember was that the Indians came and killed the men we'd been tending, saying in Cayuse that all who suffered from the pox would live if these men died, that the priests had told them this and I had confirmed it. None of the priests spoke the language; only I did. "I watched the men die and they would not let us bury them for three days. That's what I remember." It was my father's telling of the story of the baptisms that mixed like tangled night-mares. Did I even see the baptisms of the murderers? Did I hear that at the trial? My father claimed that the baptisms legitimized the killings in the Cayuse eyes so the slaughter could continue. Is that why he so hated the priests? But he hadn't been there. Had I told him this? Had someone else?

Some of what I remembered was not my own story. It was twisted like tobacco strands, tangled with a dozen other memories of people who were here and others who were not even a part of the terror.

"Tashe, my own horse that Father had been riding, was in the hands of a Umatilla man who said he was sent for Lorinda to be the wife of Five Crows. My own horse! I remember that."

Timothy smiled. "You would remember that white mount with dark dribbles across its back. You rode as one together in the wind."

"My father claimed he had left that horse and others behind with the priest when Father escaped, and he blamed the priest for sending that particular animal—so that I would recognize it—and believe my father dead. But . . . it was a roan, with frost on its back, I'm sure." Hadn't I always remembered it as Father's horse? That was how I knew he had died. I was confused, still.

"It might have been the only animal the priests had, sent not to do you harm or, what you say, kindle a fire."

"I thought my father was dead when I saw that Indian pony."

"I hear the story that the girl Five Crows took claimed the horse was gentle, she could stay on despite her hands tied and the biting cold. The horse brought comfort to her."

"That must have been Tashe, then." Confusion settled into calm. "Father's horse was high strung with a nervous step. So Tashe comforted her." There were good things that happened, sewn through the bad. Tears pooled in my eyes.

Timothy lifted a fussing baby up to me. "You were strong and saved your life. People called to you to explain the Indian words and you did this, as a comfort for them. You tasted food so all could eat. If there were misunderstandings, there is no fault. No blame. You were a child."

In that moment I saw that frightened young child among the rye grasses and wished beyond measure to put my arms around her stiff shoulders, to pull her to me in a comforting embrace. I'd tell her that the future would be fruitful; that she had done good deeds at this place, in surviving in that time. She had cared as she could, spoke words to help others. She had shown mercy. She would grow to be a tender mother, a faithful wife. She could forgive herself.

With the back of my hand I wiped tears from my cheeks, held my baby close.

"You became a hollow vessel inside in order to make room for what must be done. It served you, this hollowness. But now, you do not need it. It takes you away."

Maka shifted her weight, rested on the other hip as horses do.

"It is the thought that harms you now, not what happened. Live with what is here. A good baby. Kind children. A husband you follow and who looks after you. A father who could not protect you as I could not but who loves you. We did what we could. This is all we are asked to do. All we are asked to do. Mercy is granted to everyone."

"And I blamed everyone."

"You are forgiven for being young and frightened and not able to do what you might have done at another time or place."

I saw then that my father's vehemence when he spoke about those days, when he included in his letters and preaching the story of Lorinda's terrifying testimony of being sent to Five Crows each night, when he railed against the priests and all Indians except the Nez Perce, when he admonished me for nearly every choice I'd made. These were acts to fill his hollow places, not to blame me for them. He had thought *himself* a failure, where he was powerless to change what had happened, and so he tried to change each of us. None of us could change the past. We could only transform how we reacted to what life presented, and even then, any guarantee of certain results was as elusive as morning river mist.

I never dismounted that day, liking the safety of the place atop Maka, viewing at that height what had happened, seeing from a distance instead of in the center of the sounds and smells as when I was ten. I held Minnie, and my mare followed Timothy, who walked on foot toward the orchard as he nearly swam through the tall grasses, pushing with his arms, his long hair swinging against his back. His horse was well trained and tore at grasses that looked to be spring-fed as they still wore green.

Then we were at the stream bank where Alice Whitman had drowned. I never knew her but I remember my mother praying for Mrs. Whitman and the other missionaries and "Dear Alice," every morning between 8:00 a.m. and 9:00 a.m., their maternal hour. I was doing that with my sisters, but I could expand to Nancy Osborne. Matilda Sager. Even Rachel, give to my girls the same prayer mornings my mother had once shared with me. Maybe I could even take a different route home, to see how Matilda Sager lived her life now, tell her I was sorry. At a future Independence Day picnic or an Old Pioneer celebration we'd stand in front of bunting and tell our stories. We wouldn't need to retell these Waiilatpu tragedies except to straighten them out. But no, the stories and my own life would always be tangled not only with my mother's diaries, but with my memories of her and how much I missed her in my life, and with my father's stories and a child's memory wrapped in wounds. No matter how much I tried to control my world, no matter how much Nancy attempted to line hers up, we could not command the future nor undo the past. But we could let God set us free to weave new fabrics. I suspected each of us who survived had found a way to hold ourselves together, and those ways had worked but also taken their toll. Mine nearly cost me my husband's devotion and my sister's love and my father's affection. We could find new ways.

"It's a place of quiet rest," I said.

"It is so."

"Thank you for bringing me. And for granting me forgiveness. We can go now." I'd already begun picking up lost stitches of memories that might knit over my hollow places rather than make them wider.

I felt my heart beat, but it was not a second heartbeat of the past. It was of the present. Waiilatpu was a place of death and loss and memory. My life belonged among the living.

❧ 29 ❧
A GOLD RING

After Waiilatpu, Timothy and his band left me.
But not before he hugged me like a father hugs a
daughter.

"You do forgive me," I said.

"Forgiveness is a summer blanket meant to
ward off a chill but carrying little weight. It frees
you. This your mother said long years ago.
Forgiveness is granted, Eliza. Forgive yourself."

I watched them go. I had done my work at that
sad site. What had to be settled from that time
forward involved people as they were in this
time and my need to see them through forgiven
eyes.

Each stop along my journey home unraveled
old memories and replaced them with new ones.
The Dalles was a place where my sister married
and found happiness rather than the river town
where I fell so ill I nearly died following my
father's foolish ocean trip. It was the reunion site
where I met up with my husband after he
successfully brought cattle across the Cascades;
where he gave me the gold band I wore. And it's
where my sister Millie found us, where she rode
fast and firm, before her injury. The journey on

the steamship heading back to Brownsville would be a reminder not of hostages huddled beneath the canvas with our British rescuers but of a voyage returning me to my family. The Willamette Falls in Oregon City not with memories of a trial but of a marriage. I inhaled the mist and the thundering sounds of water.

I had kept the old memories too close and they had fed a shame in me, but their sustenance came from murky places, not from a well that quenched a thirst. With practice, I could pull happier memories from that deep well.

My girls made scarves of their arms around my neck when I brought them home from Rachel and Millie's care.

"Don't leave us ever again, Mama. You abandoned us."

"Abandoned? Such a big word for you, America Jane. No, I left you safe. It's good for Mama to be alone sometimes. Good for you too, to know I'm gone but I come back. I didn't desert you."

"What if you don't come back though?" *Such a big question.* She pooched out her lower lip as she ran her hands across the smooth ribbon at my throat. She smelled of the lavender Millie must have put into the soap, lavender my mother loved.

"Then as with my own mama, I will see you again in that heavenly place."

It was enough to satisfy her as she began telling

me stories of what she'd done while I was gone, and how she'd looked after Lizzie, her little sister.

"See, you grew strong with me away, just as I did. I'm proud of you."

"You are always strong, Mama." She pressed her head against my chest, patted my arm, then told Lizzie to "get your book. We'll read to Mama and Minnie. She hasn't seen a book for a loooong time." The oldest child, giving orders to the youngest, just as I had always done.

My husband welcomed me home and I saw him through the filter of forgiveness. Yes, friends could sway him, but he also resisted temptation. He had disappointed himself and me when he drank more than to "wet his whistle," as he called it. But he sought new paths, and I found sincerity like well water rising up to squash old stories and replace them with the hope of new. These moments when I did not try to "make" my husband do this or that, didn't interfere with my children learning in their ways different from my own, were kindling for the warming fires I built each day. I remembered a Scripture about "a bruised reed he will not break." The reed of my body had been bruised but I had not broken. Even as a child it grew strong enough to endure.

Millie married John Brown in November and they began their life on the property Father had given her when Mama died, across from the schoolhouse, a level, productive piece of ground.

I wished he'd left that plot to me, but he hadn't. It was the way of things. One didn't always get what one hoped for in this life. As time wore on I saw that while Millie got good land, her husband wasn't nearly as attentive as Mr. Warren was. She had children but she needed help to raise them, and John Brown was busy soliciting investments for rebuilding the woolen mill after it burned down. Each child Millie bore took her closer to the invalid she became.

I conceived again in the fall of '65, before the great War was over, and found I loved my husband better than I had when we first met, when I'd dragged him to the altar before I let him find his own way. My life was woven in with his, but we each also had singular threads. With God's help, we had the power to wrap present moments with memory in order to make new cloth.

Mr. Warren's herd had once again grown too large to keep constrained. We had another branding that spring and this time the whoops of the buckaroos as they lassoed calves or hooted and shouted did not remind me of a sham display. The calves moved down narrow lanes into corrals where a fire waited with branding irons to sear *AJW* into their sides, and the smell of burning flesh did not remind me of another time of scent and evil sounds. And when my husband said he and several other men planned to take the herds to Montana where a new territory thrived and settlers were hungry to start their own herds, I did not object to being left alone.

"You won't be here when our baby is born."

"No. But I'll come back with cash."

"And renewed vigor, I suspect." He tipped his Stetson hat at me. I saw him as a man who needed space, challenge, and adventure, needed to be extraordinary, to have stories to tell. As did I, I decided. My story of making my way with my girls and Little Shoot and the Ruckers, my tale of riding back alone from Lapwai with a baby in my arms always marveled folks, as much as stories others told of crossing the Oregon Trail, a journey I'd been deprived of. Maybe each of us needs to feel a little extraordinary, to believe we've used well the talents we were given to live meaningful lives. I am the mother raising children to be resilient, trustworthy, able to keep going when they want to quit, kind and generous. What greater meaning can one life have?

I think Andrew also needed time away from me, and I didn't see that desire as irresponsible on his part but rather as a natural state within the weft of our marriage weave. I rather enjoyed my time without him around, at least now and then.

I learned of that cattle drive's success in August. James Henry Warren entered the world the same month. My husband achieved a feat only once before accomplished, driving a large herd of cattle from Oregon to Montana. It was something to celebrate. We would do so when he returned home.

Rachel joined Father for a time in Lapwai and then because the Board had still not authorized them to be there, and Rachel could not find teaching work to support them, they came back to Brownsville, staying with Millie, helping with her child whose arrival put Millie back on that chaise lounge. How my father's heart must have ached. He worked in his garden, a man broken despite the lives he'd touched.

And then came the letter he'd been waiting for since my mother's death. The Presbyterian Board of Foreign Missions authorized him in 1871 to once again be in official service to the Nimíipuu at Lapwai.

"You can go back!" I hugged him. "They want you there and you go with the Board's blessing."

He patted my back, separated. "I wish your mother was here to go with me. She felt so betrayed by the Board." I looked at Rachel, who held the letter now, to see if she took offense, but she kept a warm smile as she gazed upon my father. "But it was the Catholics who hurt us most."

"Henry—" Rachel touched his arm.

"It's true." His fists tightened.

"Yes, but in part we are returning under the auspices of the Mission Board *because* of the Catholics' continued success among the natives. The Board could see many were ready for conversion and understood the Presbyterians had already lost too much time. Just as you kept writing to them about."

"Maybe you're right. Maybe so." He patted her hand. "We'll celebrate God's divine guidance after all."

I saw Rachel then as a warm fire that tempered my father.

Later I asked her if we could talk.

"Of course. I love conversations with you, Eliza. They happen too infrequently, it seems to me."

Did she enjoy my company? She seemed sincere and in all these years had given me no reason to doubt.

"What can I do for you?"

"When I was young, I did something, took something that had been my mother's."

"Yes?" Her eyes had begun to cloud with age but still offered kind encouragement.

"I'd like to give it to you." I pulled out my leather pouch that held my children's umbilical cords and placed my mother's gold ring in the palm of her hand. "It was her wedding ring. My father had intended to give it to you but I . . ."

She patted my arm. "I understand. I was an intruder."

"I thought my father disloyal to my mother by marrying again. I—I was certain my mother wouldn't have wanted that, but then I read her diaries, when Father and I rode to visit Lapwai that time. You remember?"

"I do."

"Well, I was wrong. I misinterpreted and intervened where I should not have. Can you forgive me?"

"In the flash of a lamb's tail." She hugged me then, something that had rarely passed between us. "But I think you should give it to your father." She still said "father" with that rolling Boston twang that made it sound as though she said "feather."

And so I did, when we were alone in Millie's kitchen. I confessed what I'd done and said how sorry I was.

He harrumphed, turning the ring in his fingers. "You were young. You didn't know. But if I remember, you let Henry take the blame." He shook his finger at me. I found my feet of interest. He lifted my chin. "You mourned as we all mourned." He rubbed the ring on his pants, held it to the dim light from the lantern. "I thank you for this, Daughter. I'll keep it. Maybe when America Jane marries, she could use it." He clutched it in his palm.

"I offered it to Rachel."

"Did you? And she refused it?"

"She said it belonged to you to do with as you saw fit. She's a good woman and a good wife for you."

"That she is." He was thoughtful. His black eyes watered and I couldn't tell if it was from his memories or his aging. "I think I'll follow your route and see if she'll take it from me. Our eighteenth wedding anniversary is coming up. It would make a nice surprise." He wore a puzzled look then, and said, "Same number of years as your mother and I were married. Imagine. I've had as many years to make memories together with each woman. It's no wonder that I sometimes mix those recollections up."

❧ 30 ❧

LIKE A SECOND HEART

My father's past was like his second heart, a constant rhythm. Perhaps all of our memories carry such a beat. He had but three official years to serve before he died and was buried in Lapwai. Over nine hundred Nez Perce and Spokane souls found God close at hand during those last three years of my father's life. Rachel came back to Brownsville to care for Millie, and when Rachel became ill, she lived with Mr. Warren and me until she died in 1880.

My life has spiraled since that time, orphaned now. My children all married with children of their own. Lizzie died in '82, such a loss to outlive a child. I cared for her children until her husband remarried. Remarrying is a good thing when one has young children, even if the stepmother lacks certain skills, like cooking. Then Mr. Warren was called home. I think his outliving one of his children took a toll upon him. His death was long and lingering, sadly, and his skin turned the color of sunflower duff. "I want to go where you're going, Eliza," he told me at the end.

I assured him that he would.

●●●

My mother's brother Horace, who had moved back East, returned with a wife and family. He carried with him letters my mother had sent to her sisters, last letters written in the weeks before her death.

"I thought you should have them."

I thanked him, and when he and his family had bedded down in my empty house—all my children grown and gone—I read through them, startled by a few of her comments, comforted by others. While she had never said she loved me in her lifetime, she told her sisters that was so.

Beside my Lord and Mr. S, Eliza is my light. I hope she feels how much I love her. If I have time, I will write a letter to her but then I wonder what to say. She's an intelligent young girl whose bright wit and kindness has been thwarted by the tragedy at the Whitman mission. I pray for her future, that one day God will restore her, make her blind to the horrors she witnessed and instead bring new sight to her weary eyes. May she cry tears of joy one day instead of sorrow. May she laugh beside the rivers of her life without wondering at her witness, her having survived. I pray for my dear Mr. S. He pushes at the rivers that God controls and doesn't see that everything that happens can be converted into good. We simply do not know the good of it, our world being so vast and wide and us but a small part in it. Why were we chosen to come to the precious Nimíipuu? Why have we lived and the Whitmans did not? Why were we forced to leave the work of our hearts? Why has my husband taught and preached in this little Calapooia River place some call Brownsville? Is this to be his life? He seems angry here. I cannot bring him peace. These are questions without answers. I can live without the answers, but I'm not certain Mr. S can or my dear Eliza who I pray will not take on his impulsive ways. I pray Mr. S remarries soon, another teacher, someone to share his work and who will allow my dear Eliza to have the chance to be a child again, to laugh and cry in joy.

What does a child really know about their parents' lives? What do my children think of their parents' ways?

In 1888 I spoke at the Pioneer Reunion and I met up with Matilda Sager and Nancy Osborne and we told our stories just as I had one day imagined.

I reread my mother's diaries and letters, liking especially the part about my becoming a child again, someone spontaneous who didn't always regiment the days and hours and lives of those I loved.

Nearly twenty years later, in 1909, a new century, my son suggested a trip.

"We're taking a visit, Mama, to Lake Chelan." This, my son James speaking. He had moved with his family to Washington State some years before and invited me along. I was grateful they wanted an old lady tagging with them. I could still look after two little boys, and Wauna was an easy-going mother who worked hard and enjoyed her "easing time," as she called putting her feet up on the leather hassock in an evening.

Chelan is a long, clear lake in Eastern Washington, rounded at the edges like a knitted stocking. Something about the place appealed to me and I decided there and then to stay. My son tried only a little to talk me out of it. After all, I was seventy and, as he would say, a tease in his voice, "set in my ways."

"Not so set I can't build myself a little house."

"I would never try to deter you, Mother. Just tell me how I can help."

"When I'm ready, bring that woodstove out in your shed."

"The one you made me haul from Brownsville? I can get you a new modern one, have it freighted in."

"Your father gave that to me and I know just how much green wood and how much dry to get the temperature just right."

"Whatever you say, Mother." He kissed me on

the top of my head the way I once did to him.

Out in the sagebrush I built my house. On my own, hammering the walls in place, asking for brawn to set the beams but finding delight doing most of it myself as though I were a child making my own little wagon wheels out of fir ends. A young bachelor helped me arrange to pull water from the lake into my kitchen with lead pipes. Imagine! I pump right into my tin-lined sink. I heat that water on my cookstove.

I didn't try to arrange a marriage for him with one of my granddaughters. I'm past arranging the lives of others.

Sometimes I am asked to speak at pioneer picnics where we reminisce about our journeys west, north, and east. I praise the bachelors who always found time to ride hard for a doctor or raise a roof or build a chimney for someone else. And I praise the women, young and old, married and widowed, who make lives for themselves, some even doing as I did but much younger: file on a claim, build a home, and make a life there, living simply.

Nancy came to visit me once. She has lived through her husband's dying. She married a second time the year my grandson died of diphtheria. We were both already old, but she loved again and was willing to let another love her back.

"My Andrew is buried in a little Kees Cemetery

we carved out of our property not all that far from Waiilatpu, near Weston."

"Umatilla County now."

"Yes. Pretty country." I served her tea on my porch overlooking Lake Chelan. Gray laced her red hair; her freckles had faded. I noticed she left the cups alone, not moved to set them into a straight line. I commented on that.

"After my Andrew died, I sent the tortured thoughts away and vowed that if I loved again I would not waste time thinking of those events so far past. My second husband, William, tells me I am like a child with him, finding things to laugh about as much as I cry. I've buried that part of my life, Eliza. I no longer need to straighten everything out."

After she left I sat on my little rocker and looking out over the lake, I decided I needed to go back to Lapwai, one more time.

I went by steamship, up the rivers. I arrived on a Sunday. Two women serve as missionaries there —Miss McBeth and her niece, Miss Crawford. How I admire their grit! The Indians seemed pleased to greet me, though they could not have ever met me. Timothy was gone now, but they knew of me as they did my father and, yes, most fortunately, my mother. I met Old Joseph's daughter and Jim Moses, who took care of my father's grave. And then we went into the church.

I sat on the benches watching as the men and women filed in and suddenly the memories overwhelmed me—all I had been given in my life begun here.

I felt the tears come and swallowed quickly. I did not wish to cry. I listened as one of their own preached. I could not understand a word, but I didn't condemn myself for that. At the end, Miss McBeth asked if I would like to say a word or two. I stood, my feet sore from too-tight shoes. I went barefoot often at my Chelan home. Another of their ministers translated for me and I told them of how proud I was to be among them, that they had been part of the forest of God's trees, and like each of them, I was just one leaf. But that leaf had begun at Lapwai. And in keeping with the true meaning of The Peoples' name, Nez Perce, I said that I pictured my parents "walking out of the woods through the forest." Together. There were murmurs of approval. "I am proud to be the first white child born among you. Grateful I am that you helped raise me. I have done my best to bring comfort to others and bring the good words of Jesus to my family and friends too." There were smiles and nods and then they sang a song my father or mother likely taught them. They sang it in English, the gesture like a cool breeze on a warming day. It was a hymn written the year my parents came west. *"Savior, like a shepherd, lead us / how we need thy tender care.*" By the time they sang the refrain of the final verse, *Blessed Jesus, blessed Jesus, / thou has loved us, love us still,* I had begun looking at every face, every child, hoping not to lose my memory of them nor my sight through the blurring of my tears. But I was lost: lost to their singing, lost to the memories, lost to the love. I cried like a baby.

"It is all right to cry with The People. It is all right to remember your parents and your precious lives here in Lapwai." Miss McBeth put her hand on my shoulder, then held me with compassion. Although she spoke the words, I heard my mother's calming voice instead, reminding me of the healing power of memories woven new with love.

➤ Epilogue ◄

Lapwai, Idaho
September 11, 1913

My Dear Mrs. Warren,

Word came from the Presbytery that the remains were ready for shipment and should arrive here in a day or two but they did not reach here until Thursday. Many of The People had gone to the mountains already. It is that season. But Elder Jackson and the pastor went for the precious box and brought it to the church. They set it on two chairs in front of the pulpit with two dishes of lavender and asters at either end of the box no longer than three feet. These were later taken to the cemetery. The service was in Sahaptin and we sang a song she or your father had taught. Many whites from nearby Lewiston came to hear them speak of your mother's life, her faithful-ness to God and The People. At the graveside, the pastor spoke in English and we loved the picture that he painted of husband and wife arising together among the people on Resurrection morning. It is a fitting completion to their work.

Very sincerely yours,
K.C. McBeth

AUTHOR'S NOTES AND ACKNOWLEDGMENTS

Much has been written about the early continental crossings of the first non-Indian missionaries, especially Henry and Eliza Spalding and Marcus and Narcissa Whitman. But few have explored the impact of those two families on the lives of the Spalding children and what happened afterward. My story of Eliza Spalding Warren, the oldest child of Henry and Eliza, began in Brownsville, Oregon, several years ago when I was asked by Linda Lewis McCormick, a Brownsville booster extraordinaire, to speak to the Brownsville Women's Club at their one hundredth anniversary. Following that festive event, Linda told me she was working on a book about Henry Harmon Spalding, who had lived in that small Willamette Valley community one hundred fifty years earlier. Linda suggested I might want to tell Eliza the daughter's story. "His daughter stayed here most of her life, and when she married, her father went through town saying, 'My daughter is dead! My daughter is dead!' " Well, there's an unanswered question to warm a novelist's heart.

When I read Eliza's memoir, I was even more intrigued. I wanted to know more about her relationship to her mother and the ways we misinterpret our parents' lives, especially when they are no longer alive for us to ask questions of for clarification. She wrote of her mother's death in 1851 in Brownsville in her memoir and the first sentence after that was: "In 1854 I married Andrew Warren." I wondered what had happened in that very large space between 1851 and 1854.

As I researched I rediscovered the entire mission period with the Spaldings and Whitmans, Eells and Smiths, and the turbulent times following the Whitmans' deaths. I had known that Eliza was one of the hostages taken by the Cayuse but had not realized until reading her memoir that she had been the only person who could interpret Sahaptin—the language of the Cayuse and Umatila and the Nez Perce—and who also was fluent in Chinookan, the trade language made up of a mix of native and French and English words. She'd been asked to interpret, and at the age of ten, I imagined that this demand was a significant weight to carry in a sustained traumatic situation, the siege continuing for thirty-nine days before the British paid the ransom for their release. Equally demanding must have been the grief of the deaths and the month-long hostage siege. And the challenge of surviving.

Several accounts of the Waiilatpu events exist. I relied on Eliza Spalding's account, some of the trial records, Henry Spalding's later writings, a

Catholic version recounted in a 1941 book, and several online family accountings, such as for Nancy Osborne (who lived in Brownsville when Eliza did). Matilda Sager's account, along with her siblings' and Lorinda Bewley's stories and Stephenie Flora's "Whitman Massacre Roster," noted other accounts of survivors of the tragedy as well. Eliza's recalling her lowest moment having to do with the Nez Perce family friend, Timothy, is taken from her memoir. Linda McCormick's published history, *The Spaldings of the West*, proved invaluable in recreating an authentic understanding of the massacre.

Eliza's trip back to Waiilatpu with Timothy is fiction, but something in her later life changed Eliza from what local interviews of people who had known her described as "an unhappy woman" to one willing and able to leave Brownsville for good and build her own home at the age of seventy. Her memoir reflects a woman of great strength who brought four children into the world whose descendants remember the stories of her fondly. Her presentation at the Pioneer Reunion at Crawfordsville in 1888 also presents her as a stalwart and loving woman. What I read there was a devotion to family unity and to preserving the memory of her mother's work, especially among The People, who in many ways helped raise Eliza and gifted her with their own spiritual strength warmed by their conversion to Christianity. To this day there are descendants of those early converts who continue to practice the faith, just as there are descendants who returned to their native spiritual practices.

I have chosen to have Henry and Eliza Spalding use the name Nez Perce as well as Nimíipuu when they refer to The People they lived among. Eliza the daughter uses Nez Perce and The People. When the language of the Nez Perce is being spoken of, Sahaptin is the linguist group of the natives of that region. Chinookan was also used among whites and natives at that time.

The Spalding spelling was chosen as most historical, though the street in Brownsville named for Henry is spelled Spaulding and that spelling occurs on land documents from the time period. Either appears to be correct. Eliza the mother did keep a diary and many of her letters are also published. More material is also available at the Bancroft Library and the Presbyterian Historical Society's archives in Philadelphia. The diary entries in this novel are my creation, using the tone of Eliza the mother, I hope, but giving words to things she never spoke of: her surviving a terrible tragedy when the Whitmans did not; her frustration with the Mission Board's refusal to let them return to Lapwai. And I gave her an expression of some frustration with her husband, though she never criticizes him in her own diary. Still, the documented report by one of Henry's professors of his student's lack of common sense and quick temper rings true, as does that professor's high regard for Eliza as a scholar, linguist, and thinker. One gets the impression that if she had been a man, she would have been given the post that she was allowed to serve only as a helpmate for in 1836.

The history of Brownsville, the Warrens' decision to leave in 1859 and move to the Touchet country near where the tragedy took place, their return again to Brownsville, Henry's response to all his daughters' marriages, the sibling rivalry, Millie's injury, Mr. Warren's driving cattle across the Cascades where he did, and later Montana, his ups and downs and even a period when he was known to be drinking heavily (based on documents and interviews of Brownsville residents done in the 1930s), Henry's temper, Rachel's arrival and housekeeping foibles are all based on facts. Eliza Hart Spalding's wedding ring is in a collection at the Oregon Historical Society in Portland, Oregon. These facts and ephemera and love of history were provided in no small part by Linda McCormick's own passion for the story of these families. I am forever indebted to her for her willingness to share her research, to speculate with me about the weaving of those facts into fiction, and for her review of the manuscript to correct and help me refine what I hope is a story that in many ways speaks to the power of memory and the suffering that old memories can bring into our present time.

In addition to Linda McCormick, I spoke with Carol Harrison of Monterey, California, a granddaughter of James, Eliza Spalding Warren's son. She is engaged in writing her own book about her family in which she noted she has explored the political side of the Whitman and Spalding struggles. We have a shared admiration for the lives of the Elizas but differ in how their lives may have played out. I am grateful for her time and sharing with me.

A definitive work by Clifford Merrill Drury called *Henry Harmon Spalding* and his three-volume work *First White Women over the Rockies* and *Where Wagons Could Go* offer details of the lives of the first missionaries. His papers are part of the archival collection at Spokane, Washington. I relied on Joel Palmer's work *Journals of Travels over the Oregon Trail in 1845* for both the Nez Perce/Sahaptin and Chinook words I used as well as his commentary about meeting the Spaldings and the Whitmans during that year.

Eliza Spalding Warren's *Memories of the West* was an invaluable aid that not only included her memories but also several photographs and excerpts from her mother's overland journey of 1836. Laurie Winn Carlson's work *On Sidesaddles to Heaven*: *The Women of the Rocky Mountain Mission*, read while researching an earlier trilogy, was reread, and once again I am grateful for her insights about all of the early Northwest missionaries. I also found James E. Bashford's work *The Oregon Missions* written in 1918 to offer interesting insights as the bishop of the Methodist Episcopal Church. *The Mantle of Elias: The Story of Fathers Blanchet and Demers in Early Oregon* by M. Leona Nichols offered a different take on the trial of those charged for the Whitmans' deaths and hostage-taking. *Biography of Place* by Martin Winch (Deschutes Historical Society) confirmed the route over the Cascades along the Santiam River that Eliza alluded to in her memoir. Mr. Winch provided the name Mr. Wiley, attributed to having made this first crossing in 1858 or 1859, which fit perfectly for Andrew Warren to have been one of the first to move cattle through that pass, a fact Eliza proudly mentions in her memoir. The journey up the east side of the Cascades would have taken them through a meadow (where my parents are buried in the Camp Polk cemetery) and north through the Warm Springs Indian Reservation toward The Dalles. The tragic winter of 1861–62 is documented in Oregon history and Eliza's memoir, as is her journey east to Touchet following her husband but going with another couple and her four-month-old and two-and-a-half-year-old children by an oxen-pulled wagon.

Some of my readers may find the faith discussions in this book to be greater than usual. This is due in no small part to the evidence of such faith moving in the lives of these people long before they became characters in my story. Eliza the mother's conversion to Christianity as a young woman, her pull to go west with her missionary husband, her willingness to travel sidesaddle across the continent along with Narcissa Whitman (who had rejected Henry Spalding's offer of marriage but a short time before—now there's a story!), and her devotion to The People and their devotion to her are all a part of this woman's profound and humble faith. It shaped her life in much the way that Pulitzer Prize–winner Wallace Stegner once wrote in an essay about the West. "It is not an unusual life curve for Westerners—to live in and be shaped by the bigness, sparseness, space, clarity and hopefulness of the west."[1] Both Elizas were shaped by such a West and by their Christian faith.

The intricacies of Eliza the daughter's family life, the struggles with her father, her sisters sometimes living with her, sometimes not, are based on census data, letters, and a fascinating piece written by the housekeeper of Millie, Mrs. Lizzie Reinhart Weber, in her later years. In it she describes Eliza coming to the luxurious house

1. Curt Meine, ed., *Wallace Stegner and the Continental Vision: Essays on Literature, History and Landscape* (Washington, DC: Island Press, 1997), 128.

John Brown built for Millie on the original Spalding homestead to get a cutting of a flower, but she did not go upstairs to visit her invalid sister. Were there longstanding issues? Was it sibling rivalry, older sister being miffed at a perceived coddling of youngest sister? Or was Eliza simply in a hurry that day? Clearly family was important to her, and her sisters did spend much of their time with her and Andrew Warren, including following them to Touchet with their father and Rachel.

I am indebted to a Brownsville history written by Margaret Standish Carey and Patricia Hoy Hainline and to a series of columns they wrote for the local newspaper called *Past Times*. I appreciated Glenn Harrison, a Linn County and Oregon Trail historian, who provided details of churches Henry Spalding started in the area as well as other resources and access to his books by Clifford Drury. Sharon and Terry McCoy of Atavista Farm in Brownsville shared their lovely home once lived in by Amelia "Millie" Spalding Brown, youngest sibling of Eliza Warren, and provided a copy of that letter from Mrs. Weber, her housekeeper/caregiver. Most of Mrs. Weber's comments were related to Millie's invalid status and her unhappy marriage, but she did comment about Eliza's distance from her sister as well. The McCoys also had several newspaper clippings believed to be from the *Democrat-Herald* about the loss of the Warren home by fire in 1973, leaving only the smokehouse; articles about Timothy meeting Eliza years later; and a newspaper account of the mute Indian who remembered Eliza from when he cared for her as a child. The Brownsville Historical Museum provided many documents, including a copy of "In the Days of Pioneers" by Cyrus H. Walker and a newspaper story "In Earlier Days" by Fred Lockley.

An article with pictures of *American Indian Art* magazine of 1977 included information about Henry Spalding's relationship with one of the Board members and Henry's shipment of Nez Perce regalia and daily items of both a practical nature and beauty in exchange for necessities such as hoes and plows and children's clothing. The story of the first printing press and the publication of the Nez Perce primer and the book of Matthew are based on facts provided by a number of sources, but of special note was a copy of the diary provided to me by hospital chaplain and descendant Kit Hall. The diary was kept by Sarah Hall on her overland journey bringing the printing press. Eliza the mother's use of pictures she drew, her facility with languages, and the other missionaries' ire about the Spaldings teaching in Sahaptin, the Nez Perce language, rather than in English and their conversions in the native language are all documented.

There is within this story post-traumatic stress disorder, shame, and survivor guilt, but I also hope there is transformation. Everyone in the Spalding family was affected by what happened at Waiilatpu on that cold November day in 1847. In our generation, boundless articles and theories exist about post-traumatic stress, about how shame and trauma shape our life choices, but we are still coming to terms with how to walk beside those who struggle with these profoundly painful memories. They must sort out perceived guilt for action or inaction (survivor guilt) and actual culpability for a tragedy. I relied on survivor commentaries as well as on my own experience as a mental health professional and professional articles. One of particular interest was written by Kathleen Nader, DSW, "Guilt Following Traumatic Events" as part of the online PTSD Resources for Survivors and Caregivers.[2] I created a daughter, Eliza, who assessed herself a failure for what she might have done in normal circumstances without understanding that how we respond in traumatic circumstances is quite different. Both Elizas made judgments about actions that were mis-interpretations of what the human heart is capable of in those traumatic times, whether one can aid others as much as desired, whether one can stop or interfere with the harm going on. I had Eliza the

2. See http://giftfromwithin.org/html/Guilt-Following -Traumatic-Events.html.

daughter overestimate her sense of control at times and other times live with a grave sense of worthlessness. Recovery involves seeing that "traumatized self" with new eyes. I also found Brené Brown, DSW, and her work *Daring Bravely* about wholehearted living to be very insightful for understanding the Elizas' lives.

This novel explored the Elizas and their families' response to the trauma but did not delve deeply into the trauma of the Nez Perce people and their struggles from the war waged by neighboring tribes, the month-long siege by neighboring peoples, and the wrenching away of a family whom many loved and cared about, as evidenced by their absolute joy recorded when the missionaries were allowed to return to Lapwai. Timothy's being unable to rescue Eliza had a profound effect on her, but I suspect it also challenged Timothy's sense of powerlessness. Yes, the non-Indians wrote that story, and other stories of the Nez Perce and Chief Joseph's leading his people to Canada that ended in tragedy. But the natives have told stories, too, about their asking for people to come and bring them the "Book of Heaven," and many descendants still sing of the Spaldings. My own work for seventeen years with Sahaptin linguist tribes caused me to wonder if all native peoples might be dealing with PTSD based on the missed understandings, tragedies, and lost hopes that the coming of the non-Indian brought to their own communities. They have dealt with deaths by disease and wars; disconnection from homelands and relocation to reservations; and too many times to count, the forced march of their elders, women, and children to wilderness places. A contemporary book, *Lewis and Clark Among the Nez Perce: Strangers in the Land of the Nimíipuu* by Allen V. Pinkham and Steven R. Evans, published by the Dakota Institute Press in 2013, offers new insights about this tribe of remarkable people and what the "strangers" may have missed that the Spaldings discovered by living side by side with them for fifteen years. Few have missed the traditions of hospitality and kindness of The People shown to that early expedition and to the Spaldings and that continue to this generation.

With good intention the Missionary Board responded to the call for someone to go and teach the Book of Heaven, and they sent the Spaldings and Whitmans. But what happened—even without the trauma of Waiilatpu—caused as dramatic a cultural change as would the first contact of earthlings with beings of a far-off planet.

It's my hope that this story allows each of us shaped by tragic and painful events to see that we are not alone and that there is a way to weave new cloth. May it also increase our compassion for those struggling, including ourselves. As Dr. Nader noted in her article, mentioned earlier, such change may require a counselor, clergy, or a wise friend. I'd like to add the power of story and grace are also avenues to peace.

Finally, but not least, I want to acknowledge Andrea Doering, Barb Barnes, and the many team members of Revell who have lovingly carried my stories into your hands. I am humbled by their enthusiasm for these stories and for the commitment to quality at all levels of publication. Joyce Hart, Hartline Literary, my agent of many years, continues to be my champion as I champion her! Leah Apineru of Impact Author has kept me on board with social media. Paul Schumacher of AdquestInc.com designed and manages my website and makes sure my monthly *Story Sparks* appears in the hands of those who have signed up for this bit of encouragement. Thank you. I have special gratitude for Janet Meranda, Loris Webb (my Canadian prayer partner), and Linda McCormick for early readings of this work and their suggestions. Of particular note are other members of my prayer team: Carol Tedder (who also handles my event requests with grace), Judy Schumacher, Judy Card, Susan Parrish, Gabby Sprenger, and friends Marea Stone, Sandy Maynard, Blair Fredstrom, and Jean Hendrickson. These women and their families have had us in their homes, prayed for us, and offered undue support for Jerry and me and my writing life.

I'm grateful as well to independent booksellers

who continue to carry my titles all these years—this being the twentieth year of my entry into fiction—and who hand sell my titles, giving me new readers every year. My husband, Jerry, my faith community of First Presbyterian Church in Bend, Oregon, and my brother and sister-in-law, Jerry's daughter and son and families, and friends have kept me stable and loved through the writing of this book. There are many others too numerous to name whom I claim as family and friends, and especially my faithful readers. You make my hours of writing worthwhile. I hope the Elizas touch your lives as they did mine and that all your memories will nourish and transform. Thank you.

Jane Kirkpatrick
www.jkbooks.com

Discussion Questions

1. Marcel Proust is credited with writing, "Remembrance of things past is not necessarily the remembrance of things as they were." How does this quote describe events in the two Elizas' lives? What about in other characters' lives? Was it misinterpretation or guilt or shame that affected Andrew's life? Or Henry's? Have you had occasion to discover this truth for yourself? In what way?

2. Misinterpretations often happen between generations, including between mothers and daughters. What were some of the misinterpretations that Eliza the daughter held? Do you have any experience with a misunderstanding with your own mother/daughter/father/son due to a misinterpretation of intent, meaning, or memory?

3. Why did Henry Harmon Spalding ride through Brownsville claiming his daughter was dead? What was he fearful of? What did he believe to be fact? Was Henry a loving father in your mind? Why or why not?

4. What gains and losses did Eliza the mother experience by being left alone so frequently

by her husband? Are there frequent or long separations within your parents' lives? Your own? What discoveries do you think your parents have made during those separations? What might they have missed in not having time alone? What have you discovered?

5. What factors made Andrew Warren decide to leave the Willamette Valley in 1859? Did he believe Eliza would follow him? Why did she? Where did her reluctance stem from? Would you have gone with him? Do you think that Eliza's decision to go or not was affected by not having made the overland crossing as her parents and so many pioneers had?

6. Why did Henry insist that his daughter Eliza attend the trial of the Indians accused of the crimes at Waiilatpu? What impact do you think this had on a twelve-year-old girl? Was Eliza the mother's worry justified?

7. Was Eliza the daughter's sense of abandonment and betrayal by the Nez Perce warranted? Why or why not? Was Eliza the mother's sense of betrayal of the Foreign Mission Board justified? Why or why not?

8. Did Eliza's relationships with her sisters and brother ring true? How much of the tension in

their lives was typical sibling combat and how much was related to perceived slights or privileges given by parents to one sibling or another? How much might have been related to how each dealt with the tragedy at Waiilatpu?

9. Why do you think Eliza stole her mother's wedding ring? Did the author provide authentic motivation for that action and the way that Eliza dealt with it and how it affected her brother, her father, and her stepmother?

10. What made Henry Harmon Spalding decide to follow Eliza and Andrew into Touchet country? Did his action surprise you? What influence do you think Rachel had in his life? What influence did Eliza the daughter have in his life? What kind of marriage do you think Henry and Rachel wove together?

11. What drew Nancy Osborne and Eliza the daughter together? How much of their relationship was a shared guilt and how much was two young women needing companionship in a remote land? Have you shared a tragedy with anyone? How did that change your relationship, or did it?

12. Eliza the daughter used many Nez Perce names for beloved animals (*Yaka* and *Maka*)

and her father (*Papo*) and sometimes lamented the loss of her fluency in the language. At the same time, she expressed anger that the Nez Perce had sent her and her family from Lapwai. She was also disturbed that Timothy had not rescued her. How do you account for this discrepancy between a fondness for a people while carrying a sense of betrayal? Have you held on to certain negative feelings while still lamenting a loss? How does this affect your daily life, or does it?

13. The author writes in the acknowledgments that "both Elizas made judgments about actions that were misinterpretations of what the human heart is capable of in those traumatic times, whether one can aid others as much as desired, whether one can stop or interfere with the harm going on." Do you agree or disagree? What evidence is there that both Elizas dealt with survivor guilt?

14. Does the way that Eliza came to terms with the tragedy offer any insights for your own life? Do her actions inform a recent practice of veterans of wars returning with counselors and friends to the site of great loss in an effort to find reconciliation and forgiveness? Are there areas in your life that may need a

journey with a trusted friend to bring peace to your days? What next steps might you take to make that journey?

15. Author Wallace Stegner wrote, "It is not an unusual life curve for Westerners—to live in and be shaped by the bigness, sparseness, space, clarity and hopefulness of the west."[3] How do you think those qualities of the West shaped Eliza the mother and Eliza the daughter? How does the landscape you live in shape you?

Thank you for making room in your lives for my stories.

Jane

Visit Jane at www.jkbooks.com, sign up for her *Story Sparks* newsletter, and follow her on her *Words of Encouragement* blog and Facebook and Twitter.

---

3. Meine, *Wallace Stegner*, 128.

About the Author

Jane Kirkpatrick is the *New York Times*, CBA, and Pacific Northwest bestselling author of more than twenty-seven books, including *A Light in the Wilderness*, a 2015 Spur Award Finalist, and *A Sweetness to the Soul*, which won the coveted Wrangler Award from the Western Heritage Center. Her works have been finalists for the Christy Award, Spur Award, Oregon Book Award, and Reader's Choice awards, and have won the WILLA Literary Award and Carol Award for Historical Fiction. Many of her titles have been Book of the Month, Crossings, and Literary Guild selections. You can also read her work in more than fifty publications, including *Decision*, *Private Pilot*, and *Daily Guideposts*, and in her *Story Sparks* newsletter. Jane lives in Central Oregon with her husband, Jerry.

She loves to hear from readers at
http://www.jkbooks.com
and
http://Facebook.com/theauthorJaneKirkpatrick.

Center Point Large Print
600 Brooks Road / PO Box 1
Thorndike, ME 04986-0001 USA

(207) 568-3717

US & Canada:
1 800 929-9108
www.centerpointlargeprint.com